A Dark Place to Die

Ed Chatterton is the prize-winning author and illustrator of more than twenty children's novels (published under the name Martin Chatterton). Born and raised in Liverpool, he now lives in the Australian outback with his wife and two children.

A Dark Place to Die is his first crime novel and he is already hard at work on the second in the DI Frank Keane series.

ed chatterton
A Dark Place to Die

arrow books

Published by Arrow 2012

4 6 8 10 9 7 5

Copyright © Ed Chatterton 2012

Ed Chatterton has asserted his right under the Copyright, Designs and Patents Act 1988 to be identified as the author of this work

First published in Great Britain in 2012 by
Arrow
Random House, 20 Vauxhall Bridge Road,
London SW1V 2SA
www.randomhouse.co.uk

Addresses for companies within The Random House Group Limited can be found at: www.randomhouse.co.uk

The Random House Group Limited Reg. No. 954009

A CIP catalogue record for this book is available from the British Library

ISBN 9780099576679

The Random House Group Limited supports The Forest Stewardship Council (FSC®), the leading international forest certification organisation. Our books carrying the FSC label are printed on FSC® certified paper. FSC is the only forest certification scheme endorsed by the leading environmental organisations, including Greenpeace. Our paper procurement policy can be found at: www.randomhouse.co.uk/environment

Printed and bound in Great Britain by
CPI Group (UK) Ltd, Croydon, CR0 4YY

To the girl from Neston Street

1

Frank, hunched against a bastard wind knifing in off the Irish Sea, isn't sure at first where the sound is coming from. It's barely light and a soft insistent hiss sits below the whining gale, like white-noise feedback at song's end. He leans a little closer and realises the source is sand rattling against the charred skin stretched tom-tom tight across the dead man's face.

By exacting local standards it's been a while since the last body turned up on his patch, and Frank Keane has been wondering when the next one would arrive, but on this bone-cold Tuesday morning in late October, normal service looks like it's been resumed.

Someone's made a real effort this time, the victim lashed bolt upright to a length of scaffolding pole driven deep into the Liverpool sand and barbecued to a blackened crisp. His back to the still-waking city, the corpse faces seawards, just fifty paces from the turning tide. As a pig of a caffeine headache settles in behind his eyeballs, Frank squints into the melted nightmare that had once been someone's face and sees if he can recognise the corpse as one of the bottom-feeders in his patch.

You never know. Sometimes you get lucky.

The victim's features are a molten mess, the nostrils visible as clotted slits and the teeth bared, the lips peeled away. A horror show. Frank's grateful for the dull light, the details thankfully sketchy. The cold as sharp as Lennon's tongue, Keane rams his hands deeper into the pockets of his useless overcoat and curses his lack of foresight in not coming equipped with better outdoor clothing. *Harris* will have the right clothes; Frank's sure of that, but she hasn't arrived. DI Frank Keane is the first officer at the scene – not through any great zeal on his part; he happened to be on his way in when the dispatcher called – but now he is here, and freezing his bollocks off instead of still being tucked under the duvet with the wonderfully warm-bottomed Julie, he's anxious to be on with the job. Right now, that means waiting for Harris to arrive before laying so much as a finger on the crime scene. The new set of Merseyside Police regulations specifically state that the investigation must be as a team, solo efforts being prone to awkward courtroom arguments about tainted evidence, and – more pertinently in Frank's world – vulnerable to harsh punishment by the brass. Especially from The Fish, the pole-climbing prick. Difficulties in court represent blots on the copybook and The Fish wants his department's record purer than.

Besides, impatient though he is, Keane predicts that they'll discover little from the physical evidence and he's too old to be ferreting around the frozen beach like some new-minted numpty looking for 'clues', a word that in the context of modern-day policing seems almost quaint. Most of the Merseyside Police Major Incident Team cases come home thanks to one thing and one thing only. There's always someone, eventually, who talks. That's one thing about Scousers: they can't stop fucking talking. Or, it sometimes seems to Frank, slaughtering one another.

So he waits. He walks in a wide slow circle round the victim, wondering which of the likely suspects will turn out to be responsible.

There's no shortage of candidates.

While Liverpool's heavy industry has wasted away to almost nothing, the city's criminals seem to have perfected production of a steady stream of ever more violent and sharp-fanged drug predators. The latest fashion in executions has been for drama and this poor bastard on the beach, another of the gangland killings that have plagued Liverpool for decades, is supplying plenty.

DI Keane knows this victim is, in all likelihood, not someone who'll be mourned by many; certainly not by anyone in uniform. It's a five-course meal to a bacon butty that the vic'll be someone who got in the way of a bigger fish working up the food chain.

Guns or baseball bats, the staple fare of drug beefs, are the usual method of settling scores, although there has been a recent fashion for using M75 military-issue grenades to make a point. Even the battle-scarred Keane sat up and took notice when the fuckers began using grenades.

Compared to that, Keane's victim is positively artistic.

They'll explore all investigative avenues – or at least that's the official line – but there's not a copper on Merseyside worth his salt who'd waste ten seconds seriously considering this is anything other than drugs. They all are.

Keane, his back to the wind again, works his reluctant frozen fingers into a pair of surgical gloves. If Harris doesn't arrive soon he's going to make a start, regs or no regs. It's too cold to be standing out here and it's getting colder with every passing minute. Keane raises his hands to his mouth to warm them, before remembering, too late, the gloves. With the sour taste of latex on his lips, he contents himself with rubbing his palms together but it's not effective; the talced rubber too smooth to get any decent friction.

Whoever put the victim here chose a suitably miserable spot.

The low-lying city, skulking along five or six miles of heavy docks, sits behind and to the left of the corpse, while directly in front the grey-brown Mersey empties into the Irish Sea with all the enthusiasm of an hungover drunk staggering out of bed. Across the river mouth sits New Brighton, the waves white against its blackened Victorian sea walls. The ships that have carried everything and everyone, from West African slaves packed heel to head in shameful wooden clippers, to sweaty-palmed IRA bombers supping Guinness at the tilting ferry bar, have always needed to be careful coming in and out of Liverpool Bay. Sly sandbanks that guard the entrance to the river lie in wait for the unwary like a late-night stranger in the Lime Street shadows. *Mate, mate, got a cig? I'm gaspin'. Giz yer fucken money.*

It is, as Keane knows too well, a port with form as long as a docker's pocket, and today as cold and unforgiving as a bailiff's smile.

Keane turns away from the water and glances over the victim's shoulder back towards the concrete promenade for any sign of investigative life, and for Harris. Keane swears long and hard but despite his exhortations Harris doesn't appear. Apart from the two plods taking statements from the witnesses who discovered the body – a couple of stunned and shivering art students who got more than they bargained for on their early morning research

4

trip – the beach is as deserted as you might expect at 7.40 on a dank autumn morning.

It doesn't look it, though, not at first glance.

Motionless life-size figures dot the sand, strung out along a half-mile of the semi-industrial shoreline: sculptor Antony Gormley's iron men, an ambitious piece of public sculpture, once derided, now being grudgingly embraced by the city.

The work takes the form of one hundred slowly rusting, life-size iron figures standing on the beach in the same pose, arms by the side, and positioned at varying distances from the long concrete promenade according to some reasoning of the artist. Several are almost always completely submerged and will only surface as the tide recedes.

Which it will do rapidly. On the wide sand flats, the water sometimes moves faster than a man can run. As a child Keane almost drowned at Ainsdale, a few miles north, when he misjudged the water. It's a real concern for Keane, one that will give added impetus to the familiar process. If the tide comes in before they're done with the body, things will get much messier than they already are. If Harris and the SOC boys don't get here soon, someone is going to be on the receiving end of Frank Keane's legendary temper. It hasn't been off the leash for a while and, fuelled by his building headache, he can feel a legendary vent bubbling up.

To postpone the inevitable, he ducks his shoulder into the wind, flips out his mobile and gives Harris another buzz, his impatient fingers stabbing the buttons. He waits a few seconds for a reply.

Nothing. Fuck it. He might as well make a start.

Keane pockets the phone and turns his attention to the corpse. He reaches inside his jacket to put on his reading glasses and bends to inspect the hands, feeling the creak in his joints from his workout at the Boxing Club last night as he does so. Just forty and the knees already going. Bending forward, Keane concentrates, and, for the first time, touches the dead man.

The corpse's hands have been tied in place at his side using steel wire, the fingers curved into involuntary claws by the fire that has claimed him – or, if you were being pedantic, her. Keane isn't quite ready to set that in stone just yet, although he'd bet the farm on this one being male. The same steel wire has been used to tie the corpse to a four-inch-diameter steel scaffolding pole, the end of which appears to be firmly embedded in the sand. He gives the pole an experimental shake.

Rock solid. Keane reckons when they eventually dig this mess out of the beach they'll find a large lump of concrete at the base. He registers the scale of effort required to pull this execution off. Distracted and stationary, Keane feels moisture on his feet and looks down to see them sinking an inch or two into the wet sand. Cold seawater slops over the tops of his black shoes. New ones, bought less than a week ago in one of the fancy shops in L1.

'Fuck.'

He half-hops backwards to firmer territory, shaking his feet, conscious of the picture he's presenting to the slowly gathering crowd of gawpers on the prom.

Inspector Bean.

Jesus. Shit. Fuck. Bastard. It's cold enough out here without going paddling. To make matters worse, Harris chooses exactly this moment to arrive, right on cue, along with the first vanload of Scene of Crime Officers, two of whom begin wrestling a white tarpaulin across the sand, and stifling sniggers at the sight of Keane splashing about in the muck.

'Can you two useless fucking fuckwits get that fucking screen fixed before someone gets this poor bastard up on fucking YouTube?' spits Keane as soon as they get within earshot. The SOCOs' smiles vanish and they bend to their task; a difficult one in the conditions. Keane glares at them, his feet ice, his mood icier. 'Fuckers.'

Back on the promenade, police vehicles are now arriving in larger numbers and Keane spots the white estate car belonging to the photographer. Despite the wet feet, Keane senses a quickening in his blood. The crime scene, *his* crime scene, is, at last, starting to take shape.

'Careful,' says Emily Harris, as she reaches Keane and points at his shoes. 'Don't want to interfere with the chain of evidence, Roy.'

Harris is the second Detective Inspector in Keane's 'syndicate', the current jargon being used to describe the four deployments working under the banner of MIT. She has to raise her voice above the incessant wind to be heard. Unlike Keane, she doesn't seem to be feeling the cold. She's wearing a warm-looking black ski-jacket and a black knitted beanie pulled down over her short hair.

'Crime scene. That's a laugh, Em. This place will be back under water in a few hours' time. And I told you before, less of that "Roy" shite, right? And what kept you?'

Keane, a Liverpool supporter, doesn't like the nickname he's been given; that of a famously aggressive former captain of Manchester United, Liverpool's despised rivals forty miles down the 62. Emily, from the blue, Everton half of the city, and knowing exactly how deep the hatred runs, makes it a point of honour to use it as often as possible. It doesn't help Keane's cause that he bears more than a passing resemblance to the footballer; insomniac eyes under a brooding brow, cropped grey-black hair, a

7

permanent five o'clock shadow and an air about him of someone who would welcome an argument on any given subject at any time.

Emily Harris rewards him with a half-smile and holds out her hands in an insincere placating gesture. 'Sorry, *Frank*,' she says. 'I was in an interview. The Glassfield thing.'

Harris, a black woman of middle height, and with the solid build of someone with a serious gym habit, cuts a striking figure. It is one of Keane's guilty pleasures to admire that figure on a daily basis. If Em Harris has ever known he's looking, she has never let it show.

Like Keane, Harris puts her glasses on, shielding the lenses from the sand-flecked wind with her latex-gloved hand, and peers closely at the corpse, all business.

'No lifeguard on duty, I take it?' she says, without looking up.

'Very funny. No, no lifeguards. They must have been transferred to California. Or Bondi. And no reports so far of anyone else seeing so much as a fucking dog. Still, early days, eh?'

Harris, feet smugly protected by the practical rubber boots she pulled from the boot of the car on arrival, moves in close, puts her nose a millimetre or two from the victim's cheek and inhales, seemingly oblivious to the sickening stench of burnt flesh.

'Paraffin. Or some other accelerant.' She announces this in the tone someone might use to describe the bouquet of a fine wine.

Keane is only part-listening. Good officer though she is, Em does have a habit of sometimes stating the bleeding obvious.

As if he'd spoken aloud, Harris looks up and then glances past Keane who turns to see the lumbering form of Callum

8

McGettigan, one of the MIT photographers, trudging towards them. McGettigan, a portly man wheezing like a broken accordion, is rumoured to have once been seen train-spotting on Crewe station, but Keane has always found him first class. If there's something worth recording at a crime scene, you can guarantee that McGettigan will bag a crisply lit image of it, meticulously recorded and cross-referenced. Sometimes you needed the trainspotters.

McGettigan dubiously sets down his bag of tricks on a patch of dryish-looking sand and rubs his face, sweating lightly despite the cold.

'You need long, Callum? I'd like to get the examiner in before we need to use a bastard submarine.'

'Give me a chance, DI Keane.' McGettigan lifts a camera to face level and makes an adjustment. 'I'll do my best, OK?'

Keane nods and steps aside to give the man room to work. He looks down at the dun-coloured sand around the corpse. 'Shit.'

Keane's not expecting much physical evidence from the scene, but there isn't a snowball's chance of anything useful still being here. Not after, what, eight, nine hours of being rinsed by the sea and scoured by the wind. Still, they – or more accurately, someone Keane and Harris assign to do the task – will have to run a quadrant search on a large section of the beach, down on their hands and knees, before the next tide.

'We'll make this quick,' says Harris as if Keane has spoken aloud. After three years working side-by-side, the two of them have developed a shorthand way of communication. It isn't telepathy, but it's close.

The sand looks firm but, as Keane has just found out the hard way, the application of any weight close to where the pole is sunk into the beach rapidly turns it into a kind of gelatinous porridge.

'Why couldn't this one have had the good sense to be killed somewhere civilised, like a nice dry warehouse, or somewhere with CCTV at least?'

'You're getting soft.'

It begins to rain.

'Great. Fucking perfect.' Keane retracts his head down into the neck of his overcoat. He glances back at the promenade where the uniforms have begun to get things organised. At either end of the beach, crime scene tape is being strung out to stop anyone getting closer. The small crowd of onlookers is being shepherded to a suitable distance.

He flips open his mobile and checks on the arrival of the medical examiner. Stuck in traffic. Should be there within the half-hour. He pockets the phone and, leaving Harris and McGettigan with the victim, walks across the sands to where the uniform – Parkes, that was the feller, wasn't it? – is talking to the witnesses. With a jerk of his head, Keane beckons the officer over.

'They saw it? Like this? Close up, I mean, PC . . .?'

The uniform nods, his face creased into the wind. 'Norton, sir. Yes they did, sir. They say they didn't go close. They didn't need to. They've got binoculars. Pretty good ones too, so they got a real eyeful.'

The young officer gestures to where the chastened students sit quietly on the tailgate of a police Land Rover talking to a second policeman in uniform. 'The bloke puked. She seems calmer. Yorkshire lass. Might get a bit more from her, sir. My oppo's looking after them.'

'Get them back to the office,' says Keane, not unkindly. 'I want these people off the beach before they start "remembering" things they didn't see. This is a crime scene, Parkes, not a day at the seaside. They'll be wearing kiss-me-quick hats next and asking for donkey rides.'

From the blank look that flickers across the young policeman's face, Keane sees that the man has no idea what a kiss-me-quick hat is, or was. It's things like that that are starting to make Keane feel his age. He also realises that he'd got the man's name wrong.

Keane turns away from Norton, trying to commit the name to memory by silently repeating it to himself three times. He'd once been told repetition helped with this kind of thing. It's a failing of Keane's – not remembering names – that is beginning to worry him more with every advancing year. Ever a hypochondriac, the word 'Alzheimer's' hovers in the ether. Phil Donnelly, one of Keane's first section bosses, and one of the sharpest coppers Keane had ever known, went that way early and went hard.

Leaving Norton talking into his radio, Keane checks with the various new arrivals and spends the next twenty minutes attending to the organisation of the crime scene, waiting for McGettigan to finish his photography and Em to get acquainted with the corpse and make her customary extensive notes. Eventually, the delegating done to Keane's satisfaction, the machinery working as it should be, he moves back towards the beach, meeting the photographer halfway.

'Should have everything online for you inside the hour,' puffs McGettigan. With the incoming tide there is a real reason for McGettigan to hurry the photographs. If he's missed something, getting the images turned around quickly may give him the chance to come back and shoot again. Keane gives him an encouraging pat on the shoulder.

11

'Cheers,' says Keane, and leaves the photographer waddling through the rain towards his car.

As McGettigan drives away, Keane sees the medical examiner pulling up and he hurries back towards the corpse. He wants to check that he and Harris present the victim to the ME in the way that will help them most effectively; mainly by stressing the importance of *their* case so that it leapfrogs other bodies on the examiner's slab. Liverpool isn't quite Johannesburg or Baghdad, but there are still enough cadavers for a queue to form. Most of them will be domestics or Saturday night specials, the victims no less important than Keane's guy, but certainly less rich in possibilities. Spinning the case as a crucial one, or, if Keane wants to be cynical, one likely to attract publicity, is a possible method of bumping it up the ME's list.

Keane looks back along the length of the beach and is struck once more by the resemblance of the corpse to the iron men strung out along the sand. Facing the same way. At the same height. Whoever has done this has even made sure that the victim's hands have been tied at his sides in the same posture as the sculptures. It shows an attention to detail, thinks Keane, even a twisted sense of humour.

Or a love of art.

Anything is possible.

He'd read recently about an art exhibition that consisted of dismembered corpses preserved in resin and positioned in allegedly artistic poses. Austria, was it? God help us.

'Look at this,' says Harris before Keane can speak.

Harris carefully raises the legs of her trousers to minimise the damage to the crease and squats to the height of the corpse's knees, her rubber boots squeaking as she does so. Keane tries and fails to avoid peeking down the sliver of cleavage that is visible at the front of her jacket. With a silver pen, Harris indicates several areas of seemingly untouched skin that begin just below the victim's knee and run down to his feet.

'I noticed,' says Keane, remaining upright and staying on the slightly drier sand away from the base of the scaffolding pole, 'there's bruising, cuts, some discolouration.'

'But no burning,' says Harris.

'Which means . . .'

'That this poor sod had already been in the water long enough for the tide to rise when he was set alight. He's been brought out here, tied to the pole and covered in petrol –'

She stops and looks at Keane.

'And then someone's put a match to him.' Keane finishes off her story.

'Jesus,' says Harris. 'I hate this town sometimes.'

'Sometimes?'

Harris doesn't smile. Which is fine, it wasn't a joke.

'The ME's here,' says Keane. He nods back in the direction of the promenade. Three white-suited figures are walking across the sand.

'Right, Em,' says Keane. 'Let's get this wrapped up before they arrive, eh?'

Harris smiles without humour. 'And back home before *X-Factor*? No problem.'

Keane looks at the corpse's bare shins now exposed by the falling tide.

'There was one other thing,' he says. 'Did you notice?'

Harris raises her eyebrows in a question.

'The tan,' says Keane. 'This one's not from round here.'

2

Menno Koopman sits up in bed, stretches his lanky frame and blinks, momentarily unsure of his surroundings.

He's woken this way many times during the past two years.

Koop – no-one except his mother calls him Menno – shades his eyes from a bright shaft of sunlight splintering through the wooden blinds and it all clicks into place. Sunlight.

Not England.

He sinks back against the pillow, yawns and lifts his watch. Almost six-thirty. Mid-morning, if you were going on Australian country time. Which, since the move, Koop has been. Two years and a couple of months and he – they – have adjusted to that at least. In bed by ten as often as not, and up around six.

Back in the squad room in Liverpool, Detective Chief Inspector Koopman would have laughed long and hard if anyone had suggested that that would be the pattern of his days.

Eyes closed once more, he rolls over and puts his arm around Zoe, pressing his groin against her. His hand cups her breast, his fingers brush a nipple. She stirs and glances over her shoulder.

'Koop?' says Melumi.

'Oh, sorry, Mel,' says Koop. 'Zoe there?' He opens his eyes, raises his head and looks over Melumi's shoulder. The other side of the bed is empty, the covers thrown back.

Melumi shakes her black hair. 'She's working, I think.' She stretches and sits up. 'You want a coffee or something?'

Koop nods. He watches Melumi swing her feet out of bed and pad across the floor to the door. His eyes follow her all the way, enjoying the fall and rise of her smooth buttocks. He'd forgotten Mel was coming over. She and Zoe must have come to bed after him.

They have a big bed.

Ringo, the dog, takes advantage of the bed's size by jumping up and settling down in the hollow Mel has vacated. He looks so ridiculously happy about it that Koop doesn't have the energy or inclination to push him off.

A couple of minutes later Mel comes back in with a cup of coffee. She places it on the table next to the bed and stands unselfconsciously petting Ringo, her trimmed black pussy in Koop's direct line of vision.

He feels his cock stir beneath the sheets. Koop can see why Zoe would go for her. She always did have a taste for the exotic.

Not that Melumi would be particularly exotic in Osaka, or Tokyo, thinks Koop, but for Zoe, from Bootle, it was different.

'Thanks, Mel,' he says, propping himself up on one elbow.

'*Dou itashi mashite*, your Highness,' says Melumi. She bows sarcastically before bending coquettishly with a little

15

bob and picking up a t-shirt. She slips it over her head and leaves the room.

'I'll take a cup in to Zoe,' she offers over her shoulder before she and her perfect behind disappear into the kitchen.

Koop sips his coffee which, as usual, is excellent.

Definitely not England. He shivers as he recalls the bucketloads of acrid swill he'd slugged down in canteens and greasy spoons for more years than he cared to think about. The Majorca off Hardman Street springs to mind as a particularly vile brew.

From the kitchen he hears the sounds of Mel clanking cups.

Melumi Ato, a linguistics lecturer at the local university, has been on the scene for a year, the latest in a series of friendships – is that the right word? – that Zoe has had for almost as long as Koop has been with her.

She's never made any bones about her bisexuality. It's been something that Koop could accept as an integral part of life with Zoe, or object to and live without her. It isn't just the sexual side, it's part and parcel of the complete Zoe package.

Not that he's complaining. Every man's fantasy, isn't it? And he was so often included in Zoe's sexuality that, for them, a threesome – and, on more than one occasion, a foursome – is no big deal.

He knows it isn't for everybody but it suits them. He and Zoe, and Zoe's girlfriends, live in the hills tucked away at the top end of the New South Wales coast, an area Koop had never so much as heard of three years ago and yet which now feels as much a part of him as Liverpool ever had, their nearest neighbour a few thickly forested acres away. For Koop and Zoe, brought up in the terraces of north Liverpool, this lush green rolling landscape is paradise. There is no other word for it. Koop sips his coffee and tries not to look as smug as he feels.

If he knew what the day was going to bring, he'd have savoured the moment a little longer.

3

The police mortuary in the Royal – the Royal Liverpool University Hospital to give it its full, never-used name – is not high on the list of places Frank Keane would have chosen to be at any time. At 7.30 on a blustery, rain-swept Wednesday morning, in an October that is so far delivering more than its usual quota of barometric misery, it's close to being the absolute lowest. After spending the rest of Tuesday setting up the investigation and allocating staff, Frank wants to hit the ground running today. The autopsy's a good place to start.

The staff at the mortuary have worked hard to convey the idea that this is just a shiny new medical facility by the addition of bright prints on the walls and pot plants along the corridors.

Keane knows better. It's like putting make-up over a lesion. The atmosphere of the place leaches through the cream-painted walls. Perhaps it's the hush after the pandemonium of the rest of the hospital. Or maybe it's the sight of the waiting-room chairs that nobody ever sits in. The occasional muted whine from the surgical saws doesn't help.

Keane signs in and walks towards the examination room. Harris is already there, her feet encased in bright blue paper bootees. Their body from the beach – Keane is already thinking of it as *their* body – is lying stiffly on the slab between Harris and Ian Ferguson, the medical examiner, a middle-aged man with the build of a marathon runner, which is exactly what he is almost every minute outside working hours.

'Shoes,' says Ferguson. He jabs a pencil down towards Keane's feet.

'And a very good morning to you too,' mutters Keane. 'Bloody miserable Manc twat.'

'I heard that,' says Ferguson.

Ignoring the Scot, Keane goes back through the doors, finds the bootee dispenser and, suitably clad, re-enters the examination room carrying with him an air of an Edwardian gentleman having been impossibly inconvenienced by an impudent footman.

'Better?' says Keane.

Ferguson grunts. It's all Keane's going to get out of him.

'Morning, Frank,' says Harris.

'Em,' Keane looks at the medical examiner. 'Morning, Fergie.'

'Two-nil,' says Ferguson, deadpan, a man of few words, almost none of them pleasant. His team, Manchester United, managed by his red-faced namesake, are playing Liverpool later that day. Keane's six-thirty briefing included a reference to the measures the police at Anfield will be taking to keep the rival supporters apart. He imagines that he and Ferguson will manage without coming to blows.

But it could be close.

'In your fucking dreams,' says Keane. 'Three-one, to us.'

Harris rolls her eyes. 'Can we get on with it?'

Keane looks down at the body on the slab, feeling his stomach lurch as it always does in the autopsy room. He's never told anyone this still happens. It wouldn't be advisable for a senior MIT officer to admit something like that.

'Always makes my stomach turn,' says Harris. She clearly doesn't share his reticence. It's something he admires about her. Em was Em and you took her her way or you didn't. It was all the same to her. Or maybe she knew more about Keane's dirty little secret than he thought?

'Anything?' says Keane.

Ferguson pauses and looks at Keane directly for the first time since he's arrived.

'Well, he's definitely dead.'

Keane gives a sour smile at the old joke and turns his full attention to the body on the table. The corpse has been worked on overnight. Ferguson, Keane knows, would have been here most of the time. The dead man lies on his back, a ragged red slash jarring against the blackened skin, running from the thorax to the sternum. The untouched, unburnt shins and feet lend the corpse a blackly comic and surreal aspect. Although not an art lover, Keane is reminded of a painting by Magritte he once saw at The Walker of a pair of battered boots morphing into feet.

'I haven't closed him up yet in case there's something you want to check, although, quite frankly, I don't think I've missed anything. Nothing you'd spot anyway,' says Ferguson. He picks a clipboard up and reads. 'The victim was a male, height one hundred and eighty-one centimetres, aged somewhere between twenty and thirty-five, in excellent physical shape – until his death, obviously – and the cause of that death was asphyxiation.'

'Drowned?' says Harris.

Ferguson shakes his head. 'No oxygen. He was alive when he was set alight, but couldn't breathe due to the flames. He may have been unconscious through shock, or possibly already unconscious when the fire was lit.'

'I hope so,' murmurs Keane. An imagined picture of the flaming man springs to mind. It's a striking image. Horrifying, yes, but striking too.

And a question. Why had no-one seen it? Despite the relative isolation of the crime scene, a fire at night would have been visible for miles around, wouldn't it? He makes a mental note to check.

'Either way,' continues Ferguson, 'it was the fire that killed him.'

Keane nods and rubs his upper lip. It helps to block a little of the stench of charred flesh and chemicals that saturates the room. Keane had read once that the sense of smell is simply nerve endings responding to molecules of whatever you smelled drifting into your nasal cavity. Which means, if what he'd read is accurate, that bits of the dead man are inside his nose. He forces himself not to retch.

'Anything else?' He barks this out, anxious not to let his fear become apparent.

Ferguson eyes Keane curiously and hesitates before speaking.

'He'd been tortured before he died. Badly too. Although I guess there's never a good way to be tortured, eh?'

'In what way exactly?' says Harris, studiously ignoring Ferguson's weak joke.

The medical examiner's eyes brighten. He's animated. Perky.

'Quite ingeniously, actually. He'd been peeled.'

For a moment Keane thinks he must have misheard.

'What?'

'Peeled,' repeats Ferguson. He mimes the action of peeling a banana. 'Although it was closer to peeling an orange. And it was restricted to his head.'

DI Harris swallows and coughs quietly.

Keane leans closer to the body, not because he wants to see anything but because it gives him an excuse to support himself on the slab. He pauses for a moment and then looks at the victim, the fresh horror of Ferguson's observation bringing the case rushing up Keane's unofficial priority list.

'*Peeled?* How can you tell?'

Ferguson points at the framed medical certificates that can be seen through an internal window sitting in a row above a desk.

'How can I tell? That's how I can tell, *Detective*.' The Scot gives an almost imperceptible shake of the head, picks up a pair of stainless steel tweezers and bends close to the corpse. Keane and Harris lean in too.

'The fire has charred the skin, blackened it, that's obvious. But petrol burns out reasonably swiftly. It was more than enough to kill him, but you can see that the skin, or what's left of it, has lifted away from the tissue in an unusual pattern.' Ferguson delicately pulls up a flap of blackened skin from the victim's cheek and Keane feels his stomach lurch. He feels something else too, another tick upwards in his interest in the case. Even by recent local standards this victim has come in for some unusually florid treatment. 'See?' Ferguson continues. 'It's been sliced cleanly. I didn't do that – it wasn't part of the examination.'

He drops the flap and moves his hand a few centimetres down the face. He lifts another strip of charred skin in a clear line running from under the jawline to somewhere near the top of the forehead. Ferguson lets it flop down and waves a rubber-gloved hand over the victim's head.

'It's the same all the way round. Someone has taken their time with this one.' Ferguson is almost purring. 'You have to admire it in a way. Artistic.'

'Artistic?' says Keane. Another flicker. Harris gets it too and they exchange a glance.

'It would have taken some time,' says Ferguson. He straightens and walks to the other end of the slab. 'Your boys knew what they were doing.'

'Boys?' says Harris. 'So there were more than one?'

'It's not for me to say, but if I had to do something like this then I'd need someone's help. If only to keep him still.'

'That's a point,' says Keane, looking up. 'How was he restrained? Anything on that?'

Ferguson purses his thin lips and waggles a hand from side to side. 'Possible signs of a secondary ligature around the neck but nothing conclusive.'

It's only eight and Keane feels like he's been on the job for hours. Not for the first time since Menno Koopman retired, the weight of his responsibility sits heavily on him. When Koop had been his boss, Keane could remember coveting the older man's job like he'd wanted nothing before; not even the arrival of Christmas as a ten-year-old.

Now he has it, he isn't sure he wants it.

Not on days like this. He pushes away from the slab and his eyes slide towards Harris. How does she look so crisp all the time?

'And there's this, of course,' says Ferguson. He taps his finger on the victim's leg just above the ankle. 'It's what we

23

in the business call "A Clue",' he says, never missing an opportunity to use the alleged lowest form of wit.

It's a tattoo and Keane gives a silent thank you to the god of police work. Tattoos have become a kind of short cut amongst victims. Those aged under forty mostly. Almost every investigation involving body identification since Keane has been on the MIT has been helped in some way by a tattoo.

'It's a strange one, though,' says Harris, who takes out her iPhone to snap a picture of it.

The tattoo is, compared to most, understated, even a little dated. It consists of a small banner with the words 'Fortius Quo Fidelius' written in an ornate script across an unfurling scroll in the centre. It's hard to read because a great discoloured bruise has distorted the image.

'Military?' says Keane. 'A football team motto?'

Ferguson shrugs. 'Your field,' he says.

'Might be a non-league team, I suppose,' replies Keane in a voice that clearly suggests he finds it difficult to believe anyone could have an allegiance to a club outside the Premiership. He does know a couple of Tranmere fans in the city but, like those people who claim to understand opera, or rugby, or camping holidays in the Dordogne, he thinks it's probably an affectation.

Harris holds up her iPhone. 'Praise be to Google,' she says. 'Fortius Quo Fidelius is the club motto of St Kilda Football Club.'

'St Kilda?' says Keane. 'Irish?'

Harris shakes her head.

'You were right about this one not being from round here. St Kilda are an Aussie Rules team. He's Australian.'

4

'The name Jacques Derrida mean anything to you? No? Deconstruction? "No text is discrete"? Ringing any fucking bells? Didn't think so. Hit the cunt again, Sean.'

Sean Bourke faces the naked man bound to the iron pole in the centre of the container and, like always, does exactly as he is told. And immediately. It doesn't pay to hesitate around Mr Kite. He bunches his fist and drives it hard into the man's stomach. The man pukes and makes a sobbing, strangled sound.

'The reason I'm telling you about Jacques fucking Derrida, you Australian convict gobshite, is not that I expect a maggot like you to have even heard of Jacques Derrida. He's not a cricketer, or a fucking rugby player, is he?'

Keith Kite spits out the words staccato, his brick-thick nasal Liverpool accent crackling the consonants and stomping the vowels flat. He paces slowly to one end of the bare metal container, the heels of his polished boots sending a reverberating boom around the space. Evil swirls around him, thick as oil.

'Fucking terrible acoustics in these containers, isn't there? But then, I suppose there always is in art galleries.'

'Galleries?' the man on the pole croaks.

'Kick him, Sean,' says Kite, his little eyes glittering. 'In the leg, hard, and make sure it hurts. He's interrupting me train of thought.'

Bourke lashes out and kicks the naked man full in the side of the ankle with the toe of his boot. The man screams and Kite puts his hands over his ears. 'Oi, oi, keep it down, Rolf! Fuck me.'

As the sound dies away, Kite comes closer and the man flinches.

'Doesn't *seem* like a gallery, I know. But that's what it is. And you know why? Because I said so. Because Jacques says that art is whatever the artist says it is. Or some such bollocks. It's so hard to make sense what any of them fuckers are saying, isn't it? Don't speak straight, always using fancy words. Mind you, I like fancy words. Like "conceptual". You are my conceptual piece, Australian. It might not have a large or particularly appreciative audience right now.' Kite gestures behind him to include the other four men in the room. Besides Bourke, there are two men standing back against one end of the container and another operating a professional-looking video camera mounted on a tripod. The white beam from the camera is the only light in the container. 'Just Sean,' continues Kite, 'who you've already met, Mr Halligan operating the camera, another Mr Halligan against the wall along with Mr North. You'll get to know Mr North a lot better very soon; in fact, it was his suggestion that we turned this little lesson into an art piece. Him being a naughty ex-art student once upon a time, ain't that right, Mr North?'

'Very naughty indeed, Mr Kite,' says North in a soft Irish accent. 'A bit Gilbert and George.' He's carrying a

Tupperware box, and dressed in a protective white suit, such as might be worn by a worker in a toxic chemical lab.

'Now, where was I?' says Kite.

'Audience, Mr Kite,' puts in Bourke, eager to please.

Kite smiles. 'Very good, Sean. You *was* listening, you great big dumb prick. Yes, Australian, there's not much of an audience now, but in a few hours you are going to be the centrepiece in our very own work of art. We're calling it "Dead Australian Cunt". What do you think?'

'Please,' the naked man whimpers.

'I'll take that as a yes,' says Kite.

'Let me go please I won't say anything I'll disappear I'll just go you'll never see me again please . . .'

Kite puts a hand over the man's mouth.

'Shh, shh. There there. No need for all that crap, Australian,' he says quietly. 'Have some dignity.'

'I'm just the messenger I don't know a fucken thing mate not a thing Jimmy just said . . .'

'Tape his mouth, Sean,' says Kite, stepping backwards. Bourke produces a roll of duct tape and winds it tightly around the man's mouth. He jerks spastically, his eyes wide and white.

'I *know* you are just the messenger, Aussie,' says Kite. 'I know that because, despite what you fucking crocodile-hunting convict wankers obviously think, I am *not* a stupid man. The thing is, this Jimmy wanker must be working to some long out-of-date code of fucking criminal chivalry or something, thinking he could send you halfway round the fucking world, coming into my place of work and having the weird idea that you could just say whatever you liked without there being significant consequences. Very, very significant consequences, for you personally, as it's going to turn out.'

Kite spins on his heel and holds his arms out in a theatrical gesture. 'Now *you're* gonna *become* the message. You see? It's sort of poetry, really. Post-modern. Deconstruction. Or some fucking thing. Mr North would explain it better but, as you've noticed, I *do* like the sound of me own voice. Whatever it is, you might as well get used to the fact that you are already not who you once were. You are already something bigger than that now, something powerful, something wondrous. You are doubling up, son! You are the messenger and the message, the dead and the undead. Fucking beautiful. Ain't that so, Mr North?'

'I couldn't have put it better myself, Mr Kite.'

Kite takes out a cigar from a case in his jacket pocket and lights it. He bends towards the cigar, drawing the flame. He exhales and blows smoke in the naked man's face.

'And I like to make my messages very very clear, Australian. I'm not going to lie to you; you are going to die a horrible and violent death and that's going to happen very soon. No use shaking about like that, I'm just explaining my artistic intentions. In a few minutes I'll be handing you over to Mr North who will be doing the actual "hands-on" part of the piece. None of yer real modern artists do anything themselves now, you know. Jeff Koons. Damien Hirst. All of them hand it over to craftsmen these days. Look it up. They don't have to paint or draw or any of that nonsense, dear me, no. Mind you, saying that, I'm not giving Mr North the credit he deserves. Am I, Mr North? This was your little idea, wasn't it?'

North dips his head fractionally, the artisan to patron. 'Makes things a little more interesting.' North looks at the Australian. 'I think this will work very well.'

The terrified man moans and Kite steps back from him, a moue of disgust on his lips.

'Soiled yourself? That's not pleasant, is it, Australian? Still, understandable in the circumstances, I suppose.'

Kite turns towards North.

'Mr North?' he says. 'Over to you.'

North snaps a paper face mask over his mouth, places a pair of goggles over his eyes and walks towards the naked man who begins to tremble uncontrollably. North peels the duct tape from the man's mouth.

Behind him, the door to the container swings open and Kite steps out into the thin, early evening light. He pauses on the threshold and looks back towards the naked man.

'Sorry this didn't work out,' he says with a leery smile. 'Better luck next time, eh?'

The door clangs shut behind him and North turns back to the Australian. He reaches inside the Tupperware box and produces a scalpel.

'Ready?'

5

Koop doesn't shave today and still gets a small rebellious thrill after the years on the force. He brushes his teeth and runs his hand over his thatch of grey hair. 'Salt and pepper', Zoe calls it but Koop can't see it as anything other than grey. He turned fifty a few months back and everyone told him it was the new forty. Koop didn't buy that line, but he's trying not to get too wound up about the numbers. Reflexively, he checks himself in the mirror. Not too bad, he thinks. For an old codger. Tall, but not stooped, his shoulders wide from swimming, his stomach still as flat as could be reasonably expected, Menno Koopman gives silent thanks for his Dutch genes. So many of his old colleagues now look like bloated parodies of their former selves while he, through no great effort, remains essentially how he was at twenty-five. Koop pulls on jeans and a white t-shirt and, dressed, walks across the courtyard to Zoe's studio.

As he opens the door, Zoe and Melumi are kissing. Koop stops in the doorway and watches them appreciatively. It's only after they pull apart that they notice him.

'Don't stop on my account. Should I come back later

when you and the cunning linguist have finished?'

Melumi picks up her bag. 'Pervert,' she says. 'I was just going.' She strokes Zoe on the hip, a gesture Koop finds oddly erotic, and moves to the door. Koop stands aside as Melumi passes. She pauses, pecks him on the cheek and grabs his crotch playfully.

'Slut,' says Koop, smiling.

Melumi blows him a kiss and walks out towards her car, parked, as always, at a sloppy angle to the house, one wheel canting awkwardly atop a tree root. Koop sees that its balding tyre needs replacing. Thirty years in the force means that Koop still notices those sorts of details.

His current job, distributing organic coffee from the plantation which borders their property, is one he enjoys, getting him out and about and helping him and Zoe to put down some roots, but there's no denying it doesn't have the salty tang that his old life had. And living amongst the hill-dwellers and hippies means he keeps his old job quiet. Even so, the news has leaked out somewhere, and Koop has had more than one sticky encounter with a member of the alternative community.

Still, he reflects, as images of himself and Zoe and Melumi come to mind, the alternative life does have compensating factors. Mel's Prado chugs painfully down the long gravel track towards the road and Koop closes the studio door.

He walks over to Zoe, pulls her close and kisses her, tasting Melumi on her lips.

Every time Mel, or one of Zoe's previous girlfriends, stays over he wakes horny, no matter what the three of them have done the night before. This morning is no different. And Zoe, he knows, will be the same. It will only take the tiniest push from him for them to be rolling around the floor of the studio in a breathless heated muddle of clothing and sweat.

Intertwangling, Zoe had called it once. She has a habit of putting accidentally mangled words into her speech; one of the many things Koop loves about her. Zoe slips her tongue into his mouth and Koop pushes himself closer. She pulls away slightly and smiles at him.

'Not now, Koop,' she says. 'Tempting though it is. I've got that GOMA presentation thing next Tuesday, remember?'

Koop stifles a childish impulse to argue the point. But Zoe is right. Why be greedy? They have the whole weekend coming up and Friday is one of his busy days.

Zoe returns to her desk and clicks the Mac into life. Koop stands behind her rubbing her shoulders and looks at the designs onscreen.

'Excellent,' he says, meaning it.

Zoe is a good designer, turning everything she works on into clean and clever solutions. There is an unfussy elegance and sly wit about her work which Koop, while not fully understanding, is fiercely proud of. For the past six months, one of Zoe's best clients has been the shiny new Gallery of Modern Art – GOMA – two hours north in Brisbane. She started with small jobs for them and has rapidly expanded her influence until the point has come when she's close to being handed sole design responsibility for next year's prestigious BritArt show.

She has no illusions that being English helped her as much as her design skills. She's found that, in many ways, Australia still has an often unwarranted, but highly useful, respect for English design and English designers. Her arriving at GOMA's door at the same time the BritArt show was being mooted was also serendipitous.

She isn't complaining. Twenty-five years in the design business has taught her that while not *everything* is about timing and fortune, when things fall into place for you, it's best to just accept it as part of the package.

And it isn't like she hasn't made it happen. She and Koop arrived in Australia on a business visa. In addition to putting up money, they pledged to run a company employing Australians, Zoe leasing a small office in Brisbane and installing two young Australian designers along with a secretary. She called the new practice Boomerang and allowed the sexy young Aussies to look as though they ran the place. A designer to her boot heels, Zoe knew that dressing the shop window was the way to get customers through the door. So far, so good.

Koop kisses the back of her neck and pushes himself away with an exaggerated sigh.

'Well, if there's nothing on offer, I might as well go deliver coffee.'

Zoe waves over her shoulder, already concentrating on the details of the project.

'Go,' she says. 'Deliver.'

Koop leaves her to it, pats Ringo's head, gets into the ute and starts the engine. He turns around the great fig tree which spreads across fully thirty metres of their garden and sets off down the track, disturbing a noisy flock of rainbow lorikeets who fly chattering across the paddock and down towards the creek.

Another day in paradise.

6

After the autopsy, Frank returns to Stanley Road and
by lunchtime has assembled a crime wall that, by his
exacting standards, is starting to resemble something
that might produce results. The wall is an integral part of
all MIT's investigations. Frank Keane and Emily Harris's
syndicate – one of four operating under the Merseyside Police MIT remit – occupies the fourth floor at the
Stanley Road base. The place is nothing special: generic
office space, indistinguishable from thousands of others
apart from the cork boards which line three walls of the
room. These boards are divided into neat sections, each
a current active case.

The wall is not the haphazard collection of 'clues'
beloved of television detectives. Instead it is carefully
produced to serve as a central information point for the
inquiry. Daily updated sheets will be printed, each of
which relate back to the internal MIT server which is the
case's official hub.

There is, in fact, no real reason for the crime wall to still
exist, not with modern police work being encouraged to
become ever more digitally driven.

But the wall, Keane is pleased to note, is proving stubborn to change. They have already successfully resisted several Stanley Road 'initiatives', most of which involve reducing paper consumption; a laudable concept in the context of the grotesque spume of paper which spews out of MIT and all other police departments on a daily basis.

The reason for the survival of the crime walls is simple: officers, or at least most of the more effective ones, like them. Keane believes they serve the same purpose as a village campfire. In a day which seems to be filled with an almost unending list of online police procedures to fulfil, the walls are somewhere that the officers can congregate without fear of being seen to be 'not working'.

Today, though, the thin pickings on the burnt-man case are proving resistant to progress. An abundance of medical evidence from the examiner's office is beginning to make its way into the system and up onto the wall, but of the core of the case – the identity of the victim – there is still precious little.

Harris has posted what she's discovered about the tattoo in a thorough online file, limiting her wall to a single A4 sheet detailing the various lines of inquiry that require following up.

To Keane, Aussie Rules football is not something he has any knowledge of other than as a game that seems inexplicably popular in Australia. He's looked at some clips on YouTube and has not come away with any feeling as to why anyone could get excited enough about it to get a club motto tattooed on their leg. An Australian thing, clearly.

Harris has discovered some potentially useful stuff. St Kilda is a seaside suburb in Melbourne, the support for Aussie Rules being particularly virulent in that part of the country. That helps narrow things down a little but, as Ronnie Rimmer, another of the detective constables in Keane's syndicate, points out, it only narrows it down to the male population of Australia.

'And there's nothing to guarantee he's an Aussie,' says Em Harris. 'Could be an immigrant wanting to fit in? A South African? English?'

Keane shakes his head. 'An Englishman wouldn't get a tat like that. I just know it.'

Harris looks unsure, but Keane knows he's right.

'We need to talk to an Australian,' he says to no-one in particular.

At the morning briefing, Keane and Harris, while being clear to the team that they are to keep an open mind, express the view – one shared by everyone in the room – that this is a drug case. It isn't a giant leap of intellect to make the assumption and the officers greet the notion with well-worn sarcasm.

Keane still feels it's worth going through the reasons why. The level of violence used, the logistics involved in transportation, in bedding the pole in the sand, all point one way. This case isn't a domestic, or a crime of passion, or something that has been covered up. It is cold and it is public.

'Whoever did this was making a point,' Keane says.

'Like the Barry Haines hit,' puts in DC Rose. He's referring to the recent lunchtime assassination of one of the city's biggest drug barons outside a gym in Speke. The word is, so far unproved, that an East European hit man was hired. After the hit he melted back into his homeland without a trace.

Keane acknowledges Rose's contribution. 'Perhaps, but this is at another level. Haines was all business. This has a level of sadism we haven't come across before. Someone is upping the ante.'

'Could there be a Colombian connection? It's got that Faraway Place feeling. Sort of Scarface, like.' The bass voice of DC Scott Corner booms out from somewhere up near the ceiling. Corner is the tallest in the MIT team. The 'Faraway Place' was the term used by an infamous Liverpool dealer to refer to Colombia. Fond of using nicknames, the 'Flat Place' had been Amsterdam. Corner is pointlessly using the term to show off and Harris chops him down.

'The old Australia–Colombia connection, eh? I think you're looking in the wrong direction, Scott.'

A few of the team suppress smiles. 'Tim-*ber*,' says someone with a smirk. Scott Corner is a decent enough copper but prone to bouts of pomposity. It's good to see him cut down to size now and again. Corner flushes and looks at his toecaps.

Keane has already moved on.

'It's one of the big boys. I can feel it. This message is being sent to someone about a deal currently in progress – why go to all the trouble otherwise? If it's a new outfit, some thrusting young Turk, I'll be staggered. It's the usual suspects.'

Keane begins counting them off on his fingers. Boyd. The Norris Greens. Kite. Azwallah. 'Maybe the Mancs taking their beef to an away ground, although my feeling is that that's the least likely prognosis.'

There are nods from the team. They all know this is local. It's not Manchester, not unless there's been a sudden acceleration of the cross-city rivalry; something that can be effectively discounted. Manchester and Liverpool are less than forty miles apart but from the drug trade point of view it might as well be four hundred. Trade is brisker between Liverpool and Amsterdam, between Liverpool and Spain, between Liverpool and half a dozen other markets than it is with Manchester. The vicious local turf wars are just that: local. Everyone at the MIT meeting suspects it's very likely to be one of the three or four really big outfits in the city, such is the scale and professionalism of the killing. But knowing this doesn't move things along very much, not immediately anyway. The code of silence active amongst the serious Liverpool drug movers and shakers would shame a Sicilian. Someone will talk but not so soon, not with this much attention on the case. The press are going to town and that always means additional pressure on the MIT syndicates from above. Liverpool's new status as a shiny tourist spot will not be helped by a drug war played out in public.

'I want some intel from the OCS,' says Keane. The Organised Crime Squad in Liverpool is one of Europe's busiest, but they have a tendency to play their cards close to their chest. Keane knows, however, that his investigation will include them at some point, certainly once a link has been established from the victim to a person of interest to the OCS.

'I'll talk to them,' says Harris. 'I've got a friend who's a DI there.'

She notices one or two of her colleagues exchange the briefest of glances; schoolboy reactions. Harris is gay. She never mentions her sexuality but neither does she hide it and, much to her bewilderment, it seems to be a constant source of fevered adolescent lesbian fantasies for some of the team. Harris contents herself with a cold glare at the offending coppers – their smirks fade under her scrutiny – and turns her attention back to the job.

She's happy to let Frank take the lead in the briefing – he's the senior officer in years if not rank – but she carefully avoids being seen as Keane's assistant. That wouldn't help her, or DI Theresa Cooper and DS Siobhan McDonald, the two other female officers in their MIT section. Not to mention any other ambitious black coppers.

Without letting Keane cut back in, Harris continues by detailing Corner and his usual partner, Peter Wills, to contact the Coastguard and find out why no-one noticed a great big fucking fire on Crosby Beach on the night in question. They are also told to rustle up some uniform plod and do some old-school door-knocking.

'Just the houses facing the sands,' says Harris. 'They're a long way from the scene but they're the nearest. Some-one may have seen something. You can also get down to the car park later and see if there are any dog walkers. People with dogs sometimes have a routine. If they're there today, it's conceivable they were there yesterday.'

With a nod to Keane to confirm agreement, she closes out the briefing and the team disperse to their various roles.

The missing persons list has been picked over without finding any Australians who match the victim. A couple of strapping blond backpackers who'd been reported as missing by their worried families in Sydney had looked promising. Keane thought it might have been the break until the two had been turned up by the Met alive and well and earning a living as gay escorts in London.

Two of the team are checking recent Australian arrivals with Immigration. Keane knows there will be an abun-dance of matches in the list, but unless one of them has been reported missing, it is, very likely, another dead end. He instructs Caddick and Rose, the officers working that angle, to go back no further than three weeks.

'Just three weeks, boss?' says Caddick. At twenty-six and already a detective sergeant, Phil Caddick is rising fast in the force. A bit too fast in Keane's view. There's something about his clean-cut face and studied air of 'professionalism' that irks him, and would have had the same effect on Koop. Keane tries to shake the negative thought, seeing it as his own problem, not Caddick's. The guy's alright, Keane reflects, I just don't like him being younger than me. He wonders if Koop ever entertained similar thoughts about the younger Frank Keane.

'The tan, Phil,' he says, not unkindly. 'Three weeks in England and he'd have been as pasty as any of us.'

'Unless he used a tanning salon,' says Harris. 'Just saying,' she adds, catching the look on Keane's face. She returns to her screen leaving Keane tapping his pen against his drip-ringed coffee cup. The day is draining away and with each passing minute the chance of getting that crucial breakthrough is fading.

Keane looks out across the city skyline. The flat northern light compresses the array of iconic buildings and rain-streaked concrete sixties shitboxes into one jagged grey line of broken teeth. On the road running past the building Keane watches a black bin bag tumbling against a broken-down plastic roadworks barrier. It joins a drift of wet litter and crap two feet deep. A fat teenager, his shaved head almost blue, inspects the line of parked cars for opportunistic bounty as he passes, oblivious to being less than eighty feet from a large police building. And what would we do if he did crack one of the windows and leg it? Chase the little fat fuck? Keane rubs his eyes, feeling the tiredness in his bones. The case is coagulating around him. Too slow.

He turns away from the window and the thief.

When in doubt, do something. He sits down at his desk and opens his computer, the noises of the office surf in his ears. Across the partition Harris is talking on the phone, her voice rhythm businesslike, although Keane can't hear the words, even if he wanted to. She's doing something, though, and Keane gets a tiny spark of irritation and the competitor in him stirs. Partner she may be but Harris is intent on moving up and Keane wonders if she'll leave him behind. She has some obvious advantages.

Keane inwardly chastises himself for the thought. It's not Harris. It's me. He shakes his head and concentrates.

It's all about momentum. Getting momentum and keeping momentum. If you don't keep the revs up the machine can get bogged down all too easily. Forty-eight hours is the perceived wisdom on the length of time it takes for a trail to grow cold and Keane has some sympathy for that point of view. He also knows of plenty of instances where the old saw proved fallible, when patient and diligent police work ground out a result over months and years.

But he's not by instinct a patient man. So he tries something Koop taught him a long time ago. He goes fishing.

He clicks the mouse and accesses the Liverpool in-call log which lists all calls to Merseyside Police from the public. Every call across the county is fed through one central collection point before being assigned geographically by the dispatchers. As with everything now there is a detailed digital record. As always, the list is dominated by noise and public disturbances, domestic violence, petty and not so petty crime.

Keane tunes his antenna to those incidents that smell a little *off*. He couldn't have articulated what that would look like, but he'll know it when he sees it. The bobbing float dipping below the canal surface, indicating the activity below.

Like when they have a lying suspect. No matter how good they are – and Liverpool is blessed, or blighted, depending on your viewpoint, with a super-abundance of some of the slipperiest liars, con men, cheats, blowhards and out-and-out bullshit merchants ever to walk the face of the earth – Keane always *knows* when they are lying. It is contained in the stories they tell, some detail that, even though it may have nothing to do with the lie itself, alerts him to the fact that lying is taking place. A bum note. A missed beat.

After more than an hour at the list, Keane has narrowed it down to three potentially interesting calls.

He clicks Google Maps up onscreen – the modern policeman's friend – and examines each location in more detail, cross-referencing it with the location of the iron men on Crosby Beach. All three are within a few miles of Keane's crime scene.

The first, and furthest from the crime scene, is a burnt-out Transit van on an upscale golf course to the north. The almost tearful club groundsman phoned it in this morning after finding the Transit smouldering in the middle of his precious eighteenth green.

For Keane, the positioning of the vehicle looks worthy of further consideration. It's something that, as an avowed hater of all things golf and golf-related, he can almost appreciate. Provoking a volcanic reaction by depositing a blazing van in the middle of the pristine green speaks of a twisted sensibility not without humour. Pitch-black, Liverpool humour, but humour. Even so, the flaming Transit feels like the work of kids. But well worth a look.

The second call concerns a rented lock-up garage on the Dock Road. A disgruntled renter at an adjacent garage called to say that a bad smell was coming from the neighbouring property. That in itself isn't particularly interesting, so much as the name of the company listed as renting the unit in question: Gormley Creations. A coincidence that the company has the same name as the sculptor? Keane doesn't believe in coincidence.

The last of Keane's picks is a call from a 'frightened' kid – the dispatcher's word on the log – who had phoned asking for someone to take a look inside a container near the north-western end of the Seaforth Freeport. Besides the location, the nearest to the body, what piques Keane's interest is that the caller would have known it was a risk calling the police: whatever they'd been doing inside the Freeport was illegal.

'Let's go,' he says, picking up his jacket from behind his chair.

Harris, despite her outward appearance of diligence at her keyboard, doesn't need to be asked twice.

They take Keane's car, a silver VW Golf which he's had for almost two years. If cars reflect their owners, the Golf is bang on the money so far as Keane is concerned. Tougher than it looks and moves quickly when it needs to.

For his part, Keane doesn't give his car a moment's thought. Never a petrolhead, the VW is something he'd bought to get around in, no more.

He and Harris cut through Everton Valley and drop down through the red-brick badlands of Kirkdale and Bootle towards the Dock Road, the streets so familiar to Keane that he could have navigated them in his sleep;

something that, in his patrol car days, he'd come closer to doing than he cared to think about.

This area is rich in pickings for policemen. Kirkdale, Keane has read in last weekend's papers, is now officially the most deprived area in Europe. The Halligans, one of Liverpool's largest disorganised crime families, live here, a tangled network of graft, violence and intimidation spread like a cancer through the close-set Victorian-terraced streets and shabby seventies housing projects built on the bomb sites left by the Luftwaffe. Thirty years after the war, Keane can just about remember seeing the acres of rubble, the odd pub left in place; an oasis in the wilderness.

Keane and Harris automatically log incongruities as they drive: a gleaming and unmolested Porsche Cayenne four-wheel drive parked outside a house that cost less than the car's gearbox. Unmolested for a reason. A lone teenager about sixteen, mobile in hand, circles the end of a street on a bike several sizes too small, and notes the traffic.

'Halligan at three o'clock,' says Em Harris. 'Darren.'

Keane's eyes flick towards the youth, his interest piqued at the name. He slows the car a fraction.

'Siobhan had a run-in with him last week on Glassfield. Needless to say, he knew nothing.' Harris is talking about another case on Keane's slate; this one a fairly low-level turf beef between the younger members of two of the north Liverpool 'squads', which ratcheted up a notch when James Glassfield, eighteen, was killed and his body tossed onto the lines at Bootle, not far from the location of the infamous Bulger toddler murder. The theory MIT are working on is that it was an 'of the moment' crime involving a number of youths. As expected, local help from the community in finding Glassfield's killer has been precisely zero.

With good reason.

Despite his youth, James Lee Glassfield was a significant local dealer with a growing rep and people know better than to raise their heads above the parapet. The police have nominal dominion here. A grass is not tolerated. The idea that you may have talked is often enough to bring instant and brutal retribution.

They crucified someone on these streets two years back. Literally. Fixed to a billboard with a nail gun. Keane remembers the guy lost a hand but wouldn't say a word. He didn't blame him. If he lived round here he'd have done the same.

Keane doesn't live round here. Neither does Harris. No coppers do and haven't done since the late sixties when it all really started going to shit. The bizzies migrated north and south, to outlying suburbs, commuting in to police communities they're no longer part of. Thatcher's blood money poured into the force in the eighties and the cord was cut forever. Now on these granite-hard streets it's dog eat fucking dog and Keane, like everyone else in the force, gets paid to mop up the remains.

With the Glassfield case, both Harris and Keane have known from the discovery of the body that the answer to finding the killer is, most likely, not going to come from hard police work. It's going to come from an arrest down the line and some toerag rolling over to negotiate a plea deal with the Crown Prosecution Service. At that level, drug murders are almost always cleared up within two years with relatively little connection to the snow-drifts of paper that accumulate round each and every MIT case.

Keane gives Darren Halligan the eye as they cruise past. Keane is more familiar with the boy's older cousins, Matty and Dean. Darren, a new fish, still has a way to go before he rises to their giddy heights.

Darren Halligan watches Keane and Harris pass, his eyes sliding off them in the too casual way Keane has seen in thousands of encounters with his 'clients'. Without quite knowing how, the kid has clocked them instantly as filth. The skill – cop spotting – has by now taken on an almost genetic quality. Certainly there are generations of families like the Halligans that Keane and Harris have had dealings with, and they all seem to be ready to do battle the instant they leave the womb.

But the links with the families are no cosy, local affair; bobbies on their bikes chasing rosy-cheeked apple scrumpers. Darren Halligan, and thousands like him busy spotting for low-level dealers, are the first point of entry for a tidal wave of drugs going in, out, and through Liverpool, the connections reaching into areas as murky as the Colombian Cali cartel, IRA hit squads and the seriously scary East European new boys.

Keane presses the accelerator. Darren Halligan sitting astride his BMX watches them go and Keane turns his attention back to the case.

The van on the green and the smelly garage both turn out to be useless. There is no guarantee the van hasn't been used by the killers – it has, after all, been reduced to a blackened husk, much like the victim – but once Keane and Harris get a look at the scene they're convinced this has been straightforward theft and mischief. The golf club is missing trophies that have been taken from a display case in the lobby. Keane can't see the type of ruthless killers he and Harris are looking for pausing en route to steal the Rotary Shield trophy. The only detail of possible drug involvement is that two scrambler motorbikes – the light, flexible sort used in motocross – were spotted in the area immediately after the fire. The likely explanation is that they were stashed earlier and used to get away across the sand dunes and walking tracks that criss-cross the area. It's the bikes that catch Keane's ear. The use of this type of machine has become commonplace in drug-related incidents. Several drive-by shootings in recent years have involved scramblers. Invariably, if the police raid a house involved in drugs, one or two or more of the bikes are discovered. Their ubiquity is such that their existence at or near a drug raid is a signifier of guilt, at least to the investigation team. But here it looks like they've been used for exactly what they were designed for: cross-country motorbiking.

The smell at the lock-up too is a bust. Rotten fish, stolen smoked salmon to be precise, part of a month-old robbery of a refrigerated Sainsbury's truck.

Which leaves the Freeport call.

They arrive there just after four and speak to the security guard who calls a second guard to take over at the gate while he directs Keane and Harris to their destination. It takes ten minutes to wind their way through the sprawling complex. Keane pulls the VW behind the security car and they step out.

It's cold now, properly cold, and Harris is glad she's worn her Berghaus.

'That must be the one,' says the security guard. 'If your information's right. Probably just some little fucker making trouble.'

'Most likely,' says Keane. 'Stay here.' Silencing the man's meek territorial protests with a glance, he and Harris begin walking towards a relatively new-looking red container standing on its own about twenty metres from the Freeport boundary fence. Behind the mesh, the river runs west to east with Crosby Beach to the north. The container squats almost directly beneath a wind turbine, silent and still. The word 'STENZER', the logo of a shipping firm, is painted onto the side of the container in a deeper red colour.

Even before they go in, Keane knows this is the place.

He can taste it. Something bad has happened here. Keane has sensed it at other crime sites before. Not always, but often enough to recognise the sensation when it arrives.

The traffic noise diminishes as they approach; two banks of containers at right angles form a wind and noise shield. In the lee of these protective boxes there is dead air in the space occupied by the red container. Above them, off to one side, the turbine blades rotate.

Keane notes that the red container can't be seen from the city side of the Freeport and is only partially visible to anyone on the wasteland bordering the site.

The killers didn't have far to travel to place the victim amongst the iron men. Through the metal slatted fence, beyond an expanse of wasteland and beyond that the rock wall, Keane can see some of Gormley's figures.

It's high tide and several of the sculptures nearest to the docks are already almost fully covered. In the cold grey light, they contain a powerful energy that Keane isn't altogether surprised by. He doesn't think of himself as an art lover. Like most locals, he was instinctively dismissive of the Gormley installation. Modern rubbish. Cost as much as a hospital wing. He remembers going out there with Julie one sunny Sunday. They parked behind the dunes next to the lake and asked for directions from a shaven-headed man with a dog and wearing the obligatory shiny nylon football shirt – this one the royal blue of Everton – which bulged over his substantial belly.

'Don't waste yer fuckin' time, mate,' he snarled in an accent so pronounced as to render it a foreign language if he'd been speaking to anyone not born in the city. 'They're absolute fuckin' shite.' And then, to make sure they fully understood the absolute fucking shiteness of the sculptures, he jabbed a finger back towards the beach and spat out the words again. 'Ab-so-lute. Fuck-ing. Shite.'

He and Julie giggled about the art critique all the way to the beach, imagining it being used word for word in *The Observer* 'Sunday Review' section.

Gormley Piece 'Absolute Fucking Shite'.

And, in all honesty, at first Keane didn't see exactly what all the fuss was about. It was an unusual sight, that had to be admitted; the figures staring blindly out across the water. Keane kept noticing details that got in between him and the art. Bits of litter. Dog shit. A group of youths milling around a couple of younger boys on the promenade. And Keane's policeman core had been moderately outraged by the local additions to the figures.

He'd seen another Gormley piece over at Gateshead when he'd been there for a training course with Newcastle Police. The magnificent and moving 'Angel of the North' looked out over the confluence of the A1 and A167 roads, the landscape grim, industrial. The sculpture, its sail-like iron wings embracing and defying the wind, had shocked Keane by its scale, its span wider than the Statue of Liberty is high. He'd found that out because he'd parked and gawped up at it, temporarily reduced to childhood again by the sheer confidence and beauty of the thing, the first and only time an artwork had literally stopped him in his tracks. Like the figures on Crosby Beach, the Angel was constructed of the stuff of northern England – iron and steel – yet it appeared light, and was possessed of so much latent energy that Keane wouldn't have been surprised to see it take flight across the north-eastern landscape – steam-driven and belching smoke, naturally.

But until today, standing outside the container that Keane is sure was the killing place, he hadn't 'got' the Liverpool artworks in the way he had the Angel. Gradually, though, the power of the work begins to emerge. And, in a way that he doesn't want to examine too closely, an echo of what Ferguson said in the mortuary, something about the murder being 'artistic', reverberates with him.

'Ready?' says Harris. She touches him on the arm and he realises he's been standing motionless.

He nods and Harris puts a gloved hand to the container door.

7

Koop's first call is the distribution shed at the plantation, a ten-minute drive from his place. He backs the ute to the open doors of the building and gets out. He pauses for a few seconds and looks at the neat rows of net-draped coffee trees rolling down the side of the hill into the valley before going inside.

Koop passes a minute talking about nothing in particular with Annie, the spike-haired company office manager, and a couple of the boys on the packing tables, before he loads up the tray and leaves on his rounds.

Zoe was right calling him a delivery boy; that's exactly what he is, and exactly how he likes it. After a lifetime working at the sharp end of things, Koop figures he is due a little ordinariness.

In the truck he punches in The Abyssinians and the reggae loops out, sounding as fresh-minted as the day it was recorded. If this is what ordinary feels like, he can take a bucketload. He turns up the volume and snakes down the hill towards Byron and the first delivery of the day.

Strictly speaking he doesn't need the work. He holds a fifteen per cent investment in North Coast Coffee, and could easily bring in another driver on the wages they pay locally. But after spending the first six months of his new Australian life lazing around watching his gut grow, he knew he had to find an outlet for his energies other than swimming and drinking coffee, or his brain would have started dribbling out of his ears.

The deliveries keep him in close touch with the business. Working the deliveries is the ideal way to protect his investment. As a copper, Koop had known the value of attention to detail and he is no different when it comes to delivering coffee.

A café owner who had found the last batch a little bitter is given a new order free of charge, no questions. Another who confides in Koop that several other coffee companies are prowling his café is offered a discount on subsequent orders, with the discount increasing in direct ratio to the size of the order.

A café whose barista has gone absent without leave (a common problem on the cruisy North Coast) gets a couple of names from Koop of people who might be able to help them out.

Each wrinkle, each detail, is dutifully recorded on the voice recorder app on Koop's phone. At the end of each day he sits in the cab and listens, wincing at the sound of his nasal Liverpool accent, and noting down anything usable in a black notebook before gladly wiping the soundbites.

By lunchtime he has all but completed the run and stops for something to eat at a café next to a pub. A velvety flat white in front of him, and an order of bacon on Turkish to come, he sits in the café garden and hopes his face doesn't look as smug as he feels.

Koop has just taken the first sip when he becomes aware he's being watched.

He glances up and sees two men aged around thirty sitting at the bar which divides the pub from the café. Rangy and dishevelled, the pair wear the *de rigueur* hemp clothing and white-boy dreadlocks common to this area of the shire. Koop thinks there must be a way station on the Pacific Highway where the clothes are handed out to metropolitan refugees on arrival. Somewhere between Ballina and Byron maybe.

They turn their faces away but there's something familiar about one of them. Koop struggles for a moment before getting it: he's a neighbour of sorts who Koop has seen behind the wheel of a smoky ute rattling past his property now and again. The two bend their shaggy heads together over their half-empty beers, and one of them mutters something which causes the other man to snigger.

Koop feels the blood quicken in his veins, sure he's the subject of their laughter, but he contents himself with drinking his coffee. Dickheads all over. Forget it.

And then he catches Zoe's name and feels something dormant inside him begin to uncoil. This could go south, he thinks, and tries to ignore the evolutionary instincts triggering his anger. Good coppers don't get angry, they just get even. He's not going to react. He's been called everything before.

But family. That's a different matter.

Koop looks up again and this time there's no mistaking that Zoe is being discussed. The two men, growing in cockiness with each swallow of their beer, are openly snickering.

Koop sighs, takes another sip of his coffee, sets it down carefully and walks across. He's been in this situation a million times and knows exactly how it will play out. He is – was – a professional.

'I know you?' he says conversationally to the guy he thinks might live nearby, making sure his face is just that bit closer than is usually comfortable, an old copper's trick. The man leans away a fraction, as Koop knew he would. 'Because you look familiar. And I thought I heard you mention my wife's name?'

The guy glances at his mate and smirks, gains a jolt of confidence. 'Don't think so, mate. You must be goin' deaf, or something. Happens to fellers your age, I heard.'

His mate splutters and the two high five. 'Fucken classic, Thommo,' says the mate.

Koop smiles, outwardly patient. 'And your mention of my wife? I heard you say something about Zoe.'

Thommo, on a roll now, nudges his mate before replying. 'Couldn't have been the same woman, mate,' he says, eyeing Koop, weighing him up, seeing him as too old, too thin. Here it comes, Koop thinks. He's decided I haven't got the juice. 'The only Zoe I know about, I heard she was a Jap-licking pussy-muncher. That couldn't be your missus, could it?'

Koop knows enough to stop his first instinct which is to grab Thommo by the back of his stupid dreadlocks and break his sun-blistered nose across the bar. Instead he walks away and sits down. Only amateurs react. Thommo's toast. He just doesn't know it yet.

Thommo and his oppo are creased up. Koop's retreat has signalled open season and attracted the attention of the barman who shrugs apologetically. Koop makes a 'what-can-you-do' gesture before leaving, the sounds of the two drinkers ringing in his ears. Whipped.

'Didn't think so,' says Thommo as he passes. 'Bye bye, you fucken pussy.'

Koop doesn't reply. He wants Thommo to think it's

over. Wants the barman to think it's over. In case what's going to happen ends badly.

Outside, the car park deserted, Koop gets into his truck and backs it into a shaded patch behind the pub dumpster and waits, checking the delivery manifest to pass the time.

He doesn't have to wait long. Fifteen minutes later, Thommo stumbles into the car park and fumbles for his keys next to a dilapidated ute. Koop winds down his window and calls him over, making sure they have the place to themselves.

Thommo looks around.

'What the fuck?' he says. 'What do you want?'

Koop holds his palm up in a conciliatory gesture and opens up the passenger side door.

'Mate, we just got off on the wrong foot, OK?' Koop says, putting a wheedling tone into his voice. He leans over, hand out. 'No hard feelings, right?'

Thommo is positively swaggering now. He leans into the cab of Koop's truck. 'So your missus does knock off that Jap bitch? I fucken knew it! I saw them swimming in the creek once. I'll say this, she's got a body on her. For an old bird.'

Koop forces a tight smile onto his face and looks down at his outstretched hand. An invitation. Thommo takes it and, as he does so, Koop jerks him sharply forward, headbutting him square in the nose. Blood spurts out and Thommo grunts, disbelieving, as Koop grabs his dreads and smashes his face down onto his knee. Koop drags the unconscious Thommo into the cab and pushes him into the passenger footwell.

Koop checks the windscreen has no splashes of blood visible and drives slowly out of the pub car park. The remaining two deliveries on Koop's manifest for that afternoon will have to wait.

He's got plans for Thommo.

The morning has passed quickly for Zoe.

She always enjoys this stage of a project, when the arguing has been done, the arm-twisting is over, and the final designs are being tweaked and polished. All the components for the BritArt project are arranged around her, both physically and onscreen. Zoe surveys her handiwork and tries to see the potential flaws, the areas that the client will find difficult, but she sees nothing that shouldn't be there. It's good work, an elegant and clever solution. She and the guys in the Brisbane office will do the final presentation at GOMA on Tuesday and Zoe knows it will be received well.

She opens up a chat link with the Brisbane office and the face of Suze, one of her designers, appears. Zoe methodically goes over the details of what they're going to need for the Tuesday presentation. Behind Suze, Tom, the second of her team, flits backwards and forwards in front of a table piled with design printouts.

'You staying overnight on Monday, Zoe?' Suze asks.

'Probably. Depends on how organised I am, Suze. But, yes, most likely.'

Zoe glances up and out through the window as something catches her peripheral vision. A car turns into the property and Zoe tenses.

A police car.

'Suze, I have to go. Talk to you later.'

Suze waves. 'Speak soon.'

Zoe closes the chat window, instinctively saves the work onscreen and stands up, her hands smoothing the front of her blouse.

Years of life with a cop means she knows that the police arriving unannounced at your door is seldom something that turns out well. She breathes deeply and tries not to think about what they want, but in her head is one word, repeating over and over.

Koop. Koop. Koop.

The roads around the shire are noted for accidents, and she has a sudden image of her husband dead or dying, surrounded by grim-faced paramedics. She picks up her mobile, her hands trembling, and dials her husband.

'Shit.'

Koop looks at Thommo who is crying. At least, Koop thinks he's crying. It's hard to tell. Thommo has his hand cupped over his nose and his face is a streaky mess of snot, blood, matted hair and tears. He is crouched on the grass in a paddock hidden from view off Friday Hut Road. He is naked.

'You broke my fuggen dose, man!'

Koop leans across and pats Thommo on the shoulder. Thommo flinches like a whipped dog, any fight in him long gone.

'You got lucky,' says Koop.

'Lucky? How the fug is dis lucky, you fuggen loony! You're goin' down, you crazy fug! The fuggen pigs'll be round once I . . .'

Koop puts a finger to his lips and holds his gaze on Thommo. He leans in close and Thommo flinches. Thommo stops talking, his eyes wide.

'No, that's not going to happen, sunshine,' says Koop. 'Two reasons. First, as you'll have noticed, you are bollock naked and ten kilometres from home. You've got more chance of being arrested for lewd behaviour than ratting out any story about me. Second, and this is where I want you to pay attention, you little ball of pus, if I get any heat from anyone over this little . . . etiquette lesson, I may have to let the police in on your little secret.'

'Secret? What fuggen secret?'

Koop jabs his finger into Thommo's chest. 'Don't act stupid, *Thommo*. I worked drugs for twenty-five years. I chewed up and spat out grubs like you quicker than I could find 'em. The amount of hydroponic supplies you've got knocking about your place means you're either an over-enthusiastic cucumber grower, or you're farming a nice batch of weed in that slum you call home. It's a miracle you haven't been busted already. But, being a reasonable man, I'm willing to let things drop at this point if you are. OK? Now nod.'

Thommo nods and Koop straightens up. He gets back into the truck leaving Thommo staring up at him through a tangle of dirty hair.

'Wait!' says Thommo, scrambling to his feet, realisation dawning, his fear-shrivelled dick bouncing pathetically in a tangle of pubic hair. 'You can't leave me here like this, mate! Mate!'

Koop guns the engine and pulls away. He leans through the window and waves. 'I think you'll find I just have, *mate*.'

As Thommo fades into the distance in Koop's rear-view mirror, his mobile phone blurts into life.

'Oh thank God,' says Zoe as he picks up on the second ring.

'Zoe?' says Koop. 'What is it?' Her voice has a panicky quality that he hasn't heard before, and following so closely on the heels of his run-in with Thommo, it rattles him.

'It's alright, Koop. It's just that the police are here and I . . .'

'The police? What do they want?'

'I don't know. They haven't come in yet. I was working and then I saw them and I, well I just thought the worst. Gave me a shock. You know what I mean.'

Koop knows what it could mean, what it often did mean. He's thought before about what it must be like to be on the receiving end of the news they brought into people's houses, like plague carriers. Dead fathers, brothers, mothers, daughters. The victims more often men than women. And the messenger frequently met with anger or bitterness, a couple of times with actual physical assault.

'I've got to go,' says Zoe. 'They're at the door.'

She hangs up and Koop speaks into dead air.

'I'm on my way.'

Ten minutes later Koop pulls sharply into the gravel driveway and revs the ute up the sharp incline. He parks next to the police car and hurries into the house, his face set.

'In the kitchen,' shouts Zoe. Koop relaxes fractionally. Her voice, while containing something he can't yet place, doesn't contain enough to panic him.

Koop walks through to the large open kitchen that is the de facto centre of the Koopman house. Two uniformed policemen sit on stools drinking coffee, their hats upside down on the counter. They're in the process of standing up when Koop comes in. He exchanges glances with Zoe but finds he can't read her expression.

59

'Mr Koopman?' says the taller of the two, a beefy, red-faced man in his late thirties. He holds out a hand which Koop shakes. 'Sergeant Sullivan, Northern Rivers Police, as you can see. Good to meet you. This is Constable Wheater.'

Koop leans across and shakes Wheater's hand.

'Now what's this all about? Is anyone hurt?'

Sullivan hesitates and glances at Zoe. 'No, no-one's hurt, Mr Koopman,' he says. 'Well, no, that's not quite accurate.'

'For God's sake,' says Koop. 'What is it?'

Zoe steps forward and puts a hand on Koop's arm.

'It's Stevie.'

8

Stevie is such a very long time ago, and so far away, that the story has acquired the air of a fairy tale that happened to someone else. Except it wasn't a fairy tale. It had happened, and it had happened to him, and is still the most painful thing Menno Koopman has ever experienced.

The music of the period sometimes jolts him backwards in a vertiginous flush of synaptic connections. Something like the snap drum intro to Bowie's 'Young Americans' can take Koopman right back to 1975 and to Sharon and Stevie.

Sharon had been a looker, not a doubt about that. Koop doesn't really remember the physical details of what she looked like, other than a vague recollection of blonde hair, flicked back Farrah Fawcett-style, but he remembers the feeling he got when he saw her. It could be summed up in one word.

Sex.

Sweet sixteen but Sharon had most definitely been kissed. Koop hadn't had any illusions that he was the first, but he was the first who'd managed to get Sharon Carroll pregnant. They'd been standing against the iron gates of

61

Hillside High up on Breeze Hill when she told him. He still had pimples.

'We'll get married,' he'd said, not knowing what else to say and not wanting to appear as he was: a scared-shitless teenager. 'I'm goin' in the police. It'll be alright.' It was an assertion, nothing more. Even as the words came out of his mouth Koop remembers thinking that things probably wouldn't be alright. Fucking pregnant! Jesus.

If Sharon noticed his hesitation she didn't say anything. She'd agreed. It had felt like a plan. Grown up. It would be alright.

'Alright,' she said. 'OK.'

Sharon's family had other ideas.

After a gut-churning scene between his and Sharon's parents one night in their cramped terraced house – an evening that still had the power to bring a blush to Koop's face – almost as soon as Stevie was born, the Carrolls had emigrated, seemingly overnight, to Australia; one of the last contingent of the ten-pound Poms.

Koop had formed half-baked heroic ideas about following Sharon over there, of becoming an Australian, of making his new life with his woman and his baby. He'd even got as far as turning up at the Cunard Buildings to find out about applications.

But he was seventeen. And at seventeen the pain had subsided shamefully quickly.

A year after Stevie's birth Koop heard through a school friend, who'd also made the move down under, that Sharon was pregnant again and had married a local. She discouraged Koop's attempts to contact Stevie as he grew older and, in all honesty, Koop had been glad. He hadn't the heart to interfere. He hoped Sharon and Stevie were making a go of things and, once he'd started work as a cadet, had begun sending money to Australia. The envelopes came back, scrawled 'return to sender' and, year after year, little by little, Koop's will lessened. Doing the right thing was complicated, slippery, and he'd never been sure he'd managed it, or even come close.

It hadn't, in the end, been his to do. It was up to Sharon and Sharon's new family to decide, and what they'd decided was best was for Koop to fade from Stevie's life as if he'd never existed.

Koop had supposed that Stevie might, if told, eventually show some interest in following up the trail of his real father, but it had never happened. Years became decades, the details of Stevie's life being drip-fed in ever-decreasing snippets of hard-won information, and although Koop tried to conjure up the appropriate feelings it had always felt false, as if he were feigning interest. He thought of Stevie frequently, often in idealised terms. And, ever since moving to Australia himself, had once or twice entertained fanciful notions of tracing him (it would be easy) and entering his life, a late flowering of filial affection.

It had been Zoe who'd gently shown him how potentially destructive this could be, not just for Stevie but for Koop himself. Zoe who –

'Mr Koopman?'

It's Sullivan and Koop is back in his kitchen. He coughs and straightens his back.

'Stevie?' he says, looking Sullivan in the eye. 'What's happened? Why are you guys here?'

Sullivan licks his lips and flicks a glance in Zoe's direction. Koop knows what's coming isn't going to be any kind of good.

'They found a body,' says Zoe. 'In Liverpool.'

9

It's taken six weeks for the container ship *Scanda-Hap*, registered under an Indonesian flag, to make the trip from Liverpool via Hamburg and Singapore. Right now she's pushing south hard down the east coast of Australia and is less than three days from berthing in Brisbane. The ship rolls easily through a moderate swell, the bulk of her load automotive, almost all of it cars from the Jaguar and Ford factories in Liverpool. In Singapore they'd unloaded a third of the cargo and filled up with an assortment of other goods, all sealed in containers and only distinguishable by the coded tracking system.

Three particular containers, stowed by prior arrangement in the centre of a three-storeyed stack, are of special interest to the ship's cargo officer who is receiving a large sum of money to ensure that they're delivered to the right person without attracting the attention of customs officials.

The cargo officer, a jittery Pole who makes more from this trip than he makes in a year of regular work, had inspected the containers himself once the voyage was underway and had found them to contain exactly what they specified: three expensive, brand new Jaguars. No doubt there is more to it than that but he knows enough to reseal the containers and think about it no more.

At Brisbane the ship docks and, despite the acid tension knot in the cargo officer's gut, clears the customs inspection without incident. The Pole had expected nothing else, but he races to the head and unloads his stomach when the customs men have left. Later, marginally more relaxed, he leans over the side and watches the three containers being unloaded before heading below decks, his part in whatever this was over.

Once off the ship, the containers make their stately way to a huge dockside container storage park to the west of the Port of Brisbane terminal where they sit for two days unmolested. On the third day a number of legitimate car dealership delivery drivers arrive and, again after undergoing scrupulous documentation checks, drive the vehicles inside the containers a short distance to a dealership car pound where the cars sit in the sun in neat rows, waiting to be transported across Australia. It's cheaper to transport the vehicles on double-decked car transporters than for them to remain in the containers.

The three vehicles from the three special containers so carefully handled by the Pole are parked at the end of the first row nearest to the perimeter fence. They are there not so that they can be taken out under cover of darkness – that would be foolish; the vehicles can be moved easily when required – but in order that Max Kolomiets and Anton Bytchkov, who pull up on the perimeter road in a tricked-out Jeep Cherokee, can check their safe arrival. The two are very anxious to see the cars for themselves.

Between them the Jaguars contain eight hundred kilos of cocaine.

They are worth keeping an eye on.

10

'That's where the kids must have got in.' Em Harris stops, her hand on the heavy lever attached to the container door, her voice barely above a whisper, and points to a section of the mostly well-maintained fence that has one tiny piece missing, revealing a small gap at its foot just big enough for a child to fit through. Keane acknowledges what she says with a twitch of his head but can't help thinking Em is delaying going inside. He pushes past her, suddenly anxious to see if their feeling about the container is right. Keane takes the lever and leans back using his weight to open the heavy door. He lowers the lever to anchor the door and steps inside.

'Careful, Frank,' says Harris. 'This *is* the place, you know that, right?'

Keane raises his hand in acknowledgment. He hasn't got a superstitious bone in his body, but a space where someone has met a violent death has an atmosphere unlike that found anywhere else. A kind of low-level psychological hum, a suppressed howl. Keane's been in too many of them for it to be all bull.

He pauses at the entrance, produces a powerful penlight

from his jacket and sweeps the beam around the interior quickly, a first pass. It's empty apart from a metal pole which has been jacked tightly into place, braced at roof and floor in the same way Keane has seen builders supporting ceilings in houses under repair. Around the base of the pole, and leading from there in a thick ragged line towards the door of the container, is the blood trail that had frightened the kids enough to make a call to their natural enemy, the police.

Keane takes out some latex gloves and hands Harris a pair. They exchange a glance and both suppress a feeling of elation. The case is achieving momentum. The murder happened in here. There will be something useful.

The container smells of vomit. Keane points his beam and sees a small pool of the stuff splashed up against a corner. Someone sickened by the killing? He makes a mental note and steps further inside.

Once in, there is a complete silence. Even the traffic surf has gone.

The two of them move slowly towards the pole taking great care where they place their feet. Without needing to check with Keane, Harris grabs her mobile and calls for the SOC unit to be sent out. When the call is finished she uses the phone display light to help illuminate the container. Keane traces the blood pattern on the floor.

'Quite a mess,' says Harris.

There is a lot of blood. The SOC unit will check for compatibility with the victim, but both of them know they're looking at the torture site.

The blood is dry, although Keane and Harris both see that it's still fresh enough to be recognisably red. In evocative splatters and dripped ribbons it radiates out from the pole in a circular fashion. Only a narrow strip of floor near the pole has escaped the blood.

'He moved around,' says Harris. Keane knows she's talking about the killer. It doesn't take a genius to work out the victim was tied to the pole. Harris takes a number of photographs using her iPhone.

'But he couldn't do the back of his head, the bit against the pole,' says Keane, pointing a latex-clad finger at a relatively clean section of the floor. 'Hence the gap.' He feels a shiver on his neck and hopes the SOC unit doesn't take too long.

Harris bends low to the floor, careful not to step on any blood.

'These small splatters.' She points out several curving marks on the floor. 'He's flicking the blood off the blade.' Harris mimes the motion and Keane can almost see the blood falling.

Keane breathes out slowly and runs his torch over the ceiling and upper walls of the container. He can see nothing of any interest, although the SOC officers will go over the entire place in microscopic detail. Perhaps they'll turn something up.

Harris moves away from the pole and runs her phone light slowly and deliberately along the base of the metal walls. At one point a small collection of detritus has gathered, blown by the breeze through the open door. She moves along carefully, stopping every few centimetres to take a closer look at the offerings. Two items in particular seem to hold her attention for longer than the rest. She places both in a small plastic evidence bag she produces from her jacket pocket and stands up, holding the bag to the light. Keane can see she's shaken by something but he doesn't ask. Harris will tell him soon enough.

Behind them the door creaks in the wind and she and Keane both twitch.

'Let's leave it at that,' he says. 'We don't want to contaminate the scene.' Harris doesn't hesitate. Despite the absence of a body, the site is the creepiest place Keane has ever been in. There's something demented about this one and Keane can feel the container taking a permanent space in his memory, a space he doesn't want it to occupy but is now powerless to stop. It joins all the other unwelcome memories that, on bad days, or on dry-mouthed pre-dawn mornings, seem to be the only ones he has.

Outside in the welcoming cold, Keane flips open his mobile and calls the container details in to the other members of the MIT team. Siobhan McDonald takes the call and tells him the SOC unit has already buzzed the news in.

'It's here,' Keane tells McDonald. 'I'd bet my left nut. Get Corner and Rose started on tracing access to the Freeport.' Even as he's giving the order, Keane knows this line of inquiry will be unlikely to produce results. But it has to be done. The Freeport must have CCTV, gate logs, something. Corner and Rose can start digging into who had access. He signs off and pockets his phone.

'What did you get?' he says to Em, pointing at the plastic bag in her hand with his chin.

Harris, her equilibrium restored but her face grim, holds it up to Keane's eye level. In the bag is a small lens cap of the kind you'd find on a video camera. The word 'Sony' is etched into the plastic. It looks new.

'Sweet Jesus,' says Keane, the penny dropping. 'The fuckers taped it.'

11

Macksym Kolomiets, known as Max by all who fear and love him (and the former group far outnumbers the latter), has no idea this is to be his last hour. Very few people ever do. For most, the time of their death must always be at some far distant point and Max is no different. If someone had told him he was about to die, and soon, he'd have laughed. What could possibly harm him, the under-14s coach, on this perfect Gold Coast evening, out in the centre of the paddock surrounded by fifteen excited boys kicking footballs?

A lightning strike?

It would have to be something cataclysmic, because anything less wouldn't get past Anton Bytchkov, waiting in the car as always. Very few dangerous things in Max's life get past Anton Bytchkov.

In the unlikely event that anyone or anything did somehow manage that prodigious feat, they would then have to face up to Max Kolomiets himself. The Russian – although Max would have beaten anyone who called him that to his face, proudly hailing as he does from Ukraine – is a man with a big reputation up and down the Goldie. Developer. Party contributor. Criminal.

No, Max would not have believed his time had come, not even if the devil himself arrived, the Grim Reaper in tow.

He swats away a mosquito, glad he sprayed himself before coming out, blows his whistle and begins to organise the team into two shooting drills. One of the boys, Mitch Barnes, the captain of the team, trots across to Max and begins talking about the upcoming game. The season proper is over but the summer league is starting this Saturday.

In the car, Anton sits bolt upright as always, his eyes fixed on the field and his beefy forearm resting on the sill of the Beemer. He looks every inch the attentive bodyguard.

Apart from the neat hole in his temple from which dribbles a thick line of blood showing black against his lifeless Ukrainian skin.

He hadn't known a thing, thinks Jimmy Gelagotis, working up a head of steam. Fucking Russians think they're fucking invincible. Not so invincible now, eh, Anton, *malaka*?

Gelagotis puts the gun inside his zipper jacket with some difficulty, the silencer bulking out the weapon's snout. Jimmy Gelagotis fucking hates Russians. Or Ukrainians, or whatever the fuck snow-bound fucking hell-hole wasteland they fucking crawled the fuck out of. Especially fucking Russians who have the fucking cheek to fuck about with his fucking business.

Fifteen years as a card-carrying nasty bastard has taught Jimmy Gelagotis that people never expect those they are in business with to go directly for the nuclear option in the event of a dispute.

With Jimmy, the nuclear option is the favourite option. He's been brought up to believe in hitting first, hitting

71

fucking hard, and making sure it fucking counts, in that order, and it hasn't let him, or those who depend on him, down yet. Work with Jimmy and you get the benefits: girls, cars, money, the usual shit. Cross Jimmy Gelagotis and what you get is what Anton has just discovered. The motherfucking nuclear option, baby, all the motherfucking way.

And now Kolomiets is going to find out about it too.

Jimmy puts one hand in the nylon pocket of his heavy black G-Star zip-up. He is sweating lightly in the warm evening air, but the coat is needed to hide the gun. Don't want Kolomiets getting any warning, do we? Jimmy walks casually across the floodlit grass, his hand raised in greeting, the sounds of the boys getting sharper, their voices insistent, passionate about the game. He is smiling.

About twenty metres away, Max sees him. Jimmy registers The Russian's hesitation as he shades his eyes against the floods. That's right, Max, it's me. Just deal with it.

Jimmy sees Max glance towards the Beemer. Anton's head and shoulders are silhouetted against the clubhouse lights and Max relaxes a little. He and Gelagotis are in business, after all. True, there have been some minor difficulties lately, Jimmy not happy about taking a smaller cut of the Liverpool thing, but what business doesn't get the odd bump in the road now and again? And with more than one hundred and fifty million dollars floating around, did Jimmy really think he was going to continue on the same percentage?

Still, Max will have to have a word with Anton later. It doesn't look good letting anyone get so close without him being there, not even a trusted ally like Jimmy Gelagotis.

'Friend!' says Max, a warm smile crinkling his broad

face. 'This is surprise.' He pats Mitch Barnes on the head. 'You come to see future Socceroos?'

Jimmy doesn't reply. There's no point. Talking is for amateurs.

Jimmy glances at the boy, draws out his Sig Sauer and shoots Max three times in the face and chest. The boy jerks involuntarily, his eyes wide, his face speckled with blood as Max drops to the grass without a sound. Jimmy Gelagotis bends and places the barrel against Kolomiets's temple and pulls the trigger one more time. Now the boy makes a kind of squeaking sound and begins to tremble violently. Jimmy expects the boy to wet himself but he doesn't. He is paralysed.

Jimmy Gelagotis stands and looks at the boy, weighing the business decision before him. After a couple of seconds, he places a finger against his own lips and raises his eyebrows. The boy nods, his entire body shaking violently.

He understands. Say nothing.

Jimmy seriously doubts the boy will ever talk again. Even if he does, runs Jimmy's logic, his evidence will never stand up. It just doesn't seem to work that way. And killing the boy would be a mistake. A dead villain is one thing, a murdered schoolboy quite another, and the last thing Jimmy Gelagotis would want in the coming weeks is the full attention of the law. It would be bad for business.

He places the Sig Sauer back inside his jacket and, leaving the boy standing uncertainly next to The Russian's body, starts walking across the sports field towards the black-shadowed trees on the far side, and beyond them, the car. Behind him, the footballers are silent, many of them not noticing what has happened, and those who have, not computing the information – their brains unwilling to interpret what they have seen as a murder. They gather round Max and the boy like confused puppies, unclear about what to do. Not one of them would remember Jimmy Gelagotis's face if asked. Not that Jimmy cares. He knows that if it came to questions being asked he will have been at a dinner at a restaurant in Broadbeach. In court, at least.

An overweight man wearing a tracksuit runs towards the boys from the direction of the soccer clubhouse.

'Hey!'

Jimmy hears him shout. His accent is English. A Londoner. Jimmy glances back and sees the man start moving his way. A hero.

'You! Hey, you, stop!'

Jimmy sighs and comes to a halt. He turns and lifts the Sig Sauer from under his jacket. The hero is now about forty metres away. Jimmy knows that, from the other man's point of view, he will appear as no more than a black silhouette against the lights from the road. Jimmy waves the gun in the air and starts moving towards the hero. As he expects, the man begins to back off. Jimmy Gelagotis waits until the hero is sprinting away before turning around again.

It's time to go. The cops have already been called by some of the kids.

Jimmy gets to the car, moving quickly now, slides into the seat and turns the ignition. A look back shows the sports field illuminated as clearly as a stage. Several more adult figures are running in the direction of Max's body, around which his players have congregated.

Jimmy Gelagotis drives carefully away from the soccer fields, his blood fizzing, his breathing coming hard. He doesn't have to do this dirty work – he could have detailed Stefan Meeks or Tony Link to do it – but over the years he's found that doing it yourself pays big dividends. For one thing, anyone who even remotely suspected that Jimmy Gelagotis was capable of such extreme violence on a personal level would most certainly adjust their attitude accordingly. The kicker for Jimmy is that flying solo means there is no messy trail, no accomplice ready to blab when an arrest is made. Keep the story simple. That's the thing that fucks people – getting too complicated. He's been out for a meal with friends – ask them. At a restaurant he owns – check with the manager. No story, no elaborate cover-up. I was here, not there. I'm not guilty. Jimmy has seen too many hard boys take the fall due to delegating, or talking too much, or both.

Eight minutes after leaving the soccer fields he parks the stolen car at the end of a darkened, deserted industrial development on a road that leads nowhere, and gets out. He lights a match and applies it to the rag that's sticking out of a can of petrol in the back seat. As the car begins burning, he jams a black cap low on his head and jogs towards the car park of a wholesale paint warehouse in the occupied portion of the industrial complex where he's left his own vehicle; an unremarkable Commodore with no tricked-out spoilers or wheels, or any of the other shit you see every day up and down the Goldie. Jimmy has even muddied the rego plate in the unlikely event of being on CCTV. The same reason he wears the cap. He already knows there were no cameras at the soccer ground; he'd checked. Homework. Details.

After a last look to make sure the stolen car is well alight, Jimmy Gelagotis drives carefully homewards, obeying the speed signs and lights, pausing only to throw the gun over a wire fence into a deep pile of refuse at the Broadbeach council tip. The gloves he gets rid of by wrapping them round a rock and dropping them over a bridge into the river.

Free of any evidence, he punches a speed-dial number on his phone.

'Tony,' says Jimmy.

'How was it?' Tony Link's voice is urgent. Jimmy can hear the sounds of glasses clinking and the chatter of a restaurant in the background. 'Hold on, mate, let me get somewhere quiet.'

Jimmy waits slightly impatiently for a few seconds until Link comes back on, his voice clearer. 'That's better.'

'You finished fucking about?'

Jimmy doesn't wait for Tony Link to answer. 'It's done,' he says.

'Both of them?'

'You don't need details, Tony. Have the big cats arrived?'

'Stefan's got them safe and sound, Jimmy. No problem.'

'I don't want any problems. I want them watched twenty-four seven until we're good to go, got it?'

'Like I said, Jimmy, Stefan's got three of his boys on it. They're safe as.'

'They fucking better be, friend.'

Jimmy clicks the conversation closed and concentrates on his driving. The last thing he needs is a speeding ticket.

Less than half an hour after putting the bullets into Maksym Kolomiets on the soccer field, Jimmy Gelagotis turns the nose of the Commodore into the driveway of his five-bedroom, pin-neat suburban home. He flicks the garage open with the remote, rolls the car inside and closes it behind him. He gets out and sniffs his hands, which smell faintly of petrol and rubber. In the house he turns into the small bathroom situated close by the garage door and washes his hands twice. He dries them thoroughly before going into the kitchen where his wife, Eva, is talking on the phone. She waves her fingers at him and he kisses her neck and then wanders over to where his eldest daughter, Anna, is doing her homework at the kitchen table.

'Good girl,' he says, and ruffles her hair.

'Dad!' She pushes him away, smiling.

Jimmy hangs his jacket over the edge of the pool table, goes into the TV room and sits down. His teenage son, Luke, is playing some sort of computer game with a friend. Neither boy looks up as Jimmy comes in.

He picks up the *Gold Coast Bulletin* and settles into his chair.

Job done.

Now all he has to do is wait and see how Stevie is doing in Liverpool.

12

Eight hundred years old, and carrying its bloody history lightly, Liverpool has been freshly spruced up in the last couple of years, with billions of euros of European Community grants and serious private investment pouring into the city. Shiny new postmodern buildings have sprung up along the waterfront, and those that have been around for a while are being forcibly scrubbed up like an old man at Christmas.

Liverpool is looking better than she has done since her heyday. The newly gleaming white 'Three Graces' – the Liver Building, the Cunard, and the Port of Liverpool Building – dominate the waterfront approach, their size and grandeur facing west, to America, speaking of a time when Liverpool was the global hub. It's a city built on the sea, its history salt-caked, and best approached from the water.

Stevie White doesn't arrive in Liverpool by sea. Very few people, other than those who work on the merchant ships, or who come in on the cruise ships beginning to use the port in increasing numbers, did. Stevie arrives in the city of his birth by rail.

He isn't impressed.

He'd left Liverpool as a baby and hasn't, until this week, set foot outside Australia again. As the train clanks its way through the arse end of Liverpool, Stevie's beginning to wish he'd never let Jimmy know that he'd been born here. Apart from ending up running this errand – something that Stevie guesses could turn out to be unpleasant – Jimmy and the guys have begun calling him 'Pommy'. It rankles with Stevie, a St Kilda boy to the core, especially coming from Stefan Meeks, who'd also been born in the UK but seems to have escaped the jibes. Stevie hadn't given the man listed as his father a second's thought. As far as he was concerned his real father had been Australian. This Koopman meant less than nothing.

Stevie stayed overnight near Heathrow after arriving late the previous night and caught the train north around lunchtime after battling his way through the filthy, over-crowded underground system. The ride up to Liverpool hasn't been all bad. Some of the countryside looks pretty nice. Small, and all sort of squished together, but pleasant enough.

It's as the train gets closer to Liverpool that things begin changing. They rattle over a bridge that gives Stevie a view of a seemingly endless industrial landscape hugging the banks of a grey waterway that disappears into the smoggy hinterland. Even through the train's air-filtering system he can smell a chemical tang that hits the back of his throat like the aftertaste of mouthwash. And then the train dips down towards the city, Stevie's windows filling with a rushing succession of drab industrial complexes that give way to row after row of grimy red-brick houses, their backyards filled with rickety white plastic chairs, overflowing bins, lines of washing, bicycles, motorbikes, a woman smoking a cigarette, stacks of wood, the carcass of a fridge. Across the tops of the houses he sees the city getting closer and he relaxes a little as he begins spotting things he's familiar with: taller buildings glinting against the grey sky, car dealerships, shinier things, signs of affluence.

The train lurches into a series of short tunnels cut into the red stone that Liverpool is built on, its surface blackened with centuries of soot and smoke and exhaust. Here and there in this subterranean labyrinth, illuminated by shafts of unexplained light, are the tags of adventurous graffiti kids. Stevie has to admire their persistence but wonders how bad life on the surface has to be to make the hellish trek underground worthwhile.

The train slows and Stevie notices those who must travel the route regularly begin to collect themselves and their belongings. The tunnels give way to a cavernous open space and the train pulls into Lime Street under a scrubbed-up Victorian steel arch roof.

It's a myth that all Australians find England cold. Still, Stevie pulls on his thick puffa jacket around his already bulked-out frame and zips it high as he steps onto the platform. He holds his bag lightly. It's a small one. He doesn't expect to be in Liverpool, or England, any longer than is strictly necessary.

13

'Why are you telling me?' Koop asks Sullivan. 'Why not Sharon? There must be a Mr White somewhere.'

Sullivan takes a swig of coffee and wipes his mouth with the back of a finger before replying.

'You were listed on the birth certificate as father. It's mandatory in the UK to list the biological. Mrs White died three years ago. Cancer. I thought you must have known.'

Koop shakes his head. Cancer? Fuck.

For him, Sharon has remained the frightened sixteen year old he last saw on Stanley Road a day or two before she and her family left for Australia. He knows that she married and moved on with her life without him, with Stevie, and then a new man, but it's still a reach to start thinking of her as dead.

'We hadn't spoken in a very long time.'

Zoe came and stood behind Koop, her hand resting lightly on his shoulder.

There was a pause.

'So . . .' said Koop. 'I still don't know why you're here. I mean, it's a shock, if this body does turn out to be Stevie but, well, as I say, it's been a long time. I don't really know what I'm supposed to do. It's Sharon's business, or her husband's now. He's Stevie's dad, right? And Stevie has a brother. A half-brother.'

'Mr White died too, Mr Koopman. A couple of years before his wife, before Sharon. Heroin took the brother. He overdosed in 2007. That's why we're here.'

Koop feels stupid. He looks at Sullivan. There's something he isn't getting. Something he should be getting.

'You're Stevie White's next of kin, Mr Koopman,' Sullivan says, his voice quiet. 'There's no-one else.'

Keane gets the call from Australia on the third day of the investigation during the morning team briefing. They're gathered in a loose group in front of the portion of the crime wall devoted to the burning man case. The empty space has been filling up rapidly after the discovery of the container and has begun to spread outwards onto the adjoining walls. The team has gone over the container in their usual thorough manner, but other than the lens cap – and of course the blood – the scene has produced little else. What they have, though, is plenty for the forensics to be getting on with.

Keane looks round at his team. They're sitting on the edges of desks, or standing. It always feels staged to him, this situation. Like something from a cop series. But how else to do it? Memos?

'What have we got? DC Corner? Anything from the Coastguard?'

'The fire was noted,' says Corner in his usual deliberate manner, checking his notebook for the details. It's a running joke at MIT that Corner, whose wedding is next month, would consult his notebook when asked to say

'I do' at the altar. 'A call came in from a householder on Marine Crescent. A Mrs O'Rourke. 11.47 pm. No action taken. Apparently there are so many beach fires that the Coastguard has stopped doing anything and the fire service only gets involved if there's a threat to life or property. And taking the engine onto the beach . . .' Corner lets the sentence trail off and closes his notebook.

'The householder had nothing to add,' says Wills. 'Old lady. She saw the fire, reported it and then closed her curtains and went straight to bed like the law-abiding citizen she is. Saw no-one, noticed nothing.'

'Dog walkers?' says Harris. A dog owner herself, she has a feeling that this line might produce something.

'Nothing,' says Corner. So much for feelings, thinks Harris. Stick to the police work.

DS Caddick raises a hand. The gesture puts Harris in mind of an eager child in the classroom. Not altogether inaccurate when applied to Caddick, whose naked ladder-climbing simultaneously repels and amuses her, so clearly is it written on everything he does. Still, she thinks, who am I to judge his ambition?

'I think we may have got something from down under, boss,' he says. The convention in these morning briefings is to keep everything all business all the time, but Caddick can't help a flicker of smugness creeping onto his face. 'Took a bit of digging . . .'

'Get on with it,' says Keane.

Caddick's partner, Steve Rose, stifles a smile. You could always depend on Roy to stop Phil dead in his tracks.

'Right,' says Caddick. 'Sorry, boss. Anyway, we drew a blank with missing Aussies.'

Keane nods impatiently and looks at his watch. His temper hasn't been improved by the latest in a long series of nights during which he's resumed his ongoing battle with his galloping insomnia. He picks up his mug of coffee and guzzles the last of it while Caddick speaks.

'So Rosie and I looked at another angle. We asked the immigration control boys for a list of recent arrivals from Oz travelling this way on a UK passport.'

'UK?' says Keane. 'This boy's Australian.'

'With respect, sir,' chimes in Steve Rose, 'he could hold both passports.'

'Which is what it turned out to be,' says Caddick. This time he can't keep the smile off his face. 'At least we think so. I asked the Aussies to contact us when they had anything for us. Someone's scheduled to call this morning with an update.'

Keane gives Caddick and Rose a grudging nod. They've done well, and spotted something he should have been alert to.

'Good,' he says crisply. 'Anything else?'

Harris leans forward and Keane notes the men in the room flick eyes towards her curving chest. He has no doubt Em is fully aware of the effect she has, but outwardly at least she is all business.

'I checked with the Organised Crime Squad and they are very interested. So much so they want access to our files.' She breaks off with a look in Keane's direction. Keane shrugs. It's only to be expected. 'They want to run a watching brief on the case,' continues Harris. 'If anything concrete turns up linking any of their targets with this, they'll be all over us like scallies in a ram raid.'

'Anything they can give us that might actually be useful?'

'The short answer? No. There's nothing they can give up that wouldn't have the potential to spoil their ongoing investigations.'

'They do know this is a murder, Em, right?' says Keane. He leans an elbow on the window and looks out towards the river.

'Hey,' she says, holding up her hands. 'Don't shoot the messenger.'

Something in Em's words reverberates with Keane and he pauses before shaking his head. It will come back to him if he lets it. He looks at Harris and raises his own hand in a placatory gesture. Both of them know the system and don't altogether blame OCS for keeping their distance. For now. Once they step across some line drawn by the OCS, things could become a lot stickier. He'd hoped for a steer towards one of the drug boys, a name, a tip.

That doesn't look like it's going to be forthcoming and he knows he and Harris are in for a few days of tip-toeing between OCS and their own boss, DCI Perch. Keane makes it a personal mission to avoid contact with Perch as much as humanly possible.

He and Harris move the briefing to the plans for the day's work and begin prioritising the other cases their MIT syndicate has active. It takes them more than forty minutes before they break. Just as members of the unit start drifting back to their desks, Australia calls.

With a questioning nod to Keane, Caddick puts the phone on speaker.

'DI Keane?' A deep, marginally distorted, Australian voice growls across the incident room, out of place against the grey city beyond the window, which can now be barely glimpsed through a curtain of rain. 'Detective Senior Sergeant Warren Eckhardt here, Queensland Police.'

'Queensland?' says Keane. 'I thought our boy was a St Kilda nut. Aren't they Melbourne?'

'Well, out here we have planes. Some buses too and one or two cars. Your bloke might have been from Melbourne but he's on my desk now.'

'Sorry, DSS Eckhardt,' says Keane, trying to keep the excitement out of his voice. 'We're all ears.'

After a pause, Eckhardt continues. 'Thanks. I believe I may have something of interest for you blokes.'

'And the non-blokes,' puts in Harris.

'It might be morning where you are,' says Eckhardt, blithely ignoring the barb from DI Harris. 'Down here it's too bloody late to be working, blokes and non-blokes, both. But this might just be worth waiting up for.'

There is an audible rustle of paper over the speakers.

'We have, or had, one Steven Brendan White, aged thirty-four. Height one hundred and eighty-one centimetres, approximate weight ninety kilos. These measurements were taken at his last arrest.'

Harris looks at Keane and raises her eyebrows. There's a tangible increase in the atmosphere inside the incident room at the mention of an arrest. An arrest means paper-work. Facts. The lifeblood of any investigation.

'Yes, this boy's got form,' says Eckhardt as if he's seen their reaction. '*If* he's your body. Quite a bit of form too. He's a "known associate" of several of our leading Melbourne businessmen, although that's a long way outside my patch. I got that from his arrest sheet and from a call I put in to a friend of mine down there. White moved up here to banana-bender land – that's Queensland to you – four years ago. I'll email the details I have, but you'll need to speak to the Melbourne guys for older informa-tion on White's activities.'

'Any distinguishing features?' says Keane.

Eckhardt pauses – for dramatic effect, Keane is sure.

'Well, that might be the clincher, DI Keane,' says Eckhardt. 'Stevie's a big Saints fan.'

'Saints?' says Keane.

'St Kilda, DI Keane. One of our glorious footy clubs. I believe your man has a tattoo that matches?'

'Looks good,' says Keane. 'Anything else?'

'Quite a lot, now you ask. Steven White left Australia via Brisbane on October seventh flying on Qantas, as all true blue Aussies do. According to the flight manifest he went straight through to London, arriving on October the eighth. He travelled on a British passport issued only recently through the British Embassy immigration department in Canberra.'

'He's a Brit?' Keane can't keep the surprise out of his voice.

'Only just,' says Eckhardt. 'According to the records I've managed to collect, Stevie was born in the UK in 1975. In your town too, DI Keane. He's one of your own.'

'A Scouser?' says DC Rose.

'I don't know,' says Eckhardt. 'What's a Scouser?'

'Someone from Liverpool,' says Keane.

A dry chuckle comes down the line. 'It looks like Stevie came home to die,' says Eckhardt. 'Not that I imagine he expected to.'

'Thanks very much, DSS Eckhardt,' says Keane. 'You've been very helpful. Very helpful. I think we'll be talking again.'

'No problem. Always a pleasure when it all lands on someone else's plate, eh? Oh, and one more thing –'

'Yes?'

'His real father's name wasn't White. It was Koopman.'

14

After Sullivan and his taciturn partner have left, Zoe kisses Koop on the side of his head and tactfully withdraws to her studio.

Koop grabs a bottle from the fridge and pours himself a large glass of white wine. He drinks half standing at the kitchen counter and refills the glass. Ringo padding along behind him, he takes it out into the garden and walks down the rough path to the fig tree. On the side of the tree furthest from the house the land runs down towards the creek and Koop can see the hinterland rolling away into the distance, with Mt Warning just poking its sharp beak above the skyline.

It is a lovely, glorious spot.

Koop has put an old double car seat there, its back to the great trunk of the tree. Zoe keeps pestering him to replace it with something more in harmony with its surroundings but, the longer the seat is there, the more resistant Koop is to the idea of getting rid of it. He settles back into its sagging embrace and reflects that, in this case, Zoe is wrong.

That's the trouble with designers; they always want

things to be tasteful. Koop prefers them to be real. This old car seat had been lying in the shed on the property when they'd moved in. As far as Koop is concerned it has more right to be here than he does.

Besides which it's bloody comfortable.

Koop takes a pull on the wine and lies back. Ringo flops heavily to the ground and drops his head onto a patch of grass, leaving Koop to try the impossible and organise his thoughts.

Stevie is dead.

Koop, like most cops, has developed an ad hoc system of compartmentalising his emotions. It's a survival tactic which no policeman on earth could manage without. Like coral building and hardening, the years bring new layers of protection. You couldn't see the things he'd seen without that distance, that crust. The trouble is, when something like this comes along, that same protection also becomes a problem. Menno Koopman is not, he feels, an unsympathetic or cold man. Far from it. Despite his Dutch antecedents he is, if anything, somewhat hot-blooded, more Mediterranean than North Sea. But this one has him foxed.

Stevie is – was – his son. A son he'd never been a father to. Stevie may never even have known Koop existed. A son who, from what Koop had pieced together, had not chosen the high road. A son who had met a grisly end in, of all cities, his birthplace. A son who Koop has thought of through the years. He should be feeling the loss yet there is nothing from the heart and this pains him almost as much as the news about Sharon and Stevie.

The sun is low now and mosquitoes begin to find their target. Koop, wearing his usual jeans, boots and a long-sleeved shirt he'd pulled on over his t-shirt, doesn't notice.

89

A dull anger is beginning to build as he starts assessing what he knows about Stevie's death. Sullivan had said the Brits might need some DNA from Koop at some stage to confirm identification. This was because Stevie had been burnt.

Possibly, Sullivan had hinted, while alive. It had been a vicious and violent end for his own flesh and blood.

Koop had seen Stevie once. In 1975, shortly before Sharon's family emigrated, he'd waited for her to leave the terraced house and take the new-born baby for a walk. Koop had stopped her in Stanley Park and looked at his son for the only time. There had been conversation but nothing heated, at least nothing that Koop could recall now across a distance of thirty-four years.

It is the image of Stevie's head, his eyes closed as he slept that crisp Liverpool morning that lodges in Koop's mind. Stevie with his life in front of him, no pathway set, no problems. Innocent. And now someone, someone in Koop's old patch, has taken the trouble to kill him. Koop finds it difficult to examine his emotional response, but there is nothing complex about the conclusion he reaches under the fig tree.

Someone is going to pay.

15

The girl's peach-perfect buttocks rotate in front of Stevie's face, the UV black light lending her skin an erotic blue-white sheen.

She is very good.

Pale-skinned, dark-haired, and looking a little more elegant than most of the other dancers, she speaks with an accent Stevie doesn't recognise. Some sort of Eastern European thing. He doesn't care. Kite is treating him well, showing him a good time and Stevie knows that the dancing is just a preamble if he decides he wants the girl. She's on offer, as much a part of Kite's hospitality as his room at the hotel, or the French fizz bubbling in his glass. A perk.

The girl turns and straddles Stevie's thighs.

'You have fantastic body,' she whispers. She breathes into his ear. 'Most people I dance for not in so good shape. I want you, yes?'

Stevie doesn't know if it's part of her act. Quite frankly he doesn't give a shit. He's been around strippers and dancers and hookers for so long that he knows it's all bullshit and that it doesn't matter. When they are as good as this chick, it's best to just lie back and enjoy the moment.

Kite, a head-turning blonde gyrating on his thigh, raises a glass to Stevie who returns the gesture.

'Not too fucking shabby, Mr White, eh?' says Kite. 'How are you liking Liverpool?'

Stevie smiles. He's liking Liverpool just fine. Kite is right. This is very far from shabby. The trip is turning out to be better than Stevie could have imagined. The Liverpool of his imagination, in so far as he'd ever thought of the place, was formed by half-digested, out-of-date TV shows broadcast in Australia. England, they told the viewers, was either a land of upper-class types punting on rivers in Oxford, or it was feral football hooligans stabbing one another before returning to their filthy terraced slums to eat black pudding and spotted dick and other unimaginably foul 'food'.

That indoctrination hasn't prepared him for modern-day Liverpool.

Granted he is being given the five-star treatment, but from what he's seen of the place it looks like somewhere he could spend some time. The weather is shithouse, that's a given, but then St Kilda in winter is nothing to boast about. The thing that Stevie has noticed – the thing that is really getting his attention – is the money. He'd been told this place was something close to a ghetto. Instead, and despite the economic gloom enveloping the country like a shroud, he finds Porsche dealerships at the dock front, upscale apartment blocks on the market for millions. Wine bars are on every corner, populated by sharply dressed drinkers. He's been driven past funky buildings lit up like art objects.

And of course there are the drugs.

Over a lunchtime steak at a waterfront restaurant at the Albert Dock, Kite had begun filling Stevie in on the deal; the deal that Stevie is there to claim a piece of on behalf of Jimmy Gelagotis. The deal that Stevie already knows too much about.

'You know the quantity, Mr White,' Kite had said. 'Eight hundred kilos. Straight from Bogota via Gdansk and then on to your neck of the woods courtesy of The Russian's connections. Eighty million plus. That's pounds by the way, none of your Australian kangaroo dollar shit.'

Stevie already knows how much the deal is worth. He's been part of Jimmy's operations for long enough to have a comprehensive knowledge of the street value of a smorgasbord of narcotics. And Kolomiets had been relying on Jimmy's connections to disperse the stuff across Australia and over to New Zealand. It's a big shipment, perhaps the biggest ever in that part of the world, and it had proven too much of a temptation for Jimmy Gelagotis. Now, with each passing minute Stevie's in Liverpool, Kite is getting closer to talking about the nub of the problem.

Kolomiets.

The Russian is dead and it is Stevie's boss who killed him. That, Stevie thinks, is the tricky bit. And it had all been avoidable.

You could almost say it had been Macksym Kolomiets's doing. Like always, greed was to blame.

Max had told Gelagotis that, due to the size of the load, Jimmy's percentage would be lower. He wanted to go to a fixed price on this deal; a new way of doing business. New to his relationship with Jimmy Gelagotis, that is.

The way Max saw it, Jimmy would still be making an obscene amount of money so what was the problem?

It was a miscalculation that had cost The Russian his life. When Jimmy had informed Stevie that it would be they, and not Kolomiets, who would be stepping in to take over the whole deal, not just becoming the distributor, it had sounded feasible, sensible even. 'Just go over there and tell the Pommy fucks that they have a new partner. They'll play ball. They'll adjust. They have to, otherwise that shipment will never reach the customers. Max shouldn't have underestimated me, Stevie. Never forget who's coming up behind you.'

In Liverpool, Stevie is starting to see things from a different angle.

For one thing, Kite is unpredictable. You don't get to be crowned the 'King' and play ball with the Colombians and the IRA without having serious history behind you, not to mention a giant set of titanium testicles.

Keith Kite doesn't look like much: small, stocky, with the doughy features common to the Irish ancestry of much of the city. He's been scrubbed up, hair sharp, clothes tailored, and he carries an aura of power with him as tangible as the smell of his expensive aftershave.

Despite this, nothing quite manages to mask his animalistic nature and Stevie suspects that is exactly how Kite likes it. His mouth has a tiny upturn at each side of the sort that Stevie associates with those who enjoyed inflicting pain and humiliation. It reminds Stevie of Heath Ledger in that Batman flick. If he had to pick one word to describe Kite it would have been 'evil'. The fucker is straight out evil.

So Stevie is somewhat relieved that Kite seems to be in no hurry to cut to the chase. The more time that passes before the ticklish subject of Max Kolomiets comes up, the better, as far as Stevie White is concerned. In the meantime, enjoy the little tour Kite is putting on. Lunch at the docks, an afternoon at the lap dancing club owned by Kite. Earlier, while driving in Kite's Bentley, Kite ostentatiously flags down a police car to ask directions, letting Stevie see the grudgingly respectful way the coppers speak to him through the window of the car.

'Unlike you to be lost, Mr Kite,' the cop says dryly, tapping a finger against the peak of his cap in an approximation of a salute. 'You be careful around here, the place is full of rough types.'

Kite drives away, he and the Halligan brothers laughing harshly. The city is his and he knows it. Wants me to know it too, reflects Stevie.

Kite is turning his drug empire into a legitimate one, brick by brick. Bars, hotels, garages, development, development, development. Security companies, the doorman controlling distribution. A shipping company, one he'd used over the years to transport drugs, is now wholly owned by a front company run by Kite. He is making more through legitimate means than through narcotics. But the margins remain so huge in drugs that Kite won't stop.

By the time evening comes, it's all starting to make Stevie feel like a junior grade footy player making his debut in the grand final.

The dark-haired dancer is very good in bed. Skilled in a way that makes Stevie forget she has been paid for. At the hotel, he fucks her lying across a white grand piano and almost laughs out loud at the theatricality of it all. She kisses him goodbye with such a good impersonation of a lover that he forgets, for a time, she is a whore. Kite has also laid on some spectacular blow and Stevie, his system buzzing in the way that a jolt of primo marching powder always brings, steps out for dinner with a swagger in his stride. He suppresses the troubling thought that Kite is ready to talk about the shipment.

Kite has reserved a private room at one of the new breed of gourmet places imported into the city in recent, confident, years. It sits near the crest of the high ground overlooking the city, between the two cathedrals. The food is better than any Stevie has ever tasted, but is a little fancy for him, and he never feels hungry on coke. Kite shovels it down with every sign of enjoyment. The table is a small one, with only three of Kite's closest team in attendance: Declan North, along with Matty and Dean Halligan, two of the infamous and labyrinthine Huyton Halligan family who have been heavily involved in the Liverpool drug operation for as long as anyone can remember. None of them speak much during the meal, which does little to settle Stevie's nerves. Outside the restaurant, Sean Bourke waits patiently as instructed.

After the waiter brings them brandies, Kite leans forward and, without Stevie quite knowing how, the atmosphere in the room cools perceptibly. Here it comes, Stevie thinks and tries to look calmer than he feels.

'Mr White, we've been very hospitable today, I think you'll agree?' Kite says, his mouth turned up in an imitation of a smile, a row of sharp teeth revealed. 'Now I think it's time to tell us what you're here for. Something to do with our upcoming Australian venture, I imagine.'

Stevie glances at the four faces around the table who gaze back at him blankly. Kite gives an encouraging nod.

'Jimmy,' says Stevie, his voice higher than he would have liked. 'Jimmy sent me, Mr Kite. Jimmy Gelagotis?'

'I know who Gelagotis is.'

OK, Stevie, man the fuck up and tell the Pommy cunts. He takes a deep breath and forces the words to come out calmly, with authority.

'Jimmy's taking over the Australian end.'

Kite stares at Stevie. He sits back and folds his arms across his impeccable suit.

'Is he now?'

Stevie nods. He keeps his face neutral.

'And how, exactly, is *Jimmy* going to do that? I'm in business with my good friend Max Kolomiets. That's who the deal is in place with.'

'The Russian's dead.' It comes out quicker than Stevie intends. Fuck it. The Pommy cunt has to find out sometime. With the words said, Stevie feels the worst is over.

Kite looks at North and then back at Stevie, letting the silence develop. Stevie is conscious of the clatter and chatter of the other diners in the restaurant. When Kite speaks again, his eyes have dulled and Stevie feels his sphincter clench. He looks at the man across the table and he knows, as sure as he knows his own name, that the whole deal has fallen apart.

'Hear that, Mr North?' murmurs Kite, his flat eyes never leaving Stevie's face. 'Mr White here tells me that The Russian is dead.'

North purses his lips. 'That is very disturbing news, Mr Kite,' his Irish accent soft, his face hard.

'Fucking heart attack, was it?' says Kite, his voice suddenly choked with venom, his face flooded with blood and fury. He leans forward until he is right in Stevie's space, spittle flying from Kite's mouth as he hisses out the words in a low undertone. 'Stroke? Fell under a bus? Clobbered by a rogue fucking kangaroo?'

The change is savage and, even though Stevie has been expecting a reaction, takes him aback. Dean and Matty Halligan haven't moved. North looks slightly bored.

Stevie opens his mouth but Kite holds up a hand and speaks rapidly, his voice lowered so that no-one nearby can overhear. More disturbingly, he plasters a sickly smile in place and his colour returns to normal. Stevie almost thinks he prefers the angry Kite.

'Not a fucking word, you out-of-your-depth and out-of-place motherfucking Australian cunt. Max Kolomiets was *my* boy, you understand? *Mine*. Not Jimmy fucking Gellygallopipa-fucking-opolis, or whatever the fuck that Greek twat is called, *mine*! He is *mine* to dispose of or not dispose of, as I please, not some jumped-up olive-stuffer!'

Kite's eyes are glowing. 'That's the fucking problem with the fucking world today: too many fucking incomers, poking their fucking noses in what is none of their fucking business! If it's not fucking Greeks, it's Polacks, or Latvians, or fucking Somalis, or some other greasy black bastard wop fuck convict cunt trying to grab a slice of someone else's hard-won money. In this case, *my* fucking money. It's ungentlemanly, that's what it is. It's a fucking liberty, my son. A. Fucking. Liberty.'

Kite sits back, vibrating with fury, still smiling. For a moment Stevie thinks of running, such is the violence contained in the man opposite him. Then, in an instant, Kite is ice. He sips the last of his brandy and looks at Stevie. Stevie's mind is flashing one phrase over and over again: *get out*, *get out*, *get out*, an adrenaline-fuelled instinctive scream. Jimmy made a mistake with this guy. A great big fucking grade-A mistake and Stevie's left in the middle of it.

'I'll pass along your . . . thoughts to Jimmy,' says Stevie.

He pushes his chair back from the table and begins to rise. 'I'm sorry it hasn't worked out, Mr Kite.'

'Sit the fuck down, Australian,' says Kite. 'You're going nowhere.' He glances at North. Stevie follows the direction and sees North has a gun. North holds it casually under a linen napkin, its ugly snout poking straight at him.

'I know you might be thinking that Mr North wouldn't kill you, Mr White, not here in front of all these lovely people eating their lovely dinners, but let me tell you that Mr North will do whatever is fucking necessary. Even if that does get very messy, understand? And it would get very messy, trust me. Mr North doesn't want to kill you here, but he will, if you so much as fart. For all I know, he may kill you anyway. He has a dislike of people generally that I sometimes find hard to accommodate.'

Stevie nods and sits down.

'There's no need for guns, Mr Kite,' says Stevie. Under the circumstances his voice is steady but he can feel a wetness in his eyes. 'This is just business, right?'

'Just business is right,' says Kite. 'Only we do things a bit differently over here in the mother country. Which you're about to find out.'

This is heading south in a hurry. Stevie feels sweat trickle down his spine and he has an overpowering urge to go to the toilet. He tries to catch the eye of a passing waiter but the waiter looks away, suddenly busy.

At a nod from Kite, Matty Halligan leaves the restaurant.

'When Mr Halligan arrives with the car,' says Kite, 'you're going to get up, walk across the room and get in it without any fuss. You're a big lad, and you look like you've been in a few nasties, but don't think that's going to help you here. Right?'

'Yeah, yeah, OK, Mr Kite, but there's no need for any of this, none at all. And I'll need to get the message back to Jimmy.' Stevie can't keep the panic out of his voice.

'Here's the car,' says Kite. 'Now stand. There's a good lad. If you can. Jimmy will get the message.'

Stevie rises unsteadily and Kite walks him towards the door, a genial nod to the head waiter, the bill put on the tab. Kite drapes an arm over Stevie's shoulder, every inch the genial host. With North following close behind them, they reach the door and Dean Halligan holds it open, the Liverpool wind cutting through Stevie's jacket.

'Tell me, Mr White,' says North, the Irishman's lilt low in Stevie's ear as the car door is opened. 'Are you in the way of being an art lover?'

16

It's lunchtime. Keane and Harris pull up their collars against the rain and splash across the wet cobbles from the car and into Ye Cracke.

The old pub stands halfway down a side road leading off Hope Street; only one street from the site of Stevie White's last meal. There are photographs of musicians drinking in there, and the walls are hung with drawings produced by artists who'd gone on to (sometimes) better things, their bar bill paid by art, or maybe just left there. The area's stiff with artists, the art school round the corner spewing out a steady supply. The ceiling is low and coated in a thick patina of nicotine, a memory of the days when smoke was as much a part of a pub as beer and casual violence. The walls don't seem to have been repainted, the décor not altered much in the twenty-odd years Keane has been drinking there, the dead hand of modernity not reaching this far up the city, or at least not into this patch, not just yet. It's one of the reasons Keane prefers it.

He bags a seat in the corner, back to the wall as always, in a booth that gives him and Harris privacy. Keane would have preferred a seat in the courtyard, a tiny, secluded bolt-hole at the back of the pub. But the rain puts paid to that and they'll have to stick inside. The downside of being a copper is that people recognise you everywhere you go. The kind of recognition that comes when you haul someone out of bed at 4 am and arrest them.

Experiences like that tend to sour a person's view of you, Keane has always found.

Another reason for choosing the pub: to Keane's knowledge the pub is 'clean'. No history of drugs, no known gangland connections, no ex-cons working security. It's also the closest decent boozer to the police HQ at Canning Place where he's due for a meeting with his boss after lunch; The Fish himself, DCI Eric Perch, the coldest man Keane has ever encountered – and that includes a serial killer currently undergoing treatment at Ashworth. Perch is missing the tips of two fingers after an accident with a lawn-mower – at least that was the story. Keane prefers the canteen gossip that Perch is a zombie who got peckish one night.

Perch's promotion from outside MIT had been greeted with the enthusiasm usually reserved for prostate exams. But, despite the misgivings, The Fish does at least get results, Keane has to give him that. He achieves this in a very simple way: by cracking his teams hard and ruthlessly. Officers who don't produce find their careers mysteriously stalled, leave requests denied, their transfers to unpopular postings hastened.

But the man gives Keane the heaves, plain and simple. If meeting The Fish for a case status update doesn't warrant a lunchtime bevy, Keane doesn't know what does.

Harris comes back from the bar with the drinks. Cranberry juice for her, Becks for him. Faces following her as she passes.

'Thanks,' says Keane and takes a guilty pull. He's never

102

been much of a lunchtime drinker but lately finds himself drifting into having the odd one here and there. Ever attentive, and seldom slow to criticise himself, Keane has dryly noted the shortening gaps between the 'odd ones'. He'll have to watch that.

Right now, though, the beer tastes good.

'Koopman,' says Harris, raising an inquisitive eyebrow. It's both a question and a statement. She takes a small sip of her drink and looks at Keane over the top of the glass. Keane tries not to let his lust show. There is, as always, an element of sexual tension crackling between them. Just enough to help the working relationship along; not enough for it to spill over into anything messy. Keane is very happy with Julie and has been for the past three years. Harris is in a long-term relationship with a theatre nurse at Broadgreen. Keane knows Harris isn't covering up her sexuality – it's simply nobody's damn business except hers – but he also has a suspicion, never to be voiced, that Harris strays from time to time with men. He isn't sure what the lesbian community's feelings are on things like that, and he sure as shit doesn't intend to have a cosy discussion on sexual politics with DI Harris to find out. Not if he wants to keep both his testicles.

'Menno Koopman,' says Keane. 'My old boss. He'd taken an early before you arrived.'

Em Harris makes a gesture of encouragement for Keane to keep talking.

'Well, despite the clog-hopper name, he's as Scouse as me and you. And a good copper, really good, a pit bull when it came to the job. Once Koop got the sniff of something, he was on to it and wouldn't let go. A networker, before the word existed. He knew everyone and everything worth knowing. We worked on a lot of cases together and

Koop took me under his wing. I was already a copper with a solid ten years, but he turned me into something else. You know what I mean.'

'Yes,' says Harris. Most decent DIs have had some sort of similar mentoring experience, sometimes good, sometimes bad, that has turned them moment by moment into the policeman or woman they've become. The arrival of The Fish at the Canning Street HQ signalled an unwelcome change to that tradition. The Fish might get results but he is never going to be asked out on the monthly MIT Friday night sessions; a throwback to the good-old/bad-old glory days of boozing bizzies in the swashbuckling seventies and eighties that is proving highly resistant to the cultural shift. Even Harris goes along sometimes.

'And his son? Stevie?'

'I had no idea. Not until Eckhardt told us. He certainly never mentioned him, but why on earth would he? He was only seventeen, and then the kid was taken to Australia. And that was back when Australia was a long way away. Not like now.'

'It hasn't drifted closer, Frank.'

'You know what I mean. Faster planes, cheaper tickets. The internet. Globalisation. Blah blah. Everything's nearer.'

The team have done a bit of digging and discovered that Steven White, just as Eckhardt had said, had been born Steven Brendan Koopman, and his place of birth listed as Liverpool, England. It hadn't taken very long to discover that the Menno Koopman named as 'father' was the same Menno Koopman who had gone on to become a Liverpool copper. Like there'd be two fuckers with a name like that in the city.

'And now his kid's turned up kebabbed. What a fucking mess.'

'He hasn't seen him since 1975, Frank. How do you think he's going to react?'

Keane takes a drink and lifts his eyebrows. 'Good question.'

He leans forward. 'I told you he was a good copper, right? Well, there was another side to Menno Koopman. You can decide for yourself if it's a good thing or a bad thing.'

'What happened?' said Em.

'It was a long time ago,' says Keane. 'Well, it seems like it to me, anyway.'

1996. The summer of the European Championships and England in the semi-finals. Oasis in the charts. Britpop. The Spice Girls. The corruption-riddled Tories teetering at the edge of eighteen years in power. It is a rare flowering of optimism for a country almost addicted to misery.

In Liverpool the body count is rising.

A savage new breed of criminal has entered the water. Brazen assassinations, the more brutal the better, are becoming, if not commonplace, certainly more frequent than they'd ever been. The city, the criminal part of it, is awash with money. The drug business is booming; ecstasy outstripping alcohol as the chosen Saturday night special for millions. The drug has leapt from the hardcore club scene into the mainstream and the consequent rewards for those who don't mind getting their hands dirty are astronomical.

Guns begin to be used as never before, and with little discrimination. Small-time dealers, who once would have been warned off with a going-over in the pub car park, are found bound, gagged and tortured on wasteland.

Exotic gestures borrowed from half-digested movies are added to their corpses: bags of excrement, flowers, dead fish. Keane remembers one case – not a murder this time – in which a stubborn club owner, unwilling to let a rival install a new 'security firm' on the doors, woke in bed to find, not just a horse's head as a warning, but an entire horse. It is the logistics of the operation that appals and amuses the investigating team in almost equal measure: the horse stolen, not without difficulty, from a local stud. The hooker paid to slip something in the club owner's drink to ensure an unconscious state while the dead horse is placed in his bed.

By a forklift no less.

But that sort of effort is rare. In the main, the new gangsters model themselves on fictional and non-fictional Americans who use extreme violence as a brutal business tool. It's an escalating cock fight that is rapidly turning Liverpool and nearby Manchester into the Wild Wild North. Keane, freshly promoted to DC, is assigned to one of the top-level initiatives designed to damp down the volcano. Gangs are opening up hitherto undreamed of connections to the Colombians, even getting so cocky as to start double-crossing them. Links with the post-Troubles IRA are becoming worrying, especially the rumoured hook-up with the paramilitary group's feared 'Cleaners', a hit squad rumoured to have been involved in at least twenty drug deaths in the city. It is in this atmosphere that Operation Footfall is launched in 1996 and Menno Koopman becomes a DI in charge of a section.

Like The Fish, he's very clear what he wants from his team: results. Unlike The Fish, Koop sets about achieving this through turning his team into a single body, unified by a common will. It's simple, Koop tells them. We are the good guys. The gangsters are the bad guys. He wants every bad guy off the streets. Zero tolerance. A clear idea.

And equally clearly impossible.

But they give it a good try.

Koop brings in the video tape of *The Untouchables* – the one with Kevin Costner and Sean Connery – and makes the section watch it late one night in the briefing room. When Connery delivers the famous 'They pull a knife, you pull a gun. He sends one of yours to the hospital, you send one of his to the morgue,' line they all cheer. It's corny as hell but it works. Over a period of months Koop slowly turns them into a formidable force and is ruthless in his pursuit of the stated objectives.

He gives no quarter to the 'enemy' as he calls them and never, ever, stops chasing. If he can't get someone picked up for the big stuff he picks them up for the little stuff.

And then he does it again. And again.

It is a war which Koopman convinces them all they are fighting for the soul of the city, a romantic notion that doesn't sit naturally with the cynical, seen-it-all city cops. But such is Koop's conviction that Keane is sure it was embraced on some level by everyone in the section. Koopman is a crusader. He pushes his team harder, pays more attention to detail than any other copper in the city. He cuts corners but never, so far as Keane can remember, over-steps the mark. It's a heady time.

The team wades into the criminal fraternity, the extended feral families on wasteland estates in Halewood and Kirkdale and Netherley, or the semi-organised collections of city centre dealers, thugs and killers. An embryonic drug network is spreading out from Liverpool, into Amsterdam, Marbella, Turkey, and beyond to Colombia. The money is incredible – simply astonishing – and, as in past centuries, Liverpool is handily placed to act as a distribution hub. Police estimate that the world cocaine trade alone is worth over two billion pounds a year with an abnormally large percentage of that money flowing through the hands and pockets of Liverpool operators. Men who have grown up selling £5 bags of weed to schoolfriends at the sprawling comprehensives dotted around the city are now multi-millionaires. Apocryphal stories abound. In 1998 Dutch police raid the villa of one of Liverpool's big players and recover four hundred kilos of cocaine, fifteen hundred kilos of cannabis, sixty kilos of heroin, fifty of ecstasy, as well as guns, ammunition, cash and crates of CS canisters. The entire haul totals £125 million. The police also estimate this particular entrepreneur owns more than three hundred UK properties, as well as casinos, discos, vineyards, and has interests in football clubs in Spain, Turkey, Bulgaria and the Gambia. The guy makes *The Sunday Times* 'Rich List' in 1998.

And he is only one.

A crop of hustling likely lads on the make emerge from Norris Green, Croxteth, Netherley, Speke, Bootle, Kirkdale, The Dingle, and from outlying towns like Skelmersdale and Kirkby. Operation Footfall logs them into a database and uses the information in a fast-moving effort to stem the flow.

'It wasn't working,' says Keane. 'But Koop didn't give a shit. He was enjoying it, in a funny kind of way. It was why he'd gone into policing; why most of us did. It couldn't last at that pace, though, and the unit was moved on, reassigned in a shake-up in 2000. Koop went into MIT and the rest you know.'

Keane drinks his beer.

'So is there anything else about Koopman?' says Harris.

Keane looks at his partner coolly.

'Well, there is one thing,' says Keane. 'There's Carl.'

17

'You're what?'

Zoe is as angry as he's ever seen her. Koop almost smiles as he imagines cartoon steam coming out of her ears but doesn't allow himself to so much as twitch a muscle. Had he done so, he is sure she'd hit him.

'I'm going back, Zoe. You knew I would.'

'To Liverpool?'

'Of course to Liverpool. Where else would I be going back to?'

'I don't know!' she says, throwing her arms in the air. 'Zambia makes as much sense as fucking Liverpool! Why not stop off at Minsk, or Potsdam, or fucking Helsinki while you're at it!?'

At the raised voices, Ringo puts his tail between his legs and heads for the safety of the area behind the couch. Koop watches him, a wistful look in his eye. He wishes he could join him. Zoe in full flow is like a cyclone. You just had to strap yourself to the mast and let the thing blow past, hoping not to get physically injured in the process.

As she rages around the house, it doesn't help Koop that she's right.

What business does he have in Liverpool? Stevie was his son, but only technically. What does he think he'll achieve?

Nothing. That's almost certainly going to be the result. Koop is enough of a pragmatist to know that even a couple of years out of the loop will probably have rendered him, to all intents and purposes, useless.

But that doesn't mean he won't try.

Zoe pauses, leaning on the kitchen island, looking out across the garden. Her breathing is heavy and Koop stays silent. Then he notices a tear trickle down her face and he moves solicitously forward, his expression stricken.

'Don't you fucking dare!' Zoe angrily wipes her cheek with the back of her hand and begins noisily emptying the dishwasher.

'Zoe,' says Koop. He opens his mouth but doesn't know what else to say.

'I'm alright.' She clatters some plates into a cupboard and bends back to the dishwasher.

'This isn't about us,' says Koop. 'It's nothing to do with . . . you know.'

You know.

There it is, out in the open. A part of their lives they have tacitly agreed not to air.

'Yes it does,' says Zoe. 'Of course it's got something to do with you going to Liverpool. It's got everything to do with it, Koop.'

Koop hangs his head and lets out a long slow breath.

He and Zoe had tried. God knows they'd tried and they'd had plenty of fun trying. But no baby had been forthcoming. At first it was almost a relief. Neither of them 'wanted' a baby in the way that they saw amongst their friends who, seemingly overnight, became mindless

111

breeding machines, their world boundaries marked by prams and nappies and baby names and sleepless nights and stretch marks. They'd been glad not to take part in endless discussions on breast v bottle.

And then in 1995 Zoe had 'fallen' pregnant. A strange expression, 'fallen', but that described it very well. And, like clouds lifting, the two of them discovered for themselves the obsessive and claustrophobic world of expectant mothers. Zoe was welcomed back into the fold like an erring daughter who had seen the error of her ways. A nursery was painted. Hospital visits undertaken. Scans. Tests. Saturday visits to Mothercare.

On September 21st their daughter, Sarah, was born. Perfect in every detail save one. Sarah died in the birth canal.

It had almost finished them both. Koop can still recall with appalling clarity the terrible months that followed and the tests that confirmed what Zoe somehow knew in her bones: there would never be any more Sarahs.

'I'll stay,' says Koop. 'You're right. It's stupid.'

Zoe cries now. She holds her arm out straight, palm up to stop him coming close. She finishes crying and blows her nose on a sheet of kitchen roll. Then she looks at him and opens her arms. They embrace and Zoe whispers in his ear.

'If you have to go, Koop, then go. It's fucking pointless, but if you think you have to do it, then do it.'

'No, I'm being stupid, you're right.'

Zoe's words are hardly the ringing endorsement Koop might have hoped for and, like husbands down the ages, he now finds himself arguing against that which he'd been arguing for only a few minutes earlier. But Zoe wins out, as she usually does.

'Stevie *was* your only son. You didn't know him and he turned out bad, but you weren't to know that. Blood is blood, I guess.' She stops suddenly and looks at Koop, conscious she may have said too much.

Blood. People always say things like that. Blood is blood. Blood is thicker than water. Koop knows better than anyone that blood is nothing but blood. He's seen enough of it to last him a lifetime and he knows himself well enough to understand that it's not the full reason he's about to fly round the world on a wild goose chase.

Koop realises that the death is being investigated – perhaps even by someone good, someone like Keane – but it may not be given priority. Another drug argument, that would be the outcome. It's the intel value that the department would be interested in. Why was Stevie in Liverpool? Who did he see? What fresh advantage can MIT get from the new corpse?

Koop wants to find out all those things too, but it's not the only reason he's making the long trek home. He's not going to Liverpool just for closure, whatever that means.

He's going to Liverpool to see if this has anything to do with Carl.

18

Liverpool, December 1997.

It's snowing. Really snowing. A rare event in the city. The Pennines to the east, the Lakes to the north and Snowdonia across the bay to the south usually form a protective ring from the worst of the winter weather. But the snow currently bringing Britain to a grinding halt has made it into Liverpool this time and it's not helping DC Koopman's mood as the car slips and slides through the unlovely streets of Kirkby. The snow has at least helped drape the town in a sodium-tinted blanket, and driven most of the citizens inside, but it's hard going on the icy roads.

'Jesus,' Koop mutters as he slaloms perilously close to an oncoming pair of headlights. 'Where're the fucking gritters when you need them?'

There's no reply. Koop is alone in the car. The call that brought him out tonight is a personal one and he's driving his own vehicle. He turns a corner into the Hatton housing estate, the snow not managing to quite conceal the shabbiness of the area, and his car is pelted with snowballs by a group of youths who break off from building a gigantic snow penis to launch the attack. Koop almost smiles; the last time he came here, as a raw officer in a patrol car, when Kirkby was still a fresh wound, the locals used concrete and bottles. The snowballs feel like a warm welcome by comparison.

Koop leaves the youths in his rear view and drives deeper into the labyrinth of the Hatton estate. He turns right into a cul-de-sac. The road sign that should read 'Eaton Shire Place' has been doctored to read 'Eat Shit Place'. At its western end the terrace slouches against the fence of a rotting industrial complex. The homes here are little better than shacks. Built cheaply thirty years ago by back-handing builders using shoddy materials, they have not lasted well. On the side of the street that Koop is looking at, almost every one of the windows has been boarded up. There are lights burning behind some of the plywood barriers indicating life of sorts and Koop notes the serried ranks of satellite TV aerials mounted along the roofline. No money for glass but enough for pay-per-view, although Koop would bet that few of the TV watchers are paying the going rate for their soaps and football. Kirkby is the pitch-blackest part of the black economy. Most things can be bought more cheaply here, no questions asked, from clothing to electricity. Koop had once arrested a guy trying to sell a canister of nerve gas behind The Molyneux on a Sunday afternoon. He'd turned out to be a nutter, and the nerve gas to be the comparatively straightforward CS gas, but the fact that the maniac had a potential buyer was what stuck with Koop. Fucking nerve gas.

Koop arrives at a house at the very end of the terrace. It seems to lean against the steel fence of the industrial estate for support. There is a patrol car parked outside, engine running, smoke rising into the flat orange-black sky, and Koop pulls the rented Ford into line behind it. He steps out, his feet sliding on the snow and stiff legs it to the driver's window. It slides down and a plume of cigarette smoke is released into the night air.

'You took yer fucking time.' The face the words come out of belongs in another era. 'Battered' doesn't come close to describing the slab of meat that houses DC Tony Hannaway's eyes, nose and mouth. It's like looking at the survivor of a particularly violent bare-knuckle fight ten years after the worst of the damage has been badly repaired. Which is pretty much the story.

'And a lovely evening to you, too, Princess,' says Koop. 'It's snowing, you know.'

Tony Hannaway glances back along the road.

'Oh, aye, so it is. Thanks, Koop, I'd never have spotted it without one of you city plods pointing it out.'

Koop opens the rear door and slips in with a nod at Hannaway's partner, a young copper with a veteran's stare he must have been practising at home.

'PC Grimes,' says Hannaway, waving a paw in the direction of the passenger seat. Koop nods and gets a barely perceptible flicker in return. His blood flares at the not-so-gentle impertinence until he reminds himself that, senior officer or not, he's on Hannaway and Grimes's turf now. He checks the impulse to bring out the Koop temper and give Grimes a burst. Besides, this is personal, and he's in no position to pull rank.

Not tonight.

Koop looks at the house. Apart from a dull green glow around one of the upstairs windows, it looks dead.

'He's still in there, then?'

Tony Hannaway doesn't bother to reply.

'I know,' says Koop, holding up a placating hand. 'Stupid question.'

Grimes mutters something that Koop doesn't catch and he makes a mental note to cause the PC some small measure of trouble in the future. Personal or not, there's a line that Koop has and Grimes is skating too close to it to be forgotten.

But not yet.

There's still the matter of Carl to deal with.

'He's pushing it, Koop,' says Hannaway, as if Koop has spoken aloud. 'We can't keep phoning you to come running every time Carl's looking to score. Someone's going to get hurt one of these days.'

'That's if no-one's been hurt already,' adds Grimes. There's something in his voice that Koop can't quite pinpoint. Hannaway shoots Grimes a warning look but the copper ploughs on.

'We shouldn't be doing this,' adds Grimes, the emphasis on the 'this'. And Koop suddenly gets a flood of adrenaline down his spine.

'That's enough,' says Hannaway, looking at Grimes, but Koop interrupts.

'Wait.' He shifts forward in his seat and stares at Hannaway. 'Carl hasn't got anyone in there, has he?'

Koop knows before Hannaway answers that he's right.

'Jesus!' Koop can't get the door open quick enough.

'It's alright,' says Tony Hannaway. 'It was only some other druggie. And there hasn't been a peep out of them since they went in.'

Koop only half hears him. He's already at the front door. He can sense Hannaway and Grimes following but he doesn't wait. There's something about the house that has set his nerves screaming. He puts his shoulder to the door, ready to break it, but there's no need; it swings open easily and Koop is in.

'Carl?' he barks, his voice echoing around the ruined hallway and up the flimsy stairs. There's a stench of old food and urine etched deep into the fabric of the building. Hannaway and Grimes are behind him now and Koop pushes open the door into the living area. It too is a stinking mess. A back-broken couch sags against one wall and there is domestic debris strewn across every surface; old clothes, ashtrays, magazines, video cassettes. There was once a carpet on the floor but Koop can't tell where it ends and the rotting floorboards start.

The kitchen is the same except in here the smell is almost toxic. One look in the sink is enough to make Koop gag. He turns away and moves to the stairs.

'Carl!' shouts Koop.

'Maybe he went out the back?' says Hannaway.

'I thought you were watching the place?' says Koop.

'We aren't exactly doing an eight-man surveillance op, Koop. It's just me and Grimes keeping a friendly eye on the druggie cunt! He could be halfway to fucking Leeds by now, for all we know.'

As if in answer there's a dull thud from upstairs and all three coppers can hear music playing.

Koop takes the stairs two at a time then comes to a sliding halt on the tiny landing. The music is louder up here and it's coming from the bedroom. The Happy Mondays' '24 Hour Party People'. A thin strip of green light seeps out from under the door.

'Carl?' says Koop again, this time more quietly. He is conscious of Hannaway and Grimes at his shoulder and pushes open the bedroom door.

'Fuck,' says Grimes.

'Oh Jesus, Carl,' says Koop. 'What have you done?'

In the hallway, Grimes is sick.

19

It is Jimmy Gelagotis's habit to try and start each day in the same way. He rises early and makes breakfast for the family. Greek omelettes are his speciality, using only the freshest spinach and organic feta he buys from a deli in Southport. Usually it's only he and Chris who have the omelettes, and then just on Thursdays. Eva and Anna almost never eat anything, pleading diet as excuses, both of them having low-slung Mediterranean figures. Still, Jimmy always makes four, just in case. He enjoys cooking the meal; it's the only one he does cook and he likes to make it perfect every time.

Once breakfast is over, and if the timing is right, he'll take the Beemer and drop Anna at her swanky private school, all ivy-clad soft stone and rolling grounds; a surreal slice of England dropped into a sprawling Gold Coast strip of car dealerships and air-conditioned mini-malls. This morning, as usual, he chats to a few of the other parents on the school run, enjoying flirting with two or three of the hard-bodied mothers on their way to another workout. They like Jimmy – one in particular making it very plain that he'd be welcome to follow her Porsche home any time he chose to – although he also notices that a certain section of parents avoid him. That's OK, he knows exactly why they feel that way. It isn't because of what he does: few of them, if any, know that. It's because of his ethnicity.

A wog.

Most of them mistake him for Lebanese; a group that is, in these regressive, reductive times, becoming a byword for criminality. Far from feeling aggrieved at the racial slur, Jimmy is a wholehearted subscriber to this view: fucking Lebs *are* all fucking crims. If he was one of those parents hoping little Sophie, or young Miles, would become a lawyer or a doctor, he'd avoid contact with people like himself too. Even if he ain't a fucking Leb.

After school, the next stop for Jimmy is at the first of his businesses. In an echo of what's happening to Keith Kite twelve thousand miles away, Jimmy's empire is growing, almost all of it legitimate, and all of his businesses profitable in their own right.

At the first stop, a bustling waterfront café called Stone, he takes a cup of coffee and sits at a corner table to talk with the manager, Milo, about the month ahead. Jimmy notes problems in a small notebook and drinks his coffee which, he is gratified to note, is perfect. After the café he drives to a large car dealership which he has a controlling stake in. His partner is completely legit and welcomes Jimmy like the hard-working man he is. Inventory is checked and discussed and Jimmy moves on to look in on the taxi company and the three bottle shops he has scattered through Surfers. The only non-legitimate piece of business is to call Tony Link to check on the Jaguars. He tells Link to call Stefan Meeks and make doubly sure the cars haven't been touched. The last thing they need is some independent car thief screwing things up by nicking one of them.

By lunchtime Jimmy Gelagotis has taken care of business and makes his way to the Q1 building, towering above Surfers Paradise. He parks the Beemer in a reserved space in the underground car park and, using his access key, takes the resident lift to the 67th floor and lets himself into the oceanfront apartment. As always, he walks first to the windows which run from floor to ceiling and drinks in the view up and down the coast. It is staggering; well worth the cost.

Behind him, Ella, dressed as always in very little, puts aside her magazine and gets up from the sofa. She walks across to Jimmy and rubs against him like a cat.

'Hey, lover.'

Jimmy doesn't reply but she can tell that he's not being mean.

She's tall, taller than Jimmy anyway, and wears high heels which emphasise the difference. At first, when she'd become Jimmy's, she'd tried to compensate by wearing flats, but Jimmy told her to keep the heels. There's something about her being taller he likes. He enjoys hard sex with Ella, slamming into her from behind, her long thighs straining as Jimmy bends her over the bed.

Or table, or chair, or bathroom sink. He never quite knows when the urge will take him and Ella never questions. With every appearance of pleasure she comes loudly, Jimmy ripping her underwear (she has an account at La Perla in Pac Fair) before pushing his cock into her roughly. He wrongly imagines it's the roughness she likes; even going so far as to share her with one of his friends from time to time, the two of them taking her at either end, switching her round in a breathy, sweat-slicked haze of booze and cocaine.

In fact, Ella doesn't like it rough.

She doesn't actually like sex very much at all, truth be told. But she doesn't actively *dislike* it, and Jimmy only drops in every couple of days and she has the apartment, a nice car, money to spend and plenty of blow.

On this visit, Jimmy is distracted. She sinks dutifully to her knees and unzips his fly as he stands at the window. His cock is heavy and flaccid and she takes it whole in her mouth, before peeling back his foreskin and smoothly licking the underside of his tip, an expression of complete enjoyment on her face. She practises the faces she sees in porn films in the mirror, as well as some of the moves. She finds it works well enough and today is no different. Jimmy's initial distraction fades and his breathing grows heavy. She holds his balls with one hand and rotates her other hand around the base of his cock, her head bobbing back and forward as Jimmy's pleasure increases and his thrusting becomes urgent. Not long. Ella makes the noises Jimmy likes and he pulls out of her mouth just as he comes. Hot strings splash onto her chin and ear and land on her silk shift. Ella makes a mental note to get it into some cold water as soon as possible. Or should it be hot? She'll have to Google it later. She rubs Jimmy's cock, her hand movements slowing in tandem with his breathing.

At a point she feels appropriate she gazes up at him adoringly. He pats her on the head like a pet dog and she makes her way to the bathroom.

As Ella showers, Jimmy zips himself, runs a hand through his hair and gets his breathing back under control. He takes out his mobile and checks for any calls that may have come in while he's been busy. There have been two, both legitimate business calls he'll respond to later. There's also a forwarded notification that he has emails in his web email box. He hitches his black pants and sits down in front of the laptop on a desk facing the ocean. As far as he knows, Ella seldom uses the laptop for anything other than shopping, but he likes her to keep it charged and operational every time he visits.

Jimmy clicks onto his Hotmail account. Eight messages, three of them junk. Two are details of properties he's looking at in a development in Noosa. One is from a mid-level Melbourne dealer he's hooked into his network, although the content has nothing to do with drugs, being instead concerned with Jimmy helping out financially with a music festival the dealer has become embroiled in. Jimmy makes a note to remind the dealer not to use this email and stick to messaging one of the mobiles he constantly changes.

The last email is from an unfamiliar address and Jimmy would have thrown it into the trash as spam except that the subject of the email reads 'Stevie Wonder'. The phrase/name is so close to Jimmy's thoughts about Stevie that he takes the risk and clicks 'open'. Inside, Jimmy can see no message. Instead there is an mpeg movie attachment, entitled 'Another Place'. He ponders for a moment before downloading the file. It's a big one, and takes a couple of minutes to come through. The laptop system has been set up to open any downloads automatically.

The movie software flickers onscreen and a small white arrow appears in the centre of the black rectangle. Jimmy clicks play and immediately wishes he hadn't.

Stevie White's face appears in the small frame, harshly lit, his eyes wide, fear twisting his features so much that at first Jimmy Gelagotis doesn't recognise him. Stevie is speaking frantically to someone off to one side of the camera but there's no sound on the clip. Then Stevie begins to cry and Jimmy flinches. The sense of something beyond terrible about to happen is palpable. Onscreen a man dressed from head to toe in protective coveralls, his face masked by a hood, goggles and a surgical mask, appears in front of Stevie. He produces a scalpel and moves forward.

Jimmy Gelagotis watches, his fingers gouging the desk, his leg twitching involuntarily. The man onscreen works slowly and the video clip jumps, cutting forward in time, Stevie's face becoming awash with blood, his unbelieving eyes staring from the red mask.

Behind Jimmy, Ella comes out of the bathroom, towelling her hair. She approaches the laptop, looks over Jimmy's shoulder and begins to scream.

20

'There's no covering this up, Koop,' says Hannaway. 'Not this one.'

Even in the middle of this nightmare Koop is annoyed with Princess. When had he ever asked Hannaway to cover up anything? Before this, Carl's various problems have been relatively minor and all Koop has received is an early tip-off. It's helped keep Carl out of serious trouble although there's been no halting the gradual decline. But this is no time for an argument. Once the bedroom door is opened, everything changes forever between Koop and his younger brother, Carl.

Carl Koopman, amphetamine skinny and shirtless in the freezing box-room, is on his knees on the bare wooden floor in an attitude of prayer underneath a music poster. The Farm playing Spike Island. The only light comes from a crown of fairy lights he has wrapped around his head. Koop registers the dark green cord trailing towards the electrical socket set into the stained wall. The lights are set on a pattern that sees them fade slowly before lighting up again. As the red bulbs glow Carl turns his head towards the door but doesn't seem to register there's anyone there.

On a bare mattress on the narrow bed to Carl's right is the naked body of a man. He has been sliced open across the belly and his interior organs pulled out and placed on the floor. A deepening pool of blood is seeping through the mattress and dripping onto the boards beneath the bed. A large knife lies to one side. Koop steps forward and drags it towards the door with his foot. The action seems to stir Carl Koopman. He sits back and looks up again, his fingers still interlaced.

'Liam's fine,' says Carl, loud enough to be heard over the music. 'He's fine, Menno. Custy.'

Koop doesn't reply. Behind him he hears Hannaway on the radio calling it in.

'You need to come with us, Carl,' says Koop. 'You can stop praying.'

'Oh no, Menno. You can't stop praying. Not till it's all alright. See?'

'Well, maybe take a break, eh, Carlo?' Koop uses the old family name for his brother. It seems to work. Koop steps across and flicks the power button on the CD player. He uses the knuckle of his index finger, his copper instincts automatically minimising any crime scene contamination. Shaun Ryder's nasal whine dies and Carl Koopman gets to his feet.

'He'll be fine,' he murmurs, looking at the dead man.

'Of course he will, Carlo,' says Koop. He takes Carl's elbow, handling his brother like a delicate vase, guiding him past Hannaway. Grimes, recovered from vomiting, cuffs Carl and, looking at him as if he may explode, guides him carefully around the landing rail and down the narrow stairs. They turn in to the living room and Grimes sits Carl on the sagging sofa.

In the cramped bedroom Koop and Hannaway stand

for a few moments without speaking. Koop keeps finding his eyes flicking towards unimportant details in the room. The cheap woodchip wallpaper. A packet of Rizlas. Anything except the dead man. Carl's involvement has severed the link to Koop's professional detachment. If he looks at the dead junkie for too long Koop thinks he may start crying.

'What a fucking mess,' says Hannaway eventually. He looks at Koop. 'You alright?'

Is he alright? Koop doesn't know. He nods stiffly and this seems to satisfy Hannaway.

'You'll have to go downstairs, Koop.'

Koop's temper flares at the subtle insinuation that he might tamper with the scene, but the feeling fades as quickly as it arrives. Of course he'll have to go downstairs: his fucking brother is the killer. He shakes his head as if to brush away the thought and then nods at Hannaway. He goes slowly, postponing the inevitable for a few seconds more. Behind him he hears Hannaway talking on his radio. Its electric static crackles loud in the narrow hall.

In the living room no-one is saying anything. It's colder in there than upstairs. Koop takes off his coat and puts it around Carl, although he doesn't seem cold. Carl doesn't make any sign that he's noticed and Koop sees his head is somewhere else, somewhere not here. Grimes looks like he's aged five years and can't stop clicking a switch on his radio. On. Off. On. Off.

'I'd speak to someone about this if I were you,' says Koop. 'When it settles down. A counsellor. The department has them.'

Grimes tries to appear tough but only succeeds in looking young. To both his and Koop's surprise it's Carl who speaks next.

'Yeah, mate,' he says, 'get some therapy. Or that shit will keep coming back.' And both Koop and Grimes know that this person speaking is the real Carl Koopman – the dazed, knife-wielding psycho Carl has gone. 'You shouldn't try and, y'know, do the strong thing, man. Fucks you up.'

'Like you're an expert,' says Grimes. 'Fucking nutter.'

Koop gives Grimes a glance but can't seem to summon the energy to say anything. His bones are lead, his blood treacle. At least Mum never lived to see this. It's something.

Carl looks up at his brother. 'I'm right, aren't I? The lad needs counselling.'

'Quiet, Carlo. Not now, eh?'

A blue light bleeds through the ancient curtains signalling a second patrol car arriving in the snow-silent street, and then a third and the house begins the familiar transformation into a crime scene. But this time it's not Koop's scene. He's a witness. As the first rubberneckers arrive, Grimes hands over to the new officers and he and Hannaway lead Carl down the short slippery path and place him in the back seat of the patrol car. Despite Koop's involvement there's no way Hannaway's going to miss out on bringing the collar into the station.

Grimes still looks pale and Hannaway takes the keys from him before climbing behind the wheel of the Ford. Koop gets into his vehicle and follows them slowly to the station, Carl sitting peaceably in the back seat of the patrol car. On the slow drive through the white streets of the Hatton estate, Koop can see his brother's head bobbing softly to some inner rhythm, a song that Koop has never been able to hear. Or wanted to.

The rest of the night is torture. The victim is formally identified as Liam Jones, a low-level dope supplier who sometimes shared the squalid house with Carl. Carl freely admits killing him 'in order to save him'. From what, he never makes clear.

After the initial processing and interviews are over – none of which Koop is involved with, except as the subject – it's clear that, despite bouts of clarity, Carl Koopman should be hospitalised. He's examined by a medic for physical damage and then separately by a psychiatrist who recommends sectioning. Koop waits all night for the process to unwind until, around eight in the morning, Carl is picked up and taken to Ashworth High Security Hospital in Maghull, north of the city and less than four miles from the death house at Eaton Shire Place. Koop can't believe his brother will be occupying the same institution as Moors Murderer Ian Brady. It makes him feel unclean and – this is something Koop wouldn't have thought possible – even worse about the whole sorry business.

The case never makes it to court. At least not in any meaningful sense. Carl Koopman pleads not guilty by reason of insanity for the killing of the drug dealer, and is confined to Ashworth indefinitely. Koop and Zoe never really talk about what has happened. Not properly. Despite his advice to Grimes the previous evening to seek professional counselling, Koop never does so himself. After a short internal review by the force, Koop is given a clean bill and returns to work. Carl is never mentioned by anyone Koop comes into contact with on the job.

On October the eighteenth, 1998, Koop makes his monthly visit to Ashworth to check on Carl. It's the last time he sees his brother.

Until now.

21

Jimmy Gelagotis calms Ella with some difficulty, eventually convincing her that the clip of Stevie is a fake, a sick joke that someone is playing on him.

She seems to believe him, although Jimmy thinks this may be more to do with her wanting to, as much as any conviction on her part. Jimmy doesn't care less if she believes him or not but he doesn't want her hysterical, he needs time to think. She's sleeping now, having taken a couple of sleeping pills and a large vodka.

Jimmy pours himself the same over a tumbler full of ice and takes it to the armchair by the window. He sits and drinks and looks at the ocean. There's a storm flickering to the north. It'll come in hot and strong later that night. When the glass is empty, he flicks a look over at the laptop and considers watching the clip again just in case the story Jimmy has told Ella – that it's a fake – turns out to be the case.

No, decides Jimmy, there's no need to put himself through that nightmare again. That fucking thing is real, brother. Stevie's face is something Jimmy won't be forgetting in a hurry.

His first instinctive reaction is anger. He wants to get on a plane, or send an army, or do some motherfucking thing – *right now* – to get the bastard who's done this. Stevie White was a delivery boy. Nothing more. It's out of proportion, insane. Who the fuck does *that* to a messenger?

In the silence of the apartment, the answer comes back to him loud and clear.

Someone who doesn't like the message.

Someone who wants to send a message of their own. Kite telling Jimmy that his gambit has not paid off. Or, Jimmy wonders, perhaps this is an extreme way of letting him know who's boss? The Poms might be using Stevie's execution to acknowledge the change in the deal structure and simultaneously registering extreme disapproval.

That could be how it is. Stevie might just be the offering to placate the angry gods; the gods in this case taking the offering themselves. Jimmy cogitates on that one for a while before dismissing it as too extreme. This is much more than that. A message of 'unhappiness' would have been sent by putting Stevie in the hospital. Kite has taken this personally.

Jimmy swears, looks down at the line of the shore stretching south as the lights of Surfers come on, and swallows the last of his vodka. He's demonstrated an error of judgement, sure that, given the money involved, and the fact that the goods were already here, Kite would have barked a little but gone along with the thing. The king is dead and all that.

But Kite hasn't. Killing Stevie is telling him something. It's telling Jimmy that they aren't going to let him take over the Australian end of the deal, not without a fight at least. For a moment, Jimmy Gelagotis sees his true worth in the scheme of this. A small player who, despite his violent and ruthless past, has now stepped up into the ring with some truly bad boys. Even with the air-conditioning running, a bead of sweat trickles down his temple as he recalls the rumoured links Kite has with the Colombians and the Irish. Man, there are some nasty fuckers in that lot and no mistake. Jimmy feels a strange and rare sensation: fear.

Fuck it. He stands and moves to the laptop.

He clicks it into life and presses 'play' to watch the 'Stevie Wonder' clip again. What doesn't kill you makes you stronger.

As Jimmy watches the torture and death of Stevie White once more, he starts to relax a little. This is showy. This is unprofessional, needless. What sort of a businessman is Kite? He'll calm down eventually. There are a hundred and fifty million reasons for him to do so. He will, after a period of anger and paranoia, reflect that Jimmy Gelagotis and his team are ideally placed to complete the delivery. The difference between Jimmy Gelagotis and Keith Kite is that Jimmy Gelagotis knows he will be gone forever the second the smoke clears. This deal is the last deal. It has to work. It will work. And it's too big a deal for Kite to jeopardise with a war.

He'll be back in before too long, Jimmy reckons. Nothing else makes sense.

He picks up his phone and calls Tony. Business or not, they'll all have to start watching their backs.

22

Declan North looks at himself in the full-length mirror.

A naked man he doesn't fully recognise looks back at him. A man of middle height, firm but not overly muscled, his skin Belfast white, his hair black – artificially so, although only he will ever know that. A man who has, literally, killed more people than he can remember. A man who doesn't care about how many people he ends. As long as he gets to do them.

North has never been a person to dwell on what the future might hold, but he feels safe in predicting that, unless someone gets him first, he'll continue to feed his habit. He can dress it up and tie a ribbon round it, look at it any way he wants to, but there's only one reason why: he likes killing people. Everything else is detail.

He'd enjoyed the Australian. It was all business – or mostly all – for Kite. Kite, by Declan North's standards, is somewhat squeamish, even sentimental. After the business with the Australian, Kite was nervy. North has stored that information away for a time when it might be useful. Information, he's always found, is the best weapon. After Semtex.

North was raised in a Republican household just off the Falls Road and was ten years old when it all began kicking off again in 1968. By 1972 and Bloody Sunday, Declan North has lost his father and only brother to the Troubles. He hasn't been overly traumatised by their deaths, in all honesty. At fourteen, had he been properly assessed, Declan North would have been diagnosed as a full-blown psychopath.

He'd have killed wherever he'd been born, but being where he was, being part of where he was from, proves to be a godsend. He adopts a political stance – easy to do under the circumstances – and begins positioning himself to become a member of the IRA. North has no illusions about changing the face of Ireland through his actions, although, being no fan of the English, that would be a very welcome bonus. No, he is in it for the kicks and the kills. To be sanctioned, praised and rewarded for doing something he'd have paid to do is sweet indeed.

And Declan North is that rare combination of order and madness that means he always carries out his task no matter how difficult, or disgusting, and doesn't leave a trace. He is never so much as arrested by the British.

This is invaluable to The Cause. It means he can travel freely, or as freely as any Irishman at that time in mainland Britain, and his handlers use this to the hilt. They don't know quite how he does it but Declan North is a man born to kill and, a rare quality, *get away with it*.

By the early eighties, the IRA is heavily involved in a rapidly growing – and satisfyingly profitable – drugs trade. They use what they're good at – fear and terror – to ensure the security of sizeable deals. If you need someone to ensure delivery, to enforce an unpaid bill, to ease the passage of contraband, they will do it – for a price. Declan North has the good fortune to be in the right place when everything begins to go civilian. He has the experience and the skills that are in demand, and he makes a smooth transition to criminality long before the IRA is made respectable.

North caresses his naked chest. Thin scar lines, raised slightly from the skin, run laterally across his torso at intervals of a few millimetres. Beginning at shoulder height, there are approximately a hundred lines, most of them faded, some fresh. North takes out a vial of amyl nitrate, pops the cap and inhales, feeling his heart leap as the rush hits. He puts down the empty vial on the hotel dresser and picks up a fresh scalpel. He unwraps the sealed plastic wrapper and grasps the handle. He lovingly traces the flat of the scalpel blade along his engorged penis, the blade just brushing the skin, not breaking it. Under the harsh light from the single bulb, the only source of light in the black-painted room, the scalpel glitters. North slides the blade up his abdomen until the scalpel arrives at a spot just below the last transverse line on his chest. Now, gripping a little more firmly, he drags the blade across himself, his hand steady. A thin line of blood appears in its wake. North angles his arm to keep the line as straight as possible. He reaches the end, pinches the blood from the scalpel blade and licks his fingers. Taking a white towel, he presses it against the bloody line, feeling the sting as stray threads press into the wound.

On the wall to his right, Matty Halligan is lashed face-first to a wooden cross-beam. He wears a blindfold and heavy biker boots, but is otherwise naked. His buttocks are criss-crossed with lines that echo those on North's torso.

North picks up another vial of amyl nitrate and comes close to Halligan. He twists off the cap and holds it under Halligan's nose. He snorts greedily and groans with pleasure. North takes hold of his scalpel again and, kneeling, slowly traces a fresh line of blood across Halligan's buttocks.

North puts his mouth to Halligan's ear.

'You saw what I did to the Australian,' he whispers. 'You liked it, right enough.' It isn't a question.

Halligan flinches. A tremor of real fear runs through him.

'Relax, big man,' whispers North. 'You're a keeper.' He looks across the room to where a naked younger man stands, head bent, his penis erect. North beckons him forward and the younger man takes up a position behind Halligan. He turns and looks at North for permission.

North nods and the naked man presses himself into Halligan. North sucks in a deep breath and settles down to watch.

23

It's exactly like going to see the headmaster.

The Fish occupies a larger than normal office on the fifth floor at Canning Place. In his day Koop always maintained his office right next door to his MIT unit at Stanley Road, but The Fish insisted on moving to where 'the big decisions are being made'. The MIT took that to mean he could be better placed for the arse-licking he's renowned for.

'Enter.' Perch's querulous voice answers Keane's knuckle-knock and Harris pushes open the door.

'Sit,' says Perch, waving a hand perfunctorily in the direction of two armless leather chairs in front of his desk, not looking up from the folder of notes in front of him. Keane gives Harris a wry wrinkle of the eyebrows as they take their seats – lower, naturally, than Perch. Keane wouldn't be surprised to learn that Perch consulted some ladder-climbing business manual on details like that. The two of them sit back in the not-very-comfortable chairs and wait. With Perch, you always wait.

He takes his time. He flicks the pages of his notes, peering through rimless spectacles, his face never lifting in their direction. Eventually, after a number of silent minutes during which Keane has to fight the urge to check his watch, Perch closes the file with an almost unbearable air of efficiency, places his pen at exact right angles to one side and looks up at his two officers.

'Not very promising,' he says, tapping a thin finger on top of the file.

'Sorry, sir?' says Keane. God, this man was a tool.

Perch sighs. 'Your beach victim, DI Keane. Not made much progress, have you?'

'With respect, sir,' says Harris, seeing Keane's neck redden, 'we've established the identity of the victim and traced a connection between him and an Australian man –'

'Gelagotis,' interrupts Perch. Keane registers the DCI's need to let them know he's up to speed on the details. Prick.

'Yes, sir, Gelagotis. We've also found the murder site and we're awaiting forensics on material in the container.'

'And we know the victim was Koop's son,' Keane says, a little more forcefully than he'd meant to. 'Menno Koopman,' he adds, seeing Perch's facial expression.

'I know who Koopman is,' snaps Perch. He taps the file on his desk. 'I can read, DI Keane. I remember Koopman very clearly.' Perch purses his lips in distaste. 'A loose cannon. Your old boss, if I remember rightly.'

He leans forward and props the tips of his fingers together in an oddly ecclesiastical manner. 'And I'm not at all happy about his involvement.' He speaks as though Keane and Harris are personally responsible for Stevie White being the offspring of the former DCI. 'Not happy at all.'

Perch glances involuntarily upwards as if invoking a higher authority. You're looking in the wrong direction,

138

thinks Keane. Perch is more likely to be controlled from somewhere warmer.

'I've had to inform upstairs,' he says, his voice quivering with barely concealed irritation. 'They're going to want to know why a family member of one of our former heads is involved in a drug killing. And not for the first time.'

'White was hardly a family member,' says Keane. 'Sir. And Carl Koopman is still a patient at Bowden.'

'You know that?'

'We checked,' replies Keane, his voice even. 'Sir.'

'Steven White had never met DCI Koopman,' says Harris, anxious to divert any head-on collision between The Fish and Keane. 'He was seventeen when White's mother emigrated and as far as we know there has been no contact since. There's nothing to suggest that Koopman's involvement is anything except an accident of birth.'

'Really, DI Harris?' says Perch. 'Then why is Menno Koopman currently in the air somewhere between Sydney and here?'

Keane looks at Harris. 'That's news to us, sir.'

'I know it's news to you, DI Keane. The point is it shouldn't be. I shouldn't have to be told this through the grapevine like some village gossip!'

Perch judiciously neglects to mention he was passed this information less than ten minutes prior to his meeting. Instead, he lets Keane and Harris squirm. He looks at Keane sharply.

'As far as I'm concerned, Koopman is either dirty or trouble,' says Perch. 'Both of those alternatives are unacceptable and in my view he is likely to be both. The moment he sets foot in the city I want to know about it. I want an eye kept on him. And I want more detail on the brother. Got it?'

Keane doesn't trust himself to speak after the mention of Koop being dirty. He nods and gets to his feet, his neck now positively glowing.

'Will that be all, sir?' says Harris. She too gets up, mainly so that Perch won't be tempted to haul Keane over some very hot coals.

Perch waves his hand.

'Go and do your job,' he says, reaching for the phone. 'Don't make me do it for you.'

Harris steers Keane to the door, feeling his arm flex under her grip.

'Of course, sir,' she says. But Perch is already talking into the phone.

'The oily fucker!'

Keane smacks his hand on the car roof hard enough for a passing copper to shoot them a disapproving look.

'Don't let him wind you up so much,' says Harris evenly. She has to raise her voice above the roar of a passing lorry on Wapping, the six-lane road separating police HQ from the docks.

Men. It really was like taking care of small children. There is a lot, thinks DI Harris, to be said for having less testosterone.

'I'm not steaming about The Fish, Em! You expect that kind of thing from him. It's the slimy rat-fucker inside MIT who told him about Koopman's flight before we knew!'

'How do you know it's one of ours?'

Keane jams his hands in his pockets so as not to keep waving them around. He leans back against the car door and puffs out his cheeks. He lets out a long breath and then speaks more calmly.

'Because The Fish doesn't do detective work, Em. He's had a pencil jammed up his backside for so long he's got lead tonsils. No, a little birdie let this slip – didn't you hear him? He more or less told us. And since we're the only ones interested so far in the comings and goings of Menno Koopman, it follows that it was one of us who decided to take this tasty titbit up the food chain.' Keane walks a few paces and looks across the car park towards a view of the city skyline, and focuses as always on the Liver Building, indistinct in the misty sea air, the grey-green iron Liver birds on top looking west, straining to leave. Keane has always thought it a perfect image for the city: desire exceeding capabilities, but trying anyway. He once read that the original, twelfth-century symbol was an eagle but had been copied so poorly that a new creature was born. There was something about that too which resonated for Keane. Creativity from cack-handedness.

'Frank?' says Em Harris and Keane turns back towards the car.

'I bet it was that slimy bastard, Caddick. He's got an eye on leapfrogging over to HQ and it was him and Rose who've been doing the bulk of liaison with the Aussies.'

Harris shrugs. Privately she thinks Keane might be right about Caddick. It's the sort of thing an ambitious young DS might be tempted to do: drip feed potentially titillating information to a big noise like Perch in the hope of being seen as someone useful. But it's stupid thinking on Caddick's part if indeed it does turn out to be him. All it would do would be to lose him respect within MIT and lessen his chances of access to any other hot information.

Keane, she knows, will not let a slight like this pass without retribution, which in the knotty tangle of Merseyside Police can take many varied and ingenious forms.

There are coppers she knows for whom the pursuit of criminals is incidental to their wars of attrition against other officers. The level of grudge-holding on the force would make a Borgia blush. But she also knows that whatever happens to Caddick doesn't matter, not in the context of this case. The big thing that she's taken from the meeting is the confirmation that the father of the victim is heading their way. A father with a reputation for getting what he wants when it comes to criminal investigations. And whatever Keane's prior relationship with Koopman, Harris wants to make sure there's nothing that will leach negatively into her career. Harris has plans.

'Koopman,' she says. 'What do you think he wants?'

'I don't know,' says Keane, opening the car door. 'But it's just about the only thing me and The Fish can agree on. I don't like it either.'

24

Jimmy Gelagotis isn't the only person on the Gold Coast with an interest in the Max Kolomiets/Anton Bytchkov murders. The morning after Warren Eckhardt speaks to Keane at MIT in Liverpool, the Kolomiets file lands on his desk, bounced from the Organised Crime Group to his outfit, South East Queensland Homicide. Kolomiets was well known to the OCG, and there's little doubt that they'll be heavily involved, but the protocol dictates that the brief is kicked through to Eckhardt as a prelude to being handed back. Eckhardt knows before reading it that this will end up being a dual department investigation, and that he and OCG will have to share information sooner rather than later, with OCG establishing alpha domination as soon as possible. There are already emails and phone messages indicating as much in Eckhardt's inboxes.

But for right now at least, the file is his, and his alone. He fumbles in his pocket for a cigarette before remembering for the ten thousandth time that he can't smoke indoors. Eckhardt is an old-school smoker, getting through two packs a day and it's killing him. Already fifty, he looks nearer sixty, with a pronounced wheeze to his breathing.

It's been a long time since he's done anything more active on duty than walking down the office steps to the car park. He knows he should give up the cancer sticks, and quick.

But not today.

'Off to the coroner's office,' he tells Nick Matui, bent over his keyboard picking out a report on a domestic homicide in Nerang that came in overnight. Matui looks up and smiles wryly as Eckhardt pats his jacket pockets. He might be checking for his car keys but Matui knows Warren is making sure there are some smokes left in the pack.

'Sure, Ekkers. Say hello to Max for me,' Matui winks. It's safe to say the death of Max Kolomiets is not being mourned at Homicide.

Eckhardt makes his way outside to where his police issue Commodore is parked under the only patch of shade in the lot. As he leaves the chill air-conditioning and steps into the Gold Coast heat, Eckhardt coughs wetly. He immediately rummages around for a cigarette, jams it gratefully into his mouth and lights up. He takes off his jacket and draws the smoke blissfully into his diseased lungs.

More like it.

There is no real need for him to attend the coroner's office. The autopsy has already been done on Kolomiets and Eckhardt attended part of it; enough to already give him most of what he wants to know. He didn't attend the crime scene as he was laid up with a bout of flu which he'd only shaken off the day before. Matui filled in and brought him up to speed before handing the file over. Eckhardt already feels at a disadvantage with the Kolomiets case. And, like his counterpart twelve thousand miles and ten time zones away, Eckhardt has an atavistic need to get close to the victim. Just like Frank Keane, Warren

Eckhardt would be hard put to identify why, or how, seeing the corpse helps . . . he just knows it does.

He cranks up the Commodore's air-con and switches the radio to Nova. He hardly ever likes any song they play but the station's bright chatter is as much a part of his daily life as the heat. He turns the car towards the coroner's office and is there within ten minutes. The office is wedged incongruously between a downmarket Chinese restaurant and a tyre shop.

Eckhardt parks, takes a last regretful drag of his cigarette (his second since leaving Homicide) and pops a breath mint, before locking the car and entering the CO.

After the usual form-filling, he's granted access to the cold room where post-autopsy bodies are neatly stacked in two rows of stainless-steel mortuary drawers. The multi-pierced attendant snaps the lock on one and slides Max Kolomiets's body out for inspection. With a nod at Eckhardt, the assistant draws back the top sheet and leaves him to it.

'Hello, Max,' says Eckhardt softly. He speaks without rancour. He's only met Max Kolomiets once, during an investigation into a routine drug murder. Kolomiets was listed as the victim's employer and was interviewed as such by Homicide. With his high-priced lawyer in attendance, Kolomiets slid smoothly away from the investigation, the only technical connection between him and the victim easily explained. Of course, Max had nothing to do with the crime. He was simply the poor man's employer. What this man did outside working hours was his business and his alone. No further questions? Then we'll be off.

As Kolomiets left the interview room he winked at Eckhardt and Eckhardt knew exactly what Max was telling him. I did this, and there's absolutely nothing you can do about it, now or ever. Eckhardt knew, as did the whole team, that the victim was 'allegedly' skimming from Kolomiets and that could result in only one possible outcome. Proving it was another matter, and Kolomiets walked, as he always walked. 'Don't worry,' he said to Eckhardt at the door, 'you can't vin them all.' The Russian was untouchable. Except he wasn't.

Which is interesting, reflects Eckhardt: it means that something important in the safari park has changed.

He examines the neatest of Kolomiets's head wounds, the one that came as he lay already dead on the grass of the soccer pitch. It was a grace note, a shot by someone who didn't want to leave anything to chance. Forensics hasn't come back with any firm data on the gun, but from off-the-record snippets gleaned from the coroner, as well as his own experience, Eckhardt knows the muzzle was placed against the skin calmly by someone well-versed in violence. The body of Anton Bytchkov lay on a gurney in another of the coroner's steel cabinets, the wound in his head telling the same story.

The witness, the boy, won't speak.

Eckhardt doesn't blame him. It is frustrating but completely understandable. Eckhardt was over at the boy's home the previous morning and tried his best to put him at ease without success. The shrink is due for another visit that afternoon and Eckhardt is hopeful she'll have more success. A petite blonde wearing a tight-fitting skirt and a sternly professional expression, she called into the office at Homicide after the session with the witness and Eckhardt knew he'd have told her anything. The boy, of course, is another matter.

'One more session and he might begin to give us something,' the shrink explained as she left.

Eckhardt pats Max on the cheek, his flesh as unresponsive as a side of beef.

'Don't worry, Maxie,' he wheezes. 'You can't win 'em all.'

25

The only flight Koop can get, turns out – through no desire on his part – to connect via Amsterdam. As the plane dips in towards Schiphol, a disoriented and queasy Koop is unable to feel or articulate anything much about seeing his parents' homeland unroll beneath the wings of the jet. In truth, the place looks dismal, the light of the northern hemisphere flat and leaden after the sparkle of the past two years in Australia. Koopman disembarks and walks stiff-legged through the airport with an increasing sense of dislocation.

What does he think he's doing?

That feeling only increases after making the short hop on a budget airline into Liverpool. The same grey-green landscape, only this time as familiar as the pattern on his boyhood bedroom wallpaper. Koop gets off at Liverpool feeling like death and looking only marginally better. He's booked a room at a hotel down near the Pier Head. With both his parents now gone, and his brother still in hospital, Koop has no family in the city. There are friends, colleagues, that Koop might have called up to stay with but, like most coppers he knows, he prefers his own space, even if that's just a rented room. This is not a social visit and Koop doesn't want to fend off questions about his life in Australia and explain why he's back. Even he doesn't know that. Besides, staying in a hotel will keep him light, flexible.

For what, exactly? Koop grimaces. Now he's actually in Liverpool it strikes him how ridiculous his pilgrimage is. Perhaps Zoe is right.

He picks up his bag from the carousel and moves through into the arrivals hall. Amongst the business travellers and returning weekend revellers, Koopman stands out, tall, tanned, his grey hair bleached lighter by the faraway sun.

'Jesus,' says Frank Keane, moving forward and putting out a hand. 'It's Crocodile fucking Dundee.'

After a moment's hesitation, Koop smiles and shakes Keane's outstretched hand. 'Frank,' he says, holding on a fraction longer and a fraction harder than convention requires. It's taken only a second but Koop finds himself establishing – or trying to – some sort of alpha-male dominance with his old colleague. Worse, he's pretty sure that the woman with Keane is aware of it too. From the look on her face she's less than impressed. He tries to relax, slightly ashamed of his posturing, however small it may have been.

'Not sure if you know Em? DI Emily Harris, Menno Koopman.'

Harris shakes Koop's hand. Her grasp is cool and confident. 'DCI Koopman, good to meet you.'

'Call me Koop. And drop the DCI too, if you don't mind. It's been a while since anyone called me that.'

There's a short silence during which Menno Koopman regards the two Liverpool detectives. Em Harris does the same to him, not even trying to hide the fact that she's doing so. He's better-looking than Harris expected, taller too and carrying his fifty years with ease, and there's a steel in the eyes that doesn't bode well for any 'hands-off' message she and Keane might want to deliver. Other travellers drift past them, heading for the exits. Koop is aware of the sound of his hometown accent all around him, the nasal squawk as distinctive as ever, every second word a swear word.

'You greet all visitors to Liverpool personally these days, Frank?' says Koop.

By way of reply, Frank Keane hoists Koop's bag and pats him on the shoulder.

'Not all of 'em, Koop. Just the important ones.' He points to the door. 'Lift?'

Koop raises an eyebrow. 'Do I get a choice?'

Keane laughs.

'Since when has anyone told you what to do, Koop?'

'In that case I could murder a pint.'

Koop asks them to take him to The Phil, a hulking sand-stone Victorian-gothic pub straddling a corner opposite the Philharmonic Hall and under the shadow of the retro-futuristic Catholic Cathedral – 'Paddy's Wigwam'. The Phil is the only pub Koop has ever heard of that has urinals listed as tourist attractions.

'You do miss this, a bit.' He waves a hand around the pub as Keane sets down a pint of lager in front of him. 'In Australia. The history, I mean.'

Koop drinks in the ornate plasterwork and complex Victorian woodwork, the soft lights rebounding off polished brass and curving light fittings. He wouldn't have been able to tell anyone that was what he'd missed before getting back, but now he's here, it's obvious. He resolves to see more of the old stuff. A bit of kulcha, mate.

He might as well; it may be the only thing he manages to accomplish in Liverpool. The fact is, sitting in The Phil with the two detectives, Koop is feeling more than a little foolish. Both carry that air of absolute professionalism that he remembers well and it reminds him forcibly that he's nothing more than an amateur now. He delivers coffee, for fuck's sake. He knows what he'd be thinking if he was at the other side of the table.

Koop takes another drink and leans back, feeling the journey in the ache of his bones and the sand behind his eyes. He wants to take a long shower followed by an even longer sleep. He coughs, his throat dry from twenty-four hours plus inside a sealed metal tube.

'So,' he says, his eyes on Em Harris, 'what can I help you with, officer?'

'We heard you were coming.'

'Passport control,' says Koop. It's a statement. It's what he'd have done in their position. For the first time since arriving, Koop feels a tingle as something dormant stirs. He hasn't been out of the game for *that* long. It's not much but it feels good.

'We wanted to . . . to make sure you didn't do anything . . . rash, Koop.' Keane holds the gaze of his old boss. He taps his nail against the rim of his glass and Koop watches the small movement fixedly, Keane's words distant.

'Why are you here, Mr Koopman?' says Em, cutting across Koop's jetlagged stare. She leaves the prefix in deliberately and Keane glances sideways at her. Em Harris does everything deliberately and Keane can see why she's being cagey. Menno Koopman may have been something in the city once, but as far as Em is concerned he's trouble. Harris has no illusions about the dangers someone like Koopman could pose to her investigation. And as much as Frank Keane likes to put himself about as top dog, Em Harris thinks of the case as hers.

'Koop,' says Koop with a wry smile. 'Call me "Koop".' He knows why she's keeping an edge.

'Why are you here, Koop?' says Harris, her voice business-like. 'You hardly knew your son. And your brother is still safely tucked up in Bowden.'

Keane flashes Em a glance but Koop holds his hand up in a gesture of surrender. He takes another drink and leans forward, digesting Harris's welcome information that Carl is under lock and key. Coming from the patently reliable Harris, it's a relief. She's answered the question that's been at the front of his mind since the news about Stevie: was his brother involved?

Koop relaxes.

'Honestly?' he says. He feels a sneeze coming on, lifts a tissue from his pocket and blows his nose. Christ, he's forgotten how cold this country can be.

'That would be best, Koop,' says Keane. 'Em has no patience with anything else.'

'I don't know why I'm here, not really,' says Koop. He spreads his hands out, palms upwards; an oddly Italianate gesture. 'Back in Australia – back *home* – it just seemed like something . . . I don't know, something that I had to do. DI Harris, Em, is right. I didn't know Stevie, not even a little bit. But he doesn't have anyone else to . . . well, there's no-one else left for Stevie. Not unless there's some de facto who doesn't know he's dead. From what the Aussies told me, that's not the case. And Carl? Well, I don't really know about him either. I haven't seen him in more than ten years. Maybe that's got a bit to do with coming over too. Flesh and blood, y'know?'

The two cops don't reply. Koop looks at them both and smiles. It's an old copper's trick: say nothing and they'll keep talking. He continues regardless, not feeling like there's much for him to reveal.

'You don't have kids, right, Frank? Unless you've been busy over the past few years?'

Keane shakes his head.

'How about you?' Koop nods at Harris.

'Not my thing. Not yet, anyway.'

'Me neither,' says Koop, after a glance towards Harris. 'At least none since Sharon had Stevie. They just didn't come along for me and Zoe. Not after . . . well, it just didn't happen. I don't think I'm the fatherly kind, to be honest.'

Koop looks up and taps a finger on the table.

'But I *was* Stevie's father, at least technically. And since there's no-one else, it's up to me to see he's looked after. Even if it's just the funeral.'

'That won't be happening anytime soon, Koop,' says Keane gently. 'It's still a murder investigation, remember.'

'And that's all you're here for?' says Harris. 'No thoughts about taking things into your own hands?'

'Listen, I was a copper for longer than you can imagine and I might have cut corners from time to time, but I never went vigilante. Never. And I don't intend to start now.'

Another wave of fatigue sweeps over Koop. He isn't sure if it's the effect of the flights and the beer, or the fact that he's just lied through his teeth to people he respected. But it can't be helped. If there's one thing he's going to do back in the city, it's find whoever did this to Stevie.

He forces a smile onto his face.

'Do I look like a vigilante to you?' he says. 'I deliver coffee.'

He sees them relax a little. Koop sips his beer. There's a pause.

'Of course, I used to be a pretty good copper,' says Koop with a glance at Keane. 'Who knows? Maybe I could spot something that might have slipped under the radar?'

Keane looks dubious. Harris folds her arms across her chest. The movement attracts the attention of a couple of nearby drinkers who cast an appreciative eye over the DI. She's exactly Zoe's type, Koop can't help himself thinking, and a series of flash-frame images surge erotically through his head.

'Not a chance, Koop,' she says, and for a moment Koop is flustered, until he realises what she's talking about. She might be a good copper but she's not a mind reader. Thank God.

'Wait,' says Keane. 'Maybe it's worth a shot, Em. Koop knows plenty and he could be right.'

Harris drains her drink and stands. 'Nice to meet you, Mr Koopman. Sorry for your loss,' she says, as brisk as January. She shakes Koop's hand and flashes a meaningful glare at Keane. 'I'll see *you* back at the office.'

'How am I going to get back?' says Keane. 'You've got the car keys.'

'Get a cab,' says Harris. 'You can drop Mr Koopman wherever he's staying and carry on from there.'

Keane rolls his eyes but does nothing to stop his partner leaving. Both men watch her weave her way through the tables to the door, her passage leaving a procession of rubbernecking men in her wake. As the door to The Phil swings shut, Koop looks at Keane and lets out a long sigh.

'I know,' says Keane. 'Have you any idea what it's like working with a woman like that every day and remaining sane?'

Koop sucks his lower lip. 'Smart too,' he says. He smiles at Keane. 'You always do as she says?'

Keane holds up a finger in warning.

'Don't come that one, Koop. It's the oldest trick in the book. Divide and conquer.'

'You know she's wrong, though, don't you, Frank? About me, I mean. I *could* be useful. You of all people know I could.'

Keane pauses before reaching into his inside pocket and taking out a folded A4 brown envelope.

'That's why I brought this.' He hands the envelope to Koop and glowers at his drink as if it has somehow persuaded him to do something he'll regret. 'Not a fucking word.'

Koop puts the envelope on the table and pats the top of it.

'My lips are sealed. Thanks, Frank.'

'You might not thank me after you've seen it, Koop. The medicals are in there too.'

Keane leans forward and drums his fingers on the scarred wooden tabletop. 'I'm going out on a limb here, Koop. You're not going to screw me around on this, are you?'

'Cross my heart, Frank. I wouldn't dream of it.'

Keane gets up from the table and drains his glass.

'Why does that do nothing to reassure me? C'mon, let's get you to a hotel before you fall asleep in your beer.'

26

The first stop Warren Eckhardt makes after looking in on Max Kolomiets's corpse is the nearest newsagents to grab a fresh pack of smokes. The day is on its way to becoming a real bruiser, only just ten and already the mercury pushing thirty. By noon it'll become one of those heavy Gold Coast afternoons, the thick dark clouds boiling up from the west behind the hills and the threat (or promise) of rain later. In the meantime it'll be hot as Hades, and for someone like Warren Eckhardt that means trouble.

He makes a mental note – like he needs it – to stay inside air-conditioning all day like humans were supposed to do. If God had meant us to stay outside he wouldn't have invented the fucking Gold Coast on a sticky October afternoon. And it isn't even summer.

Eckhardt cranks up the air-con in the Commodore and lights up. He lets the car cool until it's ice and feels himself relax. Smoke and cold air. Nothing like it.

Now he can concentrate on the job in hand; finding out who wanted Max Kolomiets dead, and why. The second part might turn out to be something or nothing. But Eckhardt hopes it will be something. Not because he has any great burning ambition at this stage of his career, more that he plain and simple likes following something to the bitter end. I may be slow, he likes to say, but I'm steady, and I always arrive at the destination.

Yeah, like a fucking old Volvo, Nick Matui had said. And about as good-looking.

Eckhardt picks up The Russian's file and, engine running, sits in the car park outside the newsagents flicking through it once again.

The file tells him Macksym Kolomiets arrived in Australia more than twenty-five years previously, just before the fall of the Berlin Wall and at a point in time when the West was still handing out permanent residency status to anyone who managed to get across the borders. Australia, keen as always to help their friends in Washington and London, followed suit and Max Kolomiets washed up here. The first few years, as far as Ekhardt can glean, he kept his head down. He worked a few menial construction jobs on one or two big-scale projects in Tasmania and in the Kimberleys before falling off the grid for a few years. Eckhardt figures that he must have spent those years honing his criminal talents, because the next time his name crops up it's as part of a pretty serious Melbourne-based drug operation. Kolomiets wasn't charged but was interviewed as a potential witness. He didn't testify. From that point, his criminal record – at least the official one – grew steadily, the level of the charges tracing his progress upwards through the ranks. His most recent was a fraud investigation into dodgy land deals on the Gold Coast. Naturally, he walked from that one.

So much for the facts.

Warren Eckhardt knows a great deal more about Max Kolomiets that hasn't made the book. You can't survive as a cop in a place like the Goldie without knowing who does what and when and to who. You don't need to know all the details – although, given a choice, that's the way Eckhardt would prefer it – but you do have to know the big players.

Kolomiets was one of the very biggest.

Eckhardt knows he was hugely profitable, not just for himself but for those who worked with and for him. His profitability made him one of the untouchables.

Which makes his death all the more intriguing.

Eckhardt turns to the witness statements from the soccer field. He was in on most of the interviews, but reads through them again anyway. Although accurate descriptions are so far sketchy, all agree that the killer was a 'Lebanese-looking' character. As all the witnesses have an Anglo background, Eckhardt privately expands this description to include all races who aren't white-skinned. The tendency for racial simplification is one he resists at all costs. Not because of any liberal leanings in his make-up. It's because those kind of prejudices can lead to a lot of wasted time and effort. The killer on the soccer field could turn out to be almost anything: Greek, Italian, Indian, indigenous, or Pacific Islander.

Eckhardt hopes it isn't the last group. Some of those guys are hard work, even when they haven't done anything.

Next, Eckhardt goes over what he knows.

For Kolomiets to be killed like that there are only two explanations: someone bigger than him was unhappy with something he'd done, or someone smaller than him is making a step up.

Eckhardt favours the second option, mainly because Kolomiets clearly had no inkling he was being targeted. As far as the other soccer boys could judge – the key witness not having so much as opened his mouth – Kolomiets greeted the killer warmly. He certainly didn't make a run for it, or produce a weapon of his own. There were no raised voices. The killer just walked up and shot him. This was an extremely useful bit of information. In Eckhardt's experience, when someone like Kolomiets allowed people to get near enough to shoot, it meant only one thing: the Ukrainian knew whoever killed him. Which helps to narrow the field and at least gives Eckhardt something to start on. The connection between killer and victim might be thin but that one exists at all is useful.

Another thing.

The killer let the boy go.

Eckhardt considers that for some time. It could have been a practical decision, the killer's thinking running along the lines of least resistance. Offing a known criminal was ballsy. Killing an unarmed thirteen-year-old would have brought a lot more down on the shooter than Warren Eckhardt and his meagre team.

But Eckhardt also reckons leaving the boy alive shows at least a trace of sentimentality. In his practical, non-PC, real-world stereotyping experience, that usually meant a Mediterranean.

Eckhardt stubs out his cigarette and lights another. He notices a man in a suit pass him on the way into the Greek restaurant adjacent to the newsagent and shoot his smoke-filled car a disgusted glance.

What? Are the smoke Nazis going to take *that* away now? Soon he'd have to travel to the motherfucking moon for a drag. He inhales deeper and turns back to the Kolomiets file.

So who was locally in a position to make the step up to take over from Kolomiets? There aren't many candidates that Eckhardt can think of, but a few names pop into his head, Jimmy Gelagotis being one of them.

Eckhardt puts the car into drive and heads towards Surfers. He'll see if he can find Gelagotis, take a look at him and watch what happens. It isn't what you might call a scientific approach to policing but it will do for now. Besides, whoever said policing was a science?

27

Koop hasn't cried once since hearing about Stevie's death. It was like hearing about a distant relative. Sad, certainly, but not close enough for it to make much of a dent in his armour.

After reading the autopsy results and seeing the SOC photos, Menno Koopman lies on his hotel bed and weeps.

Some of it may simply be the effects of jetlag working their way through his system, but a big chunk of it is pure sorrow. As a copper, Koop thought he'd seen everything. This, though – what happened to Stevie – is in another realm. A dark knot of hatred sits in Koop's belly.

The images that are troubling him most are the SOC photographs from inside the container. That braced steel pole, the ground dark with blood – blood that contained his own genetic material – has the brooding presence of Warhol's 'Electric Chair' series that he saw at Brisbane's GOMA when accompanying Zoe on one of her frequent visits. The sense of extreme violence etched into the banal surroundings like acid on metal.

Koop rises from the bed and moves unsteadily to the bathroom. He runs cold water into the basin and washes his face. He brushes his teeth, looks out of the window and tries to regain some equilibrium. His room at one of the new hotels that has sprung up like steel mushrooms along the waterfront looks out across the Mersey towards Birkenhead and the Wirral beyond. The grey-brown river is the same as always but Koop hardly recognises parts of the city, even after only a two-year gap.

He breaks his gaze and returns to the bedroom. He collects everything Keane has given him and spreads it out methodically across the bed. It's time to forget about what he is now, and remember what he used to be: a copper, a good one.

With the contents of the file spread out, Koop organises it into chronological order beginning with the witness statements given by the art students who discovered Stevie's body. He lifts a pad of hotel notepaper from a desk drawer and begins making notes. As he does, details glossed over on first reading tingle with possibilities.

Art students.

The Gormley sculptures.

The arrangement of the body. Of Stevie.

The public display.

Koop moves on to the autopsy. He reads dispassionately the details of Stevie's torture and death. He brings a policeman's mind to it and now it reads differently.

The peeling of the skin.

Burnt alive.

The unburnt skin on Stevie's lower legs.

Koop reflects on that last note. The killers – there was obviously more than one – went to considerable trouble to set the victim on fire while he was in the water, albeit only at knee height. This would do two things: it would make any access to the victim more difficult by, say, the fire service or by a passing good Samaritan, thereby ensuring Stevie did, in fact, die. The second and potentially more revealing point to Koop is a visual one. In his mind's eye he sees the burning man – his son – and the fire dancing across the waves, reflected in the rise and fall of the ink-black water.

It would have been artistic, striking.

The site of Stevie's death has been chosen for visual effect. Koop pauses to let that sink in.

Next, Koop moves on to the site of the torture – the container.

The scaffolding pole has revealed little to forensics. It's generic, one of millions used all over the country, no handy manufacturer detail linking it to a particular yard or supplier. No unusual metals used in its construction enabling the investigation to pinpoint it as coming from one place.

The position of the container is more interesting.

The most obvious fact Koop notes is that it's close to the site of the iron men. Among other things, this would have made transportation easier. But offsetting that advantage, the Freeport is reasonably well protected. The old docks running all the way from Seaforth into Liverpool, and then south to Speke, were once a thieves paradise. Entire family dynasties were raised and nurtured on the bounty that could be shaken out of the docks.

Koop remembers entering a suspect's house to find every room filled floor to ceiling with looted goods from the containers – so much so that the family were living like lab rats in tunnels carved through teetering stacks of TVs, stereos, boxes of sportswear and the like. In one place, the back wall of a semi-detached house had been replaced by garage doors which turned the entire house into a makeshift auto chop shop by a moonlighting docker with a penchant for selling modified Bentleys to the Middle East.

Higher up the criminal food chain, organised gangs controlled entire areas of the docks and systematically skimmed both the imports and exports, as well as having a finger in every corrupt union deal or management scam. But with the arrival of the bonded Freeport, the security has been cleaned up substantially. Which raises the question of how the killers in this case had a seemingly free run at this container. Koop checks: Keane and Harris have quizzed the relevant security people, so far without making headway. Another confirmation that someone big is behind this.

Koop scrutinises the photos of the lens cap found in the container. As Em Harris spotted, it is from a video camera.

Koop, like Keane, knows what that indicates and he has to fight a fresh urge to weep.

Instead, he checks his notes and comes to a conclusion.

Stevie's murder was not intended to be covered up. It was intended to send out a powerful message to someone. And someone very powerful and very sadistic enjoyed doing it.

Koop gathers the file carefully together and places the papers back inside the envelope. He puts the envelope inside his suitcase, undresses and gets into bed. He is as tired as he can ever remember being, and falls asleep instantly.

Six hours later he wakes with a start and sits up in bed, a name at the front of his mind.

Hunter.

28

The film clip has messed with Jimmy's head. There's no way round it. He didn't sleep last night. Not a second. Left Ella at Q1 and went home late. Watched some shit on the box, the sound low with the rest of the family asleep. Anna's got some sleeping pills in the bathroom cabinet but Jimmy doesn't want them. He's not sure why but he'd like to stay wired for longer. Alert. There's a shark in the water.

By dawn Jimmy knows he has nowhere to go with it. He's considered making a trip himself to Liverpool but has decided against it. It's trickier for him than it was for Stevie, what with him being a Pom. It meant Stevie could travel freely, not many awkward questions asked. Stevie had a record, but not a long one, and nothing that would spark off too many nasty sessions at Immigration or Customs. And even if it had sparked questions, there was no debate about allowing him in on his UK passport.

Jimmy Gelagotis, on the other hand, is an entirely different concern. Jimmy tries to imagine himself landing in Liverpool and, even assuming he got through without incident, wading into Kite and his team.

It just isn't going to happen. He'd be too far from home and outgunned, outmanned, outmuscled. No, let them come over here. Then we'll see what's what.

Jimmy lets the scheming drift for the time being and concentrates on the job in hand. He tamps down the coffee in the machine and pulls the steam. Making a perfect coffee is something he can focus on. This morning Jimmy is doing barista duty at Café Stone in Surfers. With the barista on holiday, he decides to step in himself. It never does any harm to keep his hand in any of his businesses.

He rounds off the coffee and traces a heart into the head. It's a touch the customers enjoy. He places the cup on the counter and rings the bell for the waiter.

'Regular flat.'

Jimmy picks up the next order and starts working on the coffee.

Thank fuck the shipment is at this end. If the coke was still in transit, Jimmy'd be left whistling in the wind. Liverpool would have control and he'd be nowhere. Then again, killing Kolomiets and sending Stevie over was timed to coincide with the arrival of the drugs. Jimmy knows that possession of the goods is *everything*. It gives *him* power.

Which makes the 'Stevie Wonder' clip all the more disturbing. That shows real balls. He almost admires the move. And other than the torture which has never been Jimmy's style, the killing of Stevie is beginning to make a twisted kind of business sense. The nuclear option, right?

Jimmy warms the coffee cup with a blast of steam from the wand. He places it under the dripping spigot and gets the milk frothing. Coffees made, he pings the bell.

'Long black. Half-shot latte.'

Control. It all comes back to that.

And with the coke at his end he has the big bargaining chip. Everything else is details, even Stevie. This thing is moving up to another level, and sending the clip is the next stage of whatever is going to happen. Jimmy changed the playing field by killing The Russian, and now Kite is trying to regain it; first with Stevie, and now by sending the footage of Stevie.

Jimmy thinks Kite might be making a mistake emailing the mpeg. It's too showy, too Hollywood. He warms to the notion that it's an error of judgement and the thought gives him strength.

He thinks: Kite is underestimating me.

Just like Kolomiets. And if he's right about Kite going nuclear, then the response has to be the same. Whoever they send over will have to be killed and killed quickly and brutally. The next chess move.

When there's a lull in the orders, Jimmy sits on a tall chair behind the counter and calls Tony Link.

'We need to move the cats.'

Link is silent for a moment before replying. 'Sure. Where?'

'I'll text you the place. Tell Stefan.'

'OK,' says Link, but Jimmy Gelagotis has already hung up.

Warren Eckhardt just walked into the café.

29

Keane gets the momentum his case needs the day after Menno Koopman arrives.

And, as usual, the breakthrough comes because someone blabs.

This time it's Sean Bourke who's singing.

He hasn't deliberately talked, hasn't turned informer. It's much more prosaic than that. It was Bourke who vomited at the crime scene. He's seen some things, done some things, but what happened to the Australian is beyond anything Sean Bourke has ever experienced. He puked quietly in a corner as North went about his work.

Since then, Sean hasn't stopped drinking. And snorting. Keith Kite has given him tacit permission to take a short break. It never pays to have the crew hanging around after something like this, no matter how untouchable you are.

If Sean wants to blow off some steam, that's fine. He knows better than to talk.

At least when sober.

On the tail end of a three-day bender, Bourke winds up in Walton A&E getting his stomach pumped. Security personnel hold him while an Asian doctor Bourke is racially abusing in a savage torrent of spittle and bile saves his life. Afterwards, tearful and disoriented, Bourke babbles and Dr Sulami calls it in. The burnt man case has been all over the *Echo* for days and the doctor diligently writes down everything Sean Bourke says until he passes out. It's all inadmissable but the information is enough for the MIT unit to go to work on Sean.

Harris takes a sheet of paper and pins it to the crime wall. Behind her, Caddick, Rose and Corner look on. Caddick's wearing a smarter suit than he should. Or at least smarter than Keane thinks is appropriate. Keane gives him an appraising look. He wouldn't be the first or last pole-climber to pass through MIT.

'Kite?' says Rose. 'Is it solid?'

Keane is already shrugging on his jacket. 'Solid enough to pull him in.'

Harris purses her lips.

They've been arguing about this since the intel came in. Her view, forcefully expressed in the privacy of Keane's car on the way back into Stanley Road, is that they should keep a watching brief on Kite.

'We're making a mistake, Frank. Bourke's info isn't worth a thing. I can almost hear the DPP asking us what we were thinking of. Not that it'll get to court on the basis of this crap.'

'Sometimes you have to just see what happens. We haven't got the manpower to wait forever in the hope Kite gets caught with his pants down. This is something solid to go on, something we can work with.'

What he leaves unsaid is that, as the ranking case officer, it's his decision to bring Kite in and she can like it or lump it.

Which puts Harris in a difficult place.

Frank, in her view, is starting to make some bad choices. He's too close to Koopman and Koopman is bad news as far as she's concerned.

And now this. Unless a miracle happens, Kite will be out just as soon as his lawyer arrives. There isn't a scrap of corroborating evidence and Bourke's blabberings are drug-induced hearsay. She has no doubt that Kite is their man, but bringing him in will accomplish nothing except tip him off to their suspicions. And it will almost certainly also bring the OCS into the case.

They regard Kite as their pigeon; a fat juicy one that, handled properly, could make or break careers. If MIT blunders in, Perch will be bent over the table at Canning Place and, as sure as night follows day, Keane and Harris's syndicate will find themselves in a shit storm . . . and still with no case. The information from Bourke is helpful but this isn't the way to do it.

Harris thinks Frank is allowing the arrival of his ex-boss to cloud his judgement.

Fucking men.

She broods, arms folded, as Keane briefs the team. Caddick and Rose get the nod to come with them to pick up Kite. Keane anticipates no resistance and on this point Harris is in agreement. Kite will not feel threatened enough to do anything rash. His case will be that he's an innocent businessman. He's not about to start a firefight. Still, Keane assigns four support DCs as back-up. They are to remain visible but are not expected to have to do anything. Harris types a memo registering her disagreement and sends it to Frank. It's not much but it could be important down the line if it comes to an investigation. Right now it doesn't alter the most important fact.

Kite is coming in.

30

Hunter.

The name jerks Koop awake. He props himself up in the unfamiliar bed and switches on the bedside lamp. Three-thirty. Jesus. He knows instantly that sleep will be impossible.

Capitulating to the inevitable, he swings out of bed and cracks the synthetic fabric curtains. Outside, across the ink-black river, are the lights of New Brighton. They are about all he can see but the weather seems dry enough and Koop pulls on a pair of running shoes. He dresses in tracksuit pants, t-shirt and thick hooded sweatshirt, picks up a woollen beanie along with his room key and a ten-pound note, and heads downstairs.

In the lobby a bored night clerk looks at him a little suspiciously. Koop lifts his room key and waves it reassuringly as he walks to the main door. The clerk buzzes it open and Koop steps out into the city.

A light mist drifts in from the river across deserted roads. Koop takes a pedestrian walkway from the hotel and drops down onto the riverside promenade, trying to walk some of the stiffness out of his joints. At the river, he jogs south towards the newly scrubbed Liver Buildings, lit brilliantly from below.

Koop picks up the pace and works his way past a futuristic building and a canal, neither of which were there when he left town, before finding the more familiar territory of the pathway that loops around the riverfront of the Albert Dock.

He passes no-one and settles into a nice rhythm, enjoying the feeling of reconnecting with his city. His breath billows from his mouth in great white clouds and some of the edginess that's been niggling him since leaving Australia begins, fractionally, to ease.

Feeling like the last man in Liverpool, Koop runs past the end of the Albert Dock and the curving façade of the new Arena before passing through a whole series of residential developments carved from what was recently derelict land. Across the river, the shipyards still look as though they're operational. Koop spent a short time at Cammell Laird before signing up for the force.

Lurching out from a side road some fifty metres ahead, a stumbling drunk gives Koop pause. In a thin white shirt and scuffed black pants, the man would surely have been freezing if not for the buffer of alcohol. As they pass each other under a street lamp, Koop sees the drunk is young, eighteen or less, his gelled hair flattened, his still-chubby face showing a small red scuff mark on his cheekbone.

Koop slows, worried that, with the roiling Mersey protected only by a nominal iron rail, the drunk's night could end in disaster.

'You OK, son?' he says, jogging to a stop.

'F'CK*OFF!*' The drunk flails wildly and Koop steps away from him. The young man begins screeching obscenities, spittle flying from his mouth, his eyes unfocused. Then, as abruptly as he started, the drunk switches to maudlin. 'Sorry, mate, fucken sorry, like . . . I'm fucken bevvied, like.' Then he begins singing.

Koop's forgotten what it's like. Dealing with this. He feels rusty and all too aware of being a visitor. Backing off, he starts jogging again. The drunk will be fine; and if he isn't, it's none of Koop's business and the river will take him as it has taken many before.

Evolution, Koop's old sarge once called the process. 'Survival of the fittest', which, coming from Sergeant Gittings, was a bit rich.

Koop leaves the white-shirted man attempting a rendition of 'New York, New York'.

After working up a sweat he reaches the end of the riverside path and turns back towards the hotel. Nearing the point where he saw the drunk, Koop feels a tiny surge of adrenaline, his fight or flight instinct being readied, but the drunk has gone.

Home or into the river, Koop has no way of knowing.

He runs back into the city, the morning still black, the roads only marginally less deserted. He lets himself into the hotel using the security swipe and, once inside his room, showers and dresses.

Five am.

He emails Zoe with a long update that contains little actual information and gives Koop a curious homesick feeling, and spends another twenty minutes blankly channel-hopping before the hotel restaurant finally opens and he goes gratefully down for breakfast.

After the worst cup of coffee he's ever tasted and a plate of what might as well have been fried wood, Koop walks through the waking city to a car-hire place at the top of Dale Street. Twenty minutes later he's behind the wheel of an anonymous Ford. There are no signs on the vehicle that it's a hire car, a step being taken by more and more companies to deter opportunistic thieves looking for fat tourist pickings. Koop is glad; with the people who are involved in this, it wouldn't pay to stand out in any way.

He steers the familiar roads north, no need for the map of Merseyside the hire company has provided, his years of policing engraving the geography of the city on his brain forever. The traffic is still quiet, not yet into rush hour, and, in any case, he's heading against the flow, out of the city. He selects the Dock Road deliberately, surprised at the changes that have happened in the two years or so since he left. Everything that could be cleaned has been cleaned. Smart street signs, new paint, sandblasted industrial buildings are creating a shiny new corridor through some of the most benighted urban areas in Europe. Behind the scrubbed main road the estates still look like places nobody lives in through choice.

Koop drops off the Dock Road at Seaforth, leaving the sickly chemical smell coming from the industrial dock complex behind, and passes the end of the Freeport.

It's beginning to rain when he sees the first brown tourist sign guiding him left towards the Antony Gormley sculptures on Crosby Beach. He follows the road around the marine lake and parks behind the meagre dunes.

Koop turns off the engine and listens to the rain thrum against the roof. Koop remembers his mother's insistence that this particular rain was 'the sort that gets you wet'.

After a couple of minutes he picks up the bunch of flowers he'd bought in Liverpool and steps from the car. Although not particularly cold by Liverpool standards, it's enough for Koop. He shivers and yanks the zipper of his North Face jacket up to his throat and hunches his

174

chin into his chest. The Northern Rivers rain he'd left behind in Australia was straightforward, honest weather; great heavy sheets rattling straight down and bouncing off the earth. This sneaky stuff seems to soak into your bones.

Maybe his mother had been on to something.

He walks across the dunes, the claggy sand sticking to his shoes, the front of his jeans rapidly becoming sodden. As he crests the top he gets a faceful of wet sand, whipped off the top of the rise by the wind. Ahead of him, Crosby Beach stretches to his right, the Gormley figures disappearing into the distance.

Koop lopes down onto the concrete promenade and then down once more onto the sands. His first thought is that the beach is busy, before he realises almost all the people are simply sculptures. It's eerie being the only moving figure.

Koop knows the crime scene location from Keane's file. He trudges towards it now, past the flying saucer roof of the local swimming baths looking like something dropped in from a Tim Burton movie, until he reaches a point about twenty metres from one of the sculptures. The tide is out and Koop is certain he's close to the point where his son died.

There is no visible sign left that a man met a violent death at this spot.

The pole and concrete base have been taken away and successive days of tides have flattened any trace of what happened. Koop hadn't been expecting any. This is a pilgrimage.

Now he is here he feels unsure of himself. Perhaps even a little silly. He wonders – a classic Catholic reaction – if he's guilty of wallowing in an affair that he has no right to be involved with. What is it that makes Stevie *his* son? A hot flash of lust thirty-odd years ago?

Koop self-consciously places the flowers down on the sand and looks out to sea, waiting for an emotional response to come. Out in the grey haze, an enormous container ship drifts past, looking as though it's floating in a few inches of water, an optical illusion caused by the lie of the shore and the size of the craft.

The rain grows heavier and Koop turns away, disappointed with himself not to be feeling something more. He isn't sure what, but he expected more than this.

A woman with a small dog struggles down the steps onto the promenade. She carries a polythene bag containing the dog's crap in her hand.

Koop walks back to the car. There's nothing for him here.

31

Warren Eckhardt has never met Jimmy Gelagotis in the flesh before today.

He knows little about the man. Considering how well known Gelagotis is on the Goldie, Eckhardt is disappointed he's not better informed. Nor did he know much about Gelagotis's associates. Although, after a moment's reflection, perhaps he's being too hard on himself. Why should he know? Jimmy now circulates in the lofty circles patrolled by Organised Crime and seldom falls under Warren Eckhardt's radar.

Warren does know a few things. As an associate of Kolomiets, it's natural that any investigation will want to talk to Gelagotis. Eckhardt also knows that if Jimmy Gelagotis has killed Max Kolomiets, then it's a royal flush to a low pair that Gelagotis will have a signed and sealed alibi for the time in question.

But sometimes you just have to shake the tree.

Things are happening on his patch that Warren doesn't like. That's OK. Things happen all the time that Warren doesn't like. Christ, if he got his undies in a knot over every damn thing he didn't like, he wouldn't get up most mornings.

This time, though, Warren has the scent of something much bigger in the air. He spent a fruitful hour talking to DI Keane in England about the Stevie White case, during which he and Keane exchanged some highly useful information on some of the key players. At the end of the call Warren is pretty sure that Jimmy Gelagotis – if he's involved – may have bitten off more than he can chew.

Which can only mean that there's a very good reason for him to take that risk. With Stevie dead, Jimmy is going to have to attack or defend; there are no other options, apart from surrender, which Warren discounts immediately. From the background Eckhardt has been given by Frank Keane, anyone who plays games with an outfit as connected as the Liverpool cartels is not someone who would consider surrender a suitable strategy.

Besides, if Eckhardt didn't know it before, one glance at Jimmy Gelagotis tells him that. Not tall, not short, with the build of a middleweight and carrying himself like someone who knows what he is capable of but doesn't have to prove a damn thing.

'What can I get you, chief?' says Jimmy from behind the counter where he is checking the till. He's standing in front of a pin-board containing photos of the restaurant staff. Jimmy Gelagotis is in many of them, smiling and laughing. His accent contains second-generation traces of his Greek origins.

Warren Eckhardt absent-mindedly shakes out a smoke from his pack of cigarettes.

'Sorry, chief, no smoking, remember?'

Eckhardt holds up a hand in apology. Almost five years since the ban on smoking inside and he still keeps forgetting. He slides the pack back into his jacket.

'Flat white. Large, thanks.' Eckhardt hands over four dollars and pauses.

'Anything else, chief?' Gelagotis is filling a steel jug with hot water.

'You know me, Jimmy, don't you?'

Gelagotis shrugs. 'Lots of people come in here, chief. Maybe I seen you before. I don't know.'

Eckhardt smiles, revealing an uneven row of nicotine-stained teeth. 'Have it your way. When the coffee's ready perhaps you'll sit down with me for a pow-wow? Up to you, Jimmy.'

As Eckhardt picks up a handful of extra packets of sugar, his gaze is caught by one of the photographs on the café pin-board. It shows Jimmy with his arm around a taller, younger blond man. Both are smiling and holding beers.

The blond man is Stevie White.

Eckhardt turns from the photo to see Jimmy following his line of sight. Eckhardt gives him a sardonic smile, walks across to a window booth in the far corner and waits.

A few minutes later Gelagotis appears, Eckhardt's coffee in hand. He places the cup on the table and regards Eckhardt for a moment before taking the seat opposite. Any warmth that had been there has gone from his face.

'I'm sitting. What's this about?'

'You know, Jimmy. And you've got me as police, right? You're not giving much away to admit that.'

Gelagotis nods. 'Police. I see that. And I think you was pointed out one time to me. Something to do with drugs, right?'

'Look, Jimmy, I appreciate that lying is so ingrained in you that it's hard for you to think or speak any other way, so I'll make it simple.' Eckhardt stops to sip. 'Oh, good coffee.'

He puts down the cup and taps the table with a yellow finger. 'You already know I'm police. Warren Eckhardt from SE Queensland Homicide. I used to be with the Organised Crime Squad which is where you will have crossed my path – or maybe one of your tame cops knows me. I know you've got one in your pocket, at least, and I've a fair idea who that might be. But that's not all that important right now. What *is* is that you're Jimmy Gelagotis and I have a thick file on you. A great big thick juicy file.'

Jimmy makes a dismissive sound.

'Oh I know, Jimmy. Stale news. I'm not here about what's in the file. I'm here to just talk with you about what's happening. Before everything goes Wild West on us and I'm looking at you on a coroner's table. Just like I did with Max Kolomiets this morning. Yes, it didn't take very long, did it? For me to get in your face, I mean. You were expecting a little longer.'

Jimmy Gelagotis makes a motion to stand but Warren Eckhardt shoots out a surprisingly strong hand and grabs his wrist.

'Sit down, Jimmy. Really. This is going to help you.'

Gelagotis waits a beat and glances down at Eckhardt's hand. Warren opens his fingers and gestures to the seat. Gelagotis sits.

'I hardly knew Kolomiets,' he says eventually. 'If that's what this is about. Or are you after money?'

Eckhardt pulls a disappointed face.

'I know you did Kolomiets, Jimmy. I know it just as surely as I know the sun will rise, that this is good coffee, or that I will be having a cigarette the instant I'm back in my car. Given time I'll most likely prove it too. But see, here's the thing: I don't think I'll get the chance to prove a damn thing before someone gets to you, Jimmy.

That could be one of Kolomiets's boys – no, wait – you'll already have considered that, right? They must have been ready for the switch too. So, let's assume it's not one of The Russian's old team.' Eckhardt pauses. He sips his coffee and looks past Gelagotis at the pin-board. He decides to take a calculated risk.

'Does the name Stevie White mean anything to you?'

Jimmy Gelagotis doesn't blink. 'I know Stevie, yeah. So what? The guy's a customer, man.' His face shows nothing but Jimmy's thinking: this is coming home too quickly.

'He's dead, Jimmy.'

Gelagotis shrugs. 'Like I said, I hardly knew him.'

'Right,' says Eckhardt. The news of White's death is not a shock to Gelagotis, Eckhardt would bet his left nut on that.

'Aren't you curious about how he died, Jimmy? Or where?'

Gelagotis drums his fingers lightly on the surface of the table. 'Get on with it, Eckhardt.'

'I'm assuming from your reaction that the news is not a surprise to you, Jimmy. Which means you must be very worried, my friend.'

Gelagotis gives Eckhardt a level stare. 'Do I look worried?'

'No. No you don't, I'll give you that – you've managed to put a lid on it, outwardly at least. But you are worried. I see it. Because you know what'll happen. They'll be sending someone from Liverpool. Or maybe one of their friends. The Colombians. The Irish. The East Europeans. Those boys play hardball, Jimmy.'

'Do you practise this routine at home?' Gelagotis is shaking his head. 'It's fucking pathetic, man.'

Warren Eckhardt holds up a hand. He's smiling. 'OK, maybe I'm laying it on a bit. I'm a bit of a ham at heart.

Frankly, I don't care if someone does kill you, Jimmy. As far as I'm concerned it's one less cockroach I have to deal with. But this is out of your league, brother. Way out of your league. Did you hear what the Poms did to Stevie? Did you? The details, I mean?'

Jimmy feels his neck flush. The image of the video clip flashes through his mind.

'You did?' says Eckhardt, surprised at the reaction from Gelagotis. He wonders how much detail he knows and how he's come by that information. 'And you still think you're going to make this thing work out? Christ, maybe you're tougher than you look.'

Jimmy Gelagotis doesn't reply. He lets the silence build.

Eckhardt drains his coffee.

'OK,' he says, getting to his feet. 'I'm pretty sure the next time I see you, you won't be looking as fresh as you do now. Have a think about telling Uncle Warren all about it.'

Jimmy Gelagotis shakes his head. 'Like I said, I'm just a businessman. I don't know what you're talking about.'

Warren Eckhardt wipes the edge of his mouth with a paper napkin. He takes a business card and holds it out to Gelagotis. When he makes no move to take it, Eckhardt places it on the table and pushes it slightly towards the Greek.

'Well, seeing as you're a *business*man, Jimmy, here's my *business* card. Call me if you feel you want to get something off your chest. Think of me as your priest . . .'

He walks out into the heat of the day. As he reaches his car he turns to see Gelagotis pick up his card.

Tree shaken.

32

Kite is enjoying himself. Harris can see it written all over his face.

She looks across the interview room at Frank Keane fiddling with the controls of the digital recorder. Once Perch gets hold of this, it might be time to start thinking about that transfer.

Kite is their man, Emily Harris is sure of that. Just like she knows he's responsible for a large percentage of the crime on Merseyside, not to mention elsewhere. But knowing that, and proving it, are two entirely different things. As she sees the situation, hauling Kite in for questioning will accomplish nothing except give him the satisfaction of walking out with a smile on his face.

She and the tree-shaking Warren Eckhardt would not see eye to eye.

Keane, on the other hand, is at one with the Australian. He wouldn't have used the same phrase, but what he's doing with Keith Kite is precisely the same.

'9.35 am. Wednesday the nineteenth of October, 2011. DI Frank Keane and DI Emily Harris. Interview five four two, interview room three, Stanley Road Police HQ.

Interview subject, Keith Andrew Kite. Also present Constable . . .'

Keane breaks off with a quizzical glance at the PC standing next to the door.

'Parkes, sir.' Keane remembers the young copper from the White murder site.

'Constable Parkes.' Keane sits and looks at the file on the desk in front of him.

'Do you have to practise that before they give you the shiny badge?' says Kite, his mouth smiling, his eyes dark.

'We don't have badges, shiny or otherwise, Mr Kite.'

Kite gives a shake of his head. 'Fucking amateur hour,' he mutters.

'Mr Kite, we're investigating the death of one Steven White, at Crosby Beach on or around October the eleventh, 2011. We have reason to believe you may be able to shed some light on the matter.'

'Does Beyoncé here ever say anything, *Roy*? Or does she just sit there looking beautiful?' Kite turns to Harris. 'Cappuccino, luv, there's a good girl.' He sits back in his chair, his eyes black holes.

Keane wonders if Kite has already had a toot. It's early but the rumours are he's a user.

'Does the name Steven White mean anything to you, Mr Kite?' says Harris.

'One sugar, and don't forget the cinnamon sprinkles.'

'Sean Bourke's one of your lads, isn't he, Keith?' Keane says.

Kite shrugs. 'I've met him. Not sure what you mean by "one of my lads".'

'We're in the process of matching Sean's DNA to a container in Seaforth. Seems that Sean found your business methods a little too much, even for someone like him. He puked. The DNA match will put Sean at the crime scene.'

Keane waits. He and Harris both know the DNA evidence on Bourke won't be worth anything. DNA matches from vomit can be too easily contaminated for a court's liking. Frank's hoping Kite doesn't know that.

'What do you want me to say? I've met this man Bourke. What he does with his time is up to him.'

'You'd let him go just like that, Keith?' Keane's voice is hard.

Kite looks at him sadly and shakes his head. 'Fucking pathetic. You have to have more than that.'

Frank's voice is expressionless. 'You were seen, Mr Kite, dining with someone answering the description of White, the day before he was found. Sean Bourke was also there. Would you like to comment?'

Kite smiles blandly at Keane. 'I'm a busy man. I see lots of people in my game. This Bourke might have been there. I don't know.'

'What is your game exactly, Mr Kite?' Harris taps a finger on the file in front of her. 'Quite an impressive resumé.'

Kite looks at her, an expression of mock surprise on his face. 'What do you know? It can read. Well, I suppose even monkeys can be trained to recognise words, eh? No offence.' He glances at Keane and then swivels his head back to Harris. 'I'm a businessman, dear. A very successful one. As you know.'

'Does your business involve a Macksym Kolomiets?' DI Harris stares directly at Kite, an icy smile in place. There is a flicker from Kite. His smile doesn't waver but he's heard the name before, Harris is sure. 'I see you recognise the name.'

'Never heard of him,' says Kite. 'And what are you: clairvoyant? Is mind-reading now admissible in court?' Kite sits up straight in his chair. 'Now enough fucking about. I'm due at an opening tonight and I want to do a few things before it starts.'

'An art opening?' Keane breaks in. 'That's right, Keith, you're something of a culture vulture, aren't you?' He taps his pen against his teeth. 'What do you think of the Gormleys by the way?'

'Overrated. And some would say derivative.'

Keane barks out a laugh. 'Big word for you, isn't it, Keith? Been reading, have you? Mind you, you had plenty of time for that inside, didn't you? A four stretch, I believe. Some of you nightcrawlers go that way: Open University, degrees. All that crap. You want to watch that some of those big words don't get stuck in your mouth. A little knowledge is a dangerous thing.'

Kite's eyes hold Keane's. 'Yeah, you're right, it can be, Roy. Very dangerous.'

'I hope that's not a threat, Mr Kite.' Keane's voice is even.

Kite says nothing. He sits back and folds his arms.

Christ, Keane is sick to the back teeth of these low-rent fuckwits. For all his expensive tailoring and money, Kite is still one of the crop-haired, tracksuited, unlovable and unloved bottom-feeders that Liverpool's sink estates produce in their thousands. Keane experiences an adrenaline spike as he imagines smashing Kite's nose out through the back of the nasty little scum-sucking bastard's skull. Instead, in a measured tone he asks another question.

'The man you killed . . .'

Kite snorts. 'Give me a break.'

'The man you killed,' repeats Keane. He fixes Kite with a stare. 'You know whose son he is, don't you, Keith?'

Harris nudges Keane's foot with her toe. She's not happy about Keane revealing this information but he doesn't respond. For the first time in the interview Kite looks ruffled. It's the reason Keane has brought Kite into the interview; the real reason, not the bullshit he fed Harris.

'What the fuck are you talking about?' says Kite. He's recovered, but Keane can sense that this is unexpected for him. He presses forward.

'You didn't know? That's priceless, Keith. Stevie White, the man you tortured and burnt, is connected in a way you didn't know about.'

'Connected?' All pretence that Kite doesn't know about the dead man is forgotten. Keane has information Kite wants.

'Detective Chief Inspector Koopman,' says Keane. 'You remember him, don't you, Keith?'

Kite's brow furrows. 'Koopman? What's he got to do with this . . . this *alleged* murder?'

Keane allows himself a smirk. Harris is fuming but remains silent.

'White was Koopman's son, Keith.'

Kite's face darkens.

'Nothing to say?' Keane leans forward. He lowers his voice. 'You know what Koop is like, don't you? How do you think he'll take the news of your involvement?'

'Are you finished?' says Kite, all humour gone from his face. 'Because if you're not, then I'd like to speak to my lawyer. It was amusing, but time is pressing and all that.'

He looks at his watch. Harris wants to do the same. It's all she can do to not sigh out loud. This is going nowhere fast. In her view, not only has Frank chosen the wrong option in bringing Kite in too soon, he's compounded that by mentioning Koopman.

Keane perseveres for a few more minutes, but Kite's mouth remains closed. The arrival of his lawyer signals the end of questioning.

As Kite leaves the interview room, Keane does his best to avoid meeting Emily Harris's eyes. It isn't until they get back to the office that they speak. He looks out of the window at the edifying spectacle of the dual carriageway and the car park. He rubs the bridge of his nose and feels old.

'I told you so,' says Harris.

Keane raises a hand in an 'I surrender' gesture. 'At least no-one could accuse you of not stating the obvious, Em.'

Harris holds out a Post-it note. 'And Perch wants to see us. Kite's lawyer has been bending the ear of the gods.'

Keane is about to speak when he sees Kite leaving the building and getting into the lawyer's BMW.

'Shit,' says Keane.

33

Dry – or close enough after ten minutes in the car with the heater on full blast as to make no difference – and ten miles further north from the beach, Koop pulls onto the drive leading down to the new golf club complex which has risen up, seemingly overnight, in what looks like a riposte to the crusty grandees of Royal Birkdale and Hillside golf clubs a few miles further north in Southport.

The club has been an instant success and has attracted a different breed of clientele to the course and hotel: businessmen, footballers, soap stars, visiting actors, sports teams. To Koopman, the place looks like a suburban mansion on steroids wrapped around an expensive-looking golf course.

Koop walks along an impeccably groomed gravel path which meanders past a curve of unused golf carts. The weather is keeping all but the most dedicated of players at home. Beyond the carts is the pro-shop and booking centre.

Inside, the only occupant is a man wearing a golf-club polo shirt and sharply creased slacks. He is bent over a ledger on the counter in front of him trying to look busy.

At the sight of Koop, he straightens. Late October days at the club can be very slow indeed.

Then the man's eyes fall on Koop's jeans, trainers and damp North Face jacket and an almost imperceptible sneer creeps onto his face.

Golfers. A different breed, reflects Koop. He once knew a commercial painter and decorator who, working at one of the big clubs, was asked by a man wearing a cravat to 'paint more quietly' as the noise of his brush was disturbing the members. Koop is not, by nature, a golf club sort of person. Standing in the pro-shop, the rain puddling at his feet, he wonders if he might have risen further in the force if he had been. And then wonders if it would have been worth it. Probably not, if he had to dress like this twat.

'Lousy morning,' says the guy, pleasantly enough. As Koop draws closer he can smell the man's aftershave. 'How can I help you?'

'I'm interested in joining the club,' says Koop, doing his best to look convincing.

The man stares at him.

'Ah.'

'Is there a problem?'

The man smiles. 'It's just that there *is* a waiting list for membership, sir. Quite a substantial waiting list, actually. And the fees . . . well.' He looks Koop up and down and makes a sort of discouraging shrug. Koop wants to slap him. Instead he tries to appear crestfallen.

'Oh, I see,' he says. He looks at the man. 'Is there some information I could look at? A brochure?'

'A brochure?'

'Yes, a brochure. A printed document? Something that explains how I go about applying.'

'I'd have to see,' says the man doubtfully. He hesitates.

'If you would,' says Koop with an encouraging wink.

'There are some leaflets, I think.' He doesn't move. Instead, he peers around the counter as if expecting the leaflets to materialise. Koop remains still.

'A leaflet would be good,' he says, politely.

With a smile that vanishes quicker than it arrives, the man turns away from Koop and steps into a small inner office where he begins to rummage around inside the top drawer of a filing cabinet. The second he's gone, Koop reaches out a hand and rotates the ledger. As he expects, it is a booking diary containing the day's teeing off times. He slides a finger down the list until he finds the name he is looking for. He turns the ledger back as the man closes the filing cabinet.

'There you are, sir,' he says, handing Koop an expensively produced card membership booklet. 'I think you'll find everything you need to know in there.'

Koop opens the first page and tosses it back onto the counter. 'Thanks, but I think I'll stick to footy.' He turns and leaves the shop whistling. He couldn't help himself. Wanker.

At the clubhouse, and following a short discussion to establish that the bar is open to non-members, Koop has a little further difficulty with the way he is dressed before he is, eventually, allowed in. His offending jacket is stowed out of sight and Koop is shown to a seat near the window overlooking the eighteenth green.

A thin young man with a pronounced Liverpool accent, incongruous with his flawless manner, takes his order. Koop opts for a Diet Coke. His jetlag might need the caffeine later in the day. He's already beginning to flag after his night-time exertions and early start.

The waiter brings his drink and Koop settles back. Despite his anti-golf prejudice, it's comfortable in the bar. He watches a few brave golfers battle their way to the eighteenth, the drizzle making their rainwear shimmer, and reflects on less comfortable places he's had to wait in his professional life.

Koop finishes the Coke and orders a coffee. As he lifts it to his mouth, he braces himself against the expected disappointment of another English cup of slop, but this time, against all the odds, it's perfect. He picks up a newspaper and reads, keeping one eye on the eighteenth.

Almost an hour into his wait, and just as Koop is beginning to think about giving it up as a lost cause, three golfers arrive on the green and he sits up, suddenly alert.

The three finish their round, shake hands amid much exaggerated laughter and back-slapping, and head inside. A few minutes later the men appear, sans waterproofs, in the bar, their faces shining from four hours battling the elements. Eschewing the waiter service, and despite the early hour, they order beers at the bar and then head for a table. After glancing Koop's way, the tallest of the golfers disengages himself from his friends and walks across the thickly carpeted lounge.

'Koop,' says the golfer in a thick Glaswegian accent. His voice is neither friendly nor unfriendly. 'I thought you were in New Zealand, man.'

'Australia,' says Koop, making no attempt to get up.

'Close enough.'

'Sit down, Alan.'

Alan Hunter glances at his companions before taking a seat.

'How'd you know I'd be here?'

'I didn't. But it's daylight so I figured you'd be on the course. You always used to be able to set your clock by your golf.'

'Aye, true enough.'

Hunter, dour-faced, but with a flashing smile that changes him radically on the rare occasions he uses it, is in his mid-fifties, trim and dapper with sandy-coloured hair running to grey at the sides. People in the bar flash surreptitious glances at him from time to time. Hunter is famous. A Liverpool player for twelve years, before retiring and becoming one of the north-west's biggest property developers. A millionaire from his sporting days, Hunter has successfully traded his sporting spoils for an empire now worth hundreds of millions.

'So what brings you back to Liverpool, Koop, the weather?'

Koop half-smiles. 'How's Siobhan?'

Hunter looks shrewdly at Koop.

'She's fine, just fine. Second year at university. Psychology.'

'That figures,' says Koop. Alan Hunter rewards him with the smallest of nods.

Koop holds his coffee cup and lets Hunter wait.

Siobhan Hunter was one of Menno Koopman's highest-profile cases at MIT. A rape victim at sixteen, left for dead behind a nightclub in town one warm summer evening. Koop and his team found the rapist, a psychopathic bouncer by the name of Lewis. In the course of the investigation Lewis beat Koop severely, leaving him with a broken arm and fractured jaw. Despite his injuries Koop clung to Lewis until help arrived and Lewis ended up convicted for life. Lewis only lasted three weeks after the conviction, stabbed to death in his cell, assailant unknown.

Alan Hunter owes him.

Which doesn't mean that Alan Hunter likes it. His face hardens imperceptibly.

'It doesn't feel right trading on a collar like Lewis, Alan,' says Koop. 'And I wouldn't do it unless I needed to badly. Very badly.' He pauses and fixes the Glaswegian with a stare. 'It was my son who they found at Crosby last week.'

Hunter's eyes narrow. 'Son? Jesus. Sorry to hear that, Koop, really. I never knew you even had a son.'

'Long story. The thing is, I need to cut some corners.'

Hunter nods. 'Aye, I understand.'

Koop knows what he's asking. Alan Hunter hasn't reached the position he is in by playing fair. He has stood on toes and broken rules and crucially, from Menno Koopman's perspective, is rumoured to have formed an allegiance with Ali Sawarzi, a one-time Liverpool drug operator who is busy transforming himself into a pillar of the community with Hunter's help.

During the investigation into Siobhan's rape, Koop never pushed any information on Hunter towards the Serious Crime Squad. He didn't turn a blind eye, but neither did he use Siobhan's rape to delve further into Hunter's business. For that, as well as delivering Lewis, Hunter knows he owes Koop.

'What do you need?'

Koop leans forward. 'Stevie – my son – came here from Australia. He didn't know me, that's not why he came. He'd never been back to Liverpool as far as I know. And the next thing is he winds up dead.'

Koop holds Hunter's gaze.

'He was no angel, Alan. But he didn't deserve what happened. He was tortured.'

Hunter shakes his head. 'No.'

'What I need to know is have you heard anything . . . on the jungle drums about Australia, or anything like that?'

'Now wait a minute . . .'

'Anything you can give me.'

'I'm no grass, Koop.'

Koop holds up his hands, palms outstretched. 'I know that.'

Hunter seems to come to a decision. He inches forward and lowers his voice.

'I may have heard a whisper. And here's the thing, Koop. I mention something, and you connect that something to someone, that doesn't mean that someone has done this to your boy, right? It just means I've heard a story and you might want to look closer.'

'Anything you have.'

'There might be something,' says Hunter. 'There was a sniff about a down under delivery being talked about.'

'A delivery?' Koop says. 'You sure this isn't about stirring up trouble for one of your rivals, Alan?'

Hunter stands up, a smile on his face, but when he bends forward to speak to Koop his voice is ice. 'It's a fucking big delivery, Koop. The kind that people have been known to get very twitchy about. I appreciate what you did finding that scum who raped Siobhan, but that's all I'm giving you, is that clear? We're quits. And if what I told you does turn out to have been behind this, then you're on your own. Because these people are bad news, DCI Koopman. Scary bad. And I'm not someone who scares easily.'

He turns away.

'A name, Alan?'

Hunter stops.

'You much of a Beatles fan, Koop? When was the last time you listened to *Sergeant Pepper*?' Hunter walks back to his golfing buddies without another word. There is laughter as Hunter makes a quip Koop can't hear.

Koop sits for a few minutes thinking about what Alan Hunter has said, before drinking the last of his coffee and leaving the bar. Hunter doesn't look up as he walks past. Koop retrieves his jacket and walks through the drizzle to his car. He gets into the Ford and heads west towards Bowden Hospital and Carl.

Hunter's information or not, Koop has to see his brother some time. It might as well be now.

34

Eckhardt takes his information to the Organised Crime Group.

He has to. He's already held onto it a shade longer than is politically wise. There's a solid connection he can make between the recently deceased Stevie White and Jimmy Gelagotis. There's a solid connection between Jimmy Gelagotis and the recently deceased Macksym Kolomiets. Not to mention the recently deceased Anton Bytchkov. The last two he has no doubt OCG already knows about, but the White connection may be news.

In Warren Eckhardt's view, Stevie White turning up dead is unlikely to be a coincidence.

It'll be interesting to see if OCG feels the same way.

Eckhardt takes it to Chris Chakos. He and Chakos go back a few years although Chakos has, it has to be said, worn better than Warren. A trim man of forty-five, Chakos competes in triathlons, has no spare body fat and would sooner have chewed a gorilla's nutsack than smoked a cigarette. The two men are in Chakos's office on the eighth floor at the OCG Broadbeach HQ.

'It's not a lot really, is it, Warren?'

Chakos taps the thin file Warren has hastily assembled.

'Not a lot? What do you want, Gelagotis to give me a witnessed confession?'

Chakos smiles thinly. 'That would be good, yeah.' He leans back in his chair. 'Come on, Warren, look at it from my point of view. It's of interest to OCG that Stevie White's turned up dead in Liverpool, you're right. And it's of interest that he might have a connection with Jimmy Gelagotis.'

'There's no "might" about it.'

'Because of the photo in the café?'

'Yes, because of the photo in the café.'

'Well, let's say that there's a connection. That's all we have right now. All you have.'

'And White just happens to turn up dead twelve thousand miles away?' Warren Eckhardt reaches for his cigarettes before remembering. Again. 'Fuck.'

'You know that White was from Liverpool?' Chakos holds Eckhardt's gaze.

'What does that mean, Chris?'

'I don't know. That's the point, Warren. For all we know it's a local beef.'

'Local? White hadn't set foot in the place in thirty-odd years!'

'And it's worth keeping tabs on. See if there's something that links White directly to drugs in Liverpool. Have the Poms said anything about that?'

'No, not in so many words,' admits Eckhardt. 'But I'll chase that.'

'Good,' says Chakos. 'And I'd like to be kept up to date on that.'

The two men look at each other.

'Come on, Warren, you know how it is. We have real cases on the books stretching us thinner than a hooker's g-string.'

'This is a real case. An OCG case. Or it should be. What about the link between Gelagotis and Kolomiets?'

Chakos nods. 'I'll grant you that that is a bit more solid, Warren. And look, this is very, very close to being an OCG case. We're not idiots. Kolomiets was in drugs. White worked with Gelagotis. It all hangs together, but so far not as an international deal – if we discount your gut feeling. We do want to be in on the Kolomiets thing. The link with Gelagotis might be of interest, but Kolomiets had plenty of other piranhas in the tank with him. People you don't know about.'

'Then tell me.'

Chakos smiles. 'I will. If anyone pops up who I think might be useful to you. I don't want this case to cross-pollinate, Warren. We sometimes have bigger fish to fry.'

Eckhardt breathes deeply. His breath is wheezy, unhealthy. Chakos, the triathlete, winces inwardly.

'Look,' says Eckhardt, leaning forward and tapping the file. 'There's something bigger going on, Chris, I can feel it. The murders are linked. White. Kolomiets. Gelagotis.'

'Gelagotis hasn't been killed.'

'He will be. You watch.'

Chakos makes a note on a sheet of paper. 'OK, Warren, I appreciate you bringing these ideas to me. You've got some fair points, so here's what we're going to do. I'm going to expand the OCG investigation into the Kolomiets murder further, and I want you to bring anything you have back to me. The same applies to anything you get on the White murder from our Pommy colleagues.'

Eckhardt nods.

'But you'll have to work the Gelagotis/Kolomiets angle yourself. I'm not knocking your thinking and privately I think you may be on to something. But with things how they are, we have too many other possible scenarios for me to justify focusing money on that angle alone. I'll note it in the file that you're following that one on our behalf. I don't think Homicide will worry about that, will they?'

Eckhardt thinks about it. 'I'm halfway out the door there, Chris. They don't give a flying fuck what I do as long as I don't stink up the office.'

Chris Chakos stands.

'That's it, then?' says Eckhardt. 'I'm on my own?' He struggles to his feet and shakes Chakos's hand.

'For now. Until you get something a little more solid.'

Yeah, thinks Eckhardt, and if I do establish a concrete connection you'll be all over me like ticks on a dingo's arse.

35

After talking to Alan Hunter, Koop has no more excuses. It's time to see Carl.

He points the rental towards St Helens and, with sinking heart, prepares himself for an encounter he never thought would happen.

Bowden Hospital is a twenty-minute drive from Liverpool, out past the grime and crime of Huyton and into the flat fields of East Lancashire. Koop has never felt at home out here in the villages that have been gradually swallowed by the city. Even after his years on the force this is an area he can get lost in with little effort and, in fact, does exactly that before eventually finding what he's looking for.

The hospital is out on its own among farm fields. Despite the rural setting, it doesn't seem like a happy place. It presents a blank face to the world, its weatheraged Victorian stone concealed behind high walls and a security gate that wouldn't have looked out of place at Checkpoint Charlie.

It takes Koop almost half an hour and multiple identity checks before he gets as far as the second inner perimeter where he's told to wait for the duty psychiatrist to see him. Koop is shown to a waiting room situated in a steel and glass annexe where he sits in an uncomfortable chair, watching the rain fall on the main hospital building. It's a miserable sight and Koop experiences several stabs of guilt for his absence over the past decade. A bit too late for regrets, he reflects as the door opens and a middle-aged man in a rumpled jacket steps in.

'Mr Koopman?' The voice is Scottish, Glaswegian. 'Dr Burton.'

Burton has the air of a reformed boozer. Koop can't quite say exactly how he knows this but he's met this kind before. Perhaps it's the rasp in the voice matched to a clearness of eye. Burton raises an eyebrow. Koop realises he's been quiet a beat too long.

'Sorry, miles away. Yes, Menno Koopman. Thanks for seeing me at such short notice. I should have called.'

Burton sits down next to Koop. It's an awkward arrangement that further unsettles Koop's already shaky nerves. He shifts position to look at the psychiatrist.

'Do all visitors get to see you?' he asks. 'Or only those with dangerous relatives as inmates?'

Burton smiles thinly. 'Patients,' he corrects, in an intonation that makes it clear this is a correction he's made many times before. Koop nods, penitent. 'And, no,' continues Burton, 'not all visitors get this treatment. I was at the nursing station when the call came in that your brother had a visitor and I was curious.'

Koop's antenna twitches. 'Curious?'

'Yes,' says Burton. 'I wondered why he had a visitor.'

'Is that supposed to be some sort of crack at me?' Koop's voice is all business now.

'No, wait,' says Burton. His face softens and he holds his hands up in a placatory gesture. 'You misunderstand,

Mr Koopman. I'm not making any judgement on your relationship with your brother. That's not something I'd do.' Burton shifts forward in his seat. 'I was wondering why you'd come at all.'

Koop frowns. 'To see Carl, obviously,' he says. Despite the psychiatrist's soothing tone he's starting to get pissed off. He's never liked shrinks and now he's remembering why. Slimy buggers.

'Hasn't anyone told you?' says Burton.

'Told me what?'

'Your brother left Bowden on CS several months ago.'

'CS?'

'Controlled Supervision.'

Koop blinks. 'So he's not here?' he says, feeling the stupidity of the question just as he asks. 'No, wait, don't answer. What exactly is Controlled Supervision? Is he at some sort of halfway house?'

'Er, no, not quite,' says Burton. 'CS is more of a trust-based program. The patients on CS report in voluntarily.'

'Trust? Are you fucking kidding me?' Koop's voice has risen and the receptionist looks up. 'You let my psycho brother leave? Why do Merseyside Police think he's still a patient here?'

'I'd take issue with your description of your brother,' says Burton, getting to his feet. 'He has been profession-ally assessed as having made satisfactory progress towards full rehabilitation. And Carl *is* still a patient here. I am still his doctor.'

'But he's not here, is he?' Koop also gets to his feet. 'And I'm still his brother.'

'I have work to do,' says Burton.

'Wait.' Koop rubs his chin. 'Sorry, doctor. I shouldn't be blaming you.'

Burton nods. 'Carl is fine, Mr Koopman. That's what we try and do; fix people. With Carl his problems were mainly to do with his lifestyle choices. In many ways, all he needed was time.'

'Do you have a number for him?'

Burton shakes his head. 'I can't give you that, Mr Koopman. Wait,' he says, seeing the colour rise in Koop's cheeks. 'But I can give him yours. He's officially a sane and lawful free adult and can make his own mind up about contacting you.' Burton looks at Koop levelly. 'Or not.' The psychiatrist holds out a hand. 'Now I really must go.'

After the briefest of handshakes Burton is buzzed back through the security door and Koop reaches for his phone. He wants to let Keane know just how spectacularly sloppy he's been by not checking the patient status of Carl more thoroughly. Controlled supervision, my arse.

'Not in the hospital,' says the receptionist, pointing a red nail at the mobile. 'Unless it's an emergency.'

Koop pockets the phone. 'It just might be,' he says.

Half an hour later Koop steps out of the Ford. A BMW is leaving the car park and he gets a glimpse of a face in the passenger seat that dings a small bell somewhere in his memory bank. It'll come to him. He turns back towards the office blocks that were a part of his life for so long.

Only two years but it feels like a lifetime.

Maybe it's still the jetlag, or a kind of grief for Stevie, but a black wave of depression washes through Koop. What does he think he's doing? He doesn't belong in Liverpool any more. Zoe was right. He pulls out his phone and flicks onto the photos he has of her, suddenly anxious to see her face.

'Porn?' says a voice. 'Not your style, I wouldn't have thought, Koop.'

He looks up to see Frank Keane.

Koop switches off the iPhone and replaces it in his pocket. 'Checking something,' he says. He feels like he *has* been caught looking at porn. In fact, now he comes to think of it, most blokes he knows would sooner own up to looking at porn than a photo of their wife.

'Don't I get to sample the coffee again?' says Koop. He points towards the Stanley Road building.

Keane shivers. 'I couldn't do that to my worst enemy.' He gestures towards the city. 'I'm just on my way into town. Thought we might grab a pint.'

He doesn't want me to see the crime wall, thinks Koop and decides to keep the news about Carl to himself for the time being. See how forthcoming Keane is about the investigation. Quid pro quo and all that.

'Bit early, isn't it?'

'When you're working under The Fish you might as well start having scoops at breakfast. Come on, it's past twelve.'

'Just,' says Koop.

'You can give me a ride,' says Keane. 'I'll get a lift back.'

They compromise and end up in a café bar facing one of the revitalised back-street squares where Keane can get a beer and Koop something that bears a resemblance to drinkable coffee.

'Any news?' says Koop after they've exchanged some ritual observations about the football, the changes to the city, the weather.

'We're making progress,' says Keane, eventually. 'Some.'

'What sort of progress?'

Keane hesitates.

'Come on, Frank, don't be coy. It's a bit late in the day for that. You gave me the murder file, remember?'

'And I'm beginning to think that was a mistake.'

Koop looks at Keane. 'Oh?'

'You've been away, Koop.'

'You make it sound like a prison sentence.'

'Well, aren't they all fucking convicts?'

Koop smiles thinly, enough of an Australian already to feel uncomfortable at the easy jibe. He's reminded of his early days on the job, with Suggs and Gittings and all those neanderthals. He isn't putting Frank Keane in that category but it still sits uneasily, just like the free use of words like 'wog' and 'Abo' back in Australia. I'm getting too sensitive, thinks Koop. I'll be buying a bongo and heading to Nimbin next.

He's about to expand on this to Keane when it hits him like a punch to the gut.

The guy in the BMW.

Alan Hunter's hint becomes clear. Track seven. Lennon's vocal as familiar as a nursery rhyme over the swirling organ.

Mr Kite.

Koop sits back and lets the song run through his head, the lyrics as ingrained as any nursery rhyme. It's been so long since he's thought about this music. It was 'old' music when he was young, already the choice of older brothers, parents. But it's there in the blood like hymns, or chants on the Kop. Liverpool music. A source of pride.

But *Keith Kite*. Stevie, what were you thinking of? Koop's mind races down a pointless and unlikely scenario in which his son seeks him out and asks for advice before travelling to Liverpool. Koop clicks the track off in his head, the sounds of the café and the street outside suddenly sharp.

If Stevie ran foul of Keith Kite, it's no wonder he's ended up dead. Kite was already a monster when Menno Koopman first came across him. A vicious shark, circling whoever represented an obstacle. Koop can recall his bland face sliced in two by that cocky half-smile, his sharp teeth.

'Koop?' Keane is looking at him, his brows knitted together.

'I think you were drifting off a bit there,' says Keane. 'Maybe you should have a beer after all?'

'Why didn't you say you'd had Kite in?' His tone changes to one Keane has heard before, back in the days of *The Untouchables*. Hard. 'You've got Kite in the frame for Stevie, right, Frank?'

Keane sighs. He takes a drink, as much to give himself a moment as for anything else.

'Kite was in today. He left just before you.'

Koop draws both his hands down his face, a gesture Keane finds difficult to read.

'Is he looking good for it?'

Keane shakes his head. 'You can't ask me that, Koop.'

Koop is shown to a waiting room situated in a steel and glass annexe where he sits in an uncomfortable chair, watching the rain fall on the main hospital building.

'Can't I? I thought I just did.'

'Then I can't fucking tell you, is that clear enough for you?' Menno Koopman might have once been his boss but Keane is no pushover. His voice is loud enough for one or two people in the bar to look in their direction. Keane leans across the table and speaks in an urgent undertone, all business.

'Look, we got Kite in and we got nothing. I don't know if we did the right thing or if we did the wrong thing. Em Harris was deadset against it and for all I know she was bang on. I quite like him for it but Em's far from sure. She certainly didn't think bringing him in was a good move. I'm beginning to agree.'

'Was that Zentfeld in with him?'

Keane nods. 'Of course.'

Koop looks out across the square which has some sort of modern art installation rotating in the breeze. It isn't very good.

Keane drains his beer.

'So what was this little excursion in aid of, Frank?' Koop holds up his palms. 'Warn me off?'

'I've had enough of this,' says Keane. He gets to his feet and shrugs himself into his coat. 'We do go back, Koop, and I have a lot of time for you, but it was a mistake to come here, Stevie or not. I thought I might have got something from Kite by pulling him in and rattling his cage but I was wrong.'

Koop leans his forearm on the table. Something has just occurred to him. Keane has pulled a move straight out of Menno's own handbook. 'You told him, didn't you?'

'Told him what?'

'About me and Stevie being related.'

Keane shakes his head. 'It's not important. I was wrong.'

Koop gets to his feet and stands close to Keane. 'Not important? Don't come that crap, Frank. You knew exactly what you were doing getting Kite in and telling him about me.' He pauses. 'And now you're doing the same with me. Fuck, man, but you've become one crafty piece of work.'

'I had a good teacher.'

Koop and Keane stare at each other for a long moment before Keane breaks off. 'Look, Koop, I shouldn't have done it. If you start fucking around with Keith Kite it's going to end badly.'

'For me or for him?'

'For someone,' says Keane. 'Probably me. And that's the bit I don't like. You're not on the force now, Koop. You're not one of us. You're retired. Go back home and be retired. Let us sort out things at this end. Is that clear enough for you?'

Keane turns on his heel and stalks out of the bar without another word.

'As crystal, Frank,' mutters Koop to his disappearing back.

36

Zoe parks the car in the underground car park and tries to shake off the butterflies that seem to have taken up permanent residency in her stomach.

Great big Australian butterflies too. She doesn't think it's nerves about the upcoming presentation; she's done too many of those in London for much bigger, scarier fish than the friendly GOMA bunch. No, it's the feeling she remembers from Koop's early days in their marriage when he drew a late shift, or worked a particularly nasty case. The feeling she had almost every day he did that job-swap thing for a year with a cop in LA. The feeling she got when the police car turned into the driveway. She doesn't like Koop poking his nose into this terrible Stevie business.

Zoe checks her hair in the rear-view mirror and locks the car. She walks up and out onto the South Bank concourse and heads for the river. At a café close by the Gallery of Modern Art, Suze Lee and Tom Auger are waiting, looking sharp, just as Zoe knew they would be. Both are dressed in black and both are nervous, Suze showing her state of mind by talking constantly and Tom his by a continually bouncing left leg.

'All set?' says Zoe. They have half an hour before the BritArt presentation.

Suze taps her laptop. 'We're going to kill 'em!'

Tom smiles languidly. 'Which ties in very nicely with the theme.'

They have a strong presentation built around Damien Hirst's iconic shark – *The Physical Impossibility of Death in the Mind of Someone Living* – which is making the difficult journey from London to Brisbane. Zoe found an incredible photograph of the shark suspended in its tank, the wickedly curving mouth giving the work a sardonic twist. A striking image made all the more disturbing through a few judicious Photoshop tweaks. The neat fact that Hirst's shark is originally from Australia is what made their approach so clever. Tom came up with a nice line for the image: 'I'm Coming Home.'

'Suze, you'll start off the presentation for Vicki and the board. Tom and myself will follow your lead in backing you up on detail. Start with what we discussed. Go in with the big poster; everything else is secondary to that. If they don't get the references, I'll reinforce them. Tom will follow up with the support material. If they like the initial idea, then they'll love the development and the depth we've put into it. I want them to leave with a feeling that this is not only a good solution, it's the *only* solution that works, *and* it's a solution with real weight.'

Suze nods. Zoe in full flow is a force of nature.

'When it looks appropriate I'll finish things off. Don't forget, we want them to think of us as part of the team. We want to make an impression, but we don't want to simply suck up to them. This is a strong idea that will work and the rest is just fill.'

She smiles at her team feeling suddenly very old. They are babies. Maybe that's the real reason I pick them young, she thinks. An image of her own beautiful little Sarah flashes into her head, as she did often, before Zoe snaps her mind back to the matter in hand.

She gathers Suze and Tom and they walk up the steps towards the gallery to show off the shark.

She wonders what Koop is doing.

37

For the next two days Koop does what he used to do best: he asks around.

It's a myth that police work is about clues. It's about who you know. About gossip, tittle-tattle, whispers and rumour. Information.

Forensics, ballistics, financial data and computer tracking all play their part, but Koop knows that to get anywhere you have to talk to people who might know something.

He goes to Tiny Prior.

Prior, a dishevelled lump of a man, somewhere in his sixties, is neither small nor, as might have been expected, particularly large. His real name is Bertram which, to the uninitiated, sounds like as good a reason as any for Prior to be known by another name. The real reason is slightly different.

Tiny has worked the docks forever. He was there when Koop was a beat copper and he's still there now. His current official job title is Chief Foreman of Works with the Mersey Docks and Harbour Board, but everyone knows that Tiny's real title could best be summed up as 'Emperor'. He's seen governments and city councils come and go. He mutated into a left-wing militant when that was the way the wind was blowing in the city. He became a staunch defender of the free market when it was clear that the city was on an upward spiral of money and investment. He is smart, he is crafty.

He is a crook.

It's this last characteristic that Koop is banking on. Tiny came up on Koop's radar at MIT many times but always, always wriggled free. Koop came, in the end, to value Prior more highly for his information provision than for any kudos bringing him in on a collar might yield. It was a good strategy. Over the years Koop developed a symbiotic relationship: Tiny gave him stories, Koop didn't lock him up.

There was plenty to lock Tiny Prior up for. He's been skimming almost every day of his working life. Never an instigator of crime, Tiny's genius lies in finding out what crime is going on in the docks – which means plenty – and taking a small slice off the top: hence the nickname.

Tiny is never greedy – the downfall of almost all of Koop's clients – he's content with his little slice. A lot of little slices eventually turn into a great big pie. Koop knows that Tiny still lives in his council house in Seaforth. He also knows about Tiny's properties in Orlando and – get this – New York. Tiny Prior owns a Manhattan apartment, no loans, no paper trail.

Koop gets through the gate at the Freeport by the simple tactic of not telling the guard he is no longer with Merseyside Police. Koop parks in the visitors' car park and walks almost a kilometre to the base of one of the permanent cranes angled out over the river. With some trepidation he climbs the latticed iron stairs to the top and is faced with a yellow metal door.

He knocks, pushes it open without waiting for an answer and walks into Tiny Prior's kingdom.

'Mr Koopman,' says Tiny, his accent strong. 'A pleasure as always.'

He knows why I'm here, thinks Koop. It's not a surprise.

Prior is sitting in a leather armchair. To Koop's untutored eye it looks expensive. The armchair sits on an equally expensive-looking and richly patterned Persian rug. A low teak coffee table stands between Koop and Tiny and on it is a silver tea service. All of it is crammed inside the crane cab which is probably no larger than a small bathroom. The crane controls are situated at one end with a throw rug draped over them. Tiny's crane hasn't picked up anything in months.

'Just in time,' says Tiny, holding up a china cup. Without waiting for an answer, he pours Koop a cup and waves at a second armchair. Koop accepts the tea and takes a seat. Both armchairs are angled to look out through a window framed by heavy brocade drapes. The view is across the river and to the mountains of Snowdonia beyond.

'Nice view, Tiny,' says Koop. He sips the tea. Excellent.

'Yeah, not bad.'

Koop puts down his cup. Tiny leans forward and places a coaster under it.

'Teak,' he says. 'It marks.'

Koop lifts an apologetic hand. 'You know why I'm here, Tiny?'

'I did hear something, Mr Koopman. Very sorry about your lad.'

'He wasn't really "my lad", Tiny. Not like you think. But thanks anyway.'

Tiny looks at Koop. 'Always sad when something happens to family.'

Koop knows that Tiny divorced his first wife eight years ago and now lives with a twenty-two-year-old Thai girl. He has no children.

215

'Yes, too true, Tiny. Which brings me to the reason for my visit.'

'Anything, Mr Koopman. You name it.'

'Keith Kite.'

Tiny Prior's cup rattles in its saucer. 'Ah,' he says. 'I should have said, "Anything, except that," Mr Koopman.'

'You don't know anything about Kite?'

'That's not the problem, Mr Koopman, as you well know. I can't talk about that subject.'

'But he must do a lot of business through here, right?'

Tiny shakes his head. 'I can't say anything.'

Koop switches tack. 'OK, let's leave Kite out of it. What have you heard about Australia?'

'Big island a long way away.'

'Very funny, Tiny. Australia?'

'It's hard to track everything from here to the final destination, Mr Koopman. Just because a manifest says Indonesia, for example, it don't mean that shipment ends up in Indonesia, right? It could be an onward movement from there.'

'Not this,' says Koop. 'This is something going from here to Australia.'

He's taking a long shot. There's nothing solid connecting Kite with a large shipment, but Koop knows there is one, somewhere. He's looking for a glimmer from Tiny.

'There's lots going to Oz, Mr Koopman.' Tiny's voice has taken on a slight whining tone. It's time to up the squeeze level.

'You still skimming off the Norris Greens, Tiny?' Koop stares across the tea cups at Prior. 'Did they ever find out it was you who lightened the load on that Rotterdam run?'

Koop is talking about a case that came up three years

before he retired. Another murder which led him and the MIT team back to the docks. During the case Koop discovered that Tiny Prior was being paid to grease the delivery lines for 'furniture' being shipped to the Netherlands. What he wasn't being paid for was skimming a little – he was, after all, *Tiny* Prior – off the real delivery; chemicals used in the manufacture of ecstasy. The Norris Greens took a hit when MIT passed the information along to the Organised Crime Squad. Koop kept Tiny's role to himself. Something for a rainy day. Which has just arrived.

Tiny's pasty face turns even whiter. 'Don't joke, Mr Koopman.'

Koop stands up and leans over Prior. 'Do I look like I'm fucking joking, Tiny? Now give me something I can use, or I'll let the Norris Greens know it was you. And I might be tempted to bring Keith Kite in on this one too.'

'I can't.' Prior is shaking his head. 'They'll fucking kill me!'

Koop drops his voice. 'No-one will know, Tiny. Just me and you. And you don't have to outright tell me. Just a pointer will do. Anything.'

Tiny licks his lips. 'Alright. But it's nothing, really. And that's all you're getting, Mr Koopman.'

'Fire away, Tiny.'

Tiny Prior puts down his cup. 'You didn't hear this from me, right? You want to be looking at Halewood.'

'Halewood? What is this, *Give Us A Clue*?' Koop jabs Tiny in the chest. 'Halewood? What does that mean?'

Tiny Prior's face alters and Koop knows instantly that's all he's going to get from the Emperor of the Docks. 'That's it. Do what you want, Mr Koopman. You asked for something and I gave it yer. Now fuck off and leave me alone!'

Koop stands up, his head brushing the steel roof of the cab.

'Alright, Tiny. No need to get offensive.' Koop finishes his tea and replaces the cup in the saucer with a rattle. He looks out of the window and along the river towards Speke.

Halewood lies ten miles south-east of Liverpool and means one thing and one thing only.

Cars.

The troubled Jaguar factory at Halewood produces the X-Type Jag, mainly for export. If Tiny Prior has pointed him at Halewood he's telling him that this business has something to do with cars. Koop knows that if Keith Kite is involved it's unlikely that the deal is about cars and cars alone. But it could mean that the cars are being used as a cover for something else.

It doesn't take long for Koop to run into a brick wall.

Without access to the force computers there's no way to get into the delivery manifests.

Koop calls Keane and meets him in town.

'I thought I told you to leave it alone?'

'Told?' Koop arches his eyebrows. 'Are you serious, Frank?'

'I was, yes.'

Koop waves the comment away. He doesn't have time to get into a pissing contest.

'Never mind all that.' Koop tells him about the information he's got from Tiny. Naturally he leaves Tiny's name out.

'That's it?' says Keane. 'An anonymous tip about Jaguars? What am I supposed to do with that?'

'You're supposed to be a fucking copper, Frank. Or have

you forgotten that since I've been away? Christ almighty, I'm handing you a solid lead on this case. Think what we'd have done with it when I was here. We'd have been onto the thing like a dog on a rabbit.'

'You're not here any more, Koop. That's the point. Things have changed.'

'You mean *you've* changed.'

'And what if I have? What the fuck business is it of yours?'

'It's my son who was killed, Frank. I'd say that makes it my business, wouldn't you?'

Keane glares at Koop. 'Don't come that crap, Koop. Stevie was no son of yours – not in a way that means anything. So don't get all high and mighty with me.'

Koop tries to calm his breathing. He doesn't want an assault charge. And he isn't at all sure that Keane wouldn't go right ahead and kick his arse back to Australia anyway.

'Look, I've given you the information. You must have known when you gave me Stevie's file that I'd be digging around. Well, I've done some digging and I've brought you a bone. A small one, I'll give you that, but it *is* a fucking bone. Can you at least look into it?'

Keane lets out a long breath.

'Okay. Okay, Koop. I'll see what we can do. But things have really changed since Perch came in.'

'This is still a police force, isn't it?'

'Yes, it is, Koop. A force that you're no longer part of. And I'm regretting giving you that file. I told you before. It was a mistake. You coming back was a mistake. Go home.'

Keane walks away without another word.

Home?

Koop isn't sure he knows where that is any more.

38

'You're getting paranoid, Jimmy. Relax. Eckhardt's just some old fart. He's got nothing solid.'

'Relax? Easy for you to say, brother.' Jimmy rubs his fingers against his chin. He and Tony Link are at the Q1 apartment, Ella having been sent out with a wad to do some shopping.

'What do you want?' she'd asked.

'Me? I don't want fucking anything. Just go shopping. Buy something.'

Ella had shrugged and taken the money, leaving the two men drinking in the apartment.

She doesn't like Tony or Stefan coming round. Jimmy might pay for the place, but this is her home and Stefan Meeks in particular is an out-and-out creep.

Jimmy shared her with Stefan one time and since then he looks at her as if he wants to hurt her. He's careful to smile and joke, but he can't hide what's in his eyes. Tony, too, is less respectful than Ella would like. Despite their clothes and their cars and the money, they are not classy.

She's glad to leave even if she can see storm clouds

gathering outside the windows. If she parks at Pac Fair she needn't get wet.

Jimmy Gelagotis drums his fingers on the arm of his chair but says nothing. Tony Link risks a glimpse at his watch.

'You busy?' says Jimmy.

'I got a few things to do. You know how it is.'

Gelagotis nods. He does understand all about the need for keeping your eye on the details. It's how he's grown his businesses, the legit as well as the criminal. Tony is right. Except now Jimmy wants him and everyone else to focus their full attention on the shipment. This whole thing is beginning to leak like a busted bucket. First Stevie. Now this Eckhardt turning up out of the blue.

Details. Details.

'The cars?'

Tony Link lets out an almost imperceptible sigh. 'They're golden, Jimmy. Stefan's all over 'em.'

'They moved them?'

'We've been over this, Jimmy. Yes, they've been moved. They're all at the lock-up in Beenleigh. Just like we discussed. Stefan took care of it all.'

Jimmy looks at Tony Link. One of those Greek looks.

'You trust him?'

'Who?'

'Stefan. You trust him?'

Jimmy sits up in his chair.

'Fuck, yes I trust him!' says Link. 'He's a solid bloke. I can't believe you asked me that, Jimmy. Stefan's one of our own.'

Jimmy Gelagotis doesn't flinch. He nods absently. 'He's a Pom too. Did you know?'

221

Link shrugs. 'Yeah? So what? Being a Pom makes him suss?'

'The Poms sent the shipment.' Jimmy isn't asking a question but Link replies as if he is.

'Stefan's good, Jimmy. This isn't the time to be worrying about your own.'

Jimmy looks out of the window. Thinking: you're wrong, Tony. This is exactly the time to be worrying about the people around you. And about the details.

'I want to move the cars again. Get them somewhere safer. And get the stuff moving, get it sold.' Jimmy talks quickly, decisively. 'And I want to see it for myself. All of it. All the merchandise. Now.' He gets up from his chair and grabs his car keys from the table.

Link waits a beat before following Gelagotis from the apartment. The two stand at the express lift side by side. Tony glances at the man next to him, the man he's been in business with for the past four years.

He hopes to fuck that Stefan hasn't started moving the stuff already. If he has, they'll have to kill Jimmy earlier than planned.

39

The ticket is at the front desk when Koop gets back to the hotel at five. Anfield Road End, lower level, kick-off at eight. There's no note and Koop stares at the ticket for a while.

'Who left this?' Koop asks the receptionist. She shakes her head. 'Sorry, Mr Koopman, I don't know. I could ask around, see if whoever was on the last shift knows?'

Koop waves a hand. 'That's OK, it's no big deal.' A moment's reflection and he knows that he'll be using the ticket. It's a development Koop would be foolish to pass up. Chasing the delivery boy won't help. Besides, it's almost five years since he's been to the match.

Two hours later, Koop is cutting through the cobbled back alleys up from Everton Valley. He's one of thousands heading to the brightly lit shrine which looms above the terraced streets. The lights from the stadium make silhouettes of the crowd and flicker on the glass shards concreted into the back walls of the tiny houses. Home-made burglar alarms. Some residents have chosen the belt-and-braces approach of razor wire and/or a rottweiler. There are no houses without some sort of violent deterrent. Koop knows they're wise. Anfield is a tough neighbourhood. He's arrested a significant number of scallies around here.

Closer to the ground and Koop feels a surge of pride. He always did prefer the night games. At the back of the Kop the pre-match crowd scarf down burgers, chips, hot dogs. Beer too from the microscopic corner pubs, packed to overflowing and already in full song. A sign of the times: amidst the burger bars and dodgy souvenir stalls is a proper coffee stand, complete with steaming espresso machine. Lattes and cappuccinos in the lee of the Kop. Who'd have thought it?

Koop walks around to the opposite end. At the corner of Anfield Road he catches the eye of one of the mounted police who does a double take. 'DCI Koopman!' says the copper, a twenty-year veteran. 'I thought you'd gone overseas? Canada, right?'

'Australia.' He shakes the outstretched hand but cuts the reminiscences short. He's already getting the odd look from more than a few of the crowd and has no desire to raise his profile any higher. Leaving the horses behind, Koop finds the turnstile and squeezes through.

He's in his seat ten minutes before kick-off. On his right is a young family. Dad and two excited lads of about eight and ten. The father nods affably as Koop sits, but it's clear this is not who left the ticket at the hotel. The aisle seat to his left remains empty through the ritualistic singing. The Liverpool anthem works its customary magic and Koop feels a tingle down his spine at the sound of forty thousand voices in unison. Fucking hell; what a moment.

It's five minutes into the game before Koop feels someone slip into the empty seat and he looks round.

'Hello, Menno,' says Carl. 'Any score?'

*

It's one-nil to the Reds at halftime, but Menno Koopman has barely registered the details. By some tacit understanding, he and Carl have exchanged just a few words during the first half, and then only concerning the game, both of them grateful for the spectacle in front of them. That's why Carl chose here, Koop thinks, and why he waited until the whistle to take his seat.

'It's good to see you, Menno,' says Carl. The two of them are standing, shaking some feeling into their feet. 'Really.'

Koop is rocked by the warmth in his brother's voice. He feels a flood of shame at the way he's been. Or not been, to be more accurate.

'You're looking good,' says Koop. And he's right, Carl Koopman *is* looking good. Considering. Older, obviously, and with a residual wariness about him that any copper would recognise as that of someone who's spent time locked up, but fit and healthy. He's dressed conservatively but well. There's no sign to the untrained eye that Carl is anything but a reasonably prosperous middle-aged man in good shape.

'I hadn't realised,' says Koop. 'About Bowden, I mean.'

Carl raises an eyebrow.

'That you'd . . . been released.'

Carl smiles but there's a touch of grit there. 'Cured, you mean.'

Koop nods. 'Sorry.'

The word hangs in the air. The pause threatens to become more awkward than it already is. Both men begin to speak at once and laugh.

'After you,' says Menno. The phrase seems absurdly formal.

'I don't mind that you didn't visit,' says Carl. 'What I did, well, it must have been very difficult. For you, I mean.

It wasn't easy for me either, but I understand where you were coming from. Being a cop and all that.'

Menno coughs.

'I'm not saying I wasn't hurt,' continues Carl. 'But it's OK, Menno.' He looks directly at Koop and as Carl holds his gaze Koop feels vaguely uncomfortable. He forces himself not to look away.

'I was ill, you know. I know you lot – coppers – don't see it that way, but that's what it was.'

Menno doesn't know what to say. He makes a vague gesture with his shoulders, not quite a shrug.

'I am better,' adds Carl.

Menno nods. 'OK.' He looks around the stadium. 'Water under the bridge,' he says.

'I've moved on,' says Carl. 'It's over.'

'It's certainly over for Liam Jones.' The name of Carl's victim slips out before Koop can stop himself and Koop doesn't know why. The loss of one more drug-gobbling scrote certainly didn't deprive the world of anything that could be described as a productive human being and Koop feels slightly shameful using him as a moral baseball bat on his brother.

'That's true,' says Carl. 'Very perceptive, Menno. You probably didn't need to point it out.'

Koop sighs. 'Look, Carl, I don't know how to behave here. We haven't seen each other since . . . well, since the court case. I probably should have visited. I don't know. I don't know why I mentioned Jones. Who knows what's right in this kind of thing?'

'I heard about Stevie,' says Carl.

This information brings Menno up short and he feels the faintest whisper of disquiet tickle the back of his brain.

'How?'

226

'That doesn't matter.'

Koop thinks: yes, it does. He tries to stop himself behaving like a policeman but it's hard. He waits for Carl to speak again.

'Family is family, whatever happens,' says Carl, and this time there's no mistaking it; Koop's antennae are twitching. Carl hasn't changed his voice a fraction but Koop feels a charge in the atmosphere. 'I knew you'd come home.' Carl leans back and Koop lets out a breath he didn't know he was holding.

'You knew?'

'Yeah, I knew.' Carl smiles again. 'You're my brother, Menno. You can't change that. Blood is blood etc, etc.'

Koop runs his tongue against his teeth. There's something wrong here and he tries to choose his words carefully. It doesn't work and comes out too blunt.

'How did you know about Stevie, Carl?' he says. 'It hasn't been in the papers.'

Carl blinks and looks as though he's about to speak. Then his puzzled expression hardens into one of understanding.

'You think *I* had something to do with it? Loony tops nephew to get back at older brother – is that the great detective's scenario? Burton told me you'd been in. That's how I knew. Fuck, Menno, what do you think I am?'

Carl turns and stalks off towards the exit leaving Koop watching him. The fact is, Menno Koopman doesn't have the faintest clue about what his brother is, or has become.

'Jesus,' Koop mutters under his breath. 'Carl, wait!'

Koop heads in the direction taken by Carl. A minute later he's standing outside the ground looking up and down Anfield Road. It's dark and still busy. Menno spots Carl and trots after him.

'Wait,' says Koop as he taps his brother on the shoulder.

It isn't Carl. 'Sorry, mate,' says Koop to the stranger. 'Thought you were someone else.'

The man nods and walks off, leaving Menno standing in the middle of Anfield Road. He jams his hands into his coat pocket and heads towards the city.

Twenty metres away, Carl Koopman steps out from the black mouth of an alley bisecting the row of window-boarded terraces and follows his brother.

By ten, Koop is halfway pissed. Three quick pints and chasers will do that. He's somewhere round the back of Bold Street, at a bar that wasn't there when he'd left Liverpool. Across the square a chattering crowd spills out of a converted former grain warehouse. For the first time, Koop notices it's an art gallery, its warm brick façade lit from below by a series of blue spotlights which cast beams up and onto the enamelled metal of the gallery sign. In trendy lower case, the name has been cut out – *the granary* – and its enhanced shadow cants up on the brick-work. In the courtyard the people look no less shiny and modern. The sound of their chattering reminds Koop of the lorikeets gathering in his fig tree at dusk.

He swallows the last of his beer and drifts over to the gallery. No-one asks for a ticket and he lifts a glass of white wine from a passing waiter. He's already had too much but after the scene at Anfield he's past caring. This whole thing – whatever the fuck it is – is not working out. Exactly what Koop hoped to get from his trip he doesn't know. The one thing he does know is that he's getting nowhere fast. First Keane's ultimatum – there's no other word for it – and then the fucked-up thing with Carl. Koop doesn't even know if the Halewood information he gave Keane is being acted on or not.

And then he sees Keith Kite.

It's a sign, thinks Koop, although he has no patience with that sort of mystical crap. Whatever it is, as soon as Koop sees Kite he knows there's going to be trouble.

He wishes he hadn't already had a few, though. He'd have preferred a clear head for this.

Koop takes a mouthful of wine and wanders around the gallery, making a show of looking at the artwork. No longer a complete philistine, thanks to a lifetime with Zoe, he knows enough to see that this is good stuff.

Intensely worked images have been digitally treated somehow so that their content is rendered almost impossible to extract. Yet the things positively hum with a playful sexuality. Koop looks across the crowded gallery and from a distance can see that the images have been taken from hugely inflated home-made pornography – threesomes, foursomes, spit-roasts, role-play, orgies – the tangled bodies pixelated, treated, abstracted until they become whirling patterns of vibrant colour.

Beauty from porn. They're clever, sexy pieces that Koop would, under normal circumstances, have enjoyed talking about with Zoe. Now, though, there's only one thing on his mind.

Keith Kite.

Koop had history with Kite long before Stevie. Anyone at MIT worked cases that had his fingers all over them. As slippery as an eel, and protected by more than a decade of graft, Kite proved impossible to link to anything substantial that would stand up in court. Witnesses, naturally enough, after seeing what happened to others who testified, clammed up. Koop didn't blame them, and since most

229

of the cases where Kite was involved weren't homicides, his interest in Kite was marginal. Until now.

Seeing Keane bring Kite in for questioning, so soon after being given the tip by Alan Hunter, means only one thing: Kite is involved. If Kite is involved, then Kite is the person responsible for killing Stevie.

Koop takes another gulp of wine and fights to control himself. Don't lose it, Koopman.

In a corner of the gallery, a temporary bar has been installed. In front of it stands a knot of people laughing and joking. It is, to a student of Liverpool types, an interesting mix, and Koop is nothing if not a lifelong observer, even pissed. To anyone with a working knowledge of Liverpool serious crime, the majority of those gathered around the bar are instantly recognisable as trouble. Kite stands in the middle, a champagne glass in hand, a thin blonde to his right, an artistic looking middle-aged woman to his left, possibly the gallery owner. Three men in suits, two of the Halligan tribe, and an uncomfortable-looking gorilla who Koop vaguely recognises from prior encounters with Kite: Bourke, is it? A fourth man drinking water stands slightly off to one side. Koop can't tell if he's with Kite's party or not and doesn't recognise him.

The rest of the group are a ragtag of suits and women wearing very short skirts. All of them look moneyed and, to Koop's eyes, most have already had more than a toot of marching powder. Their conversation has that strident swagger that typifies a night out with Charlie.

Kite appears to be listening intently to what the arty woman is saying. Koop has heard he's an art lover. How much Kite understands about it is another matter; Koop figures he may have adopted 'art' as a way of lifting himself above what he truly is. From the adoring looks and barking laughs he's getting, the guise is working.

Without realising it, Koop drifts closer to the group and, as Kite turns his face from the conversation, his eyes catch Koop's. Kite is momentarily blank-faced before he raises his glass in Koop's direction. He turns away to the man drinking water and says something in his ear. Both of them look at Koop.

Koop realises he's grinding his teeth.

He forces himself to relax and finds a waiter, taking another glass from the tray. Even as he takes a mouthful of the wine he registers that it isn't the smartest of moves. He replaces the wine, swaps it for water and turns to inspect a large-scale piece consisting of polished silver balloons. The work has a dizzying quality that makes Koop's head swim, although whether that is the work itself, the wine, or the strain of not putting Keith Kite through the gallery window, he doesn't know.

'Fuckin' exquisite, eh?'

Koop turns.

Kite stands at his shoulder, smaller than Koop, and points at a painting to Koop's left. 'Clever little bastard. You know if you look at 'em from a distance they're all fucking?'

Koop glances back at the group at the bar. Only the man drinking water is looking in their direction.

'What do you want, Kite?'

Kite smiles. 'Me?' He tilts his glass towards Koop. 'Shouldn't the question be the other way round? I thought you'd left town, *Cunt*stable Koopman. For a land down under, where women summat and men . . . oh, I forget the fucking song. Load of shite, anyway. What brings you back to our glorious European City of Culture? Art? Or are you visiting that psycho brother of yours?'

'It was DCI Koopman, Kite. And you know exactly why I'm back.'

Kite opens his arms wide in mock outrage. 'Me? You're giving me credit for mind-reading, Mr Koopman. I'm no clairvoyant.'

'If I mention the word "Halewood" to you, would you still be such a smartarse?'

Kite's smile doesn't waver but Koop knows the word has meaning.

'Hit home?'

'You want to be very careful, Mr Koopman. You're just a civilian now, remember?'

'Fuck off, Kite, before I do something I regret.'

'Wouldn't want that now, would we, Mr Koopman? Zoe might have to start shopping for a black dress. How is the lovely Zoe by the way? Keeping well? She always was a lovely looker, your Zoe, although she's probably not getting any younger, is she?'

At the sound of Zoe's name in Kite's mouth, Koop feels something loosen inside him. Something bad.

'Is that a threat, Kite?'

Kite turns back towards the bar, his shark smile fixed. 'Take it any way you like. I don't care, you Dutch cunt. You don't have the bottle to do anything about it, anyway, not now you're not a fuckin' bizzy. Have a nice trip back to Kangaroo Country, won't you?'

Kite pauses. He looks at Koop pityingly. 'And as an art lover, you must make time to go and see the Gormley sculptures down at Crosby. Some people say they're a load of crap, but me, I love 'em.'

He turns back towards the bar and Koop slams into him from behind.

As people in the gallery scream and scatter, Koop flips Kite over and smashes his wine glass into Kite's forehead. The glass splinters and blood spatters onto the polished wooden floor. Koop grips Kite's lapels and headbutts him square in the nose. Kite's nose explodes and he howls. Before Koop can land another blow, he feels hands drag him away and a boot slam into his ribs. All the breath leaves him and he curls up against the gallery wall as three of Kite's men go to work. He manages to glance up and see one of the men reach inside his suit coat. Kite, on his feet, blood pouring from his head and nose, puts a hand on the man's arm.

'Stop,' Kite says and the kicking ceases immediately. Kite staggers forward and puts his mouth close to Koop's face. Kite's blood drips onto Koop. 'Thanks for that, you stupid cunt,' says Kite. 'It tidies up a few things at this end.' He pats Koop's cheek with a bloody hand. 'One of my associates will be visiting your fair island soon. I'll make good and sure he looks up Zoe for me.'

Koop tries to answer but all that comes out is a muted groan. Kite smiles and whispers in his ear. 'It'll make what we did to your boy seem like a warm-up.'

And then, as the ceiling of the gallery flashes blue, Koop passes out.

40

'What were you *thinking*?'

Keane paces the interview room, Harris sitting across the desk from Koop, her arms folded, her expression unreadable.

'I mean, from some wet-behind-the-ears civilian, I can believe, Koop, but from someone with your background . . .'

Koop rubs his back. The medics at Broadgreen have patched him up and he hasn't suffered any major damage, but he still feels like he's been ten rounds with a grizzly. He's been in hospital overnight. Keane woke him and brought him straight to Stanley Road and is working hard now to keep his temper in check.

'You didn't call Zoe, did you?' says Koop. 'Because I'd prefer her not to be worrying.'

'Never mind Zoe!' Keane shakes his head. 'No, we didn't. We had other shit to concern ourselves about, like why my ex-boss attacked a local businessman in front of the great and good of Liverpool. Including DCI Eric Perch.'

'Perch was there? I didn't see him,' says Koop. 'That's not good.'

'No shit? Come on, Koop, you know better than this.'

'I can't say anything. Nothing you want to hear anyway, Frank. If you're expecting me to say I'm sorry, then you'll be waiting a long time. I'm only sorry I didn't kill him.'

'You're lucky you didn't. Do you know that Perch is pushing for you to be charged with attempted murder?'

Harris looks up. 'You know that's not going to work, Frank,' she says wearily. 'It's assault. Grievous, maybe.'

'That's not the point! In Perch's eyes, we didn't control you and that means my life is going to be made much, much harder. Christ knows where this leaves Kite in the investigation.'

'He did it, Frank,' says Koop quietly. 'The fucker told me.'

There's a short silence.

'And you'd testify to that?'

'Of course, but what difference would it make? My evidence is tainted anyway. Son of the victim. I attacked Kite. It wouldn't make it to court on that.'

'He's right, Frank,' says Harris.

Keane acknowledges the statement with a frown and a grudging nod.

'Kite won't press charges,' says Harris. 'There is that. And the gallery has waived any charges too after I'd explained your . . . position. Your loss. They want payment for cleaning, though.'

'Perch may not be so understanding,' says Keane. 'Jackson was at the opening. His boss,' he adds by way of explanation. 'Perch thinks it looks bad.'

'Which it does,' says Harris.

Keane raises his hands. 'Which it fucking does – correct, Em.'

He paces around the table.

'Here's what's going to happen,' he says. He sits behind the desk. 'No charges have been filed as of now. Which doesn't mean that there won't be some coming your way soon. Apart from Perch, OCS is actively agitating for a piece of you for stirring up Kite's little nest. But they haven't put anything down officially. Which means you can, technically, leave the country.'

'Frank,' says Harris, a warning note in her voice.

'It's alright, Em,' says Keane. 'This way everyone will be happy, believe me. Or as happy as they're going to be. The Terminator here has had a pop at Kite – nice going too, by the way – so he's kept his honour intact; Perch will be glad an ex-member of his department is safely twelve thousand miles away; OCS, once they settle down, will be happy that no-one is ruffling Kite's feathers again; and lastly, we'll be glad because we can get back on track with the Stevie White case.'

'Did you chase the car thing?' says Koop. 'Halewood?'

Keane runs his fingers through his hair. Like him, it feels old and tired. 'There may be something; we're still checking a shipment of Jags that went out to Brisbane via Hamburg. I didn't call because there's nothing solid. Without the cars themselves, the lead means nothing. Does that make you feel happy?'

'Not really.'

'Good, because I'm not really interested in making you happy any more. I went out further than I should have already giving you the file.'

'You gave him the *file*?' Harris sits upright. 'You didn't tell me that.'

'Because you'd have stopped me.'

'Damn right I'd have stopped you, Frank! Christ, if

Perch gets hold of that information, we're dead whatever happens.'

'He's not going to find out. Is he, Koop?'

Koop shakes his head. 'Not from me.'

'I can't believe you did that,' says Harris, shooting a black look at Keane.

'I thought it was safe. It was . . . I owed Koop one, Em.'

Keane stands.

'So it's "Get out of town by sundown", is it, Frank?' says Koop.

'It's not quite sundown, Koop. I took the liberty of changing your return ticket. Not something I should be doing, but I'm sure you don't mind, do you? You fly out of Manchester on the 6.30 pm. You'll be back in Oz inside thirty hours.'

Koop gets to his feet too. Keane is right. He had no business here. Everything has changed and Stevie, son or no son, was involved with some nasty people. It's been a mistake coming back to Liverpool. He shakes hands with the two cops.

'You'll keep me posted?' says Koop. He thinks about mentioning Carl being out of Bowden on release but decides against it. It's Frank Keane's sloppy work that he doesn't have that information already and there's enough of the old dog in Koop to get some satisfaction from that.

Keane nods.

'Koop? One more thing.'

Koop halts. 'Yes?'

'No offence, but don't come back.'

Koop steps into the corridor and closes the door behind him.

41

The cars are still at the lock-up. Stefan hasn't moved them on, thank Christ.

The last thing Tony Link needs right now is having to off someone with the rep of Jimmy Gelagotis without expert help. Link has enough awareness of his own limitations to know that killing Jimmy unaided would be several steps above his pay grade.

'See?' Tony Link's tone is suitably aggrieved. He gestures at the gleaming Jaguar sitting to one side of the unit, half-hidden under a soft cotton tarp. It needles him that Jimmy felt the need to pull back the tarp to check it was the Jag. The three cars are side by side in a storage unit rented by the elderly uncle of one of Stefan Meeks's boys. The uncle has no idea he is the signatory on a triple-size lock-up in Beenleigh.

Stefan is too sharp to have any sort of paper trail directly connecting him to the unit. He doesn't like being around the cars any longer than is strictly necessary, and he is damn sure he doesn't like being there in the company of Jimmy Gelagotis. There's always the chance since the Kolomiets murder that Jimmy is being tailed, and Stefan doesn't want any part of that.

Of course, there's no way he or Tony can display so much as a hint that that's how they feel. The code demands a cool detachment and apparent indifference to the possibility of police involvement. Stefan follows Tony's lead.

'The stuff's in the boot.' He walks to the rear and, taking care to use the edge of the tarp to flick the lid, opens the boot. He reaches in and lifts up the carpeted flap hiding the spare.

In the space usually occupied by the wheel is a rectangular stack of tightly packed white bricks each encased in heavy shrink-wrapped plastic. Stefan moves to the side of the car and, again using the tarp, opens the rear door. He lifts the floor mats to reveal two other blocks of plastic-wrapped cocaine lying flush against the car's chassis. He glances at Jimmy who nods before Stefan lets the carpet fall back into place. Meeks closes the rear door and replaces the tarp.

Jimmy Gelagotis feels a weight lift from his shoulders at the sight of the coke. It's going to be fine.

'Good,' says Jimmy. He pats Tony and Stefan on their shoulders in turn. 'Good, good, good.' He turns and moves towards the door. 'Let's get the stuff shifting. I don't want to wait. I don't care if it does draw some attention. I want this sold and turned into easy cash.'

Tony Link and Stefan Meeks exchange a glance. Link shakes his head a fraction. Keep it to yourself, the gesture says. At least until later.

'If you say so, Jimmy,' he says. 'But you did say you wanted this to lie doggo. Let any heat fade away. Three months.'

'I do say so,' says Jimmy Gelagotis. The image of Stevie White screaming on that motherfucking video clip springs, unbidden, to his mind. 'I really do say so. There's trouble heading our way and I want to be able to meet it with full force. We might need more troops and that's going to take more money.'

Tony nods. Inside he's thinking: troops? That's Gelagotis's problem in a fucking nutshell. He thinks he's in one of those dumb mafia TV shows. Tony wants to say to him, you're Greek, not Sicilian. Tony Link smiles as the three step outside into the bright glare of the afternoon sun and Stefan slides the door shut, locking it carefully. Jimmy is right about one thing. There is trouble coming right enough. Bad trouble.

It's coming for him.

42

From the car park of a Red Rooster situated amid a tangle of fast-food outlets and exhaust-repair centres on a rise above the lock-up, Warren Eckhardt snaps off a round of photos. He's more than eighty metres away shooting from inside the air-conditioned comfort of his Commodore. Gelagotis, Link and Meeks have no idea he's there. Eckhardt continues snapping as Link and Gelagotis get into the Greek's car and drive off, Meeks following soon after.

Eckhardt tailed Gelagotis from the Q1 apartment and so far it has proven to be a bonanza decision. *If* he knew what was in the lock-up.

Eckhardt lights a cigarette and considers the options as he tails Gelagotis. Meeks peels off onto Beenleigh Road while Jimmy and Tony Link head south down the Pacific Highway. Eckhardt sticks with Gelagotis on the basis of him being the biggest shark.

That the men have something hidden in the lock-up is hardly worth commenting upon: it's obvious to a one-eyed imbecile. The key question is what to do about it.

Eckhardt calls his office and speaks to Cootes, his superior. He fills him in on the story so far and suggests a watch be kept on the lock-up. As he expected, the suggestion goes down like a bacon sanger at a bar mitzvah. Resource allocation doesn't stretch to backing the hunches of soon-to-be-extinct dinosaurs like Warren Eckhardt. Where's the evidence? Three criminals visiting a lock-up around the Goldie? Get real.

'You know and I know there's something inside there, Warren,' says Cootes. 'But we have nothing to go on. You talked to Gelagotis. You tailed him to a location. They're private citizens. We have no probable cause.'

'They're convicted drug importers. How about that?'

Cootes sighs. Eckhardt swings the Commodore behind a panel truck, masking himself from any potential spotting by Gelagotis, six or seven cars in front in the middle lane.

'Warren, you know that's not going to work. Stick with the Kolomiets thing. I have a whole team doing the work on that. You're part of that team. I'd like you back here from time to time.'

'They're going to move it. I can feel it, Phil.'

'It's Chief Inspector Cootes, Warren. You get a lot of slack from me, given the situation. But that doesn't mean you go rogue. Do the police work. Work it out until you finish. And don't call me Phil.'

'OK, Phil,' says Eckhardt. 'Sorry, Chief Inspector.' He presses the 'end' key and picks up his cigarette from the tray.

They're going to move it. He knows it as sure as he knows his right nut is bigger than his left.

Up ahead the sign comes up for Surfers and Gelagotis takes it. A hundred metres back, and cloaked in the heavy traffic, Eckhardt slides smoothly down the off ramp and heads east.

43

Feeling battered, both physically and mentally, Koop takes a cab back to his hotel. Despite wanting to slump miserably in the back seat, he rides up front as is the custom with Liverpool cabs. To sit in the back could be seen as giving yourself airs. Thankfully, and unusually, the cabbie isn't the chatty sort. After his opening gambit on the likelihood of a management change at Anfield after the latest tragic loss to the Mancs (Ferguson had won his bet with Keane) has elicited a monosyllabic grunt, the cabbie turns up the radio for the short ride down to the Pier Head. Koop stares out of the window and watches the streets of his home town drift past. It's a city in flux, being pulled in contradictory directions.

He won't be coming back any time soon.

The cab pulls up outside the hotel. He pays the guy, overtipping him, and gets into the lift. It feels like forever since he left the place yesterday morning. As the lift rises, Frank feels nauseous and dizzy.

He checks his watch. Eleven am UK, 10 pm in the Northern Rivers. He'll call Zoe when he gets to the room, tell her he's coming back. With luck, she'll have simmered down by now and if she hasn't, then, frankly, Koop is past caring. Zoe's wrath is no more than he deserves. Still, it'd be nice if she was in a forgiving mood. He needs something to look forward to.

The lift doors ping and Koop steps out into the hushed hallway. He slides the key card from his pocket and inserts it into the hotel door. The room is of the kind that requires the key card placed in a wall socket to access power. Koop slots it home and presses the light switch. As well as the light, the radio comes on, blaring out some anodyne generic R&B.

Koop walks the few paces into the bedroom and stops.

Keith Kite's corpse is tied to the hotel bed, naked save for a pair of soiled Calvin Kleins. A sock has been stuffed into his mouth and fixed in place with duct tape. Koop can see the woollen edges of the sock poking out below his nose. Kite's eyes are open, staring wildly at the ceiling through a dry mask of blood.

His throat has been cut and he has been badly beaten.

Koop realises he isn't breathing. He leans back against the hotel wall and tries to recover some sort of equilibrium. The atmosphere in the room is thick and Koop turns the air-conditioning to full.

He looks down at the floor. There are a number of blood marks on the tasteful ochre carpet. Taking care not to step on any, Koop draws closer to the bed. Kite's blood has soaked into the mattress. His aching muscles protesting, Koop squats awkwardly close to the floor and peers underneath the bed. The base looks relatively dry and there's no sign of a weapon. As he rises, Koop almost topples forward onto Kite. He puts out a hand to the wall and steadies himself, his breathing heavy.

Behind him, the curtains to the room are open. To one

side of the window is an office block. Koop can see a few shadowy figures moving around in those rooms that have lights on. He draws the curtains and sits down on a hard chair at the tiny desk to think.

After a few minutes have passed, Koop takes out his mobile and looks at it. The obvious thing is to call Keane. His finger hovers above the keys and then he closes his phone and replaces it in his pocket. He thinks about how this will play with Keane.

His thoughts aren't flowing easily and his head is pounding but those conclusions he does manage to reach aren't good.

Strike one: he fights with Kite and Kite turns up dead.

Strike two: Keane knows Koop's suspicions about Kite's involvement in the killing of Stevie.

Strike three – and this one makes Koop blink: his meeting with Carl now assumes a conspiratorial air.

Christ! Don't tell me Carl did this? Koop squeezes his forehead. Could he have? Some sort of twisted family thing? Blood is blood, said Carl. There are buckets of the stuff here. Koop tries hard to think clearly but can't. Instead, Koop does what he knows best: he acts.

He moves to the door and looks out through the security peephole. The fisheye view of the area in front of the door reveals nothing except an expanse of bland carpeting and wall. Koop opens the door a crack and peeks out. Seeing no-one, and taking care not to emerge into the catchment area of any CCTV cameras, he hangs the 'Do Not Disturb' sign on the outer handle and closes the door. He snips the security lock and goes back inside.

Koop slides open the door of the built-in wardrobe. His small suitcase is where he left it, seemingly untouched. He places it on the desk, making sure there's no blood on the surface. He opens the lid and checks the contents. He didn't unpack much on arrival, and the clothes he hung in the wardrobe he now places inside the suitcase. Koop next moves to the bathroom and, after washing his face, packs his toiletries into his carry case and puts that inside his suitcase. He fastens the case and sets it carefully by the door.

Returning to the desk, Koop calls down to reception on his mobile. He could use the hotel room phone but that would place him inside the room at that particular time. Besides, the phone is liberally spattered with Kite's blood. Koop connects to reception and tells them he'd like to stay another two nights. He directs the girl to use the credit card they swiped on arrival. He hangs up and uses the hotel directory to put him in touch with the airlines. After three unsuccessful attempts to find an economy or business flight, he books himself a first-class ticket on an Emirates flight leaving Manchester at three. It isn't much of a start but the measures might confuse them long enough to make sure he arrives in Australia unmolested.

Koop looks at his watch. Twelve, almost. He checks the room one last time. He switches off the radio and the sudden silence seems to increase the tension. Thinking about it for a moment, Koop turns the radio back on and lowers the volume enough that it won't cause complaints in the night, but loud enough for an insistent housemaid to hear should she be at the door. Again, it could buy him an hour or two.

Finally, Koop opens his phone and methodically deletes all messages, photos, notes and web history. There's nothing incriminating on there but it will make things simpler if it ends up in the hands of an investigation team.

At the door he takes pains to make sure he is unobserved

and unobtrusive. He jams a cap down low on his head, turns his collar up and exits the hotel via the emergency stairs. He walks swiftly up towards the Town Hall and hails a cab. One hour later he's at Manchester Airport and has checked in for the flight.

What the fuck is going on?

44

Kite's body is discovered by a cleaner less than an hour after Koop leaves and brings the OCS in like a plague. While Stevie White's murder may have been an 'open' case, Kite is one of theirs, no question.

Perch, rolling over like a tame pup, cedes authority to the OCS head in an instant. It's only the ongoing involvement in the Stevie White case that keeps Keane and the MIT in the loop at all.

And just so there's no doubt about who is now in charge, the OCS investigative team keeps Keane and Harris outside the hotel room while they conduct their own operation. They're told to wait as the crime scene is too small for both teams to have simultaneous access, but Keane knows it for what it is: a straightforward slap in the face; punishment for one of theirs going rogue. He paces the corridor outside while OCS officers come and go.

Harris is keeping communication with Keane to a minimum. The Kite case is fast becoming a potential career disaster and she is canny enough to know that while loyalty to Frank Keane is expected, undue or excessive loyalty would be seen as plain stupid. She notes with pain one or two OCS boys openly smiling as they pass them in the corridor.

Eventually they're waved in by DI Moresby, one of the OCS senior detectives assigned to the case, a taciturn Welshman who doesn't mince his words. His partner, Dave Reader, is talking to a SOCO in the corridor.

'All yours. Try not to screw my scene around too much, and don't take too long about it. I'm getting pressure to let the hotel get back to normal quick. They want that thing in there out this afternoon. I don't see any reason not to let that happen.' He pauses and moves a little closer to Keane. 'And I'll need what you have on Kite's earlier involvement on my desk this afternoon. Plus, if you have any inside gen on your pal Koopman, we want to know, right?'

Keane doesn't answer. He pushes past Moresby and opens the door to the hotel room.

'Didn't you hear me, Keane? I said . . .'

'He heard you,' says Harris. 'Give him a break, eh?'

Moresby shakes his head a fraction. 'My desk. This afternoon.'

Harris regards him coolly. 'We'll do our best, DI Moresby.'

'And Koopman?'

'That too,' she nods. 'If we know anything.'

She turns and follows Keane inside, leaving Moresby looking at her.

The room is coated in print dust and the detritus of the SOC unit. Keane is standing at the end of the bed staring down at Kite's spread-eagled form. Harris closes the hotel bedroom door and stands to one side of the bed.

'Not good, Frank,' she says. 'I wouldn't have thought Koopman capable of something like this.'

249

Keane doesn't say anything.

'Frank?'

'He's not,' says Keane, eventually. 'It's just not something he'd do.'

'But he's done it, Frank. Look.'

Keane shakes his head.

'No, not Koop, Em.'

Harris opens her phone and clicks onto her notes application.

'He must have been back here because his belongings are gone. He booked himself in for a couple of extra days and hung the "Do Not Disturb" sign on the door. Frank, Koopman gave himself as long as possible to get a head start. It doesn't look good.'

Keane wanders across to the desk and idly opens the drawer.

'I know,' he says. 'But at the risk of sounding like one of those TV detectives, don't you think it all seems a bit too convenient?'

'When things look straightforward they usually are.'

'Mostly. But not this time. Koop arrives here, argues with Kite in front of everyone and the next time Kite is seen he's dead in Koop's room? I don't buy it, Em, not even for a minute.'

'You said he and Kite had history. And then Kite turns out to have been the scum who tortured and murdered his only son. I'd say that was motive, Frank. Enough for anyone. Christ, he glassed the fucker at The Granary in front of a hundred witnesses two days ago. Had to be pulled off by Kite's bodyguards.'

'And given a right going-over.'

'Exactly,' says Harris. She moves towards Keane and touches his arm. 'I know he's a friend, Frank. I know he goes back a long way, but this just isn't going to have a happy outcome for Koopman.'

'Listen, Em. There are a couple of things that don't add up: Koop was in Broadgreen overnight and when he was discharged I brought him in.'

'So he says,' says Harris. 'He could have left the ward easily.'

'What, and organised this?' Keane waves his hand over the abomination on the hotel bed. 'You think it would have been easy to get Keith Kite trussed up like that? Whoever did this has done this shit before, Em. You're not saying Menno Koopman is a serial killer now, are you?'

'Of course not,' says Harris. 'But Moresby and Reader have Koopman in the frame for this one. And I think they're going to get him. You have to choose which side of the fence you're going to be on when this all gets to an arrest.'

'Is that what this is about, Em? Worried about your career? Well, you can leave the shitty end of things in my hands, if you like. I'm not leaving Koop out to dry. He deserves better than that.'

'What about me, Frank? What do I deserve?'

'I don't know, Em. You tell me. What do you deserve?'

Keane walks towards the door just as the men from the Coroner's Office arrive.

'Where are you going?' says Harris as the room fills up. She pushes past them and follows Keane into the corridor. 'Frank!'

'What?' he says as he reaches the lift.

'What are you going to do?'

'Do what we should have done at the start of all this.'

'Which is?'

'Follow the money.'

The lift arrives and Keane gets in. He holds the door open.

'Well?' he says as Harris hesitates.

She shrugs and follows him inside. Keane presses the down button.

'What money?'

Keane begins to talk.

45

Declan North arrives in Sydney, fresh and rested after a flight which lands at 6.35 am. As a first-class passenger, and travelling on his own perfectly legitimate UK passport, North moves through Immigration and Customs without incident. Without so much as a parking ticket on his record, and with several kosher business interests to support any story he might have to tell, he doesn't expect any trouble.

'Welcome to Australia, Mr North.' The border-control officer smiles and stamps his passport. No-one at Sydney has any problems with the Irish businessman coming to town. North wears a modern-cut lightweight grey suit and carries an expensive leather briefcase. He has only one small, equally expensive suitcase, which is priority checked through for him. By 8 am he's on a VirginBlue domestic shuttle flight to the Gold Coast, paying cash and using a false ID. It never hurts to muddy the waters a little on the off-chance someone in Australia is interested. Before boarding he takes out his mobile and makes a call.

On the flight north he sits next to a middle-aged woman who, on hearing his accent and working on the almost universal assumption that all Irishmen are charming, tries to engage him in conversation. He politely avoids doing so while fondly imagining working on her with his blade. The fat bitch would cut up nicely. After a few minutes during which North makes simple, non-committal answers to her chattering, she winds down like a mechanical toy and he completes the rest of the journey in welcome silence. She'll have to find another sort of Irishman, some chirpy Plastic Paddy, to get her fix of blarney if that's what she's after. North's left all that bollix behind in Belfast ten years ago. Next to her, he inches away from the touch of her elbow and passes the time imagining what he would do to her if he didn't have more pressing business at the end of his journey.

It has taken planning to get to this point. Months and months of very careful planning, which was very nearly derailed by the arrival of Menno Koopman. That was a surprise to Kite, a very nasty surprise. Not as surprising as when he woke up tied to Koopman's hotel bed with Declan North standing over him, scalpel in hand, but surprising nonetheless.

North had planned to get rid of Kite in an unremark-able fashion by shooting him and placing his body in a landfill site near Warrington. Instead, on his pathetic amateur detective hunt, Koopman presented North with a wonderful opportunity. Implicating the ex-cop in the murder of Kite would deflect attention from himself and potentially land the interfering fecker in jail. At the very least it would mean months, if not years, of Koopman becoming entangled with the Liverpool Police. Which all leaves North free and clear to step up after ten years of hearing that fucking pain in the hole, Kite. Ten years of listening to him crap on about art, when it was North who'd introduced the ridiculous jumped-up scally twat to . . .

'What?'

The fat woman is looking at him, a fearful expression on her face. North realises he's been angrily muttering to himself, his features twisted into a gargoyle snarl, something he's found himself doing on more than one occasion recently.

'Excuse the blather,' says North. He rearranges his features into something he hopes will be more acceptable to the old wagon next to him than the hellish creature that has temporarily shown her its face. 'I was on a long flight before this one. Must have been having a wee nightmare.'

The fat woman doesn't say anything. As soon as the plane arrives at the gate she springs up and, taking her bag from the overhead locker, gets off the plane as fast as she can, without ever once looking at North again.

North knows the woman has seen him for what he is. Has seen who he is at his core. And, like any sane human, has tried to put as much distance between herself and the glimpsed demon as quickly as possible.

He's seen the same look on the faces of some of those he's killed. Once or twice he's glanced in the mirror and seen it himself; another creature inside the shell of this person called North. Sometimes, in his most unhinged moments, slick with blood in the becalmed hour before dawn, he wonders if that's what has happened; that his body is simply the carrier for something elemental.

Fuck it. The woman doesn't matter. She's seen what he is but what could anyone do with that information except store it up for sleepless nights? Still, he'd have enjoyed making her nightmares come true. North brightens as he remembers Koopman has a wife out here. He smiles as an idea comes to mind. A truly *artistic* idea.

North collects his bag and walks out of the terminal into the golden sunlight. At the kerbside pick-up in front of the outdoor café is a black Range Rover. A man leans against the door, smoking. At the sight of North, he drops the butt and walks across, his hand held out.

'Declan?'

'Mr North,' says North, without a trace of a smile. 'If you don't mind.'

'Er, sure, yeah, right, whatever . . . Mr North.'

'No, man, I'm only fucking with yer. Dec'll be fine.'

North puts out his hand and the man shakes it, relief washing over him. Declan North's reputation has travelled ahead of him.

'Tony Link,' says the man. 'Welcome to the Gold Coast.'

46

Keane and Harris are back at Stanley Road. With Perch's wrath still ringing in their ears and the OCS crawling all over the Stevie White case, MIT is not a happy ship. The White investigation, seemingly so straightforward at the outset, is proving a bastard and there is a tangible sense that it is drifting beyond the control of MIT. It's not as if they don't have a full workload elsewhere. In fact, Caddick and Rose, along with several of the DCs, have been detailed to get stuck into the backlog. But no-one wants the White case to become the sole property of the OCS. Pride is at stake.

There's a side benefit to this, though. Using Caddick to housekeep also means he isn't privy to the innermost details of the remaining investigation. Keane still doesn't trust him, and after Kite's death feels more sure than ever that Caddick is a direct link to Perch's office.

In a bland interview room at Stanley Road which doubles as an ad hoc meeting room, Keane sits around the table with Harris and DC Wills. Scott Corner, slow to finish the phone conversation he was involved in when the meeting was called, is last to arrive and an impatient

Keane stifles the reflex to give him the sole of his shoe. The air is already thick with a sour feeling of failure which Keane is anxious to dissipate, and ripping Corner a new one will do nothing for the team, no matter how much Keane is tempted.

'We've been concentrating on the crime,' he says as Corner slips into a chair. He looks flushed and, to Keane's eyes, not half as sorry as he should be for holding things up. He ignores Corner and continues. 'And Koop arriving hasn't helped that. Now all The Fish wants to do is to nail Koopman for Kite. It's perfect; Perch gets to look aggressive, and one of the city's biggest criminals is off the scene for good.'

'It works for me,' says Harris. Nothing Keane's been saying or doing has stopped her worrying about MIT going out on a limb. The trick, she feels now, is to not be on the tree when – and she thinks it will be *when*, not *if* – the bough breaks.

It's a thin line between loyalty and stupidity and one that for Em Harris is becoming thinner with every passing minute. 'You said yourself that Koopman never let details get in the way of a collar.'

'A collar is one thing, Em. Doing that, even to someone like Kite, is way beyond Menno Koopman.'

Harris purses her lips although she knows Keane is probably right. 'Probably' isn't good enough, though; experience has taught her that what often looks to be the case turns out to be the case.

'We can't let Koopman go.'

'No,' says Keane. 'Of course not. Perch has already been on to Australia and they're handling things if and when he pops up. Not that he will. OCS are at Manchester now. We can't worry too much about Koopman until he's brought in.'

'So what do we worry about, boss?' says Wills. 'We have to worry about something.'

'The money. We worry about the money.'

'What money?' says Harris. She's chewing the end of her pencil.

'There's always money,' says Keane. 'Look, Stevie White came out here for a reason, correct?'

There are nods around the table.

'Which tells us . . .?'

'There's an Australian connection.' Harris sounds a little irritated. 'We know this, Frank.'

'But we haven't looked at it closely enough. Not yet.'

'What do you want us to do, sir?' says Rose. Harris looks at her sourly. She's losing her equal billing with Frank. Both DCs are giving their attention to Keane, the alpha male. It will have to stop.

'I think what DI Keane is trying to say is that we should look more closely at the possible reasons why Steven White came to be here. We need to talk to anyone from Kite's crew –'

'Won't that upset OCS?' says Caddick.

'Fuck OCS,' says Keane. He's talking quickly. Wired. 'We talk to anyone we know with a sniff. We talk to Bourke again. Things are different with Kite off the scene. He's not going to give us much, but without the threat of Kite maybe Sean will spill a little more, who knows?'

'And DCI Perch?' Wills raises his eyebrows.

'We keep DCI Perch fully informed at all times of any information we think may be relevant to the investigation,' says Em Harris crisply. She looks at Keane. 'At all times.'

Keane holds his hands up. 'I wouldn't have it any other way. Now, if there's no more business, I suggest we pull our fucking fingers out and get some traction on this again.'

As everyone shuffles papers and pushes chairs back with a series of rubbery squeaks, Keane notices that Corner hasn't moved.

'Scott?' says Keane.

Scott Corner licks his lips. 'Well . . .' he starts slowly. 'You're not going to like it. I didn't want to say owt in front of the rest of 'em.'

'For fuck's sake, spit it out, man,' Keane snaps. Morale is one thing but Corner's hesitancy is beginning to bug him.

'The phone call I was on before the meeting?' says Corner. 'It was Bowden.'

Keane raises an eyebrow. What the fuck is Bowden?

'The hospital,' says Em Harris. 'The one Koopman's brother is at.'

'That's just the thing,' says Corner, speaking rapidly now. 'I was just tidying up some loose ends in our paper-work and it turns out there's a problem.'

'What sort of problem?' says Keane, a thin finger of apprehension tickling the back of his neck.

'Carl Koopman is the problem, boss,' says Scott Corner. 'Bowden Hospital say he isn't there. He's been out on something called Controlled Supervision since August. We fucked up.'

47

As is his way, Jimmy Gelagotis is worrying about details. One particular detail.

The boy on the soccer field is a loose end.

It was a mistake leaving him alive and Stevie's death has brought it home to Jimmy that he's not invincible. With the Poms turning out to be psychos, the last thing Jimmy needs is pressure from another angle. Which is what he's got.

The boy was mentioned on Channel 7 news last night as Jimmy ate his pasta, the tray on his knee, the whole family there. 'A witness', they said. Helping police with their inquiries. Not good. I should have shot the little fucker.

He picks up his mobile and scrolls to Todd Burns's number. Burns works as a desk sergeant at the Southport police station on Scarborough Street, and has access to most useful information that can be had.

He is also into Jimmy for well over a hundred grand.

A lithe, tan surfer ten years ago, Burns drifted into recreational drugs and gambling in a big way, at the same time as maintaining – just – his regular job on the force.

Now his access to information is the only thing he has left to bargain with. If Todd Burns wasn't Jimmy Gelagotis's pet he'd have been dead years ago.

Of course Jimmy is still careful. His inquiry to Burns is about the Kolomiets case after all. Burns knows nothing substantial about Jimmy's business but he isn't entirely stupid. Pathetic, but not stupid. Jimmy talking about the dead Ukrainian is sure to tip him that Jimmy had a hand in it. Not, reflects Jimmy, that that would mean much. Burns is fully aware he'd be dead if he ever so much as breathed Jimmy Gelagotis's name to anyone investigating the Kolomiets case.

Jimmy decides to risk it.

He presses the button and wakes Burns at home, sleeping before his nightshift later that day. Burns doesn't complain. He tells Jimmy what he needs to know and puts the phone down without ceremony, neither man wanting to be connected for any longer than is strictly necessary.

Jimmy sips his coffee – long black as always. He's now in possession of two important pieces of information. The boy hasn't talked, not yet. They've been trying, Burns said, but there wasn't very much they could do with a witness that young who simply wouldn't talk. After what he's seen, persuasion and time are being used.

'They've got a shrink coming in from Brisbane tomorrow,' Burns told him. 'He's worked with silent witnesses before. Supposed to be good.'

The second piece of information is the boy's name. Burns bargained for that one and Jimmy almost yelled at the bent copper. Instead he forgave the hundred grand in exchange for the name. It didn't matter, not really. After this conversation, Jimmy is sure that the next time he sees Todd Burns he's going to kill him.

After he's taken care of the boy.

Jimmy stares into his coffee. After a minute or two he waves Chris over and tells him to go get a clean car. A throwaway, adds Jimmy. Call me when you've got it.

Some time later, Jimmy's phone buzzes. Chris has the car and is parked three streets away. He knows better than to pull up in front of the café; a good lad. *Expinos*.

Jimmy pockets his own car keys, gathers his phone and, after a word with Nils, the manager of the café, walks outside into the sun. He gets into the car and turns towards Broadbeach.

On the pavement, Chris takes out his phone and dials a number.

48

Koop gets all the way to Manchester before he realises how badly he's screwed this. In the cold flat light of a Manchester morning, running is looking like a big fat mistake; one of the worst decisions he's made. Koop rubs his head, his fingers tracing the bruising. Kite's boys must have done some fucking brain damage judging by his solution to finding the body in his room.

What was I thinking?

Menno Koopman knows more than anyone he's good for Kite's death – more than good, close to perfect – but, as an old pro, he also knows there are plenty of gaps in the case against him. Which is why running was such a dumb move. It won't make picking open those gaps any easier.

There's only one thing to do.

Koop finds a quiet seat in the Emirates lounge, takes out his phone and calls Frank. Once the connection's made Koop explains what's happened in a few short sentences.

'You fucked me over, Koop,' says Frank. Koop can hear the stress in his voice.

'Are you going to get into this now, Frank?'

'Where are you?'

'I'm in the Emirates first class departure lounge.'

'First class?'

'Don't ask. I'll wait for you here. Be less embarrassing than out on the concourse.'

'It won't be me coming, Koop,' says Frank. 'OCS have got this now.'

Koop signs off and slumps back in the armchair.

It's a pity I didn't get onto the plane, he thinks. He'd like to have flown first class at least once.

Less than three minutes after his call to Frank, two uniforms appear inside the lounge. They don't approach Koop but he knows he's the reason they're there. Friends or not, Koop's a suspect in a killing.

Forty minutes later, Dave Reader and Ian Moresby make the pick-up at Manchester Airport personally. Koop goes back a long way with both men and there is an almost apologetic air about their manner when they walk into the lounge, a couple more uniforms behind them. When he sees them, Koop stands and walks towards the detectives and shakes their hands. As Moresby cuffs Koop, he has the good grace to look a little embarrassed.

Which is good. That embarrassment tells Koop that Reader and Moresby know this is a little flaky. Still, flaky or not, they'll be only too happy to be associated with a high-profile case like Kite's, even if it is one of their own they're bringing in. He doesn't blame them. He'd have felt the same way if the roles had been reversed. A collar is a collar.

After some paper-shuffling and arm-wrestling, Reader and Moresby prise Koop from the sticky fingers of the Manchester Airport Police, who've been greedily eyeing a slice of the action, and head for the car park. A uniform opens the door to the car and Moresby uncuffs Koop.

'Don't give me the run-around, Koop,' he says. 'I won't be made a dickhead, got that?'

'There's only one dickhead around here, Ian.' Koop shakes his head. 'And you're looking at him. There'll be no more running. I phoned you, remember?'

'Personally I think whoever killed that gobshite should be given a reward,' says Moresby. 'There's no-one mourning that little scumbag, except a whole lot of nasty little scumbag scrotes just like himself. And I think the Halligan brothers are probably still out celebrating.' Koop doesn't bother protesting he didn't kill Kite. That will come later. Right now he's grateful for Moresby's 'whoever'.

Koop takes his place in the back seat of the Range Rover and Moresby slides in next to him. With a nod from Reader in the front passenger seat, the uniform points the car back west towards Liverpool.

There's silence until they reach the 62. Something Moresby said is reverberating with Koop. The mention of the Halligans, that's what it was. A fruitful line of thought begins to open up and Koop realises he's thinking like a cop again. Whether or not that's a good thing remains to be seen. He knows what Zoe would think about it.

'You know I didn't do it.' Koop makes the statement flatly. He doesn't expect Reader or Moresby to do much in the way of responding. 'This thing won't fly, Chris.'

Reader twists round to face Koop and as he does so his eyes catch Moresby's. Koop feels a flicker of something pass between them.

Interesting.

Dave Reader drapes his arm over the seat and holds his gaze on Koop. 'It's got a halfway decent set of wings right now, to be honest. You know how it is when it's an ex-cop who gets pulled in. Everyone's watching us to do one of two things: roll over and let them go, or come down hard. Prove we're not whitewashing. Right now the OCS is pressing for the second option. But we'll sort it all out back home. Maybe you're right. I hope so.'

Koop replies with a shrug before turning to stare out of the window as the monotonous and depressingly familiar landscape flies past. Reader's mention of 'home' is clicking some cogs.

He checks his watch. Only eleven. He'd be doing his deliveries right now. Back *home*. Except it isn't eleven in the morning in New South Wales, it's ten at night. Koop rubs his eyes. What a glorious, nine hundred per cent, cast-iron fuck-up he's managed to get involved with. How did he ever think coming back to the city would do anything to help Stevie? What was he, the Lone fucking Ranger?

He rests his brow against the cold glass and listens to the hiss of the Range Rover's tyres sending an arc of dirty spray out behind them. Koop had gone a long way to escape this kind of weather, this kind of life, to free himself from ever having to come into contact with pond-life like Kite again.

And yet here he is. Up to the elbows in shit.

Great job, Koopman. Mission accomplished.

'You like it out there?'

Koop blinks. 'What? Sorry?'

Reader shifts round in his seat again. 'Australia, Koop. You like it?'

'Australia?' repeats Koop stupidly. 'Yeah. I do. It's good.' His voice and words sound awkward and he realises how tired he is. He hasn't slept more than half an hour in the last twenty-four and it's beginning to tell.

'Sorry, Chris,' says Koop. 'I'm not at my best. Yeah, we love it out there.'

Reader smiles. 'I don't blame you for leaving this country, Koop. The place is going to the dogs faster than you'd believe possible. There'll be more Poles and Latvians than English before too long the way things are going. But I don't know how you could live with all that heat. It'd do my head in. And I'd miss it all. The footy. Pubs. The beer. Fish and chips. England. *Home*.'

They're passing the blue-and-yellow rain-streaked rectangular block of IKEA. A lengthy queue of cars has already formed at the entrance and Koop glimpses people hurrying loaded trolleys stacked with flat-packed bric-a-brac through the rain towards their Fords and Mazdas and Volvos. Few of them wear suitable clothing, most clad only in thin t-shirts and tracksuits, as if they entered IKEA in Spain on a sunny July day and exited to find themselves in a rainy Warrington in October. Koop remembers his first – and only – visit to the store with Zoe when they were kitting out a spare room. Its relentless corporate zeal and zombie-like customers put him in mind of the seventh ring of hell and he'd sworn never to set foot inside the place – or anything resembling it – ever again. He was mildly depressed to discover an IKEA on the Gold Coast although there, at least, the chubby customers seemed dressed for the weather.

In the Northern Rivers, the summer is just beginning. Koop pictures the late-evening sun slanting through the leaves of his lime and mandarin trees at the back of the house, where the land slopes down towards the western ranges. He thinks about early morning nude swims with Zoe on deserted white-sand beaches, within metres of dolphins surfing in perfect unison through the glassy curl of green-blue waves. He thinks about eagles taking bream from the shallows while he was drinking coffee and shooting the shit with Marius at the café, of hiking the trails around Minyon Falls, of making love with Zoe and Mel in their big bed in the shade of the fig tree as the sun was coming up.

'I know what you mean,' he says, turning away from the window and back to Reader. 'But you can get used to anything.'

'It'd be all the creepy-crawlies I couldn't stand.' This from Ian Moresby, a man who Koop had seen take a loaded shotgun from a drugged-up psychopath in the manner of a man removing a melting ice-cream from the hand of a toddler, and with no more fuss. Moresby shivers theatrically in his seat. 'No, never could stand all those spiders.'

'And sharks!' Reader chimes in. 'You couldn't go in the water now, could you?'

'I saw a program once where they said that almost everything in Australia can kill you,' says the uniform, surprising them all. 'Even the jellyfish. They've got these ones that are only the size of your thumb, but can kill a fully grown horse.'

Reader smiles at Koop and waggles his thumb at the driver. 'It talks. Like a grown-up and everything. Just concentrate on the road, David Attenborough. And when have you ever heard of a jellyfish killing a fucking horse? What's the fucking horse doing in the fucking water in the first place, you knob?'

'Irukandji,' says Koop.

'Iruki-fucking-what?'

'The name of the jellyfish. Irukandji.'

Koop appreciates what they're doing. Safe ground. Avoiding talking about anything related to the case until they're inside an interview room with the tapes rolling.

269

He spends the rest of the trip indulging in a favourite Australian sport: Pom-scaring. Huntsman spiders feature prominently. As do brown snakes, stingers, crocodiles, white pointers, cockroaches the size of Volkswagens, and stick insects that could be mistaken for logs. The cops in the Range Rover lap it up.

At Stanley Road, the atmosphere shifts as soon as they pull into the car park. Moresby slips the cuffs back onto Koop's wrists.

'Wouldn't look right if there's any brass hanging around,' he says to Koop. The car arrives at the back entrance and Reader steps out almost before the wheels have stopped turning. Moresby helps Koop out and the three of them splash through the puddles and go inside. Koop sits on a bench while Reader does the paperwork with the booking officer. Despite the friendliness of the policeman at the desk, Koop feels a chill. For the first time since finding Kite's body he feels truly vulnerable. Sitting here, he's as far from home as it's possible to be. In so many ways.

There's a flurry of movement from outside and the doors to the booking room open. DCI Perch comes in like a politician visiting a far-flung colony, Keane and Harris behind him. Neither looks particularly happy with the way things are panning out. Perch regards Koop with disdain but says nothing. He nods to Reader and Moresby who reply in kind.

'We ready?' Reader gestures towards a door leading to the interview room. Koop gets slowly to his feet and follows the OCS officer, Moresby bringing up the rear.

At the door to the corridor Koop stops and looks at Keane.

'You know this is bullshit, right, Frank?'

Keane holds out his arms in a gesture of impotence. 'It doesn't look great, Koop. You have to see that.'

'That's enough,' snaps Perch. 'This is your fuck-up, DI Keane. Don't make it worse.'

Em Harris sees the colour rise in Keane's neck but he remains silent. As does she.

Keane moves towards the corridor, in the direction Koop has been taken.

'Where are you going, DI Keane?' Perch's voice is ice. He turns to Harris. 'You sit in with the OCS interview, DI Harris. It's their case now, I know, but there's overlap and I want you there as the MIT rep. Keane, you're out. Your relationship with Koopman prejudices you. Not to mention the sloppy work concerning Koopman's brother.'

Harris hesitates and Keane catches her eye. Perch's crack about Carl Koopman slipping through MIT's checklist has hit home. The fact that it was Harris's responsibility as much as Keane's was neither here nor there, and both of them know it. Keane isn't going to bleat about the mistake: he's ready to accept the blame. The question now is which way Emily Harris will jump. Technically, as one of Perch's junior officers, she should do exactly what he wants. The question is: will Harris make any sign of her loyalty to Keane? No matter how small, an indication that she's on Keane's side is there to be made.

'You coming?' says Moresby. He's holding the door to the corridor, feeling uncomfortable. This is typical Perch; making public something that should have been said in private. Moresby looks at Emily Harris and raises his eyebrows. She brushes past Frank Keane without a word, her eyes fixed ahead.

Keane nods to himself as though something has been confirmed. At the corridor Moresby purses his lips, studiously avoiding Keane, and closes the door behind them.

Keane looks at Perch.

'Will you be needing me here today?' he says, the words thick in his mouth. 'Sir?' If Perch so much as smiles I'm going to clock the bastard, he thinks.

The Fish shakes his head, his eyes never looking in Keane's direction.

'You can get on with something else. I'll wait for Harris to update me on Koopman. Both of them.' Perch pushes through into the main office leaving Keane in the foyer. The booking officer raises an eyebrow and Keane kicks a wastebasket into the opposite wall. He holds out a finger to the booking officer.

'Not. A. Fucking. Word.' He takes out his car keys and slams through the street doors back into the city.

49

The boy is back at school. Jimmy Gelagotis knows his name by now – Mitch Barnes – but prefers to still think of him as simply 'the boy'. It will make it easier when the time comes. Jimmy has always had that facility to put his feelings in a neat box and move it to a compartment of his mind to be dealt with later, if at all. His own son is around Mitch Barnes's age and the thought of anyone harming Chris makes Jimmy feel sick to his stomach. But, in business, as in war, sometimes difficult decisions have to be made. And since the business Jimmy Gelagotis is in combines both, he doesn't have a choice.

The boy has to go.

Once it's decided, it's as good as done. Back when Jimmy was in tenth grade and already too familiar with the workings of the justice system, a court-appointed psychiatrist described him as a 'classic sociopath'. Jimmy found out what the phrase meant and wanted to kill the psychiatrist. He tried to, in a sort of ham-fisted adolescent way, by attempting to follow the man home from his clinic. He lost the man soon after and later was glad about the way it turned out. As time passed, Jimmy grew less concerned about killing for perceived slights. It was a much more effective use of his skills to use violence when it proved useful. Besides, the shrink was right on the money, Jimmy decided. He *was* a motherfucking sociopath. So what? Wasn't every successful businessman?

It's nearing seven in the evening by the time Jimmy Gelagotis turns into the road where Mitch Barnes lives. He drives slowly past the house whose number Todd has given him. He doesn't stop, driving instead to the T-junction and making a left. A second left brings him along a road which borders a rising patch of undeveloped scrub. Jimmy pulls the car off the road under a thick tangle of tree branches. The shadow renders Jimmy and the car invisible. He takes out his iPhone and clicks the GPS map application, taps in the boy's address and sets the view to satellite. A clear image of the road comes onscreen and Jimmy zooms out to gain an understanding of the terrain. The scrub to his left rises up to a small ridge before rolling down towards the back of a retail park. On the GPS Jimmy can see the rectangles of trucks nuzzling up against the rear of the shops like suckling pups. A vast car park runs around three sides of the retail complex. That will be useful.

Jimmy slides the car from the shadows back onto the road and turns the corner. With the shops closed for the night, the complex and its car park are empty. Jimmy drives to the furthest point from the main road and stops the car in the shadows of some trees backing onto the scrub. He unclips his seatbelt and reaches inside his jacket for his phone which he places face down on the dash in front of him. From a glass vial in the glovebox Jimmy shakes out a small mound of white powder onto the back of the iPhone. Using the side of a credit card, he smoothly chops the coke into two neat deliberate lines. With a rolled five-dollar note he bends over the powder and snorts the lines one after the other. He throws his head back and sniffs wetly. As the effect kicks in, Jimmy coughs before licking a finger and wiping the remaining coke from the phone. He runs a finger around his gums before replacing the phone in his jacket pocket.

Let's get this fucking party started.

Jimmy Gelagotis checks the area but it's deserted. He steps from the car and closes the door quietly behind him. It's a blustery evening and Jimmy walks a few paces along the nature strip at the edge of the car park before spotting a small gap in the waving brush. He pushes through and stands in almost complete darkness. Jimmy waits for fully five minutes as his eyes adjust, the trees roaring above his head. Eventually he finds he can see well enough to navigate his way towards the top of the small rise. At first his progress is slow as he trips over stray branches or stumbles on loose gravel. Once or twice he jerks as spider webs are blown against his face and Jimmy furiously thrashes his head, images of spiders landing in his hair. Gradually, though, as his vision improves, he grows more confident and within ten minutes of leaving the car finds himself looking at the back of Mitch Barnes's house. A security light comes on and off again at intervals, triggered by the movement of branches in the wind. A bonus; no-one will respond to the security light coming on if it's been doing the same all night.

Jimmy settles back against the base of a tree to wait. Most people in his line of business, he'd observed, tended to rush straight into things and the temptation to do what he's come here to do and leave, quickly, is almost overpowering. But he stays, checking his watch at ever-increasing intervals. The wind picks up in intensity making his task much easier. No-one will be out on the hillside on a night like this and the wind renders any sound he might make inaudible.

After almost an hour, Jimmy hits the jackpot. A light comes on in a downstairs room only partly concealed by badly drawn blinds, and a boy walks in, illuminated as clearly as if onstage. He wears a pair of shorts and a baggy t-shirt. He gets into bed and lies down, a surf magazine in his hand.

Jimmy straightens. It looks very like the boy on the soccer field but he isn't completely sure. Jimmy moves closer to the edge of the back fence and, careful to leave his face in shadow, examines the boy more closely. He tries to recall the night of the shooting and there it is in front of him. The blood spraying up and out of Kolomiets as the bullets hit, the drops spattering the face of a white-skinned, dark-haired boy with wide eyes.

It's him.

A middle-aged woman, clearly the boy's mother, comes into the room and perches awkwardly on the edge of the bed. She ruffles his hair, and sits with him for a short time until, after a few words, she leaves. The boy flicks the magazine half-heartedly before turning off the bedside lamp, the room still illuminated by a bar of light coming in through the partially open bedroom door.

Fifteen minutes later Jimmy checks his gun and climbs the fence in one easy movement. The yard is in darkness but, as he comes within range, the security lamps flood him in harsh white light. As he expects, no-one in the house notices. They might investigate if the light stays on for a long time but Jimmy won't be here long. What he's here for will only take a few seconds.

Jimmy comes to within four paces of the sleeping boy

and levels the barrel of the Sig Sauer at his head. At that precise moment, Mitch Barnes opens his eyes and looks directly at Jimmy Gelagotis standing in much the same pose as the last time he saw him.

Jimmy's finger, tight against the trigger, freezes momentarily. He stares at Mitch Barnes who seems unable or unwilling to move. Jimmy steels himself and takes careful aim.

A sharp crack cuts through the thrashing of the wind. The front of Jimmy Gelagotis's head disappears and a crimson arc splashes against the bedroom window. Through the glass Mitch Barnes looks at Gelagotis lying in the garden, a low decorative wall keeping his body cantilevered awkwardly. His left leg jerks spastically and then Gelagotis remains completely still, his blood beginning to run in lines down the glass.

Thirty metres away, invisible in the crook of a fig tree, Declan North places his rifle inside its leather carrying case and drops lightly to the ground. He sets off back up the rise, as behind him Mitch Barnes finally begins to scream. North moves purposefully.

There are things to do.

50

Before the interview Koop calls Zoe. It isn't something he's been looking forward to. Moresby takes him into a small office, places a phone in front of him and leaves. Koop has no doubt he'll be listening in on an extension.

'Koop?' Zoe's voice, half-asleep, sounds older. 'What is it? Are you alright?'

'I'm fine, there's nothing to worry about,' he says hurriedly, conscious of how stupid a statement that will turn out to be once Zoe hears what he has to say. Koop is sure there are women somewhere who would react calmly to being woken with the news that their husband is being held on suspicion of the murder of an international drug dealer, but Zoe, he strongly suspects, won't be one of them.

'Give me a minute,' she says. He hears her put her hand over the speaker and talk to someone in a muffled tone. Mel must be staying. When Zoe comes back on to the line she sounds alert.

'I'm in the kitchen,' she says. 'What's up?'

Koop tells her. Her reaction isn't any better than he imagined it would be.

'You stupid, stupid, *stupid* bastard!'

There's a whole lot more like this during which Koop realises Mel must have come into the kitchen. He can hear Zoe repeating his words to her in tones of incredulity.

'I'm coming over,' Zoe says in a firm tone.

'Don't be ridiculous.' Koop winces at the blast down the phone. It's the wrong thing to say and it takes another minute or two to calm her down.

'This won't stick,' he says, his voice sounding like his old policeman self. As he says it, his spirits rise with the realisation that it's true. Modern policing stuffs up from time to time but not on things like this, not any more. Forensics will show no traces of Kite on him. The path report would demonstrate a time problem. There will be physical evidence – or lack of – which will take him out of the loop. For all he knows the CCTV at the hospital alone will be enough to get him off the hook. Motive would only carry the case so far before it ran out of steam.

Zoe isn't convinced. At one point she swears at him and Mel picks up the phone. In the background he can hear banging and crashing noises.

'She's really mad, Koop. She's broken a couple of things.'

'I got that, Mel. Listen, don't let her do anything silly like coming out here. There's really no need. It's all a bit of a misunderstanding. I'll be coming back as soon as all this gets sorted.'

Moresby pokes his head around the door and points at his watch. Koop nods.

'You know what she's like, Koop,' says Mel. 'And it does sound bad from this perspective.'

'It sounds worse than it is.'

'Well, I'll do what I can. That's all I can say. Do you have somewhere we can reach you?'

Koop gives her the Stanley Road number.

'What about a lawyer?' says Mel.

'We're not at that stage yet,' replies Koop, although he's far from sure that's the case. 'If I do, there are a couple of good ones I know from way back.'

'She got the GOMA gig,' says Mel.

Shit, thinks Koop. I never asked.

There's a short silence. Moresby comes into the room and stands at the door. Koop holds up an apologetic hand.

'I've got to go. Look after her, Mel.'

'I'll try, pervert. Bye.'

'Bye, slut.' Koop hangs up and Moresby raises a quizzical brow.

'Slut?'

'Long story.'

Without offering any further explanation, Koop follows Moresby back down the corridor and into Interview Room 3. His conversation with Zoe has been unsettling from a personal point of view but Koop feels strangely invincible as he takes his seat. Reader and Moresby sit across the table from him, with Em Harris at the end. Koop glances at her as he sits.

'Gone over to the dark side?'

Harris looks at him coldly but Koop sees the colour rise at the base of her throat.

'Perch must be making it worthwhile,' he says. 'Frank's a good copper. I hope you know what you're doing.'

'Can we start?' says Harris, looking at Koop, but talking to Ian Moresby.

'Good idea, love,' says Moresby. He flicks an eye towards Koop who registers the none-too-subtle put-down. Harris doesn't react. Reader presses the start button on the data recorder and gives the details of those present in a quick monotone.

'Did you kill Keith Kite?' says Reader.

'Straight into it?' says Koop. 'OK, that's fine. No, I did not kill Keith Kite.'

'He was found in your room.'

'Is that a question?' says Koop.

'Perhaps you'd like to comment?' offers Moresby.

'Yes, he was found in my room. That would be the first thing that's wrong with this. Come on, Ian. Think about it. If I'd killed Kite, would I have left him there like that?'

Moresby sucks on his lower lip.

'Left him like what?' says Harris. 'You admit to seeing him?'

Dave Reader flicks her an irritated look which Harris ignores.

'Yes, I admit I saw him. And I should have called you right away. Should have, but didn't. A mistake, I admit. But I was disoriented. Tired. I'd been in Broadgreen all night.'

'Because of the beating you took after attacking Kite at The Granary?' Reader checks his file. 'Says here you glassed him, Koop. Is that how you normally greet people in Australia?'

Koop holds up his hands. 'No. Yes. Wait. Yes, I did hit him with the glass and it was a stupid thing to do.'

'Very,' says Harris.

Koop turns in his chair to look at her directly.

'You saw my son, didn't you, DI Harris? Down at the beach, I mean? It *was* your name on the sheet as the attending officer, wasn't it? You were at the autopsy too. If that had been your boy out there, how would *you* have greeted the man responsible? A frosty glare? Give me a fucking break.'

'So you wanted to hurt him?' Dave Reader's voice is soft. 'It's understandable, Koop. We'd all have felt the same way.'

'Yes, I did. I did want to hurt him and I'm glad I did hurt him. My only regret is that I wasn't the one who killed him.'

'Were you observed at Broadgreen? On the ward, I mean?' Ian Moresby is looking at his file. 'You were admitted at 11.54 pm and discharged at 8.30 the following morning.'

'You mean I sneaked out of the ward, tracked Kite down, took him off his goons and persuaded him to come back to my hotel room where he let me tie him up and butcher him? That's your theory?'

Moresby looks at Reader and there's a short silence before Moresby speaks again.

'It might not have been you who did the persuading.'

'Not me? What do you mean?'

'You have friends in Liverpool, don't you, Koop?'

'Friends?'

Moresby leans forward and crosses his arms on the table. His voice is quiet, conspiratorial. 'Alan Hunter. There's a name that can get things done in this town.'

'Hunter?' Koop rubs the bridge of his nose. He's asking the question to buy some time as much as anything else. The mention of Hunter means one thing. They aren't going to give this up without a fight. 'I know Hunter, yes.'

'You found his daughter's attacker, Koop. Good police work as I remember. Very good. Hunter must have felt like he owed you.'

Koop is impressed. They've made the connection

between him and Hunter. And then he remembers Reader and Moresby are OCS. Post 9-11 it has become acceptable, routine almost, for drug investigations to use wire-taps and bugs. Hunter may have been under investigation when he spoke to Koop. He makes a mental adjustment not to underestimate Reader and Moresby again.

'You think Hunter delivered Kite to my room like a plate of steak and chips? Hunter might have owed me something, perhaps, but not that.'

'He gave you Kite's name.' It's a statement from Dave Reader. 'Or as good as.'

So there was a wire. Or a tail. Koop flashes back and the image of the thin waiter at the golf club comes into mind. It doesn't matter; they have the information.

Koop shrugs. 'He might have given me a start. That's all. He never mentioned Kite by name. And Hunter won't sit still for something like this, Dave. He'll have you in court just as fast as Zentfeld can get here.'

Arthur Zentfeld is a colourful and high-priced lawyer with a rottweiler reputation as a career-wrecker. Quick to litigate on his client's behalf, he has a long record of painful victories against Merseyside Police. He is Alan Hunter's pet lawyer.

Chris Reader winces at the mention of his name.

'Speaking of lawyers,' says Moresby, 'this might be a good time to reiterate that you have declined one for yourself. Just for the record.'

'I don't know,' says Koop. 'I may be giving Arthur a call myself. Seeing as how I'm so tight with Hunter and all.'

He sits back and looks at the three detectives. Koop feels old. Too old for this shit.

'We've got enough on you leaving the scene, Koop. Even if you had nothing to do with Kite's death, you know better than to do something like that.' Moresby holds Koop's gaze.

Koop holds up his palm. 'Stupid, I know. I must have still been affected by the beating at the gallery. At least that's what any decent brief would suggest. It's certainly the only fucking reason I can think of.'

'Let's take a break.' Moresby leans forward and speaks into the microphone. 'DI Ian Moresby suspending interview with Menno Koopman.'

'That's it?' says Harris. 'That's the interview?'

Moresby turns to Harris. 'That's our interview so far, DI Harris. We think we may need to discuss this in private. If that's OK with you and DCI Perch?'

Reader gestures to the uniformed officer at the door.

'Take Mr Koopman to the holding cells, Lucas. Get him a cup of tea and keep him away from the regular scum.'

Lucas leads Koop from the room. As the door closes behind him he sees Reader and Moresby turn to face Emily Harris.

He almost wishes he was staying.

51

The first thing Keane feels like doing is to head for the pub to get well and truly fucked up. It is, surely, the only sensible response to what's happened. Hit the bar for a couple of hours and blot out Emily Harris's backstabbing face for a while.

Instead, he gets in the car and goes to see Gittings. There's more than one way to skin a rabbit.

Keane heads back into the city and drives down the hill towards the tunnels. He takes the Birkenhead route and slips under the river to the Wirral shore. Once in the Birkenhead badlands he follows the road east to New Brighton, parking outside a tiny pub which huddles on the promenade close to the back of the old theatre. It's an unrepentant shithole, the sort of place that Keane would have usually only entered with a kitted-up riot team.

Or when he needs information.

Like Menno Koopman, Frank Keane worked with Sergeant Gittings as a raw recruit. Ten years after Koopman was following the big racist bastard around Liverpool, Keane found himself doing pretty much the same and with similarly mixed feelings. By Keane's time, Gittings was a decade older, six stone heavier and rapidly approaching the end of a long and massively undistinguished career in uniform. But the fact that he spent almost every day of his working life on the street gives Gittings a knowledge of the inner workings of the city that can't be matched by anyone. He knows every brick, every scrote, every deal and backhander, from Speke to Southport and all points in between. He is a sponge, soaking up street information and storing it. Keane, like many other ambitious DIs, uses Gittings from time to time as a sort of sounding board. With each passing year his reach fades as he grows further away from the contacts he made as a copper. The last time Keane saw him was three years before and Gittings didn't look good then. Frank is hoping things haven't got much worse.

Keane pushes open the door of the pub. Despite the rain and wind driving in off the Mersey, the interior of the pub seems bleaker than outside. There are three people in the bar besides Keane and the terminally bored-looking barman. Two alcoholic pensioners, a man and woman, sit on a bench seat below the only window in the room. The window itself is entirely covered by grimy security screens. Whether these screens are there to keep people in, or vandals out, Keane isn't sure. Certainly the two fossilised drinkers nursing their greasy glasses look more like long-term inmates of some Siberian gulag than happy patrons in a place of entertainment. Tonight's karaoke, promised by the shrieking orange fluoro poster above their heads, seems as unlikely as a performance of avant-garde theatre.

The other occupant of the room is, as Keane expected, sitting on the same seat he's been sitting on for the past five years. The first thing Keane notices about Gittings is that his face has taken a severe beating at some point.

He was never a movie star before, but now he looks truly hideous. His boozer's nose has mutated like some fungal growth, sprouting raw red hillocks which have pushed his eyes even further back into the folds of blue-veined flesh that surround them. What little hair remains is still cut short against his scalp; a residual habit. His body is wrecked. Always fat, he now has the proportions of a bull walrus. His body bulges against the constraints of his bar chair. He wears, as always, clothes which owe more than a little to the uniform he wore all his police life. Black pants, black shoes, blue shirt and a black coat, all of them greasy and stained. He is sixty-six, but looks like Methuselah. Up close, he smells of stale food and incontinence. It's not unbearable, but it's close.

Keane orders a pint of lager and a double whisky. Neither drink is for himself. He places the whisky in front of Gittings and takes the stool next to him. It's a few moments before Gittings realises a glass has appeared and, at first, he seems to think it may have arrived through divine intervention such is the expression of radiant joy that lights up his bloated face.

'Don't encourage 'im, mate,' says the barman. 'He's a narky fucker when he's had too much.'

Keane looks at the barman and jerks his head towards the other end of the bar. *Shift.* When that produces no effect, Keane takes out his warrant card and shows it. The card doesn't impress him either.

'I know yer a bizzy,' says the barman, his accent as thick as a plate of ten-day-old scouse. 'So?'

'So fuck off out of it, you little gobshite, while I talk to my friend here in private.' Keane doesn't smile.

The barman wipes a dirty rag around some equally dirty glasses. He picks up the remote for the monstrous plasma

TV which dominates the wall behind the bar and turns the channel to show a gardening program. He glares at Keane with a look on his face that Keane has seen on a thousand scallies. They must practise it at home in the mirror. Keane waits a few seconds and the barman dawdles long enough to satisfy his own code of honour before heading off to stock the cigarette machine.

'DC fucking Keane, as I live and breathe,' mumbles Gittings. 'Which isn't somethin' I take fer granted these days, I can tell yer.' He raises the glass of whisky and takes a pull.

'Detective Inspector,' says Keane. 'I'm a DI now.'

Gittings raises his eyebrows. 'You are doing well, *DI* Keane. Been licking all the right arseholes, eh?'

'Something like that.'

The fat man shuffles around in his chair with some effort. He looks at Keane and Keane can detect the stirrings of the feral intelligence that served the man well.

'You need somethin', Frank?'

Keane waves the rat-faced barman back over. 'Another double,' he says, pointing to Gittings's glass.

'Oh ho!' says Gittings. 'You must want the good stuff!' He drains the first glass greedily and takes a slurp of the lager. Keane notices that despite the shaking hands not a drop escapes Gittings's maw. 'Go ahead. I'm all ears,' he says.

Keane waits until the fresh whisky is placed in front of Gittings and the barman has retreated safely out of earshot. Keane slips a twenty out of his wallet and slides it across the bartop.

'The Halligans,' says Keane.

Gittings takes a sip of his second glass and regards the twenty. He snakes out a fat fist and scoops it up. 'The

Halligans,' he repeats, sounding out the name like a fine wine. 'Well, there's plenty to know, Frankie boy. But you must know most of it yourself.'

Keane nods. 'Yes, but I want your take on them.'

Gittings preens. 'They've been around forever. I brought in old man Halligan, Dessie, when I was just a lad meself. They've been good customers down the years. Old-style criminals, once upon a time. You could give 'em a good kicking and they'd never complain.'

'It's not the old stuff I need, Sarge. What I want to know is about the new crop.'

'The brothers?'

Keane nods.

Gittings looks around the bar. The old couple haven't moved a muscle. Keane wonders if they're alive. For all he knows they croaked last week. Gittings lowers his voice even further.

'Matty and Dean. Bad fuckers, Frank, as you know. Foot soldiers for Keith Kite. They came up after that gym shooting six or seven years ago. They run two or three of Kite's clubs and all the usual stuff. Steroids from the look of them. Rumour is that one of 'em's queer. Matty, I think. Likes the rough stuff too. That could be something.'

'And this helps me . . . how?'

'You never said what you're after.'

Keane folds his arms. Gittings has a point. What is he looking for? He thinks about what Gittings has mentioned about Matty Halligan being queer. 'You said they were foot soldiers. You think they might have made a move on Kite?'

Gittings stops his glass at his lips. 'Oh. I see.' He drinks and sets the glass down carefully. He closes his eyes and says nothing.

'Are you asleep, or thinking, or what?'

Gittings opens his barnacle eyes and looks scornfully at Keane. 'I'm not that far fuckin' gone, *DI* Keane. No, I don't see the brothers having the juice to step up on Kite. Not alone, anyway.'

The two men sit quietly for a few minutes. On screen a floppy-haired upper-class Englishman wearing a cravat and velvet jacket is talking animatedly about the correct way to prepare gazpacho. The barman and the two zombie pensioners are gazing at him as if he's the Archangel Gabriel.

'Well, if that's all you have . . .' Keane makes to stand. Gittings shoots out a surprisingly quick hand and grabs his sleeve. 'Not so fast, Geronimo. You have any more sisters to that twenty?'

Keane takes another note out and holds it against the bar with the flat of his hand.

'That very much depends on the quality of the information.'

Gittings pulls Keane in close. Keane fights the urge to pull back. Gittings's odour is more pungent at this distance and Keane knows the old copper will be on the streets, or worse, before too long.

'There is something. Just a tickle.' Gittings glances around the pub. 'One of my old pals on Vice got a load of DVDs from one of them queer clubs at the back of Bold Street. Operating without a licence or some such. Anyway, they had to check 'em for anything good, right? See if them pooftas was using donkeys, or kids. Something that would make a collar, y'know? But it was all just ordinary bum-bandit stuff. Hardcore; whips and chains and all that carry-on, right?'

Keane nods.

'Anyway, my mate had the job of fast-forwarding through the pile so you can imagine how pleased he was about that. But he did find something.'

Gittings eyes the twenty meaningfully and Keane lifts his hand. Gittings reaches out and trousers it.

'Nothing actual criminal, as such. My mate recognised someone watching Matty Halligan get bummed. An Irishman called North. Declan North. One of Kite's.'

Keane pulls back from Gittings and breathes in the relatively clean air.

'And from what I've been hearing, this one is proper nasty, Frank. I heard he was ex-Provo.'

'You know this?'

Gittings puts his hands to his lips and makes a zippering gesture. Frank Keane takes out another twenty but, to his surprise, Gittings pushes the note away.

'No, Frank. That's my lot. I've given you enough there to be goin' on with.' Gittings flashes a shrewd eye at the barman, still intent on the gardening show. 'Loose lips sink ships and all that.'

Frank Keane stands. Gittings grips his arm and speaks in an urgent whisper.

'You never got this from me, right? Kite and the Halligans I can cope with but I don't want any old IRA nutters tracin' anything back this way. I lived through all that exploding leprechaun shite once. I can do without a bunch of mad Paddys using me kneecaps for target practice. They're fucked enough right now.'

Keane finishes his pint and pushes away from the bar with a nod to Gittings.

'Take care, Sarge,' he says. Gittings doesn't reply. He's drinking.

Outside, Keane calls the office as he walks to the car. He looks across the Mersey towards Liverpool as he waits for the connection. The air smells fresh after the pub.

'DC Rose? Keane. I'll be back in twenty. I want you to run a name for me. Declan North. Let's see what comes up.'

52

The first thing North does when he arrives back at his hotel after killing Jimmy Gelagotis is pack the rifle carefully into the cricket bag Tony Link supplied it in and stow it in the wardrobe. Then he undresses, gets into the shower and masturbates. It's what he always does after a killing. The image of Gelagotis's head erupting over the glass merges with the images in North's diseased wank bank. He comes quickly, cleans himself up and towels off. He feels energised. He is an intelligent man. He knows what he is, or what he has become, and he has no problem with it. It's for others to have regrets, or guilt, or any of the feelings that humans are supposed to have. He has, quite simply, never felt that way. He suspects Gelagotis may have been the same. The man had that look about him. He just wasn't expecting Link and Meeks to sell him out quite so swiftly. That, like many before him, was his undoing. It was certainly Keith Kite's problem.

And now the dust has settled, Declan North is the main man. Eight hundred kilos of coke and a big fecking place like Australia to play in.

North looks out of his window and down the strip of lights. It's almost twelve and the town is thick with clubbers and drinkers. Earlier in the day Declan North took a walk down to the beach and watched the surfers. They were cute enough, but he isn't sure if any of them would like it the way he likes it. Tony Link offered him women on his arrival and seemed surprised when he turned them down, raising an eyebrow a fraction. North thought Link got the message and liked the way he dealt with it. Not like Kite. North remembers Kite finding out that he and Matty were playmates. He hit the roof, in case anyone thought he was queer too. Then his insecurities subsided into years of snide remarks and 'jokes' that only Keith Kite laughed at. North considered killing Kite many times during that period but held off, waiting for the big score and swallowing a great big steaming pile of shit along the way.

He is glad, now, that he showed restraint. Kite out and now Gelagotis out. King of the hill.

North picks up the throwaway mobile phone Link has given him. He dials and gets an answer on the second ring.

'Declan.' The voice is hesitant, clipped. North realises the man has been waiting for the call and is trying to keep the fear out of his voice. Just how North likes things to be: get everyone thinking he's half a bubble off the true – an accurate assessment, all things considered – and they fall in line right enough.

'Your mammy would be proud, Mr Link. You've been promoted,' says North. 'I'll be downstairs in five.' He presses the 'end' button, stands up and puts his wallet in his back pocket. As he does so, North feels a familiar tinny whining in his ears and the room tilts under his feet until he's canted at an angle of forty-five degrees. His mind registers the fact that there's no noise, and that none of the room's objects – the lamps, the TV, the vase of dried flowers – have moved an inch. This has happened before and North lets it wash over him. He breathes in deeply and the axis of the room starts to slowly come back to normality. North remains silent for three or four minutes, concentrating on his breathing. His head seems to fill with blood and he can hear the beating of his heart loud in his ears. When he's breathing regularly again, North goes through his routines with the precision of a penitent monk.

He places his hands together at the wrists and looks up at a corner of the room, analysing the perfection of the angles and calibrating the trajectory of a series of imagined rubber balls bouncing from one to the other. After a series of ten, North switches his attention back to the opposing corner and repeats the performance. Next he turns off every electrical switch in the room and turns them back on. He checks under the bed and behind the furniture for stray outlets he might have missed. It's vital that all outlets be turned on and then off and then back on. Finally, North opens every door and closes it, paying attention to the level of engineering in each. The hotel is a five star and North finds that, in the main, the levels are of a high enough quality to satisfy his exacting standards.

Routine complete, he picks up his hotel key and, with a last look round, leaves the room.

By the time he gets to the lobby Tony Link and Stefan Meeks are there. Despite their snappy suits and relaxed bad-guy personas, North realises they've been in the lobby for some time, waiting for word on Jimmy. They were scared of Gelagotis, North thinks.

He glances at Stefan Meeks.

And now the feckers are scared of me. The thought adds to his feeling of invincibility. He is untouchable.

'You ready for a good time?' Tony Link can't quite mask the tension in his voice. Pleasing Declan North has become even more important.

North nods and smiles. 'Aye, Mr Link. But you may have a different idea of what's good to me,' he says. It would be interesting to see how Link handles that one.

Tony Link gestures towards the door. Outside, a black car is parked under the hotel-entrance canopy, a lean, well-muscled young man dressed in black leather leaning against the wing.

'I think I might have underestimated you, Mr Link,' says North. The three of them head out of the hotel. As they exit, the leather boy stands and opens the door for North.

'Good evening, sir,' he says. 'My name is Mark and I'll be your driver for this evening.'

'I bet you fucking will,' murmurs North.

Behind the black car a second draws up.

'This is us, Declan,' says Link. 'I don't think you'll be needing us again tonight, right?'

North glances at the leather boy. 'Get in the fucking car.'

'It's like that, is it?' says the boy. He smiles and saunters around to the driver's door.

North walks the few paces to Link and Meeks.

'Thanks, Tony. Very thoughtful.'

Link waves a hand. 'No problem. Anything, Declan. Absolutely anything you need.'

'There is one small thing,' says North. He pulls a sheet of hotel writing paper from his pocket and gives it to Link. 'I'd like an address for this guy. I think he's local.'

'Old friend?' Tony Link's smile fades as North's expression turns frosty. 'No problem at all, Declan. I'll get right on it.'

North smiles again. It's like switching on a light. 'Excellent, Tony. At your leisure. Don't think there's any rush.'

North turns and gets into the front passenger side of the car. As the Irishman and his gift pull away and turn left into the light traffic, Meeks lets out a sigh.

'Jesus,' he breathes. 'That is one horrible queer motherfucker.'

Tony Link pats Meeks on the side of his face. 'Look on the bright side, Stefan: he's our horrible queer motherfucker. And at least we don't have to get in that car with him. If we run out of pooftas you're gonna have to volunteer.'

'Get fucked. Christ on a bike, he gives me the creeps, man.'

Tony Link opens the door of the car and gets in. Meeks walks around to the other side and slips in beside him. He gives Chris the nod to drive.

'What's on the paper?' says Meeks as the car pulls away.

Link holds it up to the reading light and squints.

'Menno Koopman,' he reads. 'Who the fuck is Menno Koopman?'

53

'It's black and white, Eric. No question.'

Perch isn't having any of it.

'It's too early to be jumping to conclusions.' Perch is behind a desk three floors above the holding cell in which Menno Koopman sits drinking tea and chatting to a uniformed officer.

Reader rattles the paper in his hand again.

'There's no mistake, Eric. Time of death is between twelve and three. Koopman was in the A&E ward at Broadgreen until two, and then on the main ward until the morning.'

'He could have still made it.' Perch has the demeanour of a sulky adolescent. Ian Moresby sits back and folds his arms to stop himself reaching across the desk and slapping the stupid twat.

'We can't let your feelings about Koopman interfere. He didn't do it. I suppose, in some abstract universe, there are people who can leave a hospital ward, find a high-profile drug baron, take him from his minders, get him back to the hotel, kill him – slowly, mind – before trotting back to Broadgreen and getting into bed.'

Perch looks at Moresby. 'So you admit it's possible?'

Dave Reader laughs and then stops. This clown isn't joking. 'Get real, Eric. Apart from the logistics and the complete lack of forensics, why would Koopman take Kite back to his own hotel bedroom to kill him? I knew this was going to go south as soon as I heard Koopman was in the frame. The whole thing's garbage and you know it.'

'Can you imagine someone like Zentfeld getting a sniff of this?' Moresby's voice is incredulous.

'That's not a consideration,' says Perch. 'We don't worry about what some brief might do over at MIT.'

'Well, maybe you should,' says Reader. 'From what I hear, you get your arses smacked on a regular basis over there.'

Perch bristles.

'It doesn't matter, anyway,' says Moresby, before Perch can reply. 'The Kite case is OCS and we're kicking Menno Koopman out. He's muddied the waters enough without having you going off on some vendetta. Carl Koopman is still of interest but until we get some semblance of evidence against him we're keeping an open mind. Remember those?'

In the larger office outside, Emily Harris pretends to read the notice-board. She can't swear to it, but word must have spread about her defection. There's a certain something in the air. Not quite outright hostility. More the feeling of unease, as if a fox is loose in a field of sheep.

Perhaps they're all considering which way to jump. Follow her across to Perch, or stick with Frank Keane and hope he gets them through unscathed? It's a crossroads, the sort of crossroads that careers can depend on.

And, judging from the way the Koopman investigation looks like it's heading, she may have chosen the wrong road. At least in the short term. The next few months, she suspects, are not going to be easy.

Through the glass of the partition she sees the door to the small office open and Perch, Moresby and Reader step out. None of them stop at the door to MIT. Feeling herself flush and cursing herself for it, Harris darts after them. Behind her, Caddick, Wills and Corner exchange surreptitious loaded glances. Steve Rose studiously avoids her gaze and doesn't look up from his screen as she leaves.

In the corridor she feels foolish trotting after the suits.

'Sir?' Three heads turn her way. 'Is the interview over?'

'I'm going back to Canning Place, Harris,' Perch barks. 'Sit in on the rest of the Koopman interview. There have been . . . developments, which means other work now takes priority for me.' Perch speaks as though he is needed urgently at the UN.

Harris nods, an empty feeling coming to rest in her gut, and follows Moresby and Reader down the stairs. At the foot, Perch goes one way and the rest of them turn towards the interview room. On the threshold, Harris stops the two senior detectives.

'What's happened?'

Moresby looks at her, not unkindly. 'Koopman is out.' He holds up the path report. 'Kite was killed while he was in Broadgreen.'

Harris feels like she's taken a punch. Frank warned her this would happen.

'And the brother?' says Harris. 'Did Menno know Carl was out?'

Moresby shakes his head. 'We don't know. Yet. My feeling is that if Carl Koopman did have something to do with Kite's death – and that's a big if – then Menno Koopman didn't know. Either way, there's absolutely

300

nothing apart from motive connecting Koopman with Keith Kite's sad demise. If we arrested everyone with a motive for killing that sack of shit, we'd have to pull in half of Liverpool. Koopman's out.'

'Listen,' says Dave Reader. 'Don't beat yourself up too much, Harris. Keane will come round.'

'If you do the right thing,' chips in Moresby. He shakes his head. '*Perch*. Jesus, Harris, what were you thinking?'

Harris says nothing.

'We all fuck up now and again,' says Reader. 'Even coppers with your experience. Even me. Believe it or not. And you might have made the right decision, DI Harris. For all we know, Perch has got "future CC" written all over him.'

There's a short pause while they all contemplate the idea of Eric Perch as Chief Constable.

'Shall we?' says Harris. She indicates the door. Moresby pushes it open and they move inside.

54

'What do you mean "clean"? He must have got something!'

DC Rose writhes in an agony of uselessness. Like a faithful hound, there's nothing he'd rather have done than bring back the bird between his teeth and drop it at his master's feet. But there's no way round it. He's come up empty.

'Not so much as a parking ticket, boss. I ran it through everything but Declan North isn't there. Not with a record anyway.'

Keane runs his hand through his hair and leans against Rose's desk. 'Everyone has a fucking record these days. Tax evasion. Speeding. Something!'

Rose shakes his head. If he had a tail it would be well and truly tucked between his legs. 'Sorry, sir. He's clean.'

Keane walks across to the crime wall. His carefully constructed crime wall, now DI Harris's responsibility. He closes his mind at the thought of Harris. That's something that will have to be dealt with later. Right now, DCI Perch or no DCI Perch, he's fucked if he's going to stand there and let the White case – *his* case – stay across with OCS and that back-stabbing bitch.

'I've got his non-criminal data,' says DC Rose. His tone is conciliatory, as if it's his fault personally there's nothing meaty on North.

Keane turns back from the wall. He notices Caddick skulking around near the door pretending to be busy with some paperwork. Most likely seeing which way the wind is blowing before he declares his allegiance. Keane bites his lip. That kind of thinking will eat him up if he doesn't tread carefully. For all he knows Caddick is working diligently and is a loyal and trustworthy officer. Maybe.

'What do you have, Steve?' he asks Rose. Rose's face brightens pathetically at Keane's warmer tone.

'The usual stuff, sir. Birth records, some employment stuff – although not very much there – no record of him ever claiming benefits.'

Keane looks up. 'What, never?'

Rose shakes his head.

Keane reaches over and picks up the file in front of Rose. He flicks through impatiently.

'Says he was born in Belfast, lived through the Troubles?'

Rose nods agreement.

'And no benefits? In Belfast, in the eighties?' Keane looks sceptical. He flicks a finger deeper into the file. 'No employment records either.'

'That we know of, sir.' Rose makes a face. 'I'm working with the databases we have. He could have worked off the radar. Cash in hand.'

'Which makes it all the stranger he never claimed. Standard practice in the black economy, right?'

Keane puts down the file and rubs his hands together briskly. The slim information on North is not as disappointing as he first imagined. In fact, the very lack of credible records is bringing Declan North right into focus. He was doing something in Ireland, record or no record.

'There was another thing,' says Rose. 'About North. He arrived here in eighty-three and went to college.'

That brings Keane up short. 'College? What, like technical college?' In his mind he sees a bomb-maker gaining his skills on an electronics course.

Rose shakes his head. 'No, sir. Art college. At Hope Street.'

'You're telling me that North was a fucking art student? In Liverpool?'

'Yes, sir.' Rose looks at the file on his desk. 'Eighty-three to eighty-six. Studied fine art and left with a two-one.'

'Two-one?'

'It's the grade. What they give 'em at the end of the course. A two-one's pretty good, according to Siobhan.' Rose looks across to Siobhan MacDonald. That's right, remembers Keane, Siobhan is a graduate copper.

He digests the news of North's art-school past. The image of the Gormley sculptures comes to mind. Kite's new-found status as an art lover.

'That's good work, Steve. Very good work.' Keane pats Rose on the shoulder. 'Dig around some more. Military records, passport office. You know the score.'

Leaving Rose to his task, Keane checks on the other members of his syndicate. Without going into details, he brings them up to speed on the changes Perch has made to the White case structure. DI Harris is now the lead and they are to report to her in so far as the case is still an MIT case. How long that situation will remain would be determined by the OCS involvement. Keane deliberately leaves vague the direction he feels the case will go. This is as much to cover his back, should Perch check he has left it alone, as to give him some wiggle room. Feeling much more chipper than when he arrived, Keane moves to a small office off the main room, sits at a bare desk and picks up the phone.

'Joanne? Frank.'

'Frank! Good to hear from you!' Her smoky voice is full of warmth.

He and Joanne Wright have history. Three years earlier Keane worked alongside her at MIT for a while. During that time Joanne divorced and Keane was the one who on more than one occasion was there to pick up the very messy pieces. There were two or three times when it was only Keane's involvement that prevented Joanne getting into some serious trouble involving a flirtation with coke. They dated briefly for a few months after her divorce was finalised, but it didn't work out for either of them and they parted without rancour. Keane figures that Joanne could prove useful right now.

Joanne works at OCS.

After a few pleasantries Keane gets down to it. 'Declan North. What can you tell me about him, Joanne? And I need it on the quiet. I'm not the most popular DI over here right now.'

There's a short pause during which Keane realises too late that Joanne might have been hoping for a little more than business from him. When she speaks again her tone is almost imperceptibly sharper.

'Give me a minute, Frank,' she says.

'I'll hold.' Keane presses the button and replaces the phone on its cradle. He looks out across the car park to the depressing vista of Liverpool in October. He checks his mobile for messages, but there's only one from a friend asking about tickets for the next Champions League game.

Out of the corner of his eye he sees Emily Harris come into the office. She doesn't look happy, but Keane can't work out if that's simply from the situation or if something has happened downstairs while he's been out.

'Frank.'

Keane picks up the phone. 'Hi, Joanne.'

'Why do you need to know about North?'

'Why? Because I do.' Keane frowns. 'Is there a problem?'

She lowers her voice. 'Yes there's a problem, Frank. This one is hot. I could get into deep shit if Reader or Moresby find out.'

'Find out what? You've been giving information to a fellow officer? Come on, Joanne, I thought you were made of sterner stuff than that.'

'North's Irish.'

'I know that. What are you trying to say? He's IRA?'

'Something like that. We think. Or was. But that's not why he's hot, Frank. He's hot because he's heavily linked with Kite. He's been seen by us many times but is clean as can be.'

'Too clean.'

'That's right. Much too clean.'

Keane pauses. He lowers his voice.

'I'm liking him for the Kite murder. Is that the thinking at OCS?'

It's Joanne Wright's turn to pause. 'I don't know, Frank. I'm not in that loop. And I heard you were off the Kite thing.'

'Yeah. I am. But that doesn't mean I can't have a hobby, does it?'

'I can't give you any more, Frank. It's not right.'

'One thing, Joanne. I need a snap of North. Can you

email me? You must have old surveillance shots, something like that?'

'I'll see what I can do. Good to hear from you, Frank.'

Joanne hangs up before Keane can reply. He looks blankly at the phone for a second before slowly replacing it.

Harris is tapping at her keyboard, her body hunched away from Keane. He walks past her desk and over to his own. Onscreen he sees that Joanne has come through straight away. He downloads the attachment and bins the email. He looks at Declan North's face closely. He doesn't seem like anyone's idea of a hitman. Which is, thinks Keane, damn useful if you happened to be one.

'Sir?' DC Rose leans over Keane's shoulder. He holds a printout looking like a kid on Christmas Eve. It's so endearing that Keane almost laughs out loud.

'OK, Rover,' he says. 'What have you brought me?'

Rose rests his backside on the edge of the desk. He taps the sheet of paper, beaming.

'It's your man, sir. North. He's in Australia.'

55

Koop gets his first-class flight back to Australia in the clothes he left Stanley Road in and carrying a bag of stuff bought in the airport shops.

OCS retains his belongings in case they turn out to be forensically pertinent to the Kite investigation. Even though Koop is pretty much out of the picture for Kite, OCS aren't happy. They quiz him endlessly for anything relevant, but there's nothing. There is some talk of charges relating to him running, or of interfering with an investigation, but Reader and Moresby smooth it out. It would be counter-productive to drag Koop in any deeper. Koop gets the idea that as far as Merseyside Police are concerned, the further away he is from their patch, the better. His name hasn't come up in the press yet and that's exactly how the locals will want it. They allow Koop to keep his wallet and passport and release him with clearance to return home.

Ian Moresby and Dave Reader wish him well and detail a uniform to take him back into the city. At the admissions desk, Koop is given his documents and shakes hands with the two OCS detectives.

A car draws up outside and the desk clerk nods towards it. The younger policeman clearly has no idea who Koop is. Koop pushes through the double doors and trots down the steps. He pulls open the passenger door and steps inside.

'Afternoon,' says Frank Keane. 'I heard you needed a lift?'

Koop puts his seatbelt on. 'Do they usually assign detective inspectors to taxi duty?'

Keane smiles. 'I sent the lad on his way. Took the liberty of driving you myself.' He manoeuvres the car out of the gate and into the traffic.

'The lovely DI Harris not joining us?' Koop's tone is teasing.

'I think those days are over, Koop. DI Harris . . . well, let's just leave it that we won't be exchanging Christmas cards any more, eh?'

Koop looks at Keane. 'So, what's happening with the investigation?'

'Kite?' says Keane.

Koop shakes his head. 'Stevie.'

Keane brakes at a red light.

'That's what I wanted to talk to you about, Koop. There've been some developments. Interesting ones.' They accelerate down towards the Pier Head and the tangle of glass high-rises. The Liver Building appears through a gap between two new office buildings that might have been hotels or apartment blocks; Koop doesn't know, and can't tell and doesn't care. The city is changing so fast it has left him behind and he can't wait to leave.

'I want you to help me,' says Keane. 'When you get home.'

Koop stares out of the window. 'You've changed your tune.'

'Yeah, well. Like I said, there've been developments.'

'What do you mean "help"? What can I do? I've been about as useful back here as a first-year PC.'

Keane pulls into the heavier traffic as they head east towards the 62. 'Harris shafted me,' he says. 'I'm out of the loop.'

Koop sucks his lower lip. 'She's a smart cookie,' says Koop. 'From the look of her.'

'Not as smart as she thinks, Koop. She had you for Kite and went over to Perch. Now she's got to decide if that was a good move. Perch is going to distance himself from bringing you in but she might be left in limbo.'

'Screw her.'

Keane nods. 'It wasn't personal.'

'It was for me.'

'True.'

When they get to the motorway, Keane kicks the car up to a hundred.

'In a hurry?' says Koop.

'Not me, you. Your flight's at 6.30.'

'I got time to pick up some clothes?'

'Sure. Those airports are just big shopping malls now.'

Koop shifts in his seat to study Keane. Looking at the policeman is like being in a time-machine. Himself at forty. Stressed, anxious, alternately adrenalised and dragged down by the bureaucracy. He's happier than ever to be going home. Home to Australia.

'What about Carl?' says Koop. It's the first time he's mentioned his brother to anyone since seeing him at Anfield. Koop tries to sound neutral but feels Keane tense in the seat.

'You seen him since you got back?' says Keane.

Koop sits quietly for a few seconds. 'We met at the

match last week,' he says eventually. 'He's out legitimately. He's . . . cured.'

'Come on, Koop. It must have crossed your mind that Carl might have had something to do with Kite's murder.'

'Of course it did. For about two minutes.'

'What made you so sure he didn't do it?'

Koop doesn't answer. Not immediately. 'Quit the bull-shit, Frank. If Carl was in your sights I'd still be at Stanley Road.'

Keane lets out a long breath. 'Yeah. You're right. Carl didn't do Kite.'

Koop relaxes a little. 'Why are you so sure about that? I mean, I'm biased, but you must have something solid to go on.'

'He's got an alibi. Rock solid. We found him.' Keane glances across at Koop. 'In Bowden. He checked himself back in after your little reunion at Anfield. Maybe there was a moment he thought about killing Kite. Helping his brother out, something like that. Who knows? The point is, he didn't.'

'Burton did say he's been fixed,' murmurs Koop.

'Yeah, well,' says Keane, keeping his eyes on the road. 'Anyway, Carl says he followed you for a while but realised he was being stupid. Didn't know what he was following you for.' Keane pauses. 'So there's at least one of the family who knows when something's a bad idea, eh?'

'Fair enough.'

The two men say nothing while the washed-out land-scape passes the window.

'So if it isn't something to do with Carl, what *do* you want me to do?' Koop asks as they slide onto the 56. That Keane wanted something was obvious to Koop the moment he saw him behind the wheel.

311

'I think the man who killed your son is in Australia.' Keane keeps his voice even and his eyes dead ahead. 'It's a man called Declan North.'

Koop frowns. 'Never come across him.'

'You won't have. The guy's off radar.'

'What do you mean "off radar"? What is he, a ghost?'

'Something like that.' Now Keane does look at Koop. 'This character's bad, Koop. If what I've heard is right. But there's nothing on him to connect him to Stevie. Kite may be a different matter, although I think he's good enough to skip free of that one as well.'

'Anything else?'

Keane hesitates. 'He's IRA. Ex anyway. Apparently.'

'You're not sure?'

'No, not really. That's the premise we're working on but we don't *know*. Terrorist organisations don't usually keep handy records.'

Koop is silent. 'And I can do . . . what, exactly?'

Keane shrugs. 'We can't touch him. He's legit. He's there on business, travelling under his own passport, no previous convictions. What do you think the Australians are going to do? Parcel him up and send him back in chains? Christ, I can't even bring this in to MIT! You know what it's like. The DPP wouldn't touch it, Koop.'

Koop knows full well. He butted heads with the Director of Public Prosecutions many times.

'And I'm not exactly Perch's golden boy right now.'

'I don't like it,' says Koop. 'I haven't got a system. I'm retired, for fuck's sake. I deliver coffee, Frank. And my big trip home didn't exactly work out well, now did it?'

Keane reaches into his inside pocket and hands Koop a slip of paper by way of reply.

'Warren Eckhardt,' reads Koop. 'Who's he?'

'He's a detective senior sergeant operating on the Gold Coast. I spoke to him this morning and it sounds like he's joined the dots to some murders over there. Stevie's boss, Koop. A character called Gelagotis and two others. Russian names. There's a big deal going on between our two fair cities. At least that's what Eckhardt thinks and I'm inclined to agree with him.'

Keane glances at Koop. 'Your boy was involved to the hilt, Koop. You know that, right?'

'I didn't, but I do now.'

Keane points to the slip of paper. 'Get in touch with Eckhardt. I think he'd welcome your input. He sounds old school. You're the only one who's been at both ends. If we're right, that could be very useful.'

'In doing what?'

'In getting the fucking psycho who carved up Stevie, Koop. Remember what you used to say? If they put one of ours in the hospital . . .'

'We put one of theirs in the morgue.' Koop finishes the quote. 'That was a long time ago.'

Keane pulls the car into the drop-off zone and is directed to a space by a terror cop in full battle-dress and carrying a submachine gun. 'Ye Olde Englande, eh, Koop?' says Keane.

Koop nods.

'Oh, one more thing,' says Keane. 'North was an art student once.'

Koop blinks. 'What?'

'I know, difficult to swallow. But it's legit; the guy went to art school in Liverpool in eighty-three. New one on me but I guess it would have been handy?'

Koop thinking, yes, that might have been useful for someone in the IRA.

Koop reaches over and shakes Keane's hand. 'Thanks for the lift, Frank. And for, well, for everything else. You've tried to play fair by me. It's probably more than I'd have done in your shoes.'

'I don't think so, Koop. You always do the right thing.' He pulls away from the kerb and Koop watches him go, thinking, no I don't.

56

The morning after he was given the leatherboy as an offering, Declan North calls Tony Link before he's out of bed. It's just after nine and Link is still asleep when the call comes in. Like all new kings, North wakes on the first morning of his reign feeling a powerful and urgent need to inspect his realm.

'I want to see the stuff,' says North. 'All of it.'

Of course you do, thinks Link. Just like Jimmy. 'Sure, Declan. Not a problem, brother. How did it go last night? Have fun?'

'Call me when you have the details,' says North and hangs up. He steps out of bed and pads naked into the bathroom. The boy from last night has long gone. He turned out to be something of a lightweight – started crying at one point – and North booted him out, unsatisfied. Matty Halligan he wasn't, and North finds himself thinking of Matty. It's a curiously unfamiliar feeling. Is this what normal people do? Think of others?

In the bathroom mirror he looks at his bare chest. A fresh-traced line is there, but it looks feeble to North's eyes, a perfect replica of last night's pale imitation of true lust. North pees and gets into the shower. There's no repeat of the room tilting on its axis, although he does place his wrists together once more and face each corner of the shower cubicle, annoyed that one angle is offset, a designer quirk that throws off his carefully calibrated ritual. It isn't right.

Not for a king.

North feels his anger rise and his jaw working beneath the skin. If he listens carefully sometimes he can hear the meshing of muscle and ligament working together. He imagines taking his scalpel and reconfiguring his face as he's done to others.

And now the room does tilt and North sways, reaching out a steadying hand to the cold tile of the shower stall. The room turns 180 degrees and North finds himself upside down. A great roaring sound surfs through his head and he feels the blood rush to his hands and cock. He closes his eyes for what seems like an eternity and when he opens them the room has returned to its regular plane.

He steps from the shower and dries himself, the episode forgotten as always. He has things to do. Things he always does in strange places. Things that have kept him alive and below the radar for so long.

North packs his belongings quickly and efficiently and leaves the hotel, his room as bare as when he arrived. Outside he catches a taxi which takes him a few kilometres down the strip at Surfers where he checks into another, smaller hotel. Once he has his room key he takes a second taxi back to his original hotel and waits on the balcony, watching the street below and the beach. The air carries the tang of sunscreen and fast food. The people look purposeful, as if their lives have meaning. It's a puzzle to North.

The phone rings.

'It's me,' says Link. 'We'll pick you up in ten. If that's OK?'

'That's fine, Tony,' says North, his voice warm. 'And sorry about the old sharp tongue earlier, eh? Jetlag or something.'

'It's all cool, brother,' says Link.

Ten minutes later North is in the passenger seat of Link's Lexus.

'Stef's meeting us at the lock-up,' Link says.

'Good man,' says North, upping the brogue a little. He found his accent to be a useful tool. A flight magazine article once told him that the Irish accent is considered to be one of the friendliest in the world. North knows that when people said 'Irish' they usually mean Dublin Irish, or the soft, near-impenetrable accents of the West of Ireland, not the sharp wet slap of the Belfast yap. Still, to untutored ears like Link's, the difference is minimal. So North drops his 'th' sounds to 'd' sounds and exaggerates his 'i's' to 'oi's'.

'Nice car,' he says. Noice.

Link smiles, happy to be on safe territory. He was worried that Declan North would talk him through the previous night's encounter with Leatherboy. Toleration was one thing, details of what the kinky fucker gets up to is another thing entirely. 'Got a bit of class,' says Link. 'Like me, eh?' He remembers something. 'Oh, I got that thing for you.' Tony Link lifts a slip of paper from his jacket and hands Menno Koopman's address to North.

'Nashua,' says North. 'Where the fuck is that?'

Instead of answering, Link reaches forward and taps the details into the GPS on the dash of the Lexus. 'New

South Wales,' he says. 'About two hours south. Farmer, is he, this Koopman?'

'What do they farm down there?' says North.

Link shrugs. 'Coffee? Bananas? I know there's a shitload of dope growers down that way.'

'Oh?' North perks up.

Link nods. 'Load of fucking hippies originally but there are some serious players operating there now. Big properties. Plenty of places to hide a few acres of weed. Good shit too, if that's what floats your boat.'

North watches the unfamiliar landscape unroll and chews on Link's words.

Menno Koopman, the father of Jimmy Gelagotis's ill-fated messenger, lives in a dope-growing area? Interesting. Declan North lets that percolate for a few minutes as the Lexus cruises west, trying to decide where the information fits into the scheme of things.

Or *if* it fits. Could be fuck all.

North looks up at the perfect blue sky and Koopman fades from his thoughts momentarily. For someone from Belfast, brought up in the dripping lee of Cavehill, Divis and Black Mountain, the sun would always be a novelty. North feels something knotted in him begin to slowly uncoil at the sight of people in shorts, of hot pavements and air-con units poking from the backs of buildings like warts. This is another land, one in which he feels already . . . if not at home, then at least somewhere he could *be*.

Eight hundred kays of Charlie would go a long way in this neck of the woods.

North looks across at Tony Link. He and Stefan will do. They'll require training, that's obvious, but he'll need them, their network and their contacts to transform his cocaine – he already thinks of it in those terms; his, and his alone, to do with as he pleases – into liquid. North has amassed a considerable amount of assets already, but more is never enough. And he's not going to be in second place to anyone ever again. Not after those years with Kite.

Maybe he'll start some serious art collecting. The cool stuff. When they've shifted the gear.

'Is it good?' says North. Link knows he's talking about the shipments. 'No damage in transit?'

Link shakes his head. 'It's gold, brother. Pure.' He taps his nose. 'We tried a few lines from each car and it was the best. No word of a lie, the fucking best.'

'Good,' says North. 'I want it to be good.'

Link drives the rest of the way in silence. He pulls in front of the lock-up and dabs his horn. Stefan slides the metal door up and closes it behind them when they're inside.

North shakes hands hurriedly with Stefan Meeks and walks across to the three cars, covered in their soft cotton tarps, keen to see the bounty for himself.

'Jimmy wanted us to get it shifted,' says Stefan. 'Before . . . well, before you arrived.'

'I bet he did,' murmurs North. He jerks his chin at the first car and Stefan lifts the tarp. Just as he did with Jimmy Gelagotis, Meeks opens the boot and pulls back the carpet cover to reveal the white bricks. North sees that one of them has been opened; the one Link tested. Meeks draws out a small box cutter and leans forward.

'Not that one,' says North. 'Take one from the bottom.'

Meeks nods. 'No sweat.' He lifts three bricks out and then three more from the second stack. At the bottom he slides the blade of his box cutter under a single brick and prises it out. North puts out a hand.

'Let me.'

Meeks gives North the brick. He flicks a quizzical glance at Link who replies with an imperceptible shake of the head for Meeks to remain quiet. However the mad Paddy wants to play it is fine with Tony.

North takes out a folding pocket knife and selects a blade. He slices into the brick and digs down into the centre of the white powder. Angling the knife he scoops out a lump the size of a small pea. He puts the blade to his nose and snorts.

'Pretty hot shit, eh man?' says Stefan, bobbing his head.

There's a short pause while North remains stationary.

'Is this some kind of joke?' he says. His soft brogue has slipped back to Belfast staccato. 'Some of your famous Aussie humour? All I heard on the plane was how much you fucks like playing practical jokes.'

Tony Link comes close. 'What the fuck do you mean, Declan? That stuff's pure as!'

'Pure as what? Fecking soap powder?' North holds the brick out to Link. After a second's hesitation he hands him the knife.

Link takes it and repeats the process North has undertaken.

'Fuck!' Tony Link glares at the brick as if it might explode.

'What?' says Meeks, his eyes wide. 'Don't fucking tell me.'

North rips the cotton tarp off the other two Jags and opens the boot of the middle one. He pulls the carpet cover off savagely and digs deep into the pile of white bricks. He rips one open with a finger nail and lifts a dab onto his little finger. He snorts it and immediately kicks the car.

'Fuck, fuck, fuck!'

North takes a sample from a brick on the top pile. It's grade A cocaine. He tries the brick next to it with the same result. In the passenger section of the third car, Tony Link is doing the same.

'Was it you?' says North, his glance darting between Link and Meeks. His eyes have taken on a dangerous green tinge. 'Did either of you two fuckers do this?'

'Fuck, no!'

'Don't be silly, Declan! Think about it. If we'd done this, do you think we'd have brought you here to find out?'

North tries to control his breathing. He places his hands together at the wrists and looks up at the corner of the garage. His eyes are fixed on the angle.

Tony and Stefan exchange quick glances.

After a minute, North unclasps his hands and looks at them. The anger has gone from his voice.

'No,' he says. 'No. I don't think you would have done something as stupid as that, Tony.'

He wanders a few paces towards the cars, his arms crossed in front of him. 'But some slimy fucker has stitched us up. The top layers are all coke. The rest is shit.'

He looks up at Meeks.

'Who knew about this, other than you, Tony and me?'

'A . . . a couple of the lads knew there was something.' Meeks is ashamed of his stumble, of how vulnerable he feels in front of North. 'But they haven't got the balls for this!'

'Or the organisation,' says Link. He turns to North. 'They're solid, Declan. Good fellers but not exactly what you'd call officer material.'

North acknowledges Link with a gesture. He paces up and down the concrete.

'Koopman,' he says, finally. He picks up his knife from the stack of white bricks and folds the blade. 'Fucking Koopman. I didn't see that coming.'

'Who is Koopman?' asks Meeks. 'He one of your lot?'

North doesn't reply. This has changed everything. His empire crumbles in an instant. The coke on the top layer is substantial – North calculates it might be as much as ten per cent of the total, and eighty kilos of cocaine is still a fuckload of drugs – but it isn't enough for King Dec. Christ, with eight hundred kilos a man could become a god. Instead, he's reduced to scrubbing around in the dirt with the rest of the grimy little fuckers. North has seen first-hand in Colombia what serious money means, what eight-hundred-kilo money means. It means buying a country, or a big enough part of it as makes no difference. It's insulation money, get-out-of-jail money, cartel money, King money, money that could be parlayed into an empire. *His* fucking money.

And someone has taken it. Why didn't he think about Koopman? His son is the cunt they barbequed on Crosby Beach. He and Kite and everyone else assumed that Koopman turned up as the Avenging Angel, or some such shit. But what if he was the one who sent White out there? What if Koopman has been leveraging this whole scheme, working Stevie White behind Gelagotis's back? It makes sense, doesn't it? Maybe Koopman and Stevie were going to let Gelagotis step up to The Russian, get the Scousers in on the new arrangement and then move on Gelagotis themselves?

It's a big stretch but the pieces fit together too neatly for Declan North's comfort. Koopman was Stevie White's father and the fruit doesn't fall far from the tree.

Koopman has the connections in Liverpool to put a potential squeeze on the delivery.

322

Koopman is a fucking Australian now, which is where all the trouble has come from.

Every time it's Koopman, Koopman, Koopman.

'This is wrong,' says North. He stands close to Link and Meeks. 'We need to get this stuff out of here, get it sold, get it off our hands.' He looks at Link. 'Where were you going to take it?'

Link glances at Meeks. 'Stef's the mover.'

Meeks scratches the side of his face. 'It was going all over. Sydney, Melbourne, Brissy. You name it.'

'The biggest single buyer?' says North.

'Perth,' says Meeks. 'The bikies.'

North raises his eyebrows.

'They can handle eighty over there?'

'Shit, yeah,' says Meeks. 'Lazarus can shift that amount, no sweat. They were expecting fifty before . . . before, this.'

'That's the contact's name, Lazarus?'

Meeks nods. As he does so, North whips the knife he's unfolded in his pocket and jams the blade up through the underside of Meeks's jaw. It travels through his soft palate and cuts deep into his brain.

Tony Link reacts, but not quickly enough. At North's sudden movement he recoils instinctively and reaches into his jacket. North glimpses the black butt of a gun sticking up from a shoulder holster. He pulls the knife out of Meeks and slashes down across Link's arm. The blade slices into him above the elbow and Link grunts. Link swings an in-effectual left at North and staggers against one of the Jags. Blood splashes on the tarp. North moves closer as Link manages to get his left hand on his gun. But he's coming at it wrong, from the other side, and he fumbles. North headbutts him, breaking his nose, stabbing him almost

323

simultaneously in the belly. Backed up against the car, Link drops the gun and North rams his blade into Link's ear. Link screams and North stabs him again, this time driving the knife down into the man's exposed neck. Link drops to one knee and flaps ineffectually at North's wrist. North steps back as blood arcs from Link's neck and splashes against the side of the nearest car. The man falls twitching to the floor of the lock-up, his eyes wide and bubbling sounds coming from his blood-streaked mouth.

North moves out of range and waits for Link to die. Then, like a man negotiating rock pools, he steps closer and pulls the corpse away from the Jags using his collar, the man's blood leaving a fat red smear across the concrete.

Lying slumped against the rear wall of the lock-up, Stefan Meeks is still alive. Just. Taking care not to get any more blood on his clothing or shoes, North walks across to him and stabs him in the heart. Meeks clutches the air spastically and then lies still, his head against the wall, pushing his chin down onto his scarlet chest.

The lock-up is silent.

North takes a moment to control his breathing.

The instant North found out about the missing cocaine, Link and Meeks were dead men. He knows it's unlikely either of them had anything to do with the double-cross. If that was the case, they'd have little to gain from bringing him to the lock-up. His reasoning runs like this: if Meeks or Link, or both, took the cocaine, the next logical step was to kill North. He was the connection back to Liverpool, and North knows they would never have brought him in here if they weren't completely confident the cocaine was in its rightful place. And once North knew the best destination for the coke – Perth – and had a name – Lazarus – Meeks and Link simply became witnesses or, if you wanted to be mercenary, men who would need paying. And with ninety per cent of his shipment missing, Declan North is in no mood to cut two miserable Aussies in. With eight hundred kilos to distribute, their contribution was vital and their cut bearable. With eighty, they were expendable.

Now all that's left is to clean up.

North rolls Link onto his back and finds the keys to the Lexus. He checks his own clothing for obvious signs of blood and moves to the door. He lifts the metal roller and looks outside. The lot is empty, baking in the heat of a Gold Coast morning. He walks quickly to Link's Lexus and drives it into the lock-up, closing the door behind him.

Next he strips the tarps from the Jags and balls them into a corner. Then he strips nude and places his clothes on the car furthest from the blood. He carefully lifts out the cocaine and checks every brick. Whoever replaced the coke used chalk, making the fakes easy to spot. The authentic bricks are shifted to one side of the lock-up, the fakes crumbled into the back seat of the middle Jag. Eventually, North has found all the cocaine in the first Jag. He wipes his brow and repeats the process with the other two cars. The whole thing takes him well over an hour.

Satisfied he has all the cocaine, he loads the genuine bricks into the unmarked Jag.

Then comes the awkward bit.

He walks across to Link and heaves him into a sitting position. He lifts Link's gun from his holster and places it in the Jag containing the cocaine. North returns to Link and lifts him from behind. With his arms under his armpits, North levers him into the middle of the three Jags. He puts Meeks in the back and breathes deeply. His body is coated in sweat and blood, chalk and cocaine residue; a nightmare vision. He finds a litre bottle of mineral water in the Lexus. Using a section of untouched tarp, he cleans his face and hands. The rest can be covered until he has a chance to properly clean up back at the hotel.

Now North gets dressed. He replaces his clothes and checks himself in the wing mirror of the Lexus. He will pass.

North rips three long strips from another section of tarp. He opens the petrol tank of the Lexus and forces the strips inside. Once soaked, he puts a strip into the tank of two of the Jags and leaves one in Link's car. He opens the lock-up door and reverses the Jag containing the cocaine out into the sun. He goes back into the lock-up and closes the door one more time.

He produces a lighter and lights each of the rags. When they're flaming he opens the lock-up door and quickly closes it behind him. Unhurried, he gets into the Jag and pulls out of the lot and onto the road, pointing the car back towards Surfers. He waits patiently at a set of lights about fifty metres from the perimeter of the lock-up.

The first car explodes as the lights turn green. North presses the accelerator and his rear-view mirror fills with fire.

It takes him twenty minutes to get back to his hotel, the one organised by Tony Link. North checked in under a false name and, naturally, Link paid the tab. North parks the Jag on a side street, his mind rearing up at the unpalatable thought of leaving eighty kilos of coke parked in the middle of Surfers Paradise. But there's nothing else for it. He doesn't want the Jag caught on hotel CCTV.

North crosses the lobby and goes to his room. He showers thoroughly and changes into fresh clothes; board shorts and t-shirt. He puts sunglasses on his forehead and thongs on his feet, turning himself from businessman to pale-skinned tourist.

He cleans the room, taking particular care to wipe surfaces he may have touched. Then he takes his suitcase to the lift down to the basement car park, avoiding the hotel lobby. He exits, walking, less than half an hour after coming back. He puts his suitcase in the thankfully unmolested Jag and drives to the back-up hotel, where he parks in the secure underground garage.

Job completed, North sits on the bed and looks at the slip of paper Link has given him, the vein pulsing in his temple.

Koopman is up to his neck in this.

57

It's over.

It stands to reason. With Kite dead, it's obvious to Koop that whoever killed him has moved a few rungs up the food chain and taken over whatever deal Stevie was involved with. It sounds very much like the same thing has happened in Australia, if what Keane told him about Gelagotis is accurate.

A feeding frenzy. Blood in the water.

Koop's seen it before in Liverpool at first hand. The money getting bigger, the temptations greater, and the young sharks circle, looking for their bite out of the carcass.

There are always younger sharks. Kite was one once, back when Koop was putting together The Untouchables. A nasty, vicious scally who clambered his way out of the slime and up the ladder until it happened to him.

It must have been a hell of a shock, reflects Koop. Kite was so cocksure, so certain of his own invincibility, that he forgot Rule One: watch your back. If Keane was right it was this North who did it. North must have been the guy at The Granary. He has a vague recollection of an unsmiling and unremarkable face, of a hand reaching inside a jacket . . .

Koop steps from the shower and reaches for a towel from the stack. He dries himself and shaves, careful not to cut himself as the A380 bobbles through some minor turbulence.

Flying at thirty-eight thousand feet, the Emirates flight is two hours out of Dubai with another twelve to go before Sydney, and Koop plans to have at least one more shower on board before landing. He seriously doubts he'll ever get the chance to do it again. The first-class flight is Koop's reward to himself after what has happened. He could have changed his ticket, but he simply didn't want to.

He sips his bourbon and looks at himself in the mirror. The events of the past days have not left any visible signs on Menno Koopman. He's a little tired, and his ribs still ache from the beating he took at the gallery, but the decadent surroundings of the flight are beginning to work on him. He feels rejuvenated, filled with desire for Zoe. Not to mention Melumi. Zoe is mad at him, he knows that – he's already tried calling her twice from the airport and once from the plane on the leg to Dubai – but he also knows it'll be fine when he gets back. That there'll be retribution coming his way somewhere down the track, he has no doubt, but nothing too terrible. He expects that she'll probably simply take off for a time, perhaps with Mel in tow. Punishment by denial of privileges. The age-old female prerogative.

Koop dresses and returns to his seat. A gorgeous, smiling hostess has made it up into a full bed while he's been showering. Koop lies back and thinks about what Keane said. With every passing mile he draws nearer to home, the thought of getting back into harness with this Eckhardt character is becoming less and less attractive.

He'll see him, Koop decides, out of politeness, but that will be as far as it goes. This North can do whatever he wants so long as he stays out of Koop's life. And he can't think of a single reason why North wouldn't do exactly that. Koop has failed. Kite was dead, but that was nothing to do with him. From what Koop could put together, North is now the main player in whatever deal Stevie was mixed up with. The idea of pursuing North in Australia seems as deranged as chasing a great white into the surf.

No, Koop thinks, it's over. He lies back and drifts effortlessly into sleep.

North can keep the drugs.

58

'More chips, love?'

Dot Halligan fusses over her boys as she has done every Sunday of their lives; those that they have spent outside prison, that is. She ladles fried chips onto their plates without waiting for an answer. Dean wades in, spearing his fork into the fresh stack, his eyes not leaving the football showing on the vast plasma TV set. By contrast, Matty only nibbles the end of a chip as onscreen a flamboyant Suarez flashes a volley over the bar.

Dot, who watches her boys like a lioness, is beginning to worry about Matty. Well-dressed and immaculate as ever, he looks too thin. Dot prefers a man to have some padding. Like Dean, who resembles his father – God rot his eternal frigging soul, the lazy fat fucking bastard – more and more with every passing day.

Dot takes her place on her favoured armchair after a final check that the boys have everything they could possibly need. Beans, chicken, carrots, peas, chips, bread and butter on their plates, and sauce bottles – tomato for Matty, HP for Dean – standing like sentries on the opposing arms of the sofa.

What conversation there is centres around the hopes for Liverpool's season, and exactly how useless each and every player in red is, with the exception of the sainted Stevie G. Dot doesn't listen. She enjoys the sound of the male voices in her living room. She doesn't like football. After spending all of her sixty-five years living within walking distance of Anfield, she doesn't know the rules of the game, although, like all Liverpool women, she knows the names of those players who feature heavily in almost all discussions in every house or social function she has ever attended.

As she eats, Dot notices that it's Dean who is more animated, Matty doing just enough to keep the talk flowing. Matty's eyes are dark and she notices lines beginning to appear at the corners of his mouth.

'Everything OK, son?'

At his mother's question, Dean looks up from his plate and across at Matty, a sly smile on his face. 'Yeah, you alright, la?'

'Yeah, course, why?' Matty says, avoiding Dean's grinning face.

'You havin' too many late nights? Chasing girls again?'

Dean turns back to the TV, unwilling to trust himself not to laugh. He shakes his head a fraction, a gesture noticed by Matty who throws a chip at him. Unseen by his mother, Dean mouths the words 'you big poof' at him.

'I've been working too hard, Ma,' says Matty. 'We both 'ave.'

'Well, eat up, son,' says Dot. 'You're fadin' away. I've seen more friggin' meat on a butcher's apron.'

'OK,' says Matty. 'I'll do that.'

As the three finish their meal, Liverpool pull a goal ahead while Dot is clearing the plates, temporarily blocking Dean's view of the screen.

'Fuckin' 'ell, Ma!' says Dean, pushing his mother to one side and leaning to catch the replay. 'Out the fuckin' way!'

'Language, Dean! What would Father Flaherty say?'

'He'd say, "Out the fuckin' way, please,"' whispers Matty as Dot retreats to the kitchen. Dean creases up and takes out a cigarette.

'Not in the house, Dean!' His mother's voice cuts through the excited chatter of the commentary.

'Come on, dick 'ead,' says Dean, getting to his feet. He looks at Matty. 'Ready, you big shirt-lifter?'

Matty stands and fakes a punch to Dean's balls.

'In yer dreams,' says Dean. He walks into the kitchen and kisses his mother.

'You goin' already? You've only just got 'ere!'

Dean jerks a thumb in the direction of the street. 'We're meetin' up with some of the lads,' he says. 'Watch the second 'alf in the pub.'

Matty takes a length of kitchen roll and wraps a leg of chicken in it. He places it into a plastic zip-lock bag and drops it into his jacket pocket.

Dot washes her hands and dries them on a tea towel. She kisses both her boys and walks them to the door. Both were born in this house and if Dot Halligan had her way, both would stay there for the rest of their lives.

Matty opens the front door which exits directly onto the terraced street. 'See you, Ma,' he says and presses a thick wad of banknotes into her hand. As always, she pretends not to want it and, as always, Matty insists she take it. It's a ritual that has been going on for two or three years, the amounts rising markedly over the past eight months in line with the Halligans' business interests expanding healthily under the Keith Kite umbrella.

Dean's Porsche Cayenne is parked directly in front of the house. Dean's sister's boy, Darren, is standing next to it on his BMX bike, along with three or four other boys, all dressed in identical fashion: light-coloured tracksuits, brand new white trainers, baseball caps.

'Alright, Dean, la,' says Darren.

Dean grabs Darren in a headlock and rubs his gelled hair wildly.

'Fuck off, nob 'ead!' Darren struggles. His high-pitched adolescent voice making Dean laugh more.

'Come on, stop dickin' about.' Matty is standing by the passenger door, his fingers drumming impatiently against the roof of the car.

Dean releases the boy and presses a fifty into his hand. 'Get some more gel, Daz. You look like a fuckin' spaz.'

Darren runs a hand through his hair as Matty and Dean get into the Porsche.

Dean notices a man across the street, one of his mother's neighbours, standing in his open doorway, glancing momentarily in his direction.

'What do you want, Simpson, you nosy fucking dick?' shouts Dean from the driver's seat, his head out of the window. Simpson does not meet Dean's stare. Instead, he drops his chin and closes the door.

'That's right, dickhead. Bye bye.'

Dean gives Darren a meaningful glance and the boy nods. Simpson's window will be smashed tonight and he will do nothing about it. Dean seldom punishes any of his mother's neighbours for perceived slights – Dot has to live here, after all – but Simpson rubs him up the wrong way. It never hurts to remind the natives that the Halligans' bark is backed up with bite. Besides, it will give Darren something to do.

Dean pulls away and passes the corner pub. He navigates the familiar labyrinth of red-brick and concrete until they're out of Kirkdale and heading south along the Dock Road. On their right, monolithic warehouses between them and the river; on their left, a ragged string of used-car dealerships, greasy spoon cafés, wood yards, scabby looking council houses, dilapidated gyms and taxi firms. At Vulcan Street, Dean turns the car into the fenced-in yard of a builder's merchant. He parks the Porsche out of sight between two empty skips and he and Matty move inside the office.

Two middle-aged men in overalls are laughing at something on a computer screen. The laughter stops abruptly as the Halligans come in.

'Porn?' says Dean, with a nod to the screen. 'You two should know better at your age.'

'Sorry, Dean,' says the taller of the two. He sits back at the desk.

'No need to sit down, Terry,' Matty says. He gestures towards the window with a thumb. 'You and Noel do one. We'll lock up.'

The men stand and move to the door.

'Any visitors?' says Dean.

'No-one. Sunday, like.'

'OK, good. Right, like Matty said, fuck off.'

When both men have driven off, Matty takes a key from his pocket and the Halligans leave the office and walk across to the large warehouse which serves as a store for the building company they own: a legitimate and profitable concern that comes in very handy for cleaning their money.

At the door they greet Tyson, the yard's rottweiler, who has been barking maniacally at their approach. Matty lifts the chicken leg from his pocket and holds it out. Tyson snuffles it up greedily and sits down heavily on the concrete.

Leaving Tyson outside, Matty and Dean unlock the warehouse and climb a set of steel stairs to a mezzanine floor which occupies the back half of the building's upper level. Planks and lengths of timber are stacked neatly against the back wall, the remaining space being taken up with an assortment of builders' equipment.

In one corner is a battered metal cabinet about two metres high and half a metre in depth. Matty slides a key into the large new padlock on the front and opens the doors wide. As his eyes fall on the contents, the hairs on his neck rise and he feels his sphincter tighten.

Bright white bricks of cocaine, shrink-wrapped and shiny, are stacked neatly, filling two-thirds of the cabinet.

Matty and Dean Halligan exchange glances.

'We fuckin' did it.' Dean's voice contains equal measures of glee and awe. He stands looking at the stack, shaking his solid head from side to side. He grips Matty around the shoulders. 'Me and me fuckin' little bum-bandit brother took the fuckin' lot!'

Matty shrugs out of Dean's grasp. He closes the doors and locks the padlock.

'Not quite the lot, Dean.'

'Alright, smart-arse. Ninety fuckin' per cent then.' Dean sticks his arms out wide and runs around the mezzanine in the manner of Stevie G celebrating a goal.

'Easy, Dean. We're not there yet.'

'Fuck that. It's done. It's over. No-one expected the fuckin' scallies to get their hands on it all. No-one.'

'North will know.'

Dean's face darkens momentarily at the mention of

Declan North. 'Will he fuck. He'll know something's happened, but he'll be looking at Koopman.'

Matty looks dubious. 'You think so? Sounds thin to me.'

Dean takes out a cigarette and lights up. 'Doesn't matter. Dracula said he was taking care of it. By the time North wakes up to the fact it was us, he'll be dead.'

'Dracula said? Well, that must be alright, then. You think you can trust that cunt?'

From the yard comes the sound of Tyson barking.

'Talk of the devil,' says Dean. 'That must be him.'

The brothers throw a dust sheet over the cabinet and walk back out into the yard. A two-year-old Ford is pulling up in front of the warehouse. Dean bends down to see the driver and Matty opens the warehouse doors. The Ford slides in and Matty closes the doors behind them.

The driver steps clear of the car and shakes hands briefly with each of the Halligans.

'Alright, Dracula,' says Dean. He drags on his cigarette and smiles.

'I told you not to call me that,' says the driver.

'Alright,' says Matty. 'We won't. What would you prefer; Eric or Mr Perch?'

'Neither,' says Detective Chief Inspector Eric Perch. 'As far as I'm concerned, we don't know each other.'

59

The two bodies in the burnt-out lock-up have changed everything.

Eckhardt is at the scene but OCG make it very clear that from here on in, the whole thing is going to be theirs. Collins, the senior assigned by Chris Chakos on the OCG side, is pleasant enough about it, but he wants all Eckhardt's files and he wants them now. When he finds out that Eckhardt has snapped Link and Meeks at the lock-up a few days before with Jimmy Gelagotis, Collins almost creams.

In truth, Eckhardt doesn't mind too much. He's used to OCG arriving late and grabbing the glory. To be fair, they've also been running a file on the Kolomiets case and, for all Warren knows, theirs may have been a fat and juicy one that contained the key to the Holy Grail.

But he doubts it. Not going on their reaction after he found Meeks and Link.

Eckhardt pokes around the edges of the crime scene for a while without expecting to get very much. Collins and his team have set up shop in a mobile unit parked at Red Rooster, although privately Eckhardt thinks they're wasting time looking for forensics other than bullets.

The place is ashes.

All that remains of Meeks and Link are two twisted black shapes who have morphed into what remained of what was once a fine Jaguar. A second Jag and a Lexus are also now just smouldering hulks.

The roof of the lock-up is gone, as is most of the back wall. There's a layer of wet ash underfoot and the place reeks of burnt flesh and rubber.

Across the parking lot, Red Rooster is doing great business.

Eckhardt walks outside, crosses the tapes and leans against the side of the mobile unit. He slides out a cigarette and sucks down the smoke. He's only taken a couple of drags when Collins joins him.

'Smoking as much as ever, Warren?' Collins says. He's carrying a card file which he uses to waft the smoke away.

What do you think? Jesus. Eckhardt lifts the cigarette from his mouth in a what-can-you-do gesture. 'I'm a slave to it. Is everyone at OCG a health nut or just you and Chakos?'

Eckhardt remembers the conversation with Keane. 'You spoke to the Poms?'

Collins nods. 'I talked to a DI Moresby. He gave me what they had at their end. The trouble is there's nothing concrete.'

Warren Eckhardt lets that pass. If OCG classes the deaths of Kite and Stevie White as 'nothing concrete', there's little to be said.

'What about Koopman?'

Collins moves to look in his file and then remembers.

'The retired cop? Moresby says he's out. Nothing to do with Kite. Which makes him nothing to do with our thing.'

'So you don't object if I talk to him? DI Keane mentioned he might be useful.'

'Keane?'

'Another Pom. He's out of the loop over there. From what he tells me.'

'Knock yourself out, Warren,' says Collins. 'I'll pick up on Koopman if I need to. I think he's a loose end at best. We have these two bodies, plus Kolomiets, Gelagotis and the bodyguard over here. That's enough to be going on with.'

Eckhardt can't work out if Collins is dumb, or is playing dumb. Can't OCG trace the connections, see that this is all one thing, that it's a straight-down-the-line dogfight over some deal? If the body count is anything to go by, it must be a hell of a deal.

And then the penny drops.

OCG *have* made the connections on this.

Or they're making them. They just don't want me involved, but Collins doesn't want to come out and say it. Giving me Koopman is his plan to ease me out of the way.

Fuck it. If they're giving him a free run at Koopman, that's exactly where he'll go.

60

North didn't know what a ute was until today, although he's seen plenty of them driving around. Tradesmen's vehicles, as commonplace as pigeons in London.

He places his suitcase in the cab behind the driver's seat and gets in. He paid cash for it at a sprawling used-car dealership near Nerang, dressing down in khaki shirt, jeans and workboots for the sale. A baseball cap and sunglasses complete the look.

After the fire, North had driven the Jag back to his hotel, and picked up his stuff. He hadn't checked out; the room had been paid for upfront for a week. By then, in the unlikely event of being traced to that hotel, he'd be long gone.

North drove the Jag to a large shopping mall where he bought clothes, including the jeans and boots. He took a cab out to Nerang and bought the truck, a plain white one with eighty thousand kilometres on the clock. The dealership looked to be a good one and the truck seemed reliable.

It would need to be.

North adds a solid box cover for the rear tray before picking up a number of supplies at a hardware store, including a large metal lock-box which he has bolted to the floor of the tray at a 4x4 specialist workshop. He takes the truck back to the mall where he parks it and the Jag at the most distant corner. In a spot hidden from most people, North unhurriedly unloads the cocaine and places it in the new lock-box. To an observer he looks like a mechanic attending to a broken car. When he reaches the last brick, he slices into it and discreetly chops out a line on the top of the lock-box. With a look round to check he is completely unobserved, North snorts the coke.

He reseals the brick, stows it with the rest and locks the box before taking the Jag to a nearby car wash where he runs it through a complete cycle. Returning to the shopping mall he wipes the interior clean using a bottle of spray disinfectant and a cloth from the supplies bought at the hardware store. He locks the car and places the keys under a large stone, one of many in the adjacent landscaped strip. He has no plans ever to return to the Jag but you never knew. He doesn't want the keys on him in the event of arrest, but to throw them away could be wasteful.

His tasks complete, North gets in the ute and drives out of the shopping mall. He has a clean car, a rifle, Link's gun, several knives, eighty kilos of cocaine, three thousand kilometres ahead of him, and a buyer at the end of it.

And one last thing to take care of.

61

Koop's Emirates flight touches down in a windy Sydney at six in the morning. Two hours later he hops a VirginBlue flight north to Coolangatta and is blinking in the Gold Coast sunshine by nine-thirty.

He tried calling Zoe from Sydney when he landed, and standing outside the arrivals gate he tries her again now, but she isn't picking up. He calls her mobile too, but since they seldom have reception out at Nashua, he doesn't worry too much about that. His best bet is that she and Mel have taken off somewhere. Zoe and Mel enjoyed a long weekend out towards Tenterfield earlier in the year and Koop hopes that's where they are.

Clutching his meagre plastic bag of belongings, he walks into the terminal, the sky over the hills behind him an ominous blue-black. Mount Warning – The Cloud Catcher – is shrouded. Rain is coming.

Inside, there's a man holding a scrawled sign with 'Koopman' written on it in black.

'Mr Koopman?' the man says in a gravel-laden voice and holds out a hand.

'I didn't order a pick-up,' says Koop.

'I know,' says the man. 'Warren Eckhardt. Queensland Police.'

Koop shakes hands. 'Frank said you might be in touch. I wasn't expecting it quite so soon.'

Warren Eckhardt rubs his chin. 'Well, I don't believe in waiting for things to happen, Mr Koopman. I've got bodies stacking up faster than I can count them and I think it's all connected to your son. I need to pick your brains. If you have any left after the journey.' He points outside the terminal towards a group of tables clustered around a bar. 'Why don't we find somewhere comfortable?'

With a perfect creamy flat white in front of him, Koop's spirits rise. Despite the first-class flight, the events of the past days have taken an inevitable toll.

He stirs a spoon of brown sugar into the foam and sips, his eyes closed.

'You have no idea how bad the coffee is in England, Mr Eckhardt.'

'Warren.'

'Warren. And please call me Koop.'

Eckhardt holds his cigarettes up for inspection. 'Do you mind?'

Koop does, but isn't inclined to get into that right now.

With almost comical relief Eckhardt drags on his cigarette and Koop is glad he hadn't objected. If ever a man looked like he needed a cigarette, it's Eckhardt. Eckhardt blows out a long line of smoke, wafting it away from Koop with his free hand.

'You were a cop, right?' Eckhardt doesn't wait for

an answer. He knows Koop's history. 'You went over to Liverpool to see what you could do about Stevie's death.' Again, it isn't a question.

Eckhardt takes another deep drag. 'We've had some bodies over here, Koop. Five in all that I think are linked to Stevie's murder. OCS might feel the same way too, but so far they're not letting me in on that information.'

'*Five?*' Keane had mentioned three.

'The last two showed up yesterday. Burnt.' Eckhardt's eyes flick to Koop.

'Like Stevie.'

'Like Stevie. But not . . . not tortured.'

'That's the link?'

'No offence, Koop, but do I look like someone who'd think that was enough? The two who turned up dead will, in my opinion, turn out to be Tony Link and Stefan Meeks.'

Koop looks blank.

'No, you won't know them,' says Eckhardt. 'They are – or were – two of Jimmy Gelagotis's boys. Just like Stevie was.'

Koop sits up a little straighter. Eckhardt is telling his story well. Koop can see why Keane wanted them to meet, but can't see where he fits in. Not yet, anyway.

'And this Gelagotis?'

'Well, this is where it all gets interesting. Or more complicated, depending on your point of view. Gelagotis also turned up dead a couple of days ago in the back yard of a potential witness against him. A thirteen-year-old boy. Gelagotis was armed and the boy was pretty clear that he was going to kill him if he hadn't been shot first.'

'The boy shot Gelagotis?'

'No, he was killed by a head shot from a high-calibre rifle from somewhere in the scrub behind the boy's house. No sign of the killer. No witnesses.'

Eckhardt stubs out his cigarette and lights another. He coughs wetly and looks at Koop ruefully. 'These things are going to kill me.'

Yes they will, thinks Koop, if you keep sucking them down like breath mints. 'Something has to,' he says.

Once his next cigarette is lit, Eckhardt continues. 'The boy that Gelagotis was after had been a witness in a murder two weeks back. A Ukrainian called Kolomiets and his minder, Bytchkov. It doesn't take a genius to figure out who was behind that. Even OCS could join the dots.'

'A take-over,' Koop says, sick that a son of his could be involved like this. Thirteen-year-old boys. Jesus.

Eckhardt nods, smoke streaming from his nostrils. He reminds Koop of a bull. 'Exactly. Gelagotis stepped up to Kolomiets to seize control of . . . something, I don't know yet. Bytchkov was in the way, which is why he died.'

'And Gelagotis came back to the boy,' says Koop. 'When he heard there was a witness.'

'Or thought better about not killing the boy first time round.'

'And where does Stevie come in? Was he involved with Gelagotis going after the boy?'

'I don't know,' says Eckhardt. 'I don't think so. Stevie had left by then. He was no angel, but there's nothing to suggest he was at that level. Let me run this past you. Gelagotis, along with Meeks and Link, work freelance for The Russian. There's a deal happening, or some sort of turf thing. I'm going for a deal because I'm of the opinion that it's linked with Liverpool. And it's linked with Liverpool because that's where Stevie turned up dead. Gelagotis

346

sends Stevie across to break the news to someone in Liverpool that there's been a change in personnel at the Australian end.'

'And that doesn't go down well with the people there.' Koop can imagine how some of the men he knows would have reacted to that news. How Kite would have reacted. 'Stevie was the messenger.'

'Exactly.'

'So who killed Gelagotis? This Link, or Meeks?'

'I don't think so,' says Eckhardt. He pauses. 'I was speaking to Frank Keane. He said that someone at his end had been killed too.'

'Keith Kite. He must have been the connection.'

Eckhardt has put this thing together nicely. To Koop, it feels right.

'They're all killing each other,' says Koop. 'But who killed these last two?'

'The same person who killed Kite, I would say. Wouldn't you?'

Koop doesn't reply. He's thinking about Keith Kite leaning in close to him at the art gallery in Liverpool, his blood dripping down from the wound in his forehead and his busted nose. He said something that Koop didn't register. Until now.

I'm sending someone your way.

Koop stands up too quickly, knocking his cup onto the concrete, his movements panicked, his bowels liquid. He sees the man who was drinking water at the gallery.

Declan North.

I'm sending someone your way.

Zoe.

62

Mel flicks a switch and the bubbles in the hot tub gurgle into life. Zoe sinks down gratefully, her spine resting against Mel's breasts, and sighs deeply. It's been hard with Koop away and she deserves – *they* deserve – to kick back. She feels Mel doing something unseen behind her that involves a number of small motions, and then a hand reaches round holding a lit joint. Zoe flicks water from her right hand as best she can and grabs it from Mel.

'Thanks, sexy,' she says, and takes a drag before passing it over her shoulder. They smoke the rest in similar fashion, safe in the knowledge that Koop is in mid-air somewhere over Asia. They do smoke in front of him from time to time, and Koop doesn't, in all honesty, care very much. But a lifetime of chasing drug dealers and being around users with less style than Zoe or Mel has left him with a jaundiced view of cannabis. So he usually chooses not to be around when they indulge. And Zoe, recognising the difficulty the dope poses to Koop, is always tactful.

Now, though, it is heavenly lying in the bubbles, the smoke drifting up into the flawless Northern Rivers night sky. A flying fox, looking like something from a vampire movie, flaps its papery wings and wheels through the darkness above the tub, black against black. It's quiet. Even Ringo has finally stopped barking, thank God. They're going to have to do something about that overactive hound.

The phone rings and Zoe lets it go. It's probably Koop again. He's already left two messages and Zoe wants him to stew. She knows he's on his way back, that's enough. In fact, her anger has worn off and if she wasn't in the hot tub with Mel, she'd have answered. Instead, she lets it ring out. She'll call him tomorrow morning when his flight gets in and tell him to hurry home.

The tub, which sits on the corner of the deck, juts out over a small escarpment, the ground falling away in front of it so that you appear to be sitting on the edge of a great precipice. Zoe likes to luxuriate in it, preferably with one or two sexy people, and, like now, smoke a pre-sex joint. No-one can see them. From where they are, the nearest house is several hundred metres away and concealed by a fold in the land. The road doesn't intrude on their view, and the pitch-black country night cloaks all sins. Zoe even likes the lights set into the bottom of the tub, the colours slowly changing. There's enough left in her of the child who grew up in grey post-war Liverpool to thrill at the sparkly Hollywoodiness of the hot tub.

If this is kitsch, she thinks, Mel lovingly caressing a nipple, then give me kitsch. She squirms the base of her spine pleasurably against Mel's pussy. Mel's legs are spread on either side of Zoe's thighs and she can feel her skin vibrating softly against her own. Zoe angles her head backwards and, taking care of what she's doing with the business end of the remaining joint, gives Mel a deep slow kiss.

'Better?' says Mel as they break apart with a smile.

Zoe nods. 'Mmm.'

'Have you heard from Koop?' Mel knows Zoe has, but it's a way into the subject. She understands Zoe's formidable temper and has plans for this evening that don't require her girlfriend to be excited. Not in that way, anyway.

Zoe grunts in the affirmative and points in the direction of the phone. 'He's phoned a couple of times and left messages. Nice ones, too. Clever bastard knows how to make me see things his way. Even if he *is* wrong.'

'Does he know when he's coming back?'

'Tomorrow,' murmurs Zoe. 'Now turn those bubbles off and let's get comfortable, shall we?'

As the hum of the pump fades, Zoe shifts to face Mel, who settles against the wall of the tub, only her head above water. Zoe reaches underneath and cups Mel's buttocks in her hands, propping the back of her thighs along her own strong upper arms. She angles Mel higher in the water until her pussy mound rises clear, steam floating from it as the night air cools. With a teasing smile, Zoe bends forward and lightly licks her. Mel groans extravagantly. God, she feels in the mood tonight. All this upset has meant a break in action and Mel is a woman who needs regular sex.

She arches forward, pushing her sex into Zoe's face. Zoe, taller and stronger than her lover, holds Mel firmly. Her mouth dances, flicking a tongue out to brush Mel again and again, each fresh touch eliciting a new groan of pleasure. Then, judging the moment precisely, she slides her tongue down and then up, pressing it deep between Mel's flaring labia. Zoe flicks Mel's clitoris and she bucks, water splashing noisily over the side as her breathing changes pitch and she clings to the edge of the hot tub as if it is a life raft.

Twenty metres away, safe from sight in the shadow of Zoe's studio, and undisturbed by Ringo who is lying dead at his feet, Declan North adjusts the focus on his binoculars and tries to control his own breathing. The binoculars are held in place by a webbing headband, freeing the hands for whatever they want. North uses the freedom to undo his belt, take his cock out and begin to masturbate.

63

Ella doesn't know what's going on.

Jimmy is dead, she knows that. It's been on the news. She keeps expecting the police to arrive and question her. But three days have gone and there's been no-one.

It begins to dawn on her that no-one knows about her. That no-one knows – yet – about the unit in Q1. Only that horrible Tony and Stefan.

And that makes her think something else: Meeks and Link are dead too. If either of those mongrels was alive she'd have heard something, even if it was just Meeks sniffing round Jimmy's leavings. There was something on the news this morning about two men found dead in a lock-up. They weren't named but Ella now reads between the lines. There was mention of a Lexus. Tony Link drives a Lexus.

She *knows* it.

Ella opens a bottle of wine. Ten in the morning but what does it matter? She pours out a big glass, sits in Jimmy's favourite chair and wonders what to do.

Staying here is possible. The unit is bought and paid for. There'd be no reason for anyone to come here; Jimmy's wife knows nothing about the apartment. Down the line Ella would have to deal with details she hasn't had to cope with before: rates, body corporate fees and all that. But right now she's safe.

And she is getting out of this shit. It's too much. That mpeg clip Jimmy was sent. He told her it was fake but she knew better. She knows the clip is real. She knows it has something to do with Jimmy's death.

And she knows it's on his computer.

Another thing she knows is that she definitely doesn't want to watch it ever again.

But someone might.

The day before, Ella found Warren Eckhardt's business card on Jimmy's desk. It's propped up against the monitor. Now she picks it up again and sees that Eckhardt has an email address.

She puts down her wine, sits at the computer and logs on. As far as Jimmy knew, she was too stupid to operate the computer, unless it was for shopping. She never corrected this misunderstanding. Computers are as natural to her as hair-straighteners or mobile phones, but she found that appearing to be an idiot often paid dividends. She spends five minutes making a new email account using fake address details. It isn't much camouflage; a forensic computer specialist would be able to track her down soon enough, but what she plans to do isn't illegal. She contemplates not sending the clip, staying under the radar as long as possible, but there's something else she wants more. She wants to be on the right side for once. With Jimmy gone, she can be. It's time to become a real person again.

Ella types Eckhardt's email address into the 'to' panel and adds the 'Stevie Wonder' mpeg. Without opening the clip, she sends it to Eckhardt with a brief message: 'received by Jimmy Gelagotis'.

Then she sits by the window and finishes her wine, a rare smile on her gorgeous face.

64

The Halligans are beginning to shift the mountain of coke.

With Eric Perch taking a few more risks to speed things along, they're able to move it out significantly faster than Kite was ever able to. Approximately one third goes in a straight shipment to Rotterdam, the cash being wired to accounts set up in advance. This shipment is the riskiest as it involves another cross-border transfer, but it's worth it for the money it brings in so quickly. The rest begins to be moved out onto the streets of Britain in the usual ways, being sold on to smaller distributors who then sell it on down the line.

A series of holding companies has been put together by a kiddy fiddling accountant saved from prison by Perch's intervention. He owes the copper his life and repays it with the sort of service usually reserved for popes, conducted at arm's length from the accountant's cottage in the Scottish Highlands.

Perch isn't stupid. He makes sure there is no more double-crossing, by the simple tactic of making the Halligans and him mutually dependent. The Halligans need his protection and his expertise; he needs the drugs they acquired by crossing Declan North. That was a master-stroke, double-crossing the double-crosser.

Assuming North doesn't come back and kill them all.

Perch and Matty Halligan discussed that at length in bed, Declan North not being the only one who shared Matty's predilection for violent sex.

'It's taken care of,' said Eric Perch.

'North's a fucking monster, Eric. You don't know what he can do.'

'Actually, I do.'

Perch has seen the autopsy report and photographs on both Stevie White and Keith Kite. And though he wouldn't have admitted as much to Matty Halligan, the thought of Declan North returning to England has caused him several sleepless nights.

But the steps he has taken will ensure that North never leaves Australia. As much as he has form as a killer, Perch is convinced that North will be no match for the men he has paid to kill the Irishman. It has cost him and the Halligans plenty, almost twenty per cent of their entire haul, but it will be worth it.

That's the thing with those East European villains.

They are the nastiest fuckers on the face of the earth.

65

The NSW cops have been at the property almost an hour by the time Koop and Eckhardt turn up. Koop recognises Sullivan from his visit to tell them about Stevie's death. It seems like an eternity ago now.

Eckhardt's Commodore brakes hard at the end of the driveway and Koop is out before it has completely stopped.

'Hey, hey!' says Sullivan. He grabs Koop's arm. 'It's OK, Mr Koopman. There's no sign there's been any violence.'

'Where's Zoe?' Koop tears his arm free and runs into the house.

'There's no-one here,' says Sullivan to Koop's back. He looks at Eckhardt. 'To be honest, we only stayed out of courtesy. The place is clean. No sign of forced entry, nothing to suggest there's a problem. We had to break a small window around the back to get in. The doors were locked.'

Koop comes outside, his face an unhealthy pallor. He can feel every mile of the past twenty-eight hours, first-class flight or not. He feels old, slow.

'What do you think?' says Eckhardt.

'I don't know,' says Koop. 'They may have left. I thought they might be in Tenterfield.'

'They?' says Sullivan.

'My wife and her friend. They like it out there. They went this year. They must have taken the dog.' Koop can hear himself gabbling and forces himself to slow down. Sullivan is right, there's no need to panic. Not yet. Zoe and Mel are probably at some lodge out west, letting him stew. Still, Koop knows he won't rest until he hears Zoe's voice again. There's something about the house that's nagging at him, but he can't put his finger on what it is.

Sullivan and his partner move towards their car. It's clear they're not buying the worst-case scenario.

'We'll keep an ear out for anything in the area,' says Sullivan. 'I'll let Central know about your concerns. I don't want you to think we're not taking this seriously.'

Koop likes Sullivan but can hear the disbelief in his voice. He doesn't blame him. He'd feel the same. An ex-IRA hitman coming to Nashua on a revenge killing spree? Really?

Koop shakes hands with the NSW cops. 'Call us if you hear anything,' says Sullivan. He exchanges a few words with Eckhardt and then Sullivan and his partner drive back down the track.

When they're gone, Eckhardt and Koop go over the house again. There's nothing. The place is clean.

Eckhardt sits at the kitchen table. He takes his cigarettes out and then thinks better of it. 'I could stay,' he says. 'If that's any easier.'

'Thanks, Warren,' says Koop, 'but I've made a big enough fool of myself already. Thanks for getting me down here so fast.'

Eckhardt shrugs.

'Zoe will turn up tomorrow or the day after. She's . . . independent. I should have known better.'

'I could use a beer if you've got one.' Eckhardt casts a hopeful look at the fridge.

Koop gets two bottles and sits down. They drink.

'Did you think you were going to find something in Liverpool?'

'I don't know. I hoped I wouldn't. Obviously. But it all seemed to make a sort of sense.'

'You think someone involved with a deal like this would break off to get revenge on you? For something you did to his ex-boss? The boss he probably diced up in your hotel room?'

'Not put like that,' admits Koop, 'no.'

'This North character. If he's got any sense he'll be long gone. Either out of the country or doing whatever he needs to do about this deal.'

Koop suddenly feels very tired. He rubs his jowls and leans forward, resting his head in his hands.

Eckhardt puts down his half-drunk beer and stands. 'Time for me to go,' he says. 'I was forgetting how tired you must be.'

Koop nods. He feels like he could sleep for a thousand years.

'It's the adrenaline,' says Eckhardt. 'Along with everything else. You get some rest and I'll call you in the morning. Your wife will probably have been in touch by then.'

Eckhardt leaves and Koop is alone in the house.

He sits for a few minutes nursing his beer and letting the silence grow. Suddenly he walks to the sink and pours out the remains of his drink.

He knows exactly what he's going to do. He's going to search the place again.

He goes through every room slowly, opening every cupboard and looking under all the beds. Thinking: like some scared kid at bedtime. Satisfied that the house contains nothing that doesn't belong there, he heads outside. It's mid-afternoon and the rain that's been threatening all day begins to fall. Koop watches a grey swathe drifting across the valley towards the property.

The first place he checks after the house is Zoe's studio. He opens the door and looks around. The place is spotless. Zoe's presentation notes for the GOMA thing are on her desk. Koop twinges with embarrassment as he remembers Mel telling him they won the job. He flicks through the papers on the desk.

Nothing.

The computer reveals a little more. Zoe last used it yesterday which means that she has, most likely, been ignoring his calls and decided to take off to coincide with his return. It was classic Zoe and makes Koop feel a little more optimistic.

He walks to his toolshed and checks it thoroughly as great fat drops begin to spatter against the tin roof. In the large tin shed they use as a garage, he checks the vehicles. He gets a jolt when he sees both cars there: his ute and Zoe's 4x4 side by side, before he remembers Mel's petrol-guzzling Prado.

He looks under both vehicles and checks them for . . . for what, exactly? For blood? For a note? A fucking lipstick-stained cigarette?

I'm too tired for this, he thinks. Zoe's in bed with Mel somewhere, laughing their arses off, while I'm out here playing Sherlock Holmes.

Koop leaves the garage and walks the rest of the property in the rain which is now coming down heavily.

He checks the copse of trees at the western edge and does what he can to check the creek. It's possible, he supposes, that something could be in there but since the water level is at the lowest he's seen it, he thinks it unlikely.

Soaked, Koop returns to the house.

He strips in the laundry room and puts his wet clothes in the wash basin to drain. He pads nude through the house and takes a long hot shower. A little refreshed, he dries off, dresses in some old clothes and makes himself a proper cup of coffee. As the scent of the roasted grounds wafts through the house, he begins to relax a little. He takes the coffee into the living room, sits on the couch and sinks back against the cushions.

More than an hour later he wakes with a start. His coffee lies cold and untouched on the low table and his mouth is dry as dust. In the kitchen he makes a fresh pot. This time he drinks it sitting outside on the deck watching the fig tree through the hammering rain.

Something is bothering him. Something he's seen that stubbornly refuses to rise to the surface.

He sits for some time as the light fades around him. He goes inside and calls Zoe and Mel's mobiles again with the same frustrating result. He calls Mel's home number and leaves another message on her answerphone, his voice now getting an edge to it. Teaching him a lesson is one thing. This is beginning to verge on cruelty.

Koop looks at his watch: 7.10 pm. His bed, their bed, is calling him but it's too early. Past experience has taught him that bed now will result in a sandy-eyed wake-up around two or three in the morning and a lousy day tomorrow. He wants to be as fresh as possible for Zoe's return.

He heats some beans and eats them standing up watching the kitchen TV.

Back on the couch he flicks through the stack of art books on the coffee table. It's one of Zoe's vices to buy more thick, glossy art books than any sane person could reasonably need. Koop can see that there's a point to this stack. All of them feature the British artists that Zoe's GOMA presentation is built around.

He turns the glossy pages. Tracy Emin. The infamous 'Myra' image by Marcus Harvey. Damien Hirst's incredible shark.

Zoe has Post-it notes in a number of places which show the shark image and Koop remembers she's used it as the centrepiece of their presentation to GOMA. He continues browsing and is brought up short at the photographs of the Gormley installation in Liverpool.

He closes the book quickly and walks out onto the decking, his breathing a little laboured. He sits in a chair and closes his eyes. The image of Stevie leaps unbidden into his mind as he knew it would. Not a live Stevie. Instead, Koop sees the brittle, charred thing that Stevie had become.

He opens his eyes. This is ridiculous. Bugger how early it is. He'll take a sleeping pill and crash out until the morning. As he turns back towards the house his eye catches a flicker of green light at the end of the deck and he remembers in an instant what it is that's been nagging away at him.

The hot tub.

In the dark of the evening a thin cast of green light has appeared along one edge of the hot tub cover that wasn't visible in the daylight.

Koop approaches the tub, his guts churning. He hasn't looked there, and neither, he suspects, has Sullivan.

Koop snaps the catches off the lid and lifts it.

Time stands still.

Mel lies in the green-lit water, face down, her pale skin beyond white, her long black hair spread out like an ink blot. Koop's hand flies to his mouth.

She's been sliced in two.

66

Eckhardt arrives back at the office from Menno Koopman's place around 3 pm. He sinks down gratefully behind his desk and pretends to do some work. In all honesty he just wants to go home and smoke and drink and then sleep.

He clicks his computer on, checks his email and forgets about sleeping.

There, in the middle of a long pile of junk and the usual internal crap, Eckhardt spots the phrase 'received by Jimmy Gelagotis'. He'd almost binned it along with the rest.

He opens Ella's email and sees the attachment. There are departmental protocols about opening unsolicited email attachments but Warren doesn't hesitate. Two minutes later he sits back and rubs his face. Just like Jimmy and Ella, the 'Stevie Wonder' clip has rendered him momentarily speechless.

That the footage is genuine he has no doubt whatsoever.

After a couple of minutes he shakes himself into action and logs it in the evidence chain.

Then he emails it to Chris Chakos and Frank Keane with an explanatory message.

He picks up the phone and calls Liverpool.

It takes Eckhardt twenty minutes to track Frank Keane down. MIT won't give out his mobile so Eckhardt has to wait until the man calls him back.

'This better be worth it,' says Keane. Eckhardt can hear the clink of bottles in the background. He looks at his watch. It's almost 3 am in Liverpool.

'You need to get to a computer,' says Eckhardt. 'I sent you a file.' He explains what's happened. 'It's nasty, Frank, but I thought you'd want to know about it right away.'

Even from twelve thousand miles away, Eckhardt can hear the excitement in Keane's voice. 'Thanks, Warren. I'll call you about this.'

Ten minutes later, Keane has sobered up faster than he's ever done in his life. He is alone in the darkened MIT office, the clip frozen on his desktop on the last frame.

'Fuck.'

Like his Australian counterpart, Keane sits motionless for a few moments. He watches the mpeg five or six times without gleaning any new information. Whoever shot the footage took care not to reveal anything that might help identify the killer or killers. It was put together as a warning to Jimmy Gelagotis. A warning he didn't heed.

Then Keane starts thinking as best he can, his alcohol haze both helping and hindering.

They like to film it.

Film has come into this before.

The Matty Halligan thing.

Gittings told him about Matty Halligan and Keane tracked down the Vice officer who got the videos from the S&M bust. Those tapes are now part of the evidence.

Keane goes downstairs, through the silent MIT offices and checks out the box of DVDs. He hauls them back upstairs. He doesn't know what he's looking for but the 'Stevie Wonder' clip has brought them into his mind.

The first he looks at is the one Gittings mentioned. Matty Halligan strapped naked across some complicated piece of sexual apparatus. There are at least two other men in the room. One of them – dressed from head to toe in black leather, his face entirely hooded – is fucking Halligan. The other man only comes into shot now and again. He too is dressed in leather. There is nothing Keane can use.

He turns off the DVD and inserts another. He's a few minutes into that one when something clicks.

He ejects the second DVD, goes back to the first and there it is. The man fucking Halligan is holding his head down from behind, his fingers splayed through Halligan's cropped hair.

Keane freezes the image and bends close to the screen. He uses the zoom feature to close in on a small section of the image.

'Fuck me,' he whispers. Sobered up or not, the room seems to tilt and Keane has to steady himself.

It can't be.

The hooded man's hand is clear against Halligan's dark hair.

Missing the tips of two of his fingers.

'Perch,' breathes Keane.

67

Zoe can't see a thing. She has a hood over her head and a ball jammed in her mouth which is cinched in place using a leather strap.

Zoe knows what it is: a gimp mask, an S&M sex toy. She feels her gorge rising and she wills herself not to vomit. With this thing on she'd choke to death.

She is nude and has been bound by someone who knew exactly what he was doing. Mel was skilled at knots too and Zoe, from time to time, allowed herself to be tied up, enjoying the frisson of vulnerability as Mel teased her.

That was nothing like this.

Her arms have been pulled behind her painfully and roped to her ankles, arching her back and forming her into a rigid bow shape. She's been wedged tightly into some sort of container; one she only just fits into. The madman has grazed her thigh forcing her into it. The container is cold to the touch, metallic, and is inside a vehicle moving at high speed.

Thankfully the road is smooth. For the first half hour or so Zoe was bounced around violently, banging her head against the roof of her container twice. Then came a smooth section before a long uncomfortable passage where Zoe deduced they were on a dirt road. It is agony.

And all of this is nothing after what happened to Mel.

Oh God, Mel.

In the dark, Zoe sobs.

Behind the wheel of the truck, Declan North is outwardly calm.

He drives steadily south through the night, the road unwinding before him in a narrow cone of light, as anonymous as any tradesman going about his business. He keeps to the speed limit and signals when required. He pulls over twice. The first time to take a piss, the second to go through his rituals. It's difficult out there under the great bowl of Australian nothingness, but North improvises by raising the rear gate on the ute and calibrating the angles while kneeling on the dirt.

No-one passes him.

He and the bitch are six hours from her home in the middle of nowhere. North has never been anywhere that is as nowhere as this place.

At 4 am, North pulls off the road and drives two or three kilometres slowly into the scrubby bush, taking care not to get stuck in any unseen ruts. He finds a fold in the land which he's confident makes a perfect hiding spot and parks the truck.

In the back of the ute he's kept things simple. His supplies take up most of the rear of the four-seat cab along with a lock-box containing the cocaine. The other, larger lock-box with the bitch inside is bolted along one side of the tray of the ute. North has placed a foam mattress down the other side. He'll sleep there tonight.

North climbs into the back of the truck and unfastens the lock-box. Zoe tries not to tremble.

It's the hardest thing she's ever had to do.

North doesn't say a word. He leans in and begins to lift her out of the box. She instinctively resists and North slaps her hard across the face. After that she does as he directs.

He takes off her hood and Zoe blinks. Even the lights coming from the truck interior seem harsh. North's face is blank. From what she can see he's calm. He unties her legs and fastens a rope around her neck. For a terrifying moment Zoe is sure he's going to hang her, or worse, drag her behind the truck.

'Walk,' he says and it dawns on her: he's exercising her, like a dog. After almost twelve hours in the lock-box she can hardly move. In fact, at first, she can't move. Her legs won't work and she drops painfully to the dirt. North prods her with the toe of his boot.

'Walk.'

Zoe, fighting the urge to cry, struggles onto all fours and tries to stand. Gradually her circulation begins to return and she's able to hobble painfully around at the end of the rope, conscious of North's eyes on her.

Walk. She wills herself to do it. Walk. Endure. Survive.

He allows her to stray about ten metres before he ties the end of the rope to the towbar on the truck. North loosens the gimp mask and takes out the ball. The pain in her jaw is excruciating and Zoe can't tell if her mouth is open or closed. She thinks about screaming but is unsure she could, even if she wanted to.

As if reading her thoughts, North speaks. 'Go ahead. Give it a whirl. Why not?'

When she doesn't reply, he throws his head back and howls like a wolf. He stops and looks up at the empty night. 'See?'

He holds a litre bottle of water to her lips and Zoe drinks greedily, her world now reduced to the basics. After a few seconds North lifts the bottle and empties it over her head.

'What?' says Zoe.

'You smell.' North's voice is non-judgemental. It's as if he's said 'you're tall', or 'you're English'. Somehow it frightens Zoe more than anything since leaving Nashua.

'You need to piss, go now,' he says.

Absurdly, after all that's happened, Zoe feels the need for privacy. North watches her, his eyes revealing nothing. She squats behind the front end of the truck and urinates into the red dirt. With her hands behind her, and the pain in her limbs, it's difficult but she manages.

North takes a second bottle of water and pours it over her. She stands dumbly while he washes her clean under the stars. With a cloth he washes her armpits and her pussy, his eyes on hers. She forces herself to remain expressionless.

Endure. Survive.

Eventually he's finished. North removes his clothes and Zoe braces herself for what is to come. He pulls off his boots, folds his jeans and shirt neatly and puts them in the rear of the cab. He slips on a pair of thongs.

Zoe wanders as far as the rope will let her. Out to where the light is at its dimmest, where she can feel at least a shred of privacy for a few moments more.

Naked, North uses another litre of water to wash himself thoroughly. Zoe sees the pale lines striping his upper body and looks away. When he's finished, North throws the bottle into the bush and hops up onto the mattress. He lies down and draws a blanket around himself.

'Get in,' he says to Zoe.

She says nothing and remains at the end of the rope.

'Suit yourself,' says North, Zoe registering his Belfast accent properly for the first time. He didn't speak much last night when he did . . . that thing to Mel. Now she can hear it clearly.

'You'll get in soon enough. It's too cold for you to stay out there all fecking night.'

Zoe remains silent but the madman is right. The water on her naked skin is adding to the cold as it dries. After a few minutes Zoe draws closer to the end of the truck.

'And if you're thinking about getting that rope untied then you can forget about that too,' says North. 'The knots are too good.'

Zoe knows this is true. The rope hasn't budged a millimetre since she's been tied up.

With difficulty she steps into the back of the cab and lies down next to her attacker, Mel's killer. Her skin recoils from the places it touches his. It's like getting into bed with a lizard.

'You know we might have seen each other back in Liverpool?'

'What?' Zoe can't work out what the freak means. Liverpool?

'Hope Street,' says North. 'We were at the same college. Eighty-three. I googled you.' His accent seems stronger now she's tuned in. Eighty-*t*ree.

Is he for real?

'Is this what this is about? You're a stalker?' It's the first thing that comes into her head.

'Feck, no!' North laughs. 'Just weird, though, hey?'

'I was there,' says Zoe. 'We didn't meet.' Thinking: keep him talking. 'What did . . . what subject did you do?'

North squeezes Zoe's breast. There's a playful tone to his voice that is more sickening than anything she's heard yet. 'Are you trying to keep me talking? Who gives a fuck what subject I did? That was then and this is now and that's all there is to it.'

Zoe can feel his cock hard against her buttocks.

She waits for the rape.

It doesn't come. The madman wraps an arm around her, his breathing close in her ear.

'Art,' he murmurs. 'I did art. At the Hannemann Buildings.'

Zoe doesn't say anything in reply. She lies still until she realises he's asleep. Cursing herself for her inability to do anything, she closes her eyes and thinks about Koop until, eventually, she too sleeps.

68

The cops are crawling all over Koop's property.

Sullivan returns, ashen and apologetic, along with a bigger team from Tweed Heads. A second team from the Gold Coast is there too, headed by John Collins who has been tipped off by Warren Eckhardt. While they establish the crime scene, and surreptitiously bicker over jurisdiction, Eckhardt shows up looking like hell.

Koop is sitting on the old car chair at the back of the fig tree, holding an as yet unopened bottle of booze, when he smells the smoke from Eckhardt's cigarette.

'I told them everything I know,' says Koop without looking up. 'Everything.'

'I don't know what to say,' says Eckhardt. He butts his cigarette and lights another. 'It's bad.'

Koop doesn't say anything for a moment. 'He's got Zoe. North's got her.' His voice is flat.

'Maybe.'

'She's not here, Warren.'

'It's fucked up, Koop. There's no getting around that.' Eckhardt's voice is low. He swats an insect from his face and holds his cigarette out. 'Can you believe it? Persistent little fuckers, eh?'

Koop looks at Eckhardt. 'What's Collins's take on it?'

'He thinks that North's involved, although as yet there's only your word that this guy is what you say he is.'

'They talked to Liverpool?'

'Of course, and there's some credibility from that end.'

'But . . .?'

'But North is clean. On paper at least. There's no way to get around that one. He landed here a few days ago on his own passport. As far as the law is concerned he's an innocent visitor.'

'Come on, Warren.'

Eckhardt holds his hands up. '*I* know you're right, Koop. Since North's arrived there's been a lot happening and that's what Collins is concentrating on. He knows you're right, if that's any consolation. It's a lot to swallow that all this is a coincidence; North's arrival and World War Three breaking out. We're not idiots here. It's just that . . .'

'That what?'

'The whole thing with you and your wife and . . . the victim.'

'With Mel, you mean?'

Eckhardt drags heavily on his cigarette and stares into the distance.

'Look, Koop, what you do in private is none of my business. But put yourself in our shoes. I know you didn't have anything to do with Melumi Ato's death. Collins knows it too. But we have to report upwards and, given that the three of you have been sharing a bed, that's enough for them to want us to not leap to conclusions.'

374

'A fucking domestic? You think this is a *domestic*, Warren? Did you *see* her?'

'Yes. I saw her, Koop. We all saw her. And you, more than anyone, should know that we can't just jump because you say, "This is the guy." There's back-up from Liverpool, of a sort, from what we can tell. But they . . . we, have to look at it closely to see if there's anything else. Think back. When you were on the job, if something like this – the information, I mean – came in, what would you have done?'

Koop doesn't reply. Eckhardt is right, of course. A triangular relationship in a murder inquiry? It's a no-brainer.

He begins scratching at the black-and-white label on his bottle. 'And in the meantime, Zoe . . .' His voice trails off and the two men wait in silence. Koop looks at the bottle. 'I don't know why I'm holding this thing,' he says.

'Well, anything we can do to find her, we're doing it,' says Eckhardt. It doesn't sound like much, even to Eckhardt. 'You have somewhere to stay tonight?'

'Tonight?' says Koop. He turns east to where the sun is brightening the sky. 'Doesn't seem much point.'

Eckhardt glances at the house which is blazing with lights. 'Fair enough.'

He traces the point of his shoe through the grass.

'Sullivan told me they found where she was killed,' says Echkardt quietly.

He points across the paddock to a distant tent which has been erected over a patch of ground. Two technicians are taking photographs, the flash from their cameras flickering across the night.

'I know,' says Koop.

'There was a lot of blood.'

Koop nods. He, along with everyone else, missed the area on his search earlier. As if he knows what Koop is thinking, Eckhardt speaks. 'You couldn't have done anything to save her.'

I could, thinks Koop. I could have stayed at home.

69

Menno Koopman had wanted Zoe as soon as he saw her.

1981. Liverpool. Another universe. A party in Gambier Terrace to which Koop has definitely not been invited, but to which he goes anyway – along with the rest of the Saturday Night Squad, nightsticks in hand and full of testosterone.

The party's in a top-floor flat smack in the middle of the long row of regal Georgian houses sitting opposite the massive bulk of the Anglican cathedral. In any other city, or perhaps at any other time, these houses would have been the most expensive. They'd been built as showpieces by merchants and bankers, on the highest ground overlooking the source of their power and influence: the city and the river. Whenever Koop goes there, it's as a copper on call.

The police know Gambier Terrace well. The houses have fallen into semi-dereliction as the money moves out of town and the place is filled with dealers, arts students, the odd squatter. The whole place still looks like those early Beatles photos, the good moody ones, the ones by Astrid Kirchherr, with the band in black jeans and leather, before Brian Epstein cleaned them up.

Koop tries to recall the exact moment he'd seen Zoe.

A Saturday night, he remembers that. Around twelve, and he and Geoff Suggs have been called to assist officers called to a party at the Terrace. It's easy to find, the music blaring out over the end of Hope Street; Lee Scratch Perry's 'Super Ape'. Reggae is popular amongst the punkers and art students, as well as with its regular West Indian constituency, Gambier Terrace marking the edge of the black section of Liverpool. Thick bass and spaced-out dub fills the air.

'Fuckin' jungle bunnies.' Suggs pulls a face.

Even now Koop squirms with embarrassment at the recall of the easy racism. He wasn't embarrassed at the time; he knows that in itself is a cause for some retro-active shame. To be a copper then was to be racist, it was that simple, as normal as breathing; the only question being what degree of bigotry each policeman brought to the job.

As the son of a Dutch father and English mother, Koop has been on the end of a milder form of it himself for much of his life. Despite being born and bred in Liverpool, his name marks him out as 'foreign' and therefore not quite right in some intangible way. He is white and European, but even that doesn't stop him getting called a lot of inventively obscene names.

The worst is when people confuse his heritage with German. In the 1970s, the wartime bombing of the city is as plainly evident as a badly sutured wound, the destruction and devastation remaining as a daily reminder of the Luftwaffe. No-one wants to be German and in Liverpool.

At twenty, Koop doesn't question the culture – the sub-adolescent canteen banter which he joins in with. The 'jokes', none of which he ever finds funny, but with which he laughs along, a bit of his self-respect ebbing away with each forced smile or chuckle, like sandstone from a crumbling cliff-edge.

God, the names they use, the way they treat the 'ethnics'. The discriminatory and subsequently volatile abuse of the 'stop and search' law. The truly foul treatment dished out to the only two black recruits he remembers seeing in those pre-riot days.

It curls his toes to think about it.

He never goes along with the beatings, or the stitch-ups. He has, perhaps, turned a blind eye on more than one occasion, bad enough in itself, but understandable in the context. The city is simmering. Toxteth will erupt in riots only months later and Koop isn't surprised when it does. He's never been in any doubt why Margaret Thatcher has been upping his pay. Revolution is in the air. Not the theoretical sort talked about by middle-class socialists. Actual revolution. Militant Tendency are in the ascendancy in the ruling Labour Party. There is credible talk of Liverpool declaring itself an independent People's Republic and seceding from the United Kingdom. In cabinet, Thatcher discusses abandoning the city.

That Saturday night they shoulder their way in through the jeering crowd, Suggs casually slapping a joint out of the mouth of a stumbling student dressed in a suit constructed out of what seems to be polythene sheeting.

'I'll be back for you later, Captain Plastic,' he hisses, jabbing a finger as thick as a Cumberland sausage in the wide-eyed student's face. 'Stay there, you cunt.'

The boy shrinks against the plaster wall, a meerkat making way for a rogue elephant, his clothing crackling against the peeling plasterwork.

The two coppers move onwards, no time for Suggs to waste on simple possession when there might be a decent ruck waiting up ahead. And the maxim of never dawdling on the way to help your brother officers (no sisters, of course, not then).

Koop pats the student's cheek and follows his partner's black-clad back through the crowded hallway and up to the first floor, Suggs making good and sure he steps on as many toes as possible on his way up, a chorus of insults bouncing off his thick hide like a sprinkle of hailstones against the Liver Building.

Up to the first-floor landing and the air is thick with dope. It's easy to see where the other coppers are: the bathroom – such as it is – is the only half-empty space in the entire building. Outside the door stands a growing ring of agitated black youth and student types. Suggs and Koop push past with some difficulty. A thin black girl lies dazed on the floor, her skin gleaming under the fluorescent light. Another girl, white, not quite so skinny, is leaning over her, whispering to her.

Zoe.

'Joined us, 'ave yer, Koopman, you fucking cheese-munching cloghopper?' says Sergeant Gittings, who is regarding the black girl much as someone would look at a hedgehog flattened in the road. He glances at Suggs. 'The darkie fell over or somethin',' he says. 'Won't wake up and the other spearchuckers are gettin' restless.'

'She's been attacked,' says Zoe. 'And you lot are just standing around doing nothing.'

'Yeah, luv,' says Gittings. 'Whatever you say. Now fuckin' shut it or we'll pull you in too.'

Zoe stands up and Koop knows it's at that point he is lost. He's never subscribed to all that love at first sight garbage until then.

She is only small, but built like an athlete, a toned body long before that became common – he finds out later that she has a passion for swimming. Her hair is very short and has some sort of arty style to it that Koop couldn't have named, but privately thinks of as 'Art School Punk'. He can't now remember much of how she was dressed – he has a vague recollection of stockings and biker boots – but it would have been something unusual and sexy: with variations over the years and allowing for the fluctuations and vagaries of fashion, that has been Zoe's underlying style.

She moves towards Gittings who looks at her, his eyebrows raised in amusement. Gittings looks around at the other coppers as if to say: have you seen this? Zoe is clearly bent on telling Gittings what she thinks of him and, knowing Gittings as he does, Koop steps smartly forward between them, surprising himself as much as anyone else.

'Let me get some details off you, luv,' he says, kindly, ignoring the leering grimaces from the rest of the Saturday Night Squad who, like him, haven't been slow to recognise Zoe's obvious charms. Koop takes hold of her arm to lead her to safety.

Which is the point at which she headbutts him.

Koop smiles at the memory and involuntarily rubs his cheek where her head struck. He should have known better. 'Luv', indeed.

It takes a lot of persuasion to stop Gittings taking Zoe somewhere quiet and pointing out the error of her ways. As Gittings's teaching methods are rumoured to include straight-out rape, Koop has to act quickly and uses up a year's worth of brownie points in one go.

'Get out of my sight, Koopman,' growls Gittings. 'Take bitch number one,' he nods down at the black girl, 'to casualty, and get bitch number two to wherever the fuck you want, just so long as I don't have to see her fuckin' face again. Suggs, you can help me spread some peace and love amongst our coloured brethren.'

Koop manages to get Zoe and her friend out without further incident and takes them to the Royal, ambulances at that point not venturing into Gambier Terrace. On a Saturday night the A&E is a zoo and Koop has to use some more valuable favours to bump Zoe's friend up the queue.

'If you think I'm going to be grateful, you've got another think coming,' she says as they wait outside the cubicle door for the girl to be examined. Koop doesn't push it. He just sits and talks a little and gives Zoe a lift home after her friend is kept in for observation, Zoe wanting her to fill out a complaint, her friend refusing.

She lives in Huskisson Street, not far from the site of the party. Koop writes his number on a sheet from his notebook and gives it to her. She looks at it scornfully but, Koop notices, doesn't throw it away as he feared she might.

She never calls.

But he sees her again, several times, soon after and in less dramatic circumstances. At a student-grant protest meeting he is policing. In town, at a few bars when they do the rounds before closing time. And then, crucially, as it turns out, off duty at a Clash gig at the Royal Court in October. Koop remembers her incredulity at seeing him there out of uniform. He doesn't know what she found more ridiculous; his liking for a band like that, or the way he's dressed. In truth, Koop is a fan.

At this gig, if not quite blending in, he is certainly unremarkable.

And while the band are onstage, no-one is looking at anyone else. With the drawn-out, punked-up chop of 'Police and Thieves' being belted out by Strummer, and surrounded by Liverpool's pale and interesting youth, Menno Koopman and Zoe Cane fall in love.

He and Zoe spent that night together and, a very large number of ups and downs in those early years notwithstanding, have remained together ever since. An unlikely pairing, but, as it turns out, a durable one. Zoe, two years younger than Koop, isn't quite as leftfield as she appears, or wants to appear; Koop not as hidebound or reactionary as his profession suggests. They were both brought up in near-identical houses and socio-economic backgrounds, attended schools within three miles of each other, both had reasonable relationships with their parents and, crucially, thrillingly, they found that in bed, the sum of the parts exceeded the whole by a ludicrous amount. They are good at sex, inventive, exciting and energetic, and revel in their passion which has not significantly altered over the years.

And now she's gone.

70

Zoe wakes with her head on the madman's chest.

She pulls away, disgusted with herself, and with her humiliation. It's almost light and she tries to step down from the tray without waking North.

Perhaps she can untie herself.

She should at least try, right?

A fresh flush of shame shoots through her as an inner voice picks away – *didn't try very hard last night, did you?*

She manages to get her feet on the red dirt before North wakes up and looks at her.

Zoe braces herself for his reaction. When it comes it's somehow harsher than being assaulted.

He laughs.

The man who cut Mel in two is laughing at her.

She knows what she looks like; naked, trembling, vulnerable. He can do whatever he likes to her. He looks at her like a bug.

But I'm going to try and kill you, she says to herself, holding his gaze. Just give me the slightest opportunity and I will do it, you motherfucker. She can taste how much she wants to kill him and knows she'd do it in an instant, no hesitation. Everything has been reduced to basics.

Live. Eat. Drink. Die. Or kill.

North steps down from the truck and stretches, nude, in front of her. He looks somehow fragile and, for the first time, Zoe thinks, *This is just a man*, and allows a faint hope to flicker into life. There is a lack of focus around his eyes and Zoe is struck with the possibility that maybe he is unravelling in front of her.

He walks to the cab and takes out the cocaine. North scoops out some on his finger and shoves it up his nose. He snuffles and coughs and wipes a gob of snot from his upper lip. He puts the coke back in the cab and comes towards Zoe, his face shining.

'Come here,' he says. His penis is erect.

Zoe does nothing.

'Here,' barks North and this time she's in no doubt what he wants. What he commands.

Zoe considers her options. Live or die.

She walks forward and drops to her knees. North smiles and thrusts his cock into her mouth. Zoe does as he wants, thinking two things. Come and get me, Koop. And, looking up at North: whatever happens, this is the last time I do this, motherfucker.

71

Koop opens his eyes and blinks.

For a moment he doesn't know where he is.

And then it comes back to him in one single, horrible rush.

He looks at his watch. It's mid-afternoon. He's been out for almost six hours, thanks to Eckhardt calling a doctor who gave him a sedative. It took all Warren Eckhardt's powers of persuasion to get the drug into him.

For one seductive thrilling moment Koop wonders if the whole thing was, movie-like, a nightmare. And then he sees he's in a motel room; he remembers Eckhardt bringing him here last night. His house – his and Zoe's house – is a crime scene and he couldn't have remained there last night even if he'd wanted to.

Koop jumps off the bed, sickened to his stomach by his sleep. What sort of man is he to lie in bed while his wife is Christ knows where with that . . . that monstrosity?

And Mel. Jesus, Mel.

Koop runs to the bathroom and is violently sick.

He cleans himself up and comes into the bedroom.

'Call me', says a note from Eckhardt propped against a lamp on a small desk. Koop doesn't know what to do with his hands. Doesn't know where to stand. He's never felt so useless, so powerless in his life.

He wanders around aimlessly for a few minutes. Then he goes into the bathroom and showers, turning the water as cold as possible. Shivering, he gets out and dresses in the clothes he picked up from the house last night. Jeans, boots, a work shirt.

Thinking: I'm dressing for action and there's nothing to do.

He calls Eckhardt. Something might have happened. Someone might know something.

'Anything?'

'Sorry, Koop, nothing as yet.'

'Has anything been done?'

'We have an alert at airports for North, but the level is only to detain. Collins doesn't want an itchy fingered cop shooting him.'

'Why not?' says Koop. 'The fucker's guilty!'

Eckhardt pauses. 'Koop, think like a cop again. Guilty or not, if North's dead there's no-one who'd know where Zoe is. Think.'

Koop breathes deeply. 'Sorry, Warren,' he says. 'It's just the whole . . .'

'I know.' Warren Eckhardt waits a couple of beats. 'We got some work done on Mel,' he says quietly. 'Do you want to know?'

'Yes,' says Koop. Think like a cop. It might be all Zoe has.

Eckhardt's voice assumes the detached tone of the professional.

'She was killed first, by a single blunt trauma wound to the head. She didn't suffer, Koop.'

'And the cutting?'

'She was cut in two – as you know – and the killer allowed her to bleed out.'

'Bleed out?'

'Drained. He drained her.'

There's silence.

'What?' says Koop. Eckhardt is waiting for him to respond. 'What do you want me to say?'

'I want you to think like a cop,' says Eckhardt, his voice a slap. 'Not a fucking amateur.'

Koop reflects. 'Why? Why did he do that?'

'Better,' says Eckhardt. 'No fucking idea right now, but it's worth thinking about.'

Yes, reflects Koop, Warren is right, it is worth thinking about. Why did that fucker go to all that trouble with Mel? If he wanted to send out a warning he would have just killed her and left her, surely?

'And you're out of the frame too,' says Eckhardt. 'Time of death places you with me, so unless Chakos and Collins think we're in this together, you're in the clear.'

'Well, that's something.'

'I've been chasing what I can on this whole drug thing from the Liverpool end – see if there's any clue about what this nut might do next.'

'And?'

'Nothing so far. Frank Keane's all jazzed about something I sent him – nothing you have to worry about – but I don't think it's going to break anything our way soon.'

'It has to be soon,' says Koop.

'I know. Listen, I've been thinking. Let's assume North killed Gelagotis.'

'Right.'

'That could be as punishment for stepping up to the guy in Liverpool.'

'Kite.'

'Yeah, Kite. So that could be why he kills him, yes?'

'OK. Where's this going?'

'Bear with me. Why would North kill Gelagotis? It's business? And if that's the case, then why not leave Gelagotis in place and carry on with the deal? They'd already taught the new boys a lesson.'

'You mean Stevie.'

'Yeah, Stevie. This deal must have been very big to get them so fired up. So why not leave Gelagotis?'

'I like it. Why not?'

'Because North was stepping in. He'd organised with the people under Gelagotis to off Jimmy and take over. He killed Kite, right?'

'Yes.'

'So the next logical step is to get shot of Gelagotis.'

Koop's brain feels clear for the first time in days. 'But what about those other two? The ones in the lock-up?'

Eckhardt sounds pleased with himself.

'Ah, well this is where Uncle Warren did good. I think North killed Link and Meeks.'

'Why?'

'Because the deal went bad, maybe? They cheated him, or maybe he just *thought* they cheated him. Or maybe he wanted it all for himself? Although that last one isn't what I think happened.'

'Why not?'

'Because North would have needed the other two to distribute. A deal of the size this one must be would need local distribution.'

'Makes sense.' Koop thinks about the labyrinth of distribution in his old patch. A newcomer would flounder. 'So North must either not have any merchandise . . .'

'Or only as much as he's able to handle with one sale.'

'Does that get us any further?'

Koop can hear Eckhardt puffing away and wonders where he is. Probably inside his car.

'I think I know why he's got Zoe,' he says.

Koop swallows. 'What?'

'He thinks you're in on it. Think about it, Koop. Your son is the one who comes to Liverpool. North has no way of knowing that he's a stranger in all but blood. They kill Stevie and that's followed by this deal being skimmed . . .'

'If your theory's right about that. You don't know anyone was skimming.'

'Well, let's assume I'm close. They all skim on the deals, you must know that. But that's not important. North took Zoe for one reason and one reason only.'

Koop waits.

'He's going to use her to teach you a lesson, Koop. And that's if he hasn't already done it. My opinion? I think she's already dead. I'm sorry to be so upfront but I figured you'd prefer that to a load of old crap.'

'She's alive.'

'Well, I understand that's what you want to believe. That's what I want to believe. But that doesn't make it so. North's going to use her to send you a message. That message will be: don't steal from me. And another thing.'

'What?'

'He'll be coming back for you.'

Koop doesn't say anything. Something Eckhardt said has rung a bell.

A message.

'Koop? Koop?'

Koop hangs up.

He knows where North is taking Zoe.

72

They drive all day. They drive for so long Zoe finds herself getting bored. Boredom is not something she'd have predicted during an abduction.

North gives her some clothes – a t-shirt and jeans – and makes her sit up front. He places the gun he took from Link in the pocket of the driver's door and tells Zoe he'll kill her if she does anything. If they're pulled over by cops and she blabs he'll kill her and the cops.

'You know I can do that.' It's a statement not a boast.

Zoe says nothing. Since he forced himself on her she's said nothing. Only nodded, as if expending words on this animal is beneath her. She'd let him come and then spat it into the red earth.

The landscape unfolds in front of them all that day, North keeping himself going by regular snorts from his brick. They stop for food once and twice for the toilet. North doesn't bother roping Zoe and she doesn't bother running. In this desolation there's no point. He's faster and stronger and armed.

So she pisses and eats and watches.

He caught her looking at the door in which the gun was stored and smiled. 'Don't even think about that, doll. I want you fresh for a few days more.'

That's good information. She believes it to be true; that he wants her alive for a little longer. Which gives her more time to watch and wait for an opportunity, or for Koop to come.

Or for a fucking lightning bolt to strike him down.

Which is about as likely, she thinks. He's going to kill you. When we get to wherever he's going, he's going to kill you.

Zoe notes the place names they drive through. They are, to the Belfast boy, unimaginable distances apart, and mostly deserted: Wilcannia, Broken Hill, Cocklebiddy. Twice North places her back in the lock-box, roping her as he's done previously and gagging her with a scarf. She presumes this is when they're passing through more populated areas although her geography isn't good enough to pinpoint exactly where. She knows they're heading west. Perth?

Several times they pass convoys of grey nomads, or supertrucks. For some hours they drive with the distant ocean visible out of Zoe's window. She falls asleep and wakes as North pulls the truck off the road. He repeats the previous night and camps several kilometres into the bush.

They eat tinned food which North makes Zoe heat over a camping stove. She racks her brains about a way to use the flaming canister of gas – seeing him exploding in a ball of flame – but even as she imagines it she knows it's pure James Bond. Easy to visualise, impossible to do.

After the meal, North ties her up while he cleans himself using a makeshift camp shower. When he's finished he makes Zoe strip and watches as she showers. She tenses as she finishes, expecting a repeat of the previous night's assault. It doesn't come. North ties her hands and feet and tethers her in the tray of the ute. He climbs in alongside and falls asleep.

The following day, they break camp and drive west once more, seeing fewer and fewer vehicles. Zoe realises they've crossed the vast Nullarbor Plain, something she'd hoped to do with Koop.

At Norseman they turn north and drive to Menzies. Zoe senses they're reaching their destination. North has been consulting his map more frequently. She was wrong about Perth.

After Menzies, North turns off onto a dirt road and drives for almost an hour. The sun is setting as he swings the truck down a small incline and Zoe sees the salt flats stretching out in front of her. In the glow of the setting sun the white of the salt is a gleaming orange glare. It is incredible. North pulls the truck onto the salt lake itself and Zoe worries that the surface will crumble beneath them. She wonders where he's going. It's time to camp but tonight North seems to be looking for something.

And then she sees it; in the far distance a figure, wobbling in the heat haze. As they approach she sees it is skeletal, black, hard against the flaring orange sky. She glimpses other figures and knows where she is.

73

Koop doesn't tell Eckhardt or Collins where he's going.

There's no point. They'd only do one of two things: stop him, or slow him. He can afford neither. He also knows in his heart of hearts that if he tells them where he thinks North is heading, he'll be branded a grieving fool. It is, at best, a half-chance that he's right. No, not even that. But there is a chance, just a chance. The police wouldn't act on such a vague and ill-thought-out possibility. Not when North is still – on paper, at least – simply a tourist.

Koop gets into his truck and heads north for Coolangatta and the airport. He's called ahead and booked himself onto the next flight west.

It was Eckhardt who accidentally tipped him off. North was going to send Koop a message. Where Eckhardt was wrong was that the message has already been sent. It was – at least once Koop saw it for what it was – clear as a bell.

Mel was the message.

She was sliced in two not out of sadism, although Koop has no doubt he's dealing with a full-blown sadistic psychopath in Declan North, but to tell him something.

The Physical Impossibility of Death in the Mind of Someone Living. It's a great title.

The Hirst shark.

The shark sliced in pieces and placed in a tank.

The image Zoe was using for the GOMA BritArt show.

Koop knows that North is telling him where he's taking Zoe. Doing it this way is sadistic. Koop knows North wants to kill her – if Eckhardt is on the money about North suspecting him of scamming him – and wants him to know about it. Wants him to know that this is a killer with some artistic flair.

But Koop is gambling that the man who killed Stevie has made a mistake by assuming he won't make the connection; that it'll all be over by the time they find Zoe's body. On his iPhone he flicks through the images on Google and there it is: Antony Gormley's *Inside Australia*, the mirror piece to his iron men in Liverpool. Fifty-one skeletal iron figures on the salt flats of Lake Ballard.

As Koop races for the 5 pm flight out of Coolangatta his mind sees an image: a burning figure against the desert sky.

74

'This is it, Zoe,' says North.

Zoe shrinks back against the car interior. It's the first time North has used her name. For some reason it makes it more frightening.

'Don't be stupid,' says North. 'Get out.'

Zoe has absolutely no doubt he's going to kill her.

Koop, Koop. *Koop.*

North stands at the open door of the truck and looks in at her. He beckons, the gun held loosely in his right hand. Behind him the sun is flattening itself against the horizon and North is surrounded by a flaming blood-red halo.

'Fuck you,' says Zoe. Tears run down her face. 'Fuck you!'

'Come on, woman.' North is outwardly calm but Zoe can see his eyes jerking. He's been coming unstuck for days now. Four thousand kilometres on cocaine. And God knows what other demons inside that grotesque skull. He's suddenly screaming at her. Spittle flies from his mouth. 'Now, you fucking *whore*!'

Zoe moves slowly towards the door, her eyes on the gun.

Come now, Koop. Please.

'Don't,' says Zoe.

'Shut up.' North reaches past her into the back of the ute and she flinches.

'Here,' says North. He flings a spade at her feet. 'Dig.'

'What?'

'Dig.'

Zoe picks up the spade and pushes it into the dirt. Fat tears roll down and splash on the salt surface. He's making me dig my own grave.

North sits on the bonnet of the ute and watches. The sky grows dark and Zoe keeps digging. When she begins widening the hole, North stops her. 'No,' he says. 'Just dig down.'

Down?

North switches on a torch and places it on the roof of the cab.

After another half-hour Zoe is up to her thighs in the hole, her arms and legs aching.

'OK, that's enough, Get out.'

Zoe climbs out and North ropes her to the truck. He takes a scaffolding pole from the ute and places it in the hole. He releases Zoe.

'Hold this.' North places Zoe's hands on the pole. He grabs a bucket from the rear of the cab and a bag of cement. North mixes the cement using a ten-litre container of water and pours it around the base of the pole.

'Hold it steady.'

North puts the bucket back into the cab.

'What are you doing?' says Zoe. She speaks slowly and carefully, anxious not to tip North into a rage.

'You think speaking like that's going to help, eh? *Don't upset the loony*,' North snorts. 'Jesus.'

'So what are you doing?'

'Hold it steady, woman.' North begins to strip. He takes off all his clothes and puts them in the cab. He walks around the pole and looks at it and Zoe. 'Fucking beauty.'

'What are you doing?' Zoe is shaking.

North stops and raises his eyebrows. It's happening and he feels the familiar tug of the earth shifting underneath him. He gives a low chuckle and rubs his fingers over the track marks on his torso.

'You should know, Zoe. I'm sending a message to that thieving pikey of a husband of yours. The fruit doesn't fall far from the tree, eh? First the son and now the father. Both of them tried to steal from me. One's gone and I'll do the other one after I've done you.'

'Steal? Koop didn't steal from you!' What is this lunatic talking about?

'Is that right? Well, in that case I'll let you go.' North smirks. 'Now move away from the pole and start filling the hole.'

Zoe pushes the dirt around the pole and North stamps it down. When he's certain it's solid he backs away and looks at Zoe.

'You know what to do,' he says. 'Take your clothes off.'

'He hasn't stolen anything,' she says. 'If this is about money or drugs you have to know that Koop had nothing to do with whatever this is. Nothing!'

'Clothes. Off.' North lifts a knife from the car. 'Or I'll gut you right now.'

Zoe can feel her breath coming fast. Tears are welling in her eyes. She slides out of her jeans and t-shirt and faces North. He takes a length of rope from the cab and nods towards the pole. 'Go kneel down and put your hands around the back.'

'Please,' says Zoe. 'You don't have to do this.'

'I know I don't. It's just that I want to. Now kneel down.'

Zoe kneels against the pole and puts her hands behind her. North wraps the rope around and jerks her arms back against the pole. Zoe gasps and North locks her off with quick, measured movements. He stands and cleans himself from the big water container. When he's finished, he hoists it onto his shoulders and pours it over Zoe. The water is cold in the desert night and she feels her skin tingle. Her nipples harden, involuntarily. He spends longer cleaning her this time, his touch lingering as he washes the desert from her hands and body.

'I like things clean,' says North and it sounds more like a mantra than information.

He puts the water container back in the cab and approaches Zoe, a smile on his face, his penis erect.

'Ready?'

Two hundred metres away, Perch's hired Serbian adjusts the settings on his night-vision goggles and tweaks the sight on his rifle.

This looks like it will be worth watching.

75

Koop drives out of Perth and into the night heading east on 94 along the Great Eastern Highway. Near Southern Cross a large kangaroo crashes into his offside fender, sending the car skidding in the dirt at the edge of the road.

Fuck it. There'll be plenty more kangaroos and Christ knows what else coming up.

Zoe.

He presses the accelerator on the hired 4x4 and races across the Boorabbin National Park without seeing another driver. He swings north at Coolgardie and hits Menzies less than three hours after leaving the airport. He's been signposted to the Gormley sculptures since the turn-off and has no problem locating the deserted visitor post.

Koop rolls the car to a halt next to a post-mounted map and gets out. With the engine off, he's struck by the complete sense of isolation. There are buildings in Menzies less than thirty kilometres back along the Sandstone Road, but out here on the edge of the salt flats he could be the only man on earth.

For Zoe's sake he's hoping he isn't.

Koop gets back in the car and drives out onto the

white salt lakes ignoring the signs that prohibit vehicles. He hopes this is a warning to protect the lake bed, and not a prediction that the surface will crumble beneath the wheels. Koop has visions of the ground opening up and him plunging down into some volcanic fissure. The land feels alien.

About two kilometres from the road is a conical hill poking somewhat surrealistically out of the flat earth. Koop can see it clearly – a blacker triangle set against the blue-black of the night sky. He switches off his lights and idles slowly across the salt. If his hunch turns out to be correct, the last thing he wants to do now is to alert North. With the headlights out, the ground seems to glow in the moonlight, doubling the effects of the rays.

Koop reaches the small hill and climbs, his feet scrabbling on the loose dirt and rock.

Once at the summit he calms his breathing and scans the area, taking care to let his eyes move slowly; he doesn't want to miss anything.

On the first rotation he sees nothing and a flutter of panic races through him like electricity. This has been a ridiculous headlong dash across the continent based on nothing more than an instinct.

He starts turning once more and again draws a blank.

There's nothing out there.

Koop thinks about calling out her name and then stops himself. No. Be patient. Think like a cop.

He decides to do one more rotation and this time catches the dimmest of glows in the west. Koop peers at it for so long his vision starts to betray him. He makes a mark in the ground at his feet and continues turning.

He's reached about three-quarters of the way round the rotation when he hears the screaming in the distance. It sounds like an animal caught in a trap; a hellish sound from an unimaginable world of pain. He can't tell where it's coming from. The screaming lasts for almost a minute and then there's silence.

Koop stares into the night.

Another minute passes and then, at a slightly deviated angle from where his gaze has been, Koop hears another scream, this time a woman's.

Koop can hardly breathe. He scrambles back to the car and careers towards the sounds.

76

No-one is coming.

Not Koop, not the police, not the man in the moon. She's out here on her own.

'Ready?' North says.

Zoe lets her head hang, defeated. This is simply not bearable. She thinks of Menno, of Mel, of past girlfriends. Most of all she thinks of her dead Sarah.

She feels North approach, looming over her in the glow from the torch.

'No,' she says, her voice calmer than she thought it'd be. 'Not tonight. It's not happening.'

North laughs. 'You think you have a fucking choice? Jesus. Look around, you dumb bitch! Blame your thieving husband for this. Not me.'

Zoe shakes her head. 'Don't talk about my husband, you fucking repulsive psycho.'

North smacks her hard across the face and Zoe feels her vision shift. Her jaw hurts more than she'd have believed possible. It isn't like the movies.

North comes closer and shoves his stiffened cock at her.

'I saw you and that Jap bitch in the tub. I watched what you did, so don't come the auld innocent with me.'

Something knots up inside Zoe. 'I loved her!' she screams. 'Have you any idea what that feels like? No? You wouldn't, would you, you fucking *cockroach*!'

'Enough,' North snaps. He takes Zoe's face in one hand and pushes his cock into her mouth. 'I like it rough.'

Zoe closes her eyes. North pushes his penis as far back as he can and she gags.

'You fucking love it, don't you?'

Not tonight, thinks Zoe. Not happening. Not now.

She opens her eyes and looks up at North. Her gaze softens. He's just a man. He feels pain just like everyone else.

'Good girl,' he says.

Zoe bites down hard and wrenches her head sideways in one sudden movement, her teeth clamping together. She feels North's flesh part in her mouth and he screams, a loud screeching, keening wail that doesn't sound human. She feels his hand hammer down hard on her head and still she grinds her jaws together with renewed determination, feeling his tissue shred under her sharp white teeth, his veins rip, warm metallic blood pulsing into her mouth as she jerks from side to side like a rottweiler with a rabbit. A blow hits her on the ear and she almost passes out.

And then he rips loose from her.

She gags, her mouth full of blood and flesh. Zoe spits and several teeth fall out.

Along with a large part of North's penis.

The Irishman drops to the floor, his screams increasing in panicked intensity. Blood is pouring from his groin and running out between his cupped fingers in thick gouts.

He looks down disbelievingly at his crotch, the blood and mangled flesh glinting black in the moonlight.

'You fucking cunt!' he screams.

He staggers to his feet and punches Zoe hard in the face. The effort drops North to his knees and sends a fresh wave of searing pain through his torso. 'You fucking cunt! Look what you've done to me! *Look!*'

Zoe can't hear a thing. North's blow has broken her cheekbone and popped an eardrum. Her head lolls and she feels blood trickle down her chest. She thinks she's screaming but she can't tell.

North staggers upright again and moves painfully to the car. Sobbing, he reaches inside and pulls out the gun.

Zoe raises her head. It feels like it weighs a hundred kilos. It feels like the connections have been broken. The universe is foggy.

She is going to die. Zoe knows that. It was worth it.

She breathes in the night air and thinks about Koop and about Sarah.

'You won't make it,' she says, forcing the words out through her injuries. 'You'll bleed out before you can get help. And even if you did get help, do you really want to live like that? You're as dead as me, you stupid fuck.'

North grips the gun with some difficulty, the grip slick with his blood.

'*You bitch. You fucking bitch.*' His voice is teary, disbelieving, the frightened tone of an adolescent boy, his Belfast accent unadulterated now. Zoe fixes her eyes on him and smiles a dreadful bloody smile. North steadies his gun hand and points it at her face. His finger curls against the trigger and he squeezes.

Koop slams into him like a stampeding buffalo as the gun goes off, missing Zoe's head by centimetres. North hits

406

the salt flats hard, and feels his skin tear as he's crushed into the ground under Koop's weight. Koop rolls up and headbutts North savagely, feeling the man's nose shatter.

Menno Koopman doesn't exist.

In his place is a natural force of white-hot hatred and he slams punch after punch into North as the man bucks beneath him. Their bodies are greasy with the Irishman's blood.

'MENNO!' screams Zoe.

As if in slow motion, North's gun is coming round, the barrel turning towards Koop's back as North's blood-slicked fingers grope for the trigger. The bullet rips a shallow path through Koop's flesh as he twists away. Ignoring the flash of red pain he places North's gun arm in the crook of his elbow and breaks it. Blood bubbles in North's mouth as he screams. He's bitten through his tongue. Koop staggers to his feet and stamps hard on North's groin. This time there's no scream from North, just an awful dull groan. Covered in blood and caked in salt, Koop slips, staggering momentarily away from the wrecked figure writhing on the white surface of the flats.

Before he can recover his equilibrium, Koop sees North twist the gun out of his smashed fingers and point it at him left-handed. Through a mask of blood, North's eyes show white. There's a feral gleam of ultimate triumph as he squeezes the trigger.

A bullet rips through the night and takes out the top of North's head just as his own gun barks. For a milli-second his confused eyes catch those of Menno Koopman before North slumps sideways, blood pooling darkly around him.

Disoriented, Koop jerks his head in the direction of the shot, but sees nothing. Instead his eyes focus on a silent

Zoe, her head slumped, a thick line of blood running through her blonde hair and splashing onto the ground, where it joins North's blood and forms one slowly growing black lake. With a strangled sob, Koop rushes to Zoe and falls to his knees.

A hundred metres away, Dragoslav Bregovic stands, deliberately gathers his kit into his rucksack and shoulders his rifle. He turns away from the scene and starts to retrace his steps back to his vehicle, feeling glad that he waited to fulfil his contract on the Irishman.

That shit *had* been worth seeing.

77

'Come.'

Keane glances at Em Harris before he pushes open the door to Perch's office. He wrestled with it before phoning her. She made the wrong choice siding with Perch but it wasn't a bad shout. In another life it might have been the call he'd have made. Pointless to rub it in any further; he and Harris have too much history to throw it away. Besides, knowing Harris, she might still end up C of C one day and Keane doesn't need any more enemies than his current abundant crop.

And here they were. Reader and Moresby were gracious enough to let MIT make the formal collar. Perch is – was – one of their own, after all.

Perch is behind his desk. He doesn't glance up, instead waving an imperial hand towards the chairs. The hand missing two fingertips.

Keane and Harris wait for Perch to look up. When he does his face pinches in annoyance.

'Keane. Harris. Sit.'

'I don't think so, Eric,' says Keane. 'Not today.'

Perch looks like he's been slapped. 'You'd better have a

good reason for that tone, DI Keane. I'm not in the mood for insubordination, is that clear?'

'Come on, Eric,' Keane says. 'It's over. We know.'

Before Perch can respond, Harris steps in. 'Let's do it by the book, Frank.' She fixes the DCI with a neutral look. 'Eric Perch, we are arresting you for conspiracy to commit murder, supplying illegal drugs with intent to distribute, and other charges that will be discussed at a later date.'

'You must be insane!' Perch is on his feet. 'Get out!'

'You do not have to say anything, but it may harm your defence if you do not mention when questioned something which you later rely on in court. Anything . . .'

'I'll have you fucking gutted, you black bitch!' Perch, snarling, moves around the desk towards Harris but Keane puts out a restraining hand. At his touch, Perch recoils.

'. . . you do say may be given in evidence.' Harris finishes the arrest caution as though Perch hasn't spoken.

'You got any cuffs?' Keane looks at Harris. 'I forgot we needed them.'

Harris takes a pair of cuffs and hands them to Keane. He moves towards Perch who makes an ineffectual attempt to push him away.

'You've got to be kidding,' says Keane, smiling. He twists Perch's arms and slams his face down into the polished wood of the desk. Placing a knee in his former boss's back, Keane slips the cuffs on and snaps them shut. His mouth close to Perch's ear, Keane whispers. 'How are you feeling, Eric? Like to add anything?' He hauls Perch to his feet, the Chief Inspector's spectacles askew. His breathing is ragged, his face red.

'Get me my lawyer,' he says. 'You clowns have stepped out of your league.'

'Seen much of Matty lately?' says Keane. Perch stops moving. Keane sees the arrow reach its target.

'Frank.' Harris's tone is half-warning. 'We can do this in interview. By the book, right?'

'It's OK, Em,' says Keane. 'We've got this fucker tied up nice and tight.' Keane looks at Perch. 'Just how you like it, eh, Chief Inspector? You and Matty taking turns. Each to his own, I suppose, although you might have thought twice about filming the fucking thing.'

'I . . .' Perch has tears in his eyes. With an effort he pulls himself together. 'That's personal. If it's me. And it proves nothing.'

'We've got it all, Eric,' says Harris. 'The tapes. The bank accounts. We have you on CCTV at the Halligans' lock-up. They kept tapes, as security, didn't you know? More diligent than most legit companies. We have what's left of the coke. Matty rolled over like a tame dog this morning. Gave you up without a murmur for a reduction at sentencing. We know the lot. They served you up to us. It's over.'

Keane opens the door to the office where Reader and Moresby are waiting. At the sight of the two OCS officers, Eric Perch slumps. The office behind is fizzing with adrenaline as news of Perch's arrest spreads like ripples on a lake.

'Look on the bright side, Eric. It could have been worse,' says Keane as he prods Perch towards the door. 'If Koop was still here we might be bagging you up for the coroner.'

78

Mel is going home to Sapporo to be buried by her family, but before that happens, there is a gathering at Nashua for everyone who knows her and Zoe.

Kenji Ato, Mel's older brother, has come out from Japan to accompany her body home; their parents too traumatised by the loss to make the trip. At the site of Mel's death, around the back of the fig tree, Kenji has built a small tower of flat stones he's collected from a beach at Lennox Head. The smooth black rocks are carefully arranged into a circular cone. On the top stone Kenji places a votive candle in a protective lantern and lights it. He and one of Mel's colleagues from the university embrace as a thin ribbon of smoke rises into the air. Some of the twenty or so people gathered in a loose circle around the makeshift altar sniff and dab their eyes.

From the steps of the deck, Koop watches the smoke drifting up into the branches of the fig. He has no idea if the ceremony has any religious meaning, or if it is simply something Kenji has cooked up to mark Melumi's death for a disparate group. He should have asked, he knows, but since coming back from Lake Ballard he's found himself to be short of some social skills. It's as if he is observing familiar things from underwater: he can recognise what they are but his responses feel sluggish.

It is two weeks since he raced across the salt flats, dodging Gormley's nightmarish black skeletons – two of which reared up in his beams – and found Zoe.

He can't get the image of her out of his head.

I'm too late. That was his first thought. He was so close, so very close.

Picked out by the harsh spotlights of the hired Toyota, she looked like a sacrificial offering. Naked and on her knees, her blonde hair showing a stark red bloom running down across her blood-spattered breasts and thighs. In front of her, North holding a gun to her head, ready to deliver the coup de grâce.

It was the worst moment of Koop's life. All his fault. Everything. He hit North with everything he had.

'You okay?' Koop feels a hand on his shoulder and turns to see Zoe. She wears a scarf wrapped around her head to conceal the bandages. North's bullet carved a path along her temple, taking off the tip of her ear on its way past and knocking her instantly senseless.

Koop reaches up and pats her hand. 'I thought you'd be out there.' He nods towards the gathering.

'Looking like this?' She points to her black eye and heavily bruised face. 'People will think you've been knocking me round.'

The medical diagnosis is promising. No internal damage from the bullet, no signs of brain damage from the beating she took. She'd have a small scar across her temple and there was nothing to be done about her ear, but in all other respects Zoe would make a full recovery.

Physically, at least. Koop knows from long experience rape victims carry more damaging scars.

He hasn't yet discussed in detail with her the days leading up to North's death, although Zoe told the West Australian Police everything. Which she then had to repeat for the Queensland OCG and for Warren Eckhardt at Homicide. Eckhardt offered to go through everything with Koop, but he declined. Zoe would tell him when – if – she felt the time was right.

'We'll be fine,' says Zoe, softly. 'You found me. You saved me.'

'And Mel? I didn't save her, did I?' Koop speaks in an angry enough tone for several of the mourners to turn their way. Zoe wraps her arms around him.

'You can't help everyone.' Zoe pulls away and holds him at arm's length. 'Listen, Koop, I'm only going to tell you this once because I don't want to think about it any more. Mel didn't suffer. She was out before . . . before he did what he did. He was an animal. We – Mel and I – just got in the way. *It wasn't your fault.*'

Koop appreciates it, he really does.

But she's wrong.

It is his fault, his foolish decision to chase Stevie's killer, and he is going to live with it for the rest of his life. As a copper – correction, ex-copper – Koop knows he has the capacity to compartmentalise things like this. He'll put Melumi Ato in a sealed room in his mind, but she'll always be carried around with him; he'll be able to function, but with part of him irrevocably damaged.

So he nods to Zoe. 'I know. I'll be fine.' The words stick in his throat. That's great, Koopman; *you'll* be fine. What about your wife? Her girlfriend butchered in front of her, abducted by a psychopath, raped, shot and left for dead in the middle of nowhere and she's comforting you? Top class.

He gets to his feet and puts his arms around his wife, feeling her involuntary and unnatural stiffness in his embrace. '*We'll* be fine.' They kiss awkwardly. Zoe is going to take some time to face physical contact after what happened. The two break apart and Zoe retreats to the kitchen to keep herself busy. Koop watches a friend put her arm across her shoulder and the two of them begin quietly talking.

'Hell of a thing.' Warren Eckhardt materialises on the deck. He casts an appreciative Aussie eye around the area. 'Nice size deck you have here, Koop.'

'It looks bigger because the, er, because the tub's gone. You know.'

'Oh, shit. Of course. Tactless as usual.'

Koop holds up a hand. 'That's OK.'

Eckhardt lifts out his cigarettes. 'You mind?'

Koop shakes his head. 'Help yourself.'

His cigarette lit, Eckhardt eases his generous backside onto the rail and puffs happily.

'Like I said, hell of a thing.'

'Did you hear from Frank?'

'Keane? Yes, they made the collar yesterday.'

Koop imagines Keane clanking the cuffs on Perch. Jesus, that would have been a thing to have witnessed. 'How did Perch take it?'

Eckhardt smiles. 'Not well. Frank said he tried the stonewall approach first – then he switched to "this was all an operation, I was undercover", all that sort of crap. When that got nowhere Keane said he let him marinate overnight. Put him in a cell next to a screamer. In the morning Perch wanted to talk. Funny thing was he was more worried about word getting out he was a poofta – sorry, gay – than he was about looking down the barrel of a life sentence. He's trying to negotiate something in return for the Halligans.'

'And the Halligans?'

'They're doing exactly the same. And giving up more than Perch in the hope that will seal the deal. Same the world over. Maggots.'

Eckhardt blows out a long plume of smoke into the night and the two men are silent for a moment.

'Any news on the shooter?' says Koop. Both know he is talking about the man who killed North as he pulled the trigger on Koop.

'Nothing. And we won't, if you want my personal opinion. This bloke knew what he was doing. North's vehicle was stripped bare of the cocaine. From the info Frank's getting in Liverpool and from what Chakos is giving me from OCG, there would have been around fifteen million dollars in that vehicle. If I'm putting it together right, and I think I am, the shooter was sent by Liverpool – meaning, obviously, Perch and the Halligans – to tie up the loose end. He will have had something worked out about getting the coke, or the money from the sale, back to Liverpool minus a cut. With that side of things all tucked up, I'd make a serious bet the shooter has pocketed the coke and is now busy making himself disappear.'

'It all came down to money in the end, didn't it?' Koop suddenly feels like getting hammered. He looks into the kitchen where Zoe is surrounded by a group of friendly faces. He turns to Eckhardt. 'Fancy a drink?'

'I thought you'd never ask.'

Koop grabs two beers from the deck fridge and hands one over. Eckhardt puts his arm around Koop's shoulder and the two clink the necks of their beers together. Koop can smell the smoke on Eckhardt's breath.

'You know, Koop,' says Eckhardt. 'This could be the start of a beautiful friendship.'

'Are you making a pass at me, Warren?'

'Get fucked. *Casablanca*, mate. Best film ever made.'

'Never heard of it.'

'Jesus,' says Eckhardt as the two of them walk slowly back into the house. 'I'd heard Poms were stupid, but this is going too far.'

Three thousand kilometres west the sun is low in the sky and a wind is picking up across Lake Ballard. It comes over the low-lying scrub and gathers a fine dusting of salt crystals from the dry surface. The only objects in the path of the wind are the iron skeletons. The salt rattles against the black metal and on the red earth marking the spot where North died. The dark stain is almost gone and in a few more days will have disappeared completely.

Acknowledgements

This book would not have been possible without the help and support of a number of people. I'd like to thank my good friends Margrete Lamond and Jenny Burgess for their early readings and sharply intelligent responses at a crucial time. I'd also like to thank Bev Cousins at Random House Australia, and Kate Burke at Random House UK, for their wonderful taste in crime fiction and their ongoing support, knowledge and hand-holding. My editor, Patrick Mangan, has done a great job ensuring I didn't make a complete fool of myself, a difficult task for anyone. My agent, Tara Wynne at Curtis Brown, deserves thanks for her steely nerve under fire, as does supersub Pippa Masson who filled Tara's shoes so capably while Tara briefly abandoned me on the flimsy premise that she was having a baby.

I have borrowed the names of characters freely from friends (almost all of whom have agreed). I'm hoping that those who didn't aren't too offended when they showed up as corpses, criminals or cops. Special mention must be made to Menno Koopman, Jim Gelagotis and Macksym Kolomiets, who very kindly agreed to the loaning of their names, if not their characters. It's not the first time that team-mates have supplied me with inspiration and it won't be the last. Needless to say, the characters in the book bear little or no resemblance to their real-life counterparts.

Antony Gormley's wonderful sculpture installation on Crosby Beach (*Another Place*) was fundamentally inspiring for me and, in some ways, was the jumping-off point for the book. As a fan of his work I hope my use of the iron men as a location is taken in the spirit in which it was intended. If you ever get the chance to see either *Another Place*, or *Inside Australia*, or indeed any of Gormley's work, you should.

Lastly – before I start weeping and thanking God and grandma – I would like to thank my patient and understanding life partner, Annie, who has had to call on all her powers of encouragement and reservoirs of blind faith to get me to this point.

Redemption

Will Jordan

A major new thriller series featuring Ryan Drake – a British CIA agent on his most dangerous mission yet.

Ryan Drake is a man who finds people who don't want to be found. Once a soldier in the British Army, he now works for the CIA as a 'shepherd' – an elite investigation team that finds and brings home missing agents. But his latest mission – to free a prisoner code-named Maras from a maximum security prison and bring her back to US soil within forty-eight hours – is more dangerous than anything he and his team have attempted before.

Despite the risks, the team successfully completes their mission, but for Drake the real danger has only just begun. Faced with a terrible threat, he is forced to go on the run with Maras – a veteran agent scarred by years of brutal imprisonment.

arrow books

Bloodman

Robert Pobi

Killer

In the quiet coastal town of Montauk, Long Island, a sadistic killer is stalking his prey, waiting for the right moment to unleash his fury.

Protector

When a young woman and her young son are found brutally murdered – skinned alive in a frenzied attack – Sheriff Mike Hauser knows he's out of his depth. There's no evidence, no clues and no motive, and Hauser needs someone who has dealt with this level of brutality before.

Avenger

FBI consultant Jake Cole has a unique ability – to recognize killers' artistic signatures at crime scenes. Called into help with Hauser's investigation, Jake enters the twisted mind of a serial killer. But when he recognizes the killer's signature as the one left on his own mother, brutally murdered thirty years before, the case becomes personal.

In a race against time, Jake knows he must find the killer before the 'bloodman' finds him…

arrow books

ROBERT HARRIS

THE FEAR INDEX

In the secretive inner circle of the ultra-rich, Alex
Hoffman is a legend. He has developed a method of playing
the financial markets that generates billions of pounds.
It is a system that thrives on panic – and feeds on fear.

And then, in the early hours of one morning, a terrifying
intruder breaches the elaborate security of his lakeside home.
So begins a waking nightmare of violence and paranoia as
Alex attempts – with increasing desperation – to
discover who is trying to destroy him.
Before it's too late . . .

'SIZZLING' *Sunday Times*, **Books of the Year**

'GRIPPING' *Mail on Sunday*, **Books of the Year**

'CHILLING' *Sunday Express*, **Books of the Year**

'INTOXICATING' *Independent on Sunday*, **Books of the Year**

'SUPERB' *Spectator*, **Books of the Year**

arrow books